SHELTER FROM THE STORM

It is 1943 and April Wilton is devastated when she is forced to leave Portsmouth and the WRENs where she has found friendship, fulfilment and love. Rejected by her mother, and facing an uncertain future, she travels to Cliffehaven. However, she carries with her a secret, one that could change her life for ever. Can the warmth and support of Peggy Reilly and those at Beach View Boarding House heal the wounds of April's past, and bring her hope amid this time of turmoil?

SHELTER FROM THE STORM

SHELTER FROM THE STORM

by

Ellie Dean

Magna Large Print Books
Long Preston, North Yorkshire,
BD23 4ND, England.

British Library Cataloguing in Publication Data.

A catalogue record of this book is
available from the British Library

ISBN   978-0-7505-4466-5

First published in Great Britain by Arrow Books in 2016,
part of the Penguin Random House group of companies.

Published in Large Print 2017 by arrangement with
Random House Group Limited

Magna Large Print is an imprint of Library Magna Books Ltd.

Printed and bound in Great Britain by
T.J. (International) Ltd., Cornwall, PL28 8RW

For the brave women who joined the services, the factories, farms and anywhere they could to take on a man's job to free him to fight for his country. I salute you.

Acknowledgements

I am indebted to Vera Brett, wartime Wren, for her help and advice on all things connected to the navy. It was terrific fun to meet you and hear your stories about your time in the Wrens during the Second World War, and to confirm that my research had mostly been right. I must emphasise that April's story is purely fictional, and is in no way connected to Vera's own experiences. Thank you, Vera, for your generosity in allowing me to delve into your wealth of knowledge, and for the lovely afternoon we spent together.

As usual, this book could not have been written without the help of my terrific and supportive agent, Teresa Chris, and the great team at Arrow. Thank you all, especially, Jenny Geras, my very understanding editor.

Thanks as ever to my wonderful husband who supports me through the trials and tribulations of getting the story told, provides coffee, advice and encouragement.

Prologue

Portsmouth, November 1942

April Wilton clung to the side of the motor torpedo boat. They were racing across the choppy grey waters of the Solent – testing the engine that she and her fellow maintenance Wren, Paula Simms, had just serviced – and she was filled with the exhilaration of the moment. She had been feeling gloomy since her few hours of home leave the previous day, but now she was determined to keep cheerful.

April's fair hair was whipped by the wind as the sea spray flew from either side of the MTB and sparkled like jewels in the weak, wintry sunlight. She'd started out on her journey home full of excitement in the hope that her mother would admire her smart uniform and be proud of her. This longing to have her mother's approval had, however, ended in the usual failure, and no compliment had been forthcoming. The sad truth was something April could no longer deny. Mildred Wilton was an exacting, selfish woman, forever finding fault and bemoaning the hardships of war as if they were a deliberate assault by the combatants on her comfortable life. But then Mildred could always lay the blame for whatever ailed her on someone else. April knew she should just accept that her mother would never change

11

and not let her spoil the wonderful new life April had discovered.

'I'm glad to see you've cheered up at last,' shouted Paula over the healthy roar of the MTB's engine. 'Was the trip home really that bad?'

Despite her resolve, April felt hurt all over again as she remembered the indifferent welcome she'd been given by her mother. She nodded and shrugged. 'Mother was preoccupied with the new stock of hats for her shop, and after hanging around a bit to listen to her usual gripes about the lack of materials and the uselessness of her hat makers, I took myself off and visited a couple of friends.'

Paula sighed and patted her shoulder. 'Parents can be very difficult, can't they? Father spent most of my day's leave shut away in his study. Still, we're free of all that now and doing our bit – life is exciting, isn't it?'

'It certainly is.' April gripped the handrail tighter as the speeding boat was taken into a sharp turn that in less capable hands would have seen them in the water. She grinned back at Paula as their hair was whipped from their faces, the spray splattered their oilskins, and the wind snatched away the possibility of any further conversation.

April revelled in the marvellous sense of freedom that always came when she was out on the water. Life in the Women's Royal Naval Service was exciting and fulfilling, a world away from the stifling atmosphere at home and the strictures of boarding school where she and Paula had forged their close bond. She hadn't regretted a single moment since she'd first heard the lecture from the recruiting officer who'd visited the sixth form, and seen the poster that exhorted her to 'Join the Wrens and free a man for the fleet!'

She and Paula were both eighteen and had enlisted on the same day almost a year ago following a short course at a secretarial college to fill in the time between school and the adult world. They'd been friends since they both started at their private school, for they not only shared a love of books, cinema and dancing, but soon discovered that their childhoods had been similarly unhappy. Paula's mother had died before Paula's sixth birthday, and her father hadn't known how to deal with his own grief, let alone that of his young daughter, and had immersed himself in his work, leaving Paula to the not-so-tender mercies of a hatchet-faced, coldly efficient nanny during the school holidays.

April's father had succumbed to a heart attack shortly after her ninth birthday, and she still missed him. Sadly, they hadn't been particularly close, for his strict upbringing meant that he kept any emotion in tight check beneath a rather formal veneer. Yet he had cared enough for April to have been a buffer between her and Mildred.

Mildred's attitude to his passing had been one of undisguised relief. She was determined to make good use of the money he'd left to forge a new life for herself. She had never told April much about her life before marriage – April had a vague idea that her mother had been a secretary – but now Mildred launched herself into a new career as the owner of the best hat shop in Tunbridge Wells, unfettered by marriage and the daughter she clearly had little time for. April had never under-

13

stood this lack of interest or affection, and Mildred had never revealed the reason for it – and so it was with a mutual sense of thankfulness that April had immersed herself in boarding school life and now in this new, exciting adventure in the WRNS.

It hadn't been easy to start with, for she'd been naïve and painfully shy, and for a while she'd felt isolated amongst the other girls who seemed so self-assured and sophisticated – but that had slowly changed as she'd begun to make friends. Now, at last, she felt she really belonged, and was an intrinsic part of something very special.

She and Paula had completed their initial training at Mill Hill in London, where the days seemed to be taken up with scrubbing floors, keeping fit, learning how to defend themselves in a gas attack, and endless marching – which they both hated. There had been a whole new language to learn now they were part of the Royal navy – beds were bunks, billets had names like HMS Midge, and bedrooms were cabins – but somehow that made it all the more thrilling.

April clung tightly to the railings as the captain of the MTB took it into another tight turn and headed back towards shore – or base, as the navy called it – to where flotillas of MTBs, motor gun boats and small, flat-bottomed landing craft were moored. April glanced across at Paula, saw her grinning, and knew she was thinking the same thing, for this had been the sight that had greeted them when they'd arrived, fresh from training to take up their maintenance drafts. They'd felt very proud in their brand new uniforms of navy blue jacket, skirt, tie and white shirt, with their sailor's hats perched at a jaunty angle over their brows, and it had been impossible not to giggle and blush at the wolf whistles and shouts of encouragement that followed their march through the docks.

They'd been permitted to choose their job in the Wrens, and rather than be stuck in an office, had cheerfully opted to join the maintenance crew – although they had no idea what that might entail. The mystery was heightened when they were issued with bell-bottom trousers, a boiler suit and oilskins, and they'd wondered what on earth they'd let themselves in for.

April's smile was wry as the MTB slowed to navigate the narrow waterways between the flotillas. She and Paula had been with three other new recruits when they'd been marched down to the harbour and taken on board an MTB for the first time. They'd scrambled down the hatch to be greeted by the sight of sailors stripped to the waist in the furnace heat of the engine room, and there had been a moment of shocked silence on both sides which was swiftly broken by the chief engineer barking out orders to his men to stop gawping and get on with their work. The sight of so many half-naked men had proved too much for one of the girls who'd clearly led a very sheltered life, for she went puce and shot back up the ladder, demanding to be drafted to an office job.

April and Paula had exchanged glances and stifled giggles as the sailors hastily went back to their duties, but over the ensuing months they'd become inured to the sight of bare, gleaming chests, for they'd spent most of that time in the stifling, sweaty heat of engine rooms, learning to

15

change plugs, strip down gearboxes and distributor heads, and anything else that was needed to keep the boats ready for action.

The MTB came to a halt and rocked gently by the docking pier. April and Paula saluted the captain and quickly negotiated the rusting iron ladder to reach the more stable wooden boards of the dock. With a cheerful wave to the crew, they hurried through the melee of the vast port, eager to get back to their billet, HMS Firefly, to prepare for their night out. The committee for the combined services was laying on a party in one of the large municipal buildings requisitioned by the navy, and they'd been invited.

HMS Firefly was in fact a large guesthouse which had also been requisitioned by the navy, and when the English traitor, Lord Haw-Haw, had declared in one of his propaganda broadcasts that the victorious Luftwaffe had sunk her, it had caused great hilarity to all.

It stood back from the seafront, and was home to fifteen Wrens who worked as dispatch riders, typists, telephonists, plotters and the many other jobs that were available so men could be released for sea duties. The civilian population had mostly been evacuated, but Portsmouth was still bustling despite the almost daily bombing raids which had shattered the town. HMS Firefly was only one of many billets to accommodate girls from the Wrens, WAAF and ATS, and with an American army base nearby, an RAF station on Thorney Island, and thousands of Allied sailors, airmen and marines on shore leave, the vastly outnumbered girls were in constant demand – which

16

was all very exciting.

They clumped through the front door in their thick sea-boots and ran up the two flights of stairs to the cabin they shared beneath the eaves, which had a lovely view of the sea and the flotillas of warships which were anchored in the lee of the Isle of Wight. To their disappointment, the island had suddenly been put out of bounds, and it was rumoured that the joint forces were conducting special training over there – perhaps even preparing for an invasion into France – so she and Paula had not been able to satisfy their curiosity and visit the famous coloured cliffs and sandy beaches.

April pulled off her sodden oilskins and kicked off her boots before sinking onto one of the single beds and stripping off her boiler suit. The room was quite small, and sparsely furnished, but the blue and white navy issue counterpanes made it feel a little more homely. Any clutter was tidied away in the single chest of drawers and wardrobe, for the cabin was inspected each day by their petty officer Wren, and penalties were dished out for the slightest infringement of the strict rule of orderliness.

'I don't know about you,' said Paula from the depths of the sweater she was pulling over her head, 'but I'm starving. I hope the Yanks are laying on some decent food, because navy rations are getting worse by the day.' She shook out her dark curls, her brown eyes gleaming with anticipation.

April laughed and stripped down to her regulation underwear of unattractive bra and black-out bloomers. 'They usually do, and of course the navy will provide extra grog rations.' She glanced across at her friend and they shared a grin of delight for the evening ahead. The combined services' parties were becoming quite legendary, and they counted themselves very fortunate not to be on fire-watch duty tonight.

They quickly bathed in the regulation few inches of water in the draughty, freezing bathroom on the lower landing, and then carefully dressed in their smart uniform which was the envy of all the girls in the other services. It was a strict rule that uniform had to be worn at all times – even for parties – and although it would have been lovely to wear a proper frock now and again, it certainly saved on clothing coupons. The navy blue suited them both, the well-fitting double-breasted jacket and pencil-skirt enhancing their slender figures; the black stockings were rather thick lisle, but added a touch of glamour that even the unattractive and rather clumpy lace-up shoes couldn't diminish.

April brushed out her shoulder-length fair hair and swiftly pinned it into a chignon. She carefully applied mascara, powder and lipstick and then donned her cap so that the blue insignia was at the perfect angle. Adjusting her tie until the knot was set dead centre, she nodded with satisfaction and went to fetch her navy issue gabardine coat.

'Let's just hope we don't have an air raid tonight,' she said as she waited for Paula to find her umbrella. 'It would be such a shame to miss the party.'

'I don't think Jerry's too bothered about spoiling our chance for some fun, unfortunately,' Paula muttered. Banging doors and loud voices reverb-

18

erated through the house, heralding the departure of the other girls. 'Come on, we don't want to miss out on the food – you know what gannets those girls from dispatches are.'

They ran down the stairs and out of the door to discover that darkness had fallen and it had started to rain. The streets gleamed in the pale moonlight that shone fleetingly from between scudding clouds, and water was dripping from the ornate metal trellis above the narrow porch. Unfurling their umbrellas, they made a dash across the road just as their bus wheezed, and rattled into view. Having paid the clippie, they greeted the other girls on board and within minutes were excitedly discussing all the wonderful possibilities of the evening ahead.

There was a distinct division amongst the girls, for although they were mostly from respectable middle-class families, there were some who'd been born with the proverbial silver spoon in their mouths and thought themselves far superior. With their plummy voices and rather snooty bearing, they set themselves apart, while the rest preferred to stay within their own sets – just as they had in their private school days.

As the bus trundled past the yawning bomb sites and shattered remains of buildings, April began to feel uncomfortable at some of the rather vulgar banter that was going back and forth between the girls around her. She enjoyed the dancing and the fun of these parties, but she had certainly never let any of the boys take liberties. Like many of the other girls, Paula had no such hesitation, and the sudden freedom from her restrictive home and

19

school life meant that she'd thrown herself whole-heartedly into whatever was on offer – especially the lure of the rather flashy Americans with their candy, nylons and cigarettes which garnered a kiss and cuddle – and maybe more besides, which April found rather shocking.

Paula had teased April about being such an innocent, and had even tried to set her up on several blind dates, but April was happy to keep them all at arm's length until the right man came along – even if some of the girls thought she was in danger of being a bit of a prig.

The bus groaned its slow way through the town and arrived on the corner by the municipal building where the sound of the party drifted out to greet them. It was clearly already in full swing. April and Paula hurried off the bus and everyone swarmed towards the sound of the big band music.

The noise was terrific, the vast room crammed with men and women from all the Allied services. The Americans were there in great numbers, with their smart uniforms, their charm and almost childlike openness, and amid the fray were service-men from Norway, Sweden, Denmark, Poland, New Zealand and Australia – all vying for the at-tention of the comparatively small number of girls.

April and Paula handed in their coats and gas-mask boxes to the woman in charge of the cloak-room and quickly made their way back into the hall. The band was twenty strong and made up of American marines. They were playing Glenn Miller's 'In the Mood', and before they'd had time to survey the food and drink on offer, both girls were whirled onto the dance floor.

The jitterbug was exhausting, but exhilarating too, and April discovered that her partner, an American sailor, was very good at it. She grinned at him in delight, conversation being impossible in all the noise, and threw herself into the dance, noting fleetingly that Paula was dancing nearby with a magnificently moustached RAF squadron leader.

The crush on the dance floor became greater and April was now so out of breath and thirsty that she nodded her thanks to the sailor and forced her way through the melee to the tables which were positively groaning with food and drink. She helped herself to slices of tinned ham, sausage, potato salad, coleslaw and squares of yellow corn bread which the Americans seemed to prefer to the national wheat loaf that she and the rest of the population of England hated – not only for its un-appetising colour but for its leaden and rather gritty taste. There were pats of golden butter too – an absolute luxury – and bowls of trifle piled high with whipped cream. The Yanks certainly knew how to cater for a party.

She found a corner to sit and eat her food, watching the fun on and around the dance floor. There was a pall of cigarette smoke curling along the lofty ceiling, and the chatter had risen to be heard above the music. A huge cargo net was suspended from the ceiling, loaded with hundreds of balloons. The Americans had certainly done their best to create a party atmosphere.

It must feel strange for these boys to be so very far from home. She thought about how it would be for them at Christmas. They would miss their families terribly at such a time, she thought wistfully, whereas she would be happier to spend Christmas here than with her mother. They had discussed it on her recent leave, and Mildred had clearly been relieved that April had no plans to stay over the holiday, for she was booked into a hotel for the two days and was adamant that it would have been impossible for April to join her there. April suspected her mother had a new admirer – another in a long line of rather pompous older men since father had died – and was therefore equally relieved that she was on duty.

April finished the delicious meal and sipped at her glass of beer, not quite ready to join in the crush on the dance floor again, when she caught sight of a group of African-American GIs standing on the sidelines surrounded by a gaggle of girls from the ATA. She'd heard about this special tank regiment which had arrived less than a week ago to do their training before they were sent to the front line. Like others before them, they seemed to be enjoying all the female attention – although she knew from past experience that sometimes this could cause trouble, for not all the other Americans appreciated them being here.

As the girls flirted, she watched in amusement, fully understanding their attraction to these rather exotic-looking men who seemed so handsome in their uniforms. And then her gaze shifted and her heart suddenly skipped a beat.

He was taller than the others and the most beautiful man she'd ever seen: broad-shouldered and lean in the hip, with dark brown skin. His aquiline nose was carved perfectly beneath winged black brows, dark eyes, and high cheekbones, and with his firm jawline and almost regal bearing, he stood out amongst his comrades as someone who knew he was very special.

April couldn't take her eyes off him as he talked to the girls surrounding him and his friends, but when he seemed to feel the intensity of her gaze and looked towards her it was as if the room and the noise had faded into insignificance and they were the only two people there.

His gaze was like a fiery, magnetic touch, driving into her core; drawing her towards him, her body responding in a way that made her pulse race and her insides tremble. She was ensnared by him, unable to look away even as she heard the girls around him giggling and felt the heat and colour rise into her face. He was walking towards her now, those brown eyes holding her as captive as a butterfly in a web.

'Would you care to dance, ma'am?' he asked in an almost lazy drawl, so deep and melodious it sent ripples of pleasure right through her.

April nodded, unable to speak, and as he took her hand it was as if he'd bewitched her, for she was hardly aware of floating to her feet and into his arms as the music slowed to a waltz.

'Sergeant Daniel Clement, at your service, ma'am,' he said in that dark, deep brown voice.

'Wren April Wilton,' she managed as she dared to look back at him and noted how his brown eyes were flecked with gold beneath those long, thick black lashes – and how his lips were sensually formed above the square chin. She hastily looked away, terrified he might read her thoughts.

'Nice to meet you, April Wilton,' he said as he drew her closer. 'I guess we're goin' to get along just fine.'

She breathed in the scent of him, felt the strength in his body as he held her close and fell gloriously, hopelessly in love.

He moved with liquid grace around the floor, sweeping her effortlessly from one dance into another until she felt as if she was lighter than air – at one with the music and with him. And when the countdown to midnight began and the lights dimmed, neither of them noticed the balloons drifting down or the raucous yells and cheers from those around them, for they were totally absorbed in one another.

April gazed up at him in that breathless moment as his large hand gently cupped her neck, his eyes questioning. Her whole being was drawn to him, and her lips parted as his fingers caressed her nape and then slowly slid up through her hair.

His beautiful mouth captured her lips and she closed her eyes as she was swept away in a tumult of emotions. His kiss was fire and electricity – it stoked in her wondrous sensations she'd never experienced or even imagined – sensations that made her feel wanton and greedy for more.

He finally drew back and looked down at her with an expression of warm surprise. 'Wow,' he breathed. 'That was some kiss, little lady.'

She gazed at him, her body alive with heat and longing, her lips parted in the hope he would kiss her again.

'Let's go somewhere quiet,' he murmured.

'Then I can have you all to myself for a while.'

The warnings of where that might lead clamoured in her head, but she tried desperately not to listen to them – to ignore the memory of her mother's voice lecturing her about the dangers of men and the need to stay pure until her wedding day. Something powerful had awakened inside her and she wanted his kisses, yearned to feel his hands on her skin – to share the heat of his body, and feel the strength of his arms around her. She was wavering, so close to capitulating despite the fact that she hardly knew him.

'Come on, April. We have to get back to base before lights out.'

Paula's voice startled her and broke the spell, and April didn't know whether to be annoyed or grateful. 'Yes, I suppose we must,' she said reluctantly.

'This is Saul,' said Paula with a broad smile as she drew the coloured GI forward. 'I'm sure that if we ask nicely, he and your friend will walk us back.'

Saul was light-skinned, with tight, curly black hair and the same Southern drawl – but not half as handsome as Daniel, who she quickly introduced to Paula. Daniel didn't seem at all fazed by the rude interruption as he shook Paula's hand and smiled cheerfully at his colleague. The four of them left the dance hall arm in arm, and started on the long walk back to HMS Firefly, heedless of the drizzling rain and the cold wind that was coming off the sea.

As they finally reached their billet, Saul led Paula into the deep shadows of the garden wall and Daniel drew April into his arms. His kiss was soft and very gentle, but it caused chaos within April and she was quite breathless by the time he drew back from her.

'Can I see you again?'

Her racing pulse missed a beat, and before she had time to think about how unwise it was to be over-eager and gauche, she'd blurted out, 'I'm off tomorrow night.'

His smile was wide, showing wonderfully white, even teeth. 'That's a date then,' he drawled. 'I'll come by and pick you up at eight.'

Paula emerged from the shadows, hastily trying to set her cap back in place and her hair into some kind of order. They stood outside the house and watched the two men walk away until they were lost in the blackout.

'Even when they walk, it's as if they're dancing,' murmured Paula with an appreciative sigh before she unlocked the door and led the way upstairs.

The house was settling down for the night, with only the soft murmur of a wireless and the occasional mutter of voices coming from behind the many closed doors. They reached the attic room and with sighs of weariness laced with pleasure, began to prepare for bed.

April was still trying to come to terms with the storm of emotions she'd gone through that evening, and she noted wryly that her hands were unsteady, her fingers fumbling as she attempted to undo her jacket buttons and loosen her tie.

'My goodness, you have got it bad, haven't you?' Paula teased. 'Not that I blame you. He's as handsome as any film star and quite devastating on the dance floor. You were absolutely the centre of attention there for a while.'

April blushed and tried unsuccessfully to un-button her shirt. 'I didn't realise,' she murmured.

Paula giggled. 'No, I don't expect you did. You were certainly taken up with each other all evening.' Her expression became more serious. 'I do hope you'll be careful, April. You're such an innocent, and those boys are after only one thing – you do know they can't be trusted, don't you?'

April's happy mood disintegrated. She knew it was the common consensus, but she didn't want to believe it of Daniel. He'd been so tender, so sweet, and hadn't objected at all when Paula and Saul had interrupted them, or tried to get fresh during their last kiss. 'I might be an innocent, but I'm not daft,' she replied lightly. 'I'll take care, don't you worry.'

Paula regarded her for a moment and then sighed. 'I've got an appointment at the birth control clinic on the twenty-seventh. Why don't you come with me?'

April knew that Paula had fixed herself up shortly after joining the WRNS because she'd been going steady with a rating at the time. However, the thought of going to such a place was quite shocking to April, for it all seemed terribly calculating and actually rather seedy for a single girl to even contemplate doing so. And it wasn't as if she was planning on sleeping with Daniel – of course she wasn't. Daniel might have stirred something very powerful and thrilling in her, but now the heat of the moment had passed and she could think clearly, she knew she would find the strength to resist things going any further.

'I'm on duty early that day. Perhaps another time,' she murmured.

'Well, see that you do, April. From the way you and Daniel were carrying on tonight, things could get out of hand very quickly. And I'd hate to see you getting into trouble.'

April knew Paula meant well, but although she had been quite carried away with Daniel tonight, she had absolutely no intention of letting her feelings for him get out of hand. 'If things look as if they're getting serious, I'll go to the clinic,' she said in appeasement. 'Now, can we drop the subject and get some sleep?'

April's resolve weakened over the next ten days as they met at every chance they could snatch during their busy schedules. He'd taken her dancing, and out to dinner; had sat beside her in the darkened cinema, and in the confines of the air-raid shelters, talking, laughing, getting closer as they discovered more about each other. He made her feel cherished, protected and respected – something she'd yearned for all her short life – and as Daniel's kisses became more demanding and her body cried out to be loved by him, she blocked out the loud warning bells in her head, ignored the irritating niggles of doubt and kept putting off a visit to the clinic. There was a war on and time was precious – and as Daniel had said repeatedly, he'd be shipped out the moment his training was over, and she couldn't bear the thought of wasting even a minute they could be together.

They'd been dancing and drinking cocktails in

the ballroom of a smart country hotel a little way down the coast from Portsmouth, and the heady mixture of alcohol and sensual tension was too much to resist, so when he confessed that he'd taken the liberty of booking them a room for the night, she'd silently taken his hand and gone with him up the stairs.

He'd known this would be her first time, and although she was suddenly overcome with an almost crippling shyness, he'd been gentle and patient, coaxing her to relax and enjoy the sensations his lips and hands were arousing within her. And when it was over and she lay sated and overwhelmed in his arms, he told her he loved her and wanted her to be with him always.

1

Portsmouth, March 1943

They had been seeing each other at every opportunity since that night, and April was still wildly, deeply and deliriously in love. She had no doubt at all that Daniel would fulfil the promises he'd made during those wondrous hours of lovemaking which had made her feel reborn and able to face anything and everything – and even though this new-found courage would soon be put to the hardest test, her faith in him held firm.

He'd proved to be a quiet, thoughtful man who was still in awe at the exhilarating freedom from

29

the colour bar here in England where he was welcomed everywhere. It was all so different to the segregation and restrictions of his home town in South Carolina – and to the prejudice he had to withstand in the army camp. April had been deeply shocked by the severity of the segregation imposed in America, and wondered how such prejudice could be permitted in a country that was so wealthy and powerful – and yet she was enchanted by the almost childlike delight he took in exploring this brave new world, and fiercely defended his right to do so if there was even a hint of trouble.

There had been moments over the past three months when things had turned ugly owing to some of the more hidebound racists amongst the American troops taking exception to him being with April, or daring to drink at the same bar as them. These nasty episodes had mostly come to nothing, for Daniel knew the consequences if he retaliated, and he'd simply turn on his heel and find somewhere less threatening to go. Yet these instances overshadowed April's happiness, and she'd quickly realised how very difficult Daniel's life must have been back in America, which only made her love him more.

'I simply don't understand it,' she said to Paula as they got ready to go out for the evening. 'He's not even really what you'd call black, not like some in his regiment – and as we're all fighting for the same cause, you'd think the Yanks would accept them. But they have to live in separate barracks, eat in different mess halls and shop at specific hours in the PX – and put up with the most awful verbal and physical abuse.'

Paula turned from the dressing-table mirror and regarded her solemnly. 'It's the way things are, unfortunately,' she said. 'I'm just thankful we Brits are more liberal-minded.'

'But it's quite frightening at times,' April said. 'They gang up and push him around, calling him the most awful names. I don't know how he can stay so calm and not retaliate.'

'Probably because he knows the MPs will arrest him if he lays a finger on one of those white boys,' said Paula tartly. 'All is certainly not fair in love and war.'

April knew that Paula was still trying to get over Saul who, unlike Daniel, had hit back at his tormentors and been thrown into the glasshouse to await court martial. She put her hand on Paula's shoulder in sympathy. 'Did you ever find out what happened to Saul?'

Paula bit her lip, her eyes glassy. 'He was found guilty of assault and shipped out to North Africa the next day. I doubt I'll see him again.'

April felt a pang of distress for her friend, and gave her a comforting hug. 'I am sorry,' she murmured. 'Sorry that I haven't been much of a friend just lately – and sorry that you're still upset.'

Paula shot her a wavering, watery smile and began to briskly tidy up the mess on the dressing table. 'There's plenty more fish in the sea and sailors on shore,' she said with false brightness. 'It's not as if either of us was terribly serious about the whole thing. There is a war on, and these things happen, don't they?'

April nodded realising that her friend didn't

31

want to continue the conversation. Yet the guilt still lingered, for she'd been so taken up with her own concerns – and with Daniel – that she hadn't really noticed how badly Paula had taken Saul's enforced departure. She turned away from the mirror and slipped on her jacket so she could surreptitiously undo the button on her skirt. The waistband was uncomfortably tight all of a sudden.

'I'm dreading the day Daniel is shipped out,' she said quietly. 'His training's almost over, so it will probably be quite soon.' She gave a tremulous sigh. 'From now on every moment we can snatch is precious.'

Paula's gaze was direct. 'I know you're sleeping with him, April,' she said softly, 'but I do hope you took my advice and went to the clinic.'

April went scarlet and couldn't look her friend in the eye, for she had gone – eventually – and it had all been horribly embarrassing. 'Of course I did,' she muttered.

'When, exactly? Before or after you stayed out all night with him?'

'What is this?' she asked on a shaky laugh. 'The third degree?'

'If you want to call it that,' Paula replied solemnly. 'Look, April, I don't mean to be bossy and overbearing, but I care about you, and I know how these things can get out of hand. A moment of passion overrides common sense and before you know it you're in trouble.'

'I'm fine, really,' April insisted.

Paula crossed the room and took her hand. 'Are you?' she said softly.

April felt cornered. She desperately wanted – needed – to talk to someone, but although Paula would understand, she couldn't face the shame of having to confess how stupid she'd been. 'Just drop it, Paula,' she said sharply.

Paula folded her arms, her gaze steady and her chin set determinedly. 'Not this time, April. You see, I've heard you being sick every morning for the past week or so – and I know that you haven't been sleeping well. You're off your food, suddenly hate the taste of tea, and you haven't used any sanitary towels for at least two months.'

April struggled to stay calm in the face of her friend's determination to get to the truth. 'Who said you could go through my personal things?' she countered.

'I'd run out and I thought you wouldn't mind if I used a couple of yours until I got fresh supplies,' Paula said flatly. As the silence stretched between them her expression softened. 'You're pregnant, aren't you?'

April was determined not to cry or let the emotional storm she'd been concealing over the past few weeks boil over. 'Don't be silly, Paula,' she said. 'Your imagination's running away with you. It was just a stomach upset, that's all.'

Paula regarded her evenly and gave a deep sigh. 'When you feel you can talk to me honestly about it, you know where I am,' she said sadly. 'But don't leave it too long, April, because if you do then I won't be able to help you.'

April didn't really understand how Paula could possibly help her, and she didn't want to appear naïve and even more foolish by asking her. 'We're going to be late, and Daniel will be waiting,' she muttered as she checked her watch and reached for her cap.

They left the house and walked quickly down the street to catch the bus into town. There was a heavy and unusual silence between them as they sat side by side on the uncomfortably narrow seats, each focused determinedly away from the other.

April's thoughts were in a whirl. Paula didn't know that she'd sneaked off base to visit a civilian clinic, more than once. The second time, they'd given her a pregnancy test. It had proved positive – and now she was over three months pregnant. The news had come as a terrible, frightening shock, and she'd prayed that the test had been wrong, that there'd been some awful mix-up. But as the weeks had gone on and the changes in her body had become more apparent, she'd withdrawn into herself, the doubts and fears as to how Daniel would take the news haunting her days and bringing torment to her nights.

She clenched her fists on her lap, thinking how stupid she'd been not to take Paula's advice earlier and go to the birth control clinic *before* she'd succumbed to Daniel's irresistible charms, and not two days later. By then, although she hadn't known it, the damage had already been done.

And yet, despite the wondrous, terrifying things that were happening to her body, she was too shy and embarrassed to discuss it even with Paula. It was such a personal thing, something that she needed to share with Daniel before she confided in Paula, for this was their baby, made from the love they'd found in one another. Tonight she would finally pluck up the courage to tell him, she decided firmly. And yet the doubts and fears that had troubled her over the past weeks began to cloud the faith she had in him to do the right thing, and she had to battle to dismiss them as she clung grimly to the belief that everything would turn out all right.

She'd seen little of him just lately, for his training schedule had been increased. Their time together was coming to an end, and soon – pray God not too soon – the American army would ship his regiment out to a war zone.

As the bus groaned and wheezed up the steep hill and began to wind through the narrow cobbled streets, April rehearsed what she would say to him, silently editing and adapting the words until she was satisfied that she could deliver them quietly and without any hint of desperation. They would have time then to talk it over and make their plans for the future.

She felt more settled and confident now she was prepared, and was even beginning to feel quite excited about the thought of what would happen once the war was over and they were free to do what they wanted. Daniel had talked of taking her home to America as his bride once he'd been demobbed. He'd painted a wonderful picture of the family's ranch where they raised beef cattle, corn and tobacco – and she had listened in awestruck silence as he described his beautiful mother who was the daughter of a Sioux chief, and his ruggedly handsome African father, whose family roots could be traced back to before the American

Civil War which had finally freed his people from slavery.

It had all sounded so romantic despite the prejudice they would encounter – and she vowed she would fight that every inch of the way, for his deep, melodious voice had painted such vivid pictures in her mind that she longed for this war to be won so they could be together and forge a new life in the more accepting world that peace must surely bring.

As they got off the bus, she reached for Paula's hand. 'I'll see you back at base,' she said. 'And I'm sorry I was sharp with you. We'll talk later.'

Paula's smile was wan. 'I hope things work out for you, April.'

'Of course they will,' she said brightly, her gaze flitting towards the dance hall door where she could see him waiting. She gave her friend a swift hug and then ran towards him. 'I'm sorry I'm a bit late, but the engine repair took longer than–'

'Well, you're here now,' he interrupted. 'Come on, let's get a drink.'

She frowned as she hurried in after him, for she hadn't seen him in a week and yet he hadn't kissed her as he usually did, or even taken her hand. A small dart of fear shot through her as they headed for the bar, and as she watched him order their drinks, she noticed a small muscle pulsate in his jaw and wondered what could be worrying him. Perhaps it wasn't the right time to tell him about the baby? Maybe she should leave it a bit until he was in a more pliant mood? But no. It had to be tonight.

She sipped at the warm beer feeling slightly sick

from the smell and the stifling great clouds of cigarette smoke. The noise was deafening, the crush on the dance floor impenetrable, and his demeanour strange and rather distant. She surreptitiously watched him as his gaze lingered over the dancers. There was a tension in him tonight that she didn't understand, and it was beginning to make her feel uneasy.

He turned then and looked down at her, his golden-flecked brown eyes seeming to delve right to her soul. 'I guess this will be the last night for us, honey,' he said. 'They're shipping us all out in three days and we're confined to camp after tonight.'

April froze, unable to speak as he cupped her chin and brushed his lips almost distractedly against hers.

'It's been great being with you, April, and I'll never forget the fun we had together. But there's a war to be won and the army seems to need me to help them fight it.'

'Daniel, I... Daniel, there's something I need to tell you,' she stammered.

His smile was almost bashful as he looked down at her. 'Well, I guess there's a coupl'a things I should have told you, honey,' he drawled, 'but you know how it is.'

His smile broadened and usually would have warmed her heart and made her feel cherished, but she noted that it hadn't reached his eyes, and the deep-seated uneasiness returned.

'I tell you what, little lady, why don't you tell me your secret, and then I'll tell mine and we can get on with having some fun instead of standing

37

around here wasting time?'

April stared up at him in bewilderment. He was acting strangely, and for the first time since she'd met him, she felt distanced from him. It was probably because he was nervous about going to a war zone, but she sensed that it might be better to hear what he had to say before she told him about the baby.

'Why don't you go first? My news can wait a bit longer,' she said with a lightness she didn't feel.

His gaze dropped to the floor and he shuffled his feet. 'I guess I should have told you about the wife and kids back home,' he muttered. 'But you know how it is – what with the war and everything...'

April felt the shock of his words knife through her, and she had to reach out to steady herself against the nearby table. 'A wife? Children?' she stammered. 'But you said... You promised...'

His sigh was sharp with impatience as he ran his fingers through his thick black hair. 'Aw, hell, April. It was only supposed to be a bit of fun, and the things a guy says in the heat of the moment shouldn't be taken too seriously. Surely even *you* knew that?'

April shook her head and stared back at him, feeling like a small creature caught in the headlights of a vast, fast approaching steam train.

He lit a Lucky Strike and snapped the Zippo shut before putting his arm round her waist and pulling her to him. 'How about you tell me what's on your mind, and then we can slip away and find somewhere quiet and private for one last time? I happen to know a nice little place where the landlady turns a blind eye for some nylons and gum.'

Stung by his words, lack of respect and care, she pushed hard against his chest. 'You lied to me,' she rasped through angry tears. 'You lied and cheated until you got what you wanted and now you think it's all right just to tell me about your wife and children and expect me to jump into bed with you.' She pummelled her fists against his chest. 'You're a lying rat, and I...'

'Is this guy bothering you, ma'am?'

April felt Daniel's arm fall from her waist as she turned to face the group of grim-faced white GIs. 'This is a private conversation,' she snapped. 'Go away.'

Despite her words, her expression must have betrayed her inner turmoil, for they moved as one to carefully set her apart from Daniel and close in on him. 'Okay, chief,' one of them drawled nastily. 'You wanna take this outside?'

'I'm not going anywhere,' said Daniel, standing his ground, eyes narrowed and watchful, his fists clenched at his sides.

'Hear that, you guys? The injun's got balls, I'll give him that.' There was a burst of humourless laughter and as the ringleader egged them on, they began to poke, push and jostle Daniel until he was backed up against a wall.

'Come on, *boy.*' It was a contemptuous snarl accompanied by a hard jab of a finger into Daniel's chest. 'Show us what you're made of – or are you too chicken?'

They began to make clucking noises as they continued to push and jab. April pressed back against the table, unable to do anything but watch in horror. Daniel might have been a liar and a

39

cheat, but he didn't deserve this foul-mouthed, vicious baiting. 'Stop it,' she begged. 'Stop it now.'

Her plea was lost in the loud music that was still playing and in the thud of feet on the wooden floor as Daniel's tormentors were joined by yet more of their cronies. She looked wildly round for someone to come and stop this, but there was no sign of the military police, or even the local copper.

And then suddenly Daniel was no longer alone. A platoon of black GIs closed in beside him and began to jab and punch back.

'Yeeha,' yelled one of the younger boys. 'Oh, man, we got ourselves a fight. Stick it to 'em, boys!' With that the fists started flying on both sides. A pair of combatants went reeling into the table loaded with glasses and bottles and everything crashed to the floor.

April had to leap out of the way to escape being trampled or caught by a flying fist or boot. 'Stop it. Please stop. Someone help,' she implored, but no one took any notice.

Stoked by drink and bravado, the fight was enthusiastically joined by groups of Australians, New Zealanders and Rhodesians who appeared to have a few scores of their own to settle. The music came to an abrupt halt and the dancers fled as the more senior officers bellowed for order.

April watched in horror as blood poured from Daniel's nose and mouth. His right hook met a corporal's nose dead centre, and as it exploded into a spray of blood, the corporal's fist arced in a vicious uppercut which rocked Daniel's head on his shoulders and sent him stumbling into the line of chairs at the side of the dance hall.

As girls screamed and scattered, and men shouted, more and more GIs joined the fray and the fighting became even fiercer. Tables and chairs were upended and smashed against heads, and glasses were shattered, and soon the dance floor was a heavy, grunting mass of flying fists and trampling boots that slithered in the gore now slicking the floor.

April was in tears, but Paula had managed to circumnavigate the chaos, and now she pulled her friend towards the doorway. 'We've got to get out of here,' she shouted. 'Quick, before the MPs arrive.' But there was no time to make their escape, for a great shout came from the doorway and a whole platoon of American military police came thundering into the hall. With batons raised they charged into the melee with relish, not caring who they bludgeoned in order to quell the fighting.

April and Paula cowered in terror in a corner, watching as bloodied, bruised men left the fray, heading for a swift exit through the nearest door or window to escape arrest. Some continued fighting, heedless of the baton blows, but the strength in numbers of the police proved too great and at last it was all over. The main protagonists were roughly handcuffed and hauled outside to the waiting trucks, while the injured were manhandled onto stretchers and carted off to the military hospital in ambulances.

Daniel was roughly shoved towards the door, his hands tied behind his back. He had cuts and swellings all over his face, one eye was almost closed and there was blood drying on his mouth and down his tattered uniform. April stared,

41

numb with shock. 'Daniel, I'm sorry,' she called out.

He stumbled past her and didn't even spare her a glance.

April clung to Paula. 'What will happen to him?' she sobbed.

Paula's expression was grim. 'The same as happened to Saul, I expect. I just hope the others get the same treatment, otherwise it wouldn't be fair, seeing as how they started it.'

'But they didn't,' April protested. 'It was because of me. It was all my fault.'

'I very much doubt that,' Paula replied briskly as she helped April to her feet. 'Come on, let's gather up your things and get out of here. Petty Officer Rainsworth has offered us a lift back to base, and we don't want to keep her waiting.'

April could only nod, for a heavy weight of pain had settled somewhere near her heart, and she no longer had the will or the strength to argue.

They arrived back at the house to be greeted by the other girls demanding to know what had started the fight, and how April had become involved. Petty Officer Rainsworth's expression brooked no argument as she ordered everyone into their rooms, threatening severe punishment if she saw or heard anything from them again that night.

Paula and April prepared for bed in silence, but once the light was off, April felt the need to talk, to let out all the anguish the evening had brought her. As she sobbed out her story, Paula perched on the bed beside her and put a comforting arm around her shoulder.

'How far gone are you?' she asked quietly when April fell silent.

'Over three months.'

Paula sighed. 'It's far too late to do anything about it, then. I do wish you'd told me sooner.' As April remained silent, Paula continued. 'There's a doctor, you see – a lot of the girls have used him and he's reliable. But you're too far gone, April, and no amount of money would persuade him to give you an abortion now.'

April shuddered at the thought, her mind filled with horrifying images gleaned from overhearing the stories told by the girls who'd experienced such a thing, or knew someone who had. 'I could never do that,' she murmured. 'Let alone be able to live with the guilt.'

'So what are you going to do, April? You won't be able to hide your condition for much longer, and if the navy finds out ... well, you know what will happen.'

'Yes, I do.' Her thoughts were in a jumble, her emotions so tangled that she was finding it hard to remain coherent. 'I'll just have to hide it for as long as possible and start saving up enough to rent somewhere once that day comes. Then, when the ... when the baby ... when it's born, I'll have it adopted.'

'You could go home.'

April shook her head. 'I can't face Mother. She's bad enough as it is, and something like this... She'd throw me out and never speak to me again.'

'She might surprise you and be supportive,' said Paula, without much conviction.

'I'll manage on my own – the way I always have,'

43

April said brokenly.

'I suppose you could try and get the US army to make Daniel support you.'

'He'd only deny it was his,' April said bitterly.

'Bastard,' muttered Paula. She gave April a fierce hug. 'Never mind, April. We'll see this through together for as long as we can. Now, you get some sleep. We've an early start in the morning.'

April lay awake long after Paula had fallen asleep, her restless thoughts tumbling over one another, until the heartbreak of his betrayal and the fear for her future and that of her unborn baby became such torture that she left her bed and went to stare out of the window at the black, black night, hoping for some respite and an answer to her terrible dilemma.

2

Cliffehaven, March 1943

Peggy Reilly stood on the platform, tightly gripping the pram handle as she watched her younger sister's train slowly chug and puff its way around the bend until it was out of sight. Her emotions were mixed, for she would miss Doreen, with her sparky nature and loving heart, but on the other hand, Doreen was making the right decision. She'd be much safer with her girls in Wales and have the tranquillity to enjoy and prepare for the precious baby she was expecting. Still, it was a wrench, and Peggy felt it keenly.

Ron shuffled his feet and gave her an awkward hug as his brindled lurcher, Harvey, went off to investigate the long grass beneath the hump-backed bridge. 'Ach, to be sure, Peggy girl, Doreen will be back before you know it.'

She looked at her father-in-law, who was dressed, as usual, in baggy corduroy trousers held up with garden twine, wellington boots, a faded, fraying shirt, disreputable, tatty old cap and long, grubby poacher's coat. He might look like a tramp, but he was stout-hearted and one of the kindest, bravest people she knew. She gave him a watery smile. 'Let's hope so, Ron. I'm getting awfully weary at having to say goodbye to the people I love.'

He wriggled his wayward brows. 'Never mind, Peggy. You'll always have me and Harvey to look after,' he teased with a twinkle in his eyes.

Peggy was strangely comforted by his words, for although Ron and Harvey could be ruddy nuisances at times, and tested her patience to its very limits, they were the defining glue that held her together when she most needed it, and she couldn't imagine Beach View, or life itself, without them. She watched as he whistled to the dog, waved goodbye to the portly stationmaster, Stan, and tramped away, no doubt heading for the hills in search of something for the cooking pot – but if it was rabbit yet again, she'd scream.

Stan tickled baby Daisy's rosy cheek and earned a beaming, toothy smile. 'I've always liked Doreen,' he said. 'It's a shame she had to leave. I got quite used to seeing her around the place again.'

45

Peggy nodded, fiercely blinking back her tears. 'This damned war has a lot to answer for,' she said. She tucked the pram blankets firmly around a chuckling Daisy, and adjusted her knitted mittens. 'Doreen and her girls should be here with us, not isolated over there in Wales amongst strangers.'

Stan rocked on his heels, his burgeoning belly putting a great strain on his waistcoat buttons. 'It's tough for everyone, Peg,' he muttered. 'I'm just thankful that I don't have the same problem.'

Peggy gave him a sympathetic pat on the arm. Stan had been an institution at the station for as long as she could remember. He'd fought in the first shout alongside Ron, Fred the Fish and Alf the butcher, and had taken over the stationmaster's little cottage on his father's retirement. He'd been widowed for many years, and she knew that the sad lack of any children was something he never quite managed to get over; which was probably why he took such a fatherly interest in the waifs and strays who arrived at his station, and made certain they were found decent billets. Ruby had been one such girl who'd come to Beach View through him, and there had been others who'd found his advice and genuine kindness a real help during the tough times.

'I thought you had a younger sister, Stan. Didn't she come and stay with you for a little while some years back?'

He heaved a great sigh. 'Aye, she did for a bit after Barbara passed away, but I've not seen hide nor hair of her since.'

'That is a shame,' Peggy murmured. She looked

46

fondly at Daisy, who was crowing delightedly at an early butterfly flitting above the wild flowers that grew on the railway embankments. 'At times like these we all need our family around us.' She shot him an encouraging smile. 'But you've got Ethel and her Ruby now, so life isn't too lonely, is it?'

'Aye, I'm a lucky man.' His lugubrious expression cleared and he beamed down at her. 'I'm going to ask Ethel to marry me now she's free of that toe-rag. Bought the ring and everything. Thought I might pop the question tonight.'

'Oh, Stan, how lovely. I'm so pleased for you.'

He looked suddenly uncertain. 'You don't think it's too soon, Peg? After all, she only got the telegram a couple of weeks ago.'

Peggy knew all about Ethel's brute of a husband. Far from lamenting his loss in the battle for Tunisia, Ethel and her daughter, Ruby, felt they'd been given a second chance to make a decent, settled life here. 'She's probably wondering why you didn't pop the question the night she had that celebratory dinner,' she said, smiling.

Stan nodded thoughtfully. 'It didn't feel appropriate, even though I knew she wasn't mourning him. But she does harbour a sense of guilt that she felt nothing but relief when she got that telegram.'

'Then she shouldn't,' said Peggy stoutly. 'He was a bully who made her life a misery, and Ruby's husband was just the same. The pair of them are well out of it, if you ask me – and Ethel should thank her lucky stars that she's got someone like you to look after her.'

Stan reddened and his eyes became watery. 'She's a grand girl. I'm the lucky one.'

47

Peggy giggled and playfully poked him in the stomach. 'You're certainly looking well on it, Stan. But if you put on any more weight, you're going to have to get her to sew in an extra piece on that waistcoat. Those buttons look as if they're about to pop off like bullets.'

He smiled shyly and patted his belly. 'Ethel says she likes a bit of meat on a man.'

Peggy managed to resist pointing out that there was a world of difference between a bit of meat and an entire carcass. 'I'd better get on, Stan. It's wash day, and the laundry has piled up something awful.'

She stood on tiptoe and kissed his cheek. 'I won't wish you luck with the proposal, because you don't need it,' she said softly. 'I know you'll both be very happy.'

Daisy waved goodbye, burbling happily, and Peggy pushed the pram out of the station and headed for home. It was a lovely spring morning, with just enough of a breeze to get the washing dry, and the sun was sparkling on the patch of sea that was visible at the bottom of the High Street. Despite the bomb craters, the skeletal remains of blasted buildings and the piles of sandbags outside the entrances to the civic buildings, there was romance in the air and Cliffehaven had a feeling of hope about it.

Stan watched fondly as Peggy headed off down the High Street. He admired her tremendously, for although she was small and slender and looked as if a puff of wind might blow her away, she possessed a core of steel and an uncompromising belief in working hard, and doing the right thing.

He gave a happy sigh and unlocked the Nissen hut which had replaced the booking hall and ladies' waiting room soon after the firebombs had destroyed them, along with the slum housing that had sprawled along the eastern perimeter of the station. Peggy's stalwart character reminded him of his late wife, Barbara, who'd always championed the underdog, helped those in need and never had a bad word to say about anybody. He hoped that, like Peggy, Barbara would have approved of his proposal to Ethel. He'd been alone for too long, and although some might say that, at forty-nine, Ethel was a bit young for him, the rather fierce little Cockney woman had brought liveliness, laughter and companionship back into his life, and he was excited at the prospect of making their relationship official.

Stan opened the hatchway that had been cut in the corrugated iron door and propped up the makeshift counter. The nine-eleven would be arriving soon, and people might want to buy tickets – though with the strict travel restrictions, that was highly unlikely. He put the kettle on the primus stove, poured some treacly black Camp Coffee into his favourite china mug, and added a dollop of milk and two teaspoons of sugar. Giving it a good stir, he reached for the lunch tin Ethel had brought to him earlier, and smiled with pleasure at the doorstep mutton sandwich, and the two rock cakes nestled in with a lovely sausage roll.

With the kettle boiled and the coffee cooling nicely on the counter, Stan sat down to enjoy his early elevenses. Ethel was a good cook, and even in these difficult times managed to get hold of butter, sugar and dried fruit. He knew that the butter, eggs and cheese came from the land girls who worked up at the Cliffe estate, in return for Ethel cleaning their billet and doing their mending – but the fruit and sugar? He suspected she'd made friends with someone up at the factory canteen, for she'd recently been coming home with aprons and overalls to mend. There was no doubt about it, he thought as he munched contentedly, his Ethel was a worker – and clever with it.

Brushing the flaky pastry crumbs from his dark uniform, he licked the sausage roll grease from his fingers and gave a soft belch. 'Beg pardon,' he muttered to the empty Nissen hut. His thoughts turned back to Ethel and Ruby. He knew there was a party planned for the following week to celebrate Ruby's engagement to her young Canadian, Mike Taylor, and he was delighted that she'd found such happiness here in Cliffehaven. When Stan had first seen her arrive on the train that dark, cold night a year ago, she'd borne the bruises of a nasty beating and looked half-starved and terrified of her own shadow. Stan's smile was soft as he remembered feeding her his sandwiches and tea and setting her up for the night in the Nissen hut. She'd had her ups and downs here at first, but once he and Ron had seen her secure with Peggy, she had never looked back.

'Who would have thought I'd end up being her stepfather?' he murmured. He grinned and reached for a rock cake as he went over his plans on how he was going to pop the question tonight. Ruby had arranged to meet Mike at the Anchor and Ethel was cooking him tea, so he'd wait until they'd finished that before going down on one knee. The ring was safe in its box in his jacket pocket; the bouquet of flowers would be made up during his afternoon break – there were some lovely early blooms in his allotment – and he'd taken special care to press his best suit for the occasion.

Perhaps he should nip down later to the Crown and see if Gloria Stevens had a bottle of wine tucked away – she usually had something under the counter for special celebrations, did Gloria. Though it would probably not be wise to mention where it had come from to Ethel – she and Gloria had never really got on since she'd caught the landlady of the Crown giving him the glad eye under the mistletoe at Christmas.

Stan heaved a contented sigh as he finished the rock cake, burped again and brushed crumbs from his chest. It was rather gratifying to have two women vying for his attention at his age. Then again, his friend Ron was also in his mid-sixties, and he was stepping out with the very desirable Rosie Brathwaite who owned the Anchor – which proved that a man was never too old to enjoy the attentions of a good-looking woman.

He felt the need to burp again. Perhaps he would go to the chemist while he was in town: he was out of liver salts, and he didn't want his indigestion and heartburn spoiling his proposal.

Peggy walked contentedly down the High Street, nodding to friends, but not stopping to chat. It was Monday morning, the washing had piled up, and if she didn't get on with it there wouldn't be time to get it dry before the sun lost its warmth. The nights were still damp and cold, but the promise of spring was in the air, which lifted the spirits just as much as the continuing good news from North Africa and Russia. She could almost believe that this war was getting closer to being won.

As she reached the corner of Camden Road she paused, wondering if she should go and see her older sister Doris. Havelock Road was only one street down, and she was rather miffed that Doris hadn't bothered to come to the station this morning to see Doreen off. Perhaps she was still simmering from Doreen's rather too truthful dressing-down – or preoccupied with the fact that her husband Ted was insisting upon a divorce, and her son and pregnant daughter-in-law were about to leave for the Midlands. Either way, it was pretty disgraceful not to bother to show up. There was a war on after all, and it could be months before it was safe for Doreen to return home.

Peggy dithered as she stood there. Doris might have ideas above her station and be the rudest person she knew, but there was little doubt that she was unhappy at the moment, and it would be the sisterly thing to just go and see if she was all right. Yet, as she continued down the High Street towards the seafront and Havelock Road, she saw Doris drive past in her car, nose in the air, studiously ignoring her when it was obvious she'd seen her.

'That does it, Daisy,' she said. 'She can stew in her own juice.'

Daisy clapped her hands and blew a raspberry.

Peggy giggled and began to push the pram along the promenade. It was the long way round to get back home to Beach View, and would entail climbing the steep hill at the end, but on such a lovely morning, the walk would set her up for the day.

As the gulls wheeled and mewled overhead, Peggy felt the familiar pang of regret she experienced every time she took this walk, for Cliffehaven seafront looked very different to how she remembered it before the war. And they were fond memories, not only of her childhood, but of Jim's courtship too.

The mellow days of summer spent on the beach with a picnic; Jim and her canoodling in the shadows of the Victorian shelters, and the evenings spent dancing, or going to one of the shows on the end of the pier, which had always been lit up like a Christmas tree... Coloured lights strung along the promenade, the delicious smell of fish and chips and vinegar mingling with the honeyed scent of candyfloss and toffee apples as the town's brass band entertained the holidaymakers who sat in deckchairs or on the terraces of the big hotels... They were sweet, poignant memories that belonged to another time and another world – like faded sepia photographs of a bygone age that had silently slipped away unnoticed. She felt an ache of longing for them – and for Jim – to return.

Peggy drew back from her memories and stoically faced the reality of what war had brought to her beloved home town. The pretty coloured lights had been taken down, the deckchairs stacked away, and the stalls selling ice cream, candyfloss and beach toys had been dismantled and stored in one of the municipal buildings.

The horseshoe bay between the chalk cliffs was now threaded with ugly concrete shipping traps; the shingle beach was mined and bore the evidence of sunken ships and downed aircraft in the great clumps of stinking oil that clung to the flotsam and jetsam that had been washed ashore on the tides. Vast coils of barbed wire closed off the beach, gun emplacements had been erected along the promenade, and the poor old pier had been severed from the shore and was now no more than a blackened skeleton, the remains of a German fighter plane embedded in its ribs.

Peggy kept walking, determined to remain positive and enjoy the early spring day. Hitler's armies were taking a pounding now, and the Japs were being given a run for their money by the Americans in the Pacific. The brave, indefatigable Allies would win this war. Doreen would bring her children back from Wales, Jim would come home from India, and her children and grandchildren would once again gather round her kitchen table. Life would get back to normal, the hated rationing would come to an end and Cliffehaven would be rebuilt, the beach opened once more to the holidaymakers.

She reached the end of the promenade, glancing only briefly at the spot beneath the chalk cliffs where Cliffehaven's fishing fleet used to be hauled up the shingle, the nets hung to dry in the tall black sheds which now stood empty. She studiously ignored the great bomb crater that marked the demise of the Grand Hotel, for she had too many memories of happy times there dancing the

54

night away with Jim, and started the long climb up the hill towards home.

Beach View Boarding House didn't actually have much view of the beach unless one stood on tiptoe by the top window, but that didn't matter in the slightest as the seafront was only a matter of minutes away. It was one of the many four-storey Victorian villas which lined the easterly side of the hill in neatly arranged terraces, and had been home to Peggy for most of her life. When her parents had retired, she had taken over the business while Jim worked as a projectionist at the Odeon cinema, which sadly was no more since taking an indirect hit during an enemy raid.

The holiday trade had been brisk in those early years, and she and Jim had happily raised their four children in the belief they were set for life. But as the rumours of war became a reality, the visitors had stopped coming. The debts had mounted, and Peggy had been fearful of losing her family home, so she'd applied to the billeting office for evacuees to come and fill the empty rooms. And she'd never looked back, for the girls she'd taken in had become her chicks – helping to fill the aching void left by her older children, who were now scattered and mostly living far from home.

There were four girls living with her at the moment: Fran, who worked as a theatre nurse in the hospital; Sarah, who ran the office for the Women's Timber Corps up at the Cliffe Estate; Rita, who was a driver and mechanic in the local fire service; and Ivy, who'd recently moved in and was working up at the aeroplane parts factory alongside Ruby.

55

Dear little Cordelia Finch had been a permanent resident for many years, and although she was rapidly approaching eighty, she had been invigorated by the arrival of the young ones, and revelled in the opportunity to be the grandmother of the house. She and Ron adored one another despite their endless bickering, but it was a bit of a battle to make her turn up her hearing aid, and conversations could get very convoluted and quite hilarious at times.

Peggy smiled at Daisy, who was clapping her hands and chortling at the antics of two seagulls squabbling over a paper bag. Peggy had thought her child-bearing years were over when the doctor had told her she was pregnant, so it had all come as a bit of a shock – especially as her eldest daughter Anne had only recently given birth to Peggy's first grandchild. But Daisy was sixteen months old now, and Peggy was determined to enjoy every minute of her babyhood, for she would be the last.

Peggy was puffing a bit as she trudged up the hill. Daisy was getting rather big and heavy for this old coach-built pram, and the hill never seemed to get any shorter. Perhaps it was time to dig out the pushchair from the clutter in the basement? It had served her well over the years, and once Ron had oiled the wheels, it should be absolutely fine. And yet she would find it very difficult to make the change, for it would mark the end of Daisy's babyhood, and she wasn't quite ready for that yet.

Peggy's thoughts turned to her eldest daughter Anne, who was down in Somerset with her two little girls and much younger brothers, Bob and Charlie. Bob was nearly sixteen now and Charlie was twelve. Peggy feared that if this war went on much longer, the boys wouldn't want to come home – and if they did, they'd be like strangers, for she hadn't been able to see them for years. As for Anne, she was constantly worried about her husband Martin, who was now on almost continuous bombing ops over Germany. His luck had held so far, but with so many casualties, that luck was getting very tenuous.

Cissy, on the other hand, was thankfully still in the area and could manage a fleeting visit now and again from Cliffe aerodrome where she was a driver in the WAAF. She would turn twenty-one in May, and it seemed her earlier ambitions to be a star of stage and screen had been set aside for the sophistication of a smart uniform and the company of dashing airmen.

Peggy sighed as she reached the twitten that ran between the backs of the houses. Cissy had taken on the mannerisms and language of the rather upper-class boys and girls up at Cliffe, and to Peggy's mind was becoming a little too full of herself. Yet she'd definitely sobered up a bit at the horrendous loss of so many of those brave young airmen who'd flown sortie after sortie in their efforts to defeat the enemy. It was a shame that her young American flight lieutenant had been posted some miles away at Biggin Hill, for Cissy had at last found someone to really love.

Peggy understood how keenly Cissy and Anne worried about their men and she wished she could offer her daughters some comfort – but having to rely on letters and the occasional telephone call to do so was highly unsatisfactory and left her feeling frustrated and tearful.

She opened the back gate and contemplated the garden which Ron had turned into a vegetable plot. The Anderson shelter huddled by the flint wall, the turf on its roof sprouting spring vegetables; the chicken coop and outside lav were to the right of the back door, along with the almost empty coal bunker and the tarpaulin strip which covered the bicycles. Thankfully, Ron had retrieved her bike from the factory estate after the awful bombing which had almost killed Ivy, but having Daisy in tow most of the time, it was rare for Peggy to use it these days.

She wheeled the pram into the basement scullery, hoisted Daisy out and climbed the concrete steps to the kitchen. What she needed now was a lovely cuppa and a bit of a sit-down before she started on the laundry.

3

It was lunchtime, so Stan locked up his Nissen hut and plodded down the hill to the chemist. The next tram wasn't for another two hours, so he had time to get something for his indigestion and nip into the Crown for a pint and to see Gloria.

The Crown Hotel was large and sprawling, with three bars, a function room and bedrooms to let upstairs. It was usually quiet at this time of day, for most of the servicemen and women were on duty and the factory shifts wouldn't change until after Gloria had closed for the afternoon. He shot a hasty glance up and down the High Street to make sure no one was watching him and then stepped into the gloom of the saloon bar with its dark panelled walls and dim lights.

He nodded a greeting to the two old men who were sitting by the fire nursing their pints as they puffed tranquilly on their pipes, and doffed his hat to the group of elderly women who were gossiping in the corner over bottles of milk stout. The furniture was scarred, the ceiling yellowed by years of tobacco smoke; the stained-glass windows had been heavily taped, which only added to the gloom, and the piano was so battered, it was a miracle anyone could get a tune out of it. But in the lull of the quiet lunch hour, it had a welcoming, warm atmosphere, helped enormously by the friendly smile of the landlady, Gloria Stevens.

The Crown had a bit of a reputation for being a rowdy place at night, when fights often broke out, and most things could be purchased on the black market if you knew who to approach. Gloria had run the place for years without the aid of her husband – a feckless rogue who'd run out on her and their baby son for another woman. Gloria certainly didn't seem to miss him, for it was rumoured that she spread her favours about when the fancy took her – although just lately she'd been downcast and not herself. Stan had heard that her only son had been killed in the Far East, and something like that could defeat the strongest person – even the redoubtable Gloria Stevens.

Gloria was originally from the East End and stood no nonsense from anyone. She was as sharp as a tack when it came to spotting troublemakers or girls touting for business, and sorted both out swiftly and efficiently. She was a tall, rather forceful-looking woman with large breasts that swelled like ripe melons above her low-cut dresses and blouses, and her hair had been bleached to within an inch of its life. She had surprisingly good legs for a woman her size, and a voice that could drown out an air-raid siren and give the thundering Luftwaffe a run for its money when she bellowed for order from behind her bar. With her cheap jewellery, heavy make-up and tight clothes, she was the epitome of everyone's idea of a pub landlady, and she seemed to relish the role, thumbing her nose at the less charitable women in Cliffehaven who considered her to be no better than she should be.

Stan had always liked her, for under all that brassiness was a heart of gold, and he knew that not only was she looking after her widowed daughter-in-law and two grandchildren at the moment, but she was keeping an eye out for her nephew, Andy, who'd just started at the fire station. Gloria was also a generous and enthusiastic participant when it came to charities and fund-raising, and there was always a tin on the bar for donations to something. Today it was for the Red Cross.

He smiled as he approached the bar. 'Good morning, Gloria, and how are you today?'

'A bit bored, if the truth be known, Stan. I hate it when it's this quiet.' She reached for the beer pump. 'Your usual, is it?'

Stan nodded and watched admiringly as her sturdy arm wielded the pump up and down, which made her breasts do rather delightful things above

60

the low-cut neckline of her dress. Ethel would kill him if she could see him now, but he was only human and a look did no harm.

Gloria smiled knowingly at him as she placed the frothing glass on the bar and took his money. 'Fancy something to eat with that, Stan? I've got a nice bit of 'am in for a function this afternoon, and they won't miss a slice for a sandwich.'

A bit of ham was tempting, but Gloria would be closing soon, and the thought of sitting on his own with her made him a bit hot and bothered. 'Better not,' he mumbled. 'I'm supposed to be on duty.'

'You mean Ethel wouldn't like it,' she retorted without rancour. She tossed back her candyfloss hair, which made her earrings swing, and then proceeded to vigorously wipe down the bar as her other customers drank up and left. It was almost two o'clock.

He grinned sheepishly and concentrated on drinking half of his pint before speaking again. 'How's your Betty getting on?' he asked. 'It can't be easy for her with the children and everything.'

The shadows beneath Gloria's eyes seemed to darken. 'She's bearing up, Stan. But yer right, it ain't easy for neither of us.' Her eyes became glassy and she blinked rapidly before continuing. 'Our Andy's found 'er a nice flat in Camden Road, so she'll be moving in there next week. Can't say I'll be sad to see 'em go,' she said on a sigh. 'Them two kids are holy terrors, and it's the devil's own job to keep 'em out of the bars and guest rooms.'

Stan had seen the two little boys about the town and they were certainly too lively for their poor, grieving mother to control. 'Still, she'll be close

61

enough for you to be able to pop in and keep an eye,' he said comfortably. 'And with Andy across the road at the fire station, she'll feel right at home.'

'It'll be easier for Betty when them kids start school,' said Gloria. 'But they need a firm 'and, and no mistake.' She gave a deep sigh, and suddenly, for all the make-up and bright jewellery, she looked every one of her forty-eight years. 'It's a cruel world, Stan, when mothers lose their sons and kids have to grow up without their dad.'

Stan nodded and reached for her hand. 'But you managed on your own, Gloria,' he said consolingly. 'And Betty will too, you'll see.'

Gloria sniffed and shook back her hair in an effort to dispel the dark mood that had overcome her. 'Yeah, well, when the going gets tough, the tough get going as they say, and Betty will 'ave me to help her along, never you mind.'

She folded her arms and shot him a brittle smile. 'So, Stan, you don't often pop in 'ere for a drink at lunchtime. What can I do you for today, then?'

His returning smile was wry. He might have known she'd realise he was here for more than just a pint and a chat. 'I was wondering if you've got a special bottle of something under that counter,' he said hopefully. 'Only me and Ethel – well, we're going to celebrate tonight.'

Gloria raised a fiercely plucked eyebrow. 'Blimey, Stan. Don't tell me you're going to make an honest woman of her at last?'

He went red and puffed out his chest. 'That's the idea.'

She laughed uproariously. 'There ain't no accounting for taste, but good luck to the pair of yer. I'll see what I've got.' With that she slid a key out of the till, turned on her heel and went through to unlock the back room, which Stan knew was like an Aladdin's cave filled with all sorts of things the authorities would frown upon if they ever got the chance to see them.

He was a bit put out by her remark, not knowing if it applied to him or to Ethel, but knew better than to probe, for the answer would have been unsettling either way.

She returned to the deserted saloon bar just as the clock struck two, and triumphantly placed a bottle of champagne on the counter. 'That do yer?'

It was a very posh bottle with gold foil over the cork and French writing on the label. 'How much?' he asked warily.

'Seeing as it's you, two quid. That's proper stuff, that is – all the way from France.'

Stan blanched. Two pounds was a bit steep. 'Where'd you get it?'

She tapped the side of her nose. 'Ask no questions and I'll tell you no lies. D'ya want it or not?'

Stan hesitated. 'I can give you one pound ten for it,' he said hopefully.

Her eyes narrowed. 'Two quid, Stan – and that's a bargain. I can sell it for a fiver to anyone else.'

Stan eyed the bottle with its fancy label. He'd never tasted champagne and it would be a real treat for Ethel – and as it was for such a special occasion, he supposed he should just pay up and not try to haggle with someone like Gloria, who could tie him in knots with the bat of a false eyelash. 'All right,' he said on a sigh. 'But can you wrap it up or something? I don't want half of Cliffehaven seeing me carrying that back to the station.'

'Bloody hell, Stan. What you think this is – bleedin' Harrods?' She clucked her tongue and went off again, her heels clattering on the bare floorboards. She returned with a large brown paper bag and fastened it round the neck of the bottle with a length of string. 'There. Satisfied?'

Stan opened his wallet and took out two pound notes, which were swiftly whisked away and stuffed in her black lace brassiere.

'Keep that under yer coat, Stan, and go out the back way. You know what the nosy parkers are like round 'ere.'

He nodded, finished his pint and pushed back from the bar. 'Thanks, Gloria.'

'Nice doing business with you, Stan,' she replied with a cheeky grin as she returned from locking the front door and leaned on the bar, giving him an eyeful of burgeoning breasts. 'See you again soon.'

Stan tore his gaze away. Clutching the bottle to his chest beneath his jacket, he turned towards the back door just as it opened.

Harvey came rushing in, closely followed by Ron.

The two men froze and regarded one another in a tense silence. They both knew they shouldn't be in here – and that if their women found out they'd be for the high jump – and yet to question the other's presence was not something close friends did in such circumstances.

Stan was the first to break the silence. 'Hello,

64

Ron. Nice day, isn't it?'

Ron glowered from beneath his thick brows. 'Aye, for some, maybe,' he growled. 'Haven't you got a station to run?'

Stan frowned, for it was clear he'd caught Ron on the hop – and if ever a man looked shifty it was his old friend. 'You know me, Ron,' he blustered. 'Always finding something to do between trains.' He leaned closer so Gloria couldn't hear. 'We'll keep this to ourselves, eh?'

Ron still looked uneasy. 'Mind you do, 'cos your Ethel is about as discreet as the *Cliffehaven Clarion*.'

'My Ethel won't hear about it, Ron,' he murmured, aware that Gloria was watching them keenly as she headed towards them. 'You can be very sure about that.'

They nodded in tacit agreement and Stan slipped outside into the yard. He hurried down the narrow alleyway and then turned up the High Street towards the station, his thoughts in a whirl. If Rosie got even a hint that Ron was visiting Gloria after hours there would be hell to pay. It was definitely not something to tell Ethel, for she liked Rosie and would make sure her friend was made aware of Ron's secret visit. But what on earth was Ron doing there in the first place?

Stan fretted over the situation as he put the bottle of champagne in a bucket of water to cool. He hated secrets, especially when they could cause trouble between the people he was fond of, but he couldn't help but wonder what Ron was up to.

Rosie Braithwaite was thinking much the same thing as she locked the Anchor's door behind her last customer. Ron always popped in to help her change the barrels after the lunchtime session, or at least he had until recently. This was the third time in the past week that he'd gone missing, and there had been other unexplained absences of an evening too – but when she'd questioned him about it last night, he'd given her the old excuses and shrugged off her concern with his usual blarney.

She swept back her platinum curls and stared out of the heavily taped window into the street, wondering if her intuition was proving wrong for once. She knew he had lots of commitments with the Home Guard as well as at home in Beach View, but they had never encroached on their private time before, so why the difference now?

She had wondered if he was getting frustrated by her keeping him at arm's length, but he'd seemed to accept the situation and they'd rubbed along cosily enough these past few years. The thought that he might be playing around with someone else just didn't sit right. For all his banter and dodgy ways, Ron had always been honest with her, and she couldn't find it in her heart to believe that he was playing her false.

She gave a sigh and eased out of her high-heeled shoes. The old, uneven flagstones were lovely and cool beneath her aching feet, but her troubled heart was not soothed. She took one last look out of the window at the empty street and headed past the bar to the stairs which led up to her private rooms.

Monty, her brindled cross-breed pup, climbed off the couch and greeted her joyfully, so Rosie fondled his ears and made a fuss of him before going into her tiny kitchen to make a cup of tea. Ron's lurcher, Harvey, had sired Monty during a tryst with a pedigree whippet. Needless to say, the owner of the whippet had not been best pleased and had dumped the pup on Ron and Peggy. It had all proved too much for Peggy, and as Rosie had instantly fallen in love with Monty, she'd taken him on. She was glad of his company, especially once the doors were locked and she was alone – glad too that having to walk him regularly meant she had a proper reason to get some fresh air and exercise away from the smoky, noisy atmosphere of the Anchor's bar.

Monty was dancing on his toes with little whining encouragements to be fed, so she filled his bowl with the leftover scraps from last night's supper and then made herself a Spam sandwich to go with the tea.

She took her meal into the sitting room and plumped down on the chintz-covered couch, all too aware of how quiet it was apart from the clang of Monty's collar tag hitting the metal dog bowl. It was at times like this that she wondered why she held so fast to the vows she'd taken in church all those years ago, for the loneliness she suffered was no real life at all – and if she ever lost Ron, it would become unbearable.

As she finished her tea and Monty came bounding back into the sitting room to clamber up on the couch beside her, she once again felt a great wave of sorrow. She loved Ron so much,

67

and he'd been so very patient, but he was after all a lusty man – and lusty men had needs.

'Oh, Monty,' she sighed as he rested his long nose on her lap and looked up at her with trusting amber eyes. 'Why can't I just ignore my Catholic upbringing and build a proper new life with the man I love?'

Monty whined as his tail thumped on the cushions.

'Darling Monty,' she murmured. 'You don't realise how lucky you are not to have such things to worry about.' She stroked his brindled coat and silently answered her own question. She couldn't ignore the Catholic teachings that had been drummed into her since infancy and make a life with Ron, because she could never live with the guilt and the sense of betrayal she'd feel. It would cast a cloud over everything. And as long as her poor, sick husband James was incarcerated in that asylum she too was a prisoner – not only of her guilt, but of the laws of the land which forbade divorce in such circumstances.

'It's not an easy situation for either of us, and I couldn't blame Ron for straying.' She took a quavering breath. 'But if I discover that he has, then I don't know what I'll do.'

Monty licked her hand in sympathy and then began to sniff at her untouched sandwich.

Rosie pushed him away and carried the sandwich back into the kitchen… She was no longer hungry, and poor Monty had been shut up here all morning. 'Come on, little man, let's go for a walk and see if we can't blow these old cobwebs away.'

Railway Cottage had miraculously escaped the firebomb attack which had flattened almost everything around it back in 1940. It stood beside the railway line, surrounded on three sides by beds of vegetables, its old stone walls covered in tendrils of honeysuckle and roses. A sway-backed peg-tiled roof hung low over the four diamond-paned windows and single wooden door, and a brick path led to a gate in the picket fence that surrounded the plot.

There was a large butt to store rainwater from the iron guttering, a wooden outside lav and a dilapidated lean-to which housed logs for the fire and Stan's bicycle. A few chickens scratched about in the sturdy pen that Ron had helped to build, and the stray cat that had adopted Stan at the start of the war now lay supine in front of the range.

The cottage had been Stan's childhood home, and although it was a bit shabby now, and rather cramped for a man of his size, it was nonetheless cosy and full of memories. He'd returned home from the First World War and moved back in with his young bride when his father retired as station-master, and he and Barbara had been very happy here. The only thing to overshadow this happiness was their inability to have the large family they'd so longed for – but as it turned out, it was probably for the best, for Barbara had died during the devastating flu epidemic in the twenties, and it had been heart-breaking enough for him without having to deal with grieving, motherless children.

Stan took a deep breath and tried to dismiss these gloomy memories. He was about to start a new chapter in his life, and should be looking forward, not back.

With a glance around the single room that served as parlour and kitchen, his gaze flitted from the sleeping ginger cat to the fireside chairs and brass pots hanging from the rafters, then on to the china ornaments Barbara had so loved, and the neatly stitched cloth over the small table. The memories of Barbara were everywhere, and Ethel had respected that as she'd cleaned and polished and cooked him meals on the rather old-fashioned range.

Stan wasn't a fanciful man, he didn't believe in ghosts and spirits living on, but he could feel Barbara's presence tonight, and was comforted by it. She'd loved him well, if only for a few short years, and he knew that she wouldn't have begrudged him this chance of a new start after all the years he'd been on his own.

He moved away from the range and went up the narrow, creaking stairs to the tiny bedroom he'd once shared with her. The large iron bedstead took up most of the small space, but it was where he and his two sisters had been born, so he'd been unwilling to get rid of it even though it was uncomfortable. He regarded the faded hand-stitched quilt which had been lovingly sewn by his mother, as had the embroidery on the pillowcases, and hoped that Ethel wouldn't want to make too many changes when she moved in, for the familiarity was consoling in these dangerous and uncertain times.

He picked up the photograph that had stood by the bedside since 1927. Barbara smiled back at him from behind the glass, her sweet face reminding him of how lovely she'd been. 'I'll never forget you, my love,' he murmured before kissing the image, 'but now it's time to say our last goodbye.'

He was misty-eyed as he carefully wrapped the frame and photograph in one of Barbara's silken scarves and tucked it away in a hatbox that was full of such mementos, which he kept on top of the wardrobe. It would feel strange to share that bed with Ethel, but a good kind of strange, for he missed the softness and warmth of a woman's body lying next to him, and the intimacy of snuggling up when the rain hammered on the roof and rattled the windows.

With this happy thought, Stan returned to the kitchen and picked up the large bouquet of flowers he'd gathered from his allotment earlier, and then stepped outside to where he'd placed the bottle of champagne on the doorstep to keep it cool. Placing the flowers and the bottle carefully in the basket of his bicycle, he patted his suit pocket to make sure the ring was safely in there, put the clips round his trouser legs and set off.

Ethel and Ruby lived in a bungalow that was owned by Cordelia Finch, who'd inherited it from her sister. Ethel and her daughter had made it snug and homely once Stan and Ron had painted it throughout and mended the rotting windows. Situated almost at the top of the steep hill that led eventually to the factory estate and the dairy, it had magnificent views over the town to the sea from the front room.

Stan's emotions were all over the place as he puffed and panted his way up that hill, for although he was excited and eager for a future with Ethel, they had yet to discuss where they'd

71

live once they got married. It could be a bit tricky, because Ethel loved the modern conveniences of the bungalow, and found the quirky layout of his tied cottage rather cramped. But as long as he was stationmaster, he was expected to stay there, and he couldn't actually imagine living anywhere else.

Stan wobbled to a halt and stood for a moment to catch his breath before pushing the bicycle up the path and leaning it against the wall beneath the front window. Straightening his tie and smoothing his waistcoat over his belly, he mopped his sweaty face with a large handkerchief, gathered up his gifts and rapped the doorknocker.

The door opened and there stood Ethel, looking lovely in a blue dress and cardigan, her dark, curly hair freshly washed and set. 'Hello, Stan,' she said warmly.

Suddenly overcome with shyness, Stan could only mumble a reply.

Ethel laughed. 'Oh, Stan, you are a one,' she teased. 'Are those for me?'

Stan shoved the bouquet at her and held out the champagne. 'I got this too,' he blurted. 'Thought we might have something to celebrate.'

She cocked an eyebrow at him. 'Did ya now? Well, you'd better come in then,' she said with a chuckle. 'Can't have you going down on one knee on the doorstep, can we?'

'How did you know?' he stammered as he stepped into hall and she shut the door.

'Blimey, Stan, I ain't blind. You've been on the verge of it for days!'

He looked down at her with a tentative smile, his heart hammering with love as he looked into her laughing eyes and pretty face – and then all his plans went out of the window and he dropped to his knees.

'Ethel, I know you're twenty years younger than me and probably don't want to be saddled to an old man,' he rattled off, terrified she'd turn him down before he had time to finish what he'd started. 'But I love you, and you would make me the happiest man alive if you would agree to be my wife.'

Ethel placed the flowers and champagne on the floor, then leaned down and cupped his face before she softly kissed him. 'Yer a soft old thing, Stan Dawkins. Of course I'll marry ya, yer daft bugger. Now get up off them knees before you seize up altogether, and give me a proper big kiss.'

It was a bit of a struggle to get to his feet, but he made it eventually and kissed her thoroughly. 'I must be the happiest man in Cliffehaven,' he murmured as he slipped the ruby and diamond ring onto her finger.

She let the light glitter on the ring and grinned back at him in delight before giving him another long kiss. 'Well, I reckon I'm the happiest woman in the world, Stan – but if I don't get into that kitchen pronto, we'll both go hungry. I can smell something burning.'

Stan laughed and followed her bustling little figure down the hall and into the kitchen. It felt as if he was walking on air.

4

Portsmouth, April 1943

Portsmouth was shrouded in a blanket of early morning fog, the grey battleships and frigates that lay at anchor now invisible as the horizon disappeared within the thick haze, and the sea and sky merged as one.

April stood at the window and stared out at the swirling mist, her spirits low after yet another restless night of little sleep. There had been no word from Daniel, or news of what had happened to him over the past two days, and although he'd proved to be a liar and a cheat, she needed to talk to him, to see if he had the decency to offer some help and support. It was a tenuous hope, but one that she clung to with determination, for without his financial assistance over the coming months, she wouldn't be able to cope.

April shivered and drew the thick dressing gown around her, huddling into its warmth, but the coldness lay within her, and her future was as bleak as the view from the window. This wasn't how she'd planned to spend her nineteenth birthday.

Paula seemed to understand how low she was feeling for she put her arm over her shoulder and gave her a hug. 'It's not much of a birthday, is it?'

she said sympathetically. 'Why don't you treat yourself to a lie-in while I bring you up some breakfast? We're not on duty until later, and I know you had another bad night.'

'That's a sweet thought, Paula.' April gave her friend a wan smile. 'But I'm not hungry and in no mood to go back to bed. I'm too restless and wound up, so I think I'll just get dressed and go for a walk.'

'In that?' Paula pointed to the swirling fog outside the window. 'You're mad.'

'I shall go mad if I stay cooped up in here with my thoughts.' April began to get dressed. 'I thought I might go up to Daniel's barracks and try to get to see him. His regiment is due to leave today, and it could be my last chance.'

'They won't let you past the gate,' Paula protested. 'You know how tight security is up there.'

'I have to try, Paula. He's got to be made to face up to what's happened.'

Paula was about to reply when a sharp rap on the door startled them both, and a cheery Wren poked her head into the room. 'Sorry to barge in, but I just heard on the grapevine that your chap's train leaves in half an hour, so if you want to wave him off, you'd better get your skates on.'

April and Paula exchanged glances as the girl rushed off. 'Oh, no,' April breathed as she reached for her jacket. 'I have to get there in time. I just have to.'

'It's really not wise,' Paula warned.

'Probably not. But I have to try and talk to him.'

'I doubt you'll get the chance,' said Paula grimly. 'Security will be high and there will probably be a complete scrum of girls wanting to say goodbye.'

'It's a chance I have to take,' April said stubbornly.

'Then I'm coming with you.'

She shot Paula a grateful smile and swiftly finished dressing, her thoughts racing, her fingers clumsy as she tried to knot her tie. Time was rapidly running out, and she could only pray that luck was on her side and she managed to get to him; to explain her predicament and make him understand how vital it was he believed her and was willing to help.

Paula stilled her hand. 'April, are you really sure about this? There will be a lot of other girls there milling about, and he might be...'

'Still under arrest, and therefore unable to speak to me,' finished April for her. 'Yes, I know, but I'll just have to take that chance.'

'That wasn't really what I meant. You see, there's a...'

April wasn't listening as she grabbed her raincoat and opened the door. She raced down the stairs, barely aware of Paula following her as she stepped out into the murky morning and headed for the dockyard station.

April shared Paula's misgivings about the wisdom of this mission, but her situation called for drastic action, and Daniel was her last hope. She'd gone over and over the things he'd said over the weeks they'd been together, and the way he'd been so attentive and loving until that awful night – yet, despite everything, she clung to the tenuous belief that he must possess at least a shred of decency and would do the right thing by her.

76

The mist chilled her face and emphasised the iciness inside her as their hurrying footsteps echoed in the muffled gloom of this early morning. If he rejected her and flatly refused to believe the child was his, then she didn't know what she would do. The thought of being alone was terrifying.

'Good grief,' muttered Paula as they saw the mass of girls trying to get past the phalanx of military guards at the gates. 'There's no way we're going to get past that lot. Come on, April. Let's go back and find some breakfast instead.'

'No.' April shook off her friend's tugging hand as she regarded the girls who were calling out to the black GIs already on the platform or leaning out of the train windows to shout and wave back. Some girls were openly weeping, and others were tussling with the guards to try and gain entry through the gate onto the platform.

She saw a gap and darted to one side of the shifting mob, easing her way through until she was pressed up against the sturdy torso of a grim-faced military policeman. 'You have to let me through,' she pleaded. 'I need to talk to Sergeant Clement. It's urgent.'

'Stay back, ma'am. Only American personnel permitted through today.'

There were shouts of defiance at this, and the press of girls became more determined until one great surge saw the blockade breached.

April found herself caught up in the stampede and was swept onto the platform, to be jostled and shoved by the women who were desperate to get to their sweethearts before the train pulled out. She searched in anguish for sight of Daniel

77

amid the chaos. 'Daniel!' she called. 'Daniel, where are you?'

The thick fog mingled with the steam and smoke coming from the engine, and as it was momentarily shredded by a blast of cold wind she saw him stepping down from the train, his handsome face still bearing the bruises and cuts of that terrifying fight. But at least he didn't seem to be handcuffed, or under some sort of guard.

'Daniel, I'm here! Over here!' she called out as she jumped up and down and waved to him. But she was short and dwarfed by the surrounding people and he didn't see or hear her in the hubbub.

April began to push and shove to get to him, ignoring the angry retorts as she elbowed her way past the embracing couples and trampled on toes. The military police were trying to bring order to the chaos, and as one of them reached to grab her she only just managed to give him the slip.

Her pulse quickened as she caught a glimpse of Daniel's profile and realised she was almost at his side. About to call out to him, she froze. The swirl and eddy of the people around her faded into a blur as all sound was drowned by the thunder of her beating heart.

He was smiling down at a girl in an ATS uniform, his arm about her waist. She was looking at him tearfully as she spoke to him, her hand touching his face with an intimacy that spoke of a history between them.

April watched in stunned disbelief as they kissed, and when he gathered the girl tightly into his arms to prolong that kiss, her head seemed to fill with black clouds and her legs felt as if they'd been turned to water.

A firm hand grasped her waist and stopped her from falling before gently drawing her back into the surrounding mass until Daniel and the girl were lost from sight. 'Come on, April,' murmured Paula. 'Let's get you back home.'

April was numb as she let Paula lead her away from the station. Barely aware of putting one foot in front of the other, or that the tears were streaming down her face, she was almost in a trance, the image of him kissing that girl imprinted on her mind. That had not been a soldier's farewell to a stranger, or the kiss of someone caught up in a fleeting moment of excitement – it had been one of far deeper intimacy. But when had he got to know that girl? How could he have had the time to build such an intimacy when he'd spent every available free moment with April?

She tramped up the stairs and slumped onto the bed, defeated and overwhelmed by profound hurt and utter bewilderment. 'I don't understand,' she choked out through her tears. 'How? When? Who *was* that girl?'

When Paula didn't answer, she looked fiercely up at her. 'Who was she, Paula?'

Paula sat down beside her and took her hand. 'Her name is Olive Bradshaw,' she said reluctantly. 'That's what I was trying to warn you about earlier,' she added softly.

April stared at her through her tears. 'You knew?' she muttered hoarsely. 'You knew all about her and Daniel and said nothing?'

'I only found out yesterday,' Paula admitted,

'and as there wasn't much chance of you seeing him again, I decided it wouldn't be kind or helpful to tell you about her.' She squeezed April's fingers. 'I'm sorry, April. I thought I was doing the right thing.'

April could see the genuine regret in her friend's eyes and knew that she'd been in a difficult situation – yet she still felt cross with her. 'You should have told me before I went to the station,' she said, snatching her hand away.

'I did try. But you were in no mood to listen,' said Paula flatly. 'He's not worth your tears, April – and certainly not worth us falling out over him. I was trying to protect you from him, that's all.'

April's tears slowly slid down her face as cold reality sank in. She did understand, really she did, but Paula should have made her listen – should have stopped her from going down there no matter what. And yet that treacherous little scene had shown her his true colours, and Paula was right – Daniel Clement was a complete and absolute bastard.

'Perhaps it was for the best,' said Paula. 'If I'd told you about Olive you probably wouldn't have believed me. You've been so sure that he'd do the right thing by you.' She gave a deep sigh. 'At least you've seen for yourself that he's a liar and a cheat and couldn't be trusted to tell you the right time of day.'

Something cold settled around April's heart and her tears dried as the scene at the station ran repeatedly in her head. 'Was he seeing her when he and I...?'

'Don't do this, April. Why torture yourself when

there's absolutely no chance of changing things?'

'Because I need to know,' she said dully. 'Tell me, Paula. Tell me everything.'

Paula took a deep breath, and after a momentary hesitation, managed to return April's steady gaze. 'He met her just after you started going out with him. But there were others,' she admitted softly. 'Lots of others. A man that handsome can easily get what he wants, and there were plenty of girls eager to oblige.'

April thought about this as cold contempt swept through her. 'But why bother with me at all? Why did he make me fall in love with him when he could get what he wanted elsewhere?'

She met Paula's concerned gaze and suddenly the bitter truth dawned. 'He saw me as a challenge, didn't he? I was a silly, naïve little virgin – hopelessly dazzled by his looks and charm – and stupid enough to believe every lying word he said.' She gave a scornful snort. 'I bet he keeps a score somewhere – and a virgin has to be at the top of his list, don't you think?'

'Don't, April,' Paula pleaded. 'Don't punish yourself like this.'

April got up from the bed, dry-eyed and furious with herself as well as him. 'I almost feel sorry for his wife,' she muttered. 'Do you think she's aware of what a rat he is?'

'I don't know, April, and I don't care. Neither should you. It's time to concentrate on yourself and that baby, and whatever happens in the next few months, I want you to know, that I'll do all I can to help.'

April turned from the window and embraced

81

her fiercely. 'You're such a good friend, Paula,' she murmured tearfully. 'Thank you.'

They drew apart, both feeling a little embarrassed by this show of raw emotion.

'We'd better go down and get some breakfast,' said Paula. 'It's almost time for work, and that motor gun boat's engine service is bound to be tricky.'

April nodded before going to the dressing table to clean her face and hide the tracks of her tears with make-up. She would come through this, she vowed silently. And she would learn to be strong and focused in the difficult months ahead. It was time to grow up, to face reality squarely – for although Paula was a stalwart friend who would stand by her for as long as possible, she really was on her own in this.

5

Cliffehaven, April 1943

Doreen had been down in Wales for a few weeks now and it seemed from her letter to Peggy that she and her girls were happily settling into a small rented cottage on the outskirts of Swansea. She'd managed to get a secretarial job at the girls' new school, which suited them all, and her pregnancy was progressing very well.

Peggy was relieved that her younger sister was contented, and it seemed that things were picking up all round, which was a tremendous boost to her spirits. Ethel and Stan had announced their engagement, and Ruby and Mike had thrown a terrific party at the Anchor to celebrate their own. Further afield, the news from Russia and the Pacific was heartening.

The routine at Beach View went on as normal, however, and Peggy was faced with the usual stack of ironing on this Tuesday afternoon. She stood at the end of the kitchen table where she'd folded a towel to use as an ironing board, and as the iron smoothed the wrinkles and creases from the sheets and pillowcases, she kept an eye on Daisy.

The toddler was making her unsteady way around the kitchen by clinging to chair and table legs in pursuit of Queenie, the black kitten. Queenie didn't appreciate being hugged by Daisy and she darted away, shot up the curtain beneath the sink and sought sanctuary in her usual spot on the shelf by the window.

Peggy smiled wryly at this, for she couldn't blame Queenie. Daisy could be quite rough with her, not understanding that cats didn't like being half-strangled and carted about under her arm or shoved into her doll's pram. She continued to watch Daisy's progress, realising it wouldn't be long before she found her feet properly and became even more adventurous.

'Don't let her get into the coal scuttle, Cordelia,' she said sharply. 'She'll get filthy and spread it everywhere.'

Cordelia Finch quickly sidetracked Daisy from the scuttle by flapping one of the rag books at her. Her smile was soft with affection as she

83

struggled to draw the small girl up onto her lap. 'She's a little imp,' she said fondly as she ruffled Daisy's dark curls. 'But eating anthracite isn't good for you, Daisy, and not at all ladylike.'

Daisy laughed up at her and clapped her hands before shoving the rag book into Cordelia's face. 'Nan-Nan,' she said. 'Boo. Boo.'

'Yes, I'll read your book. Just let me put on my glasses.' She patted her cardigan pockets and delved into the sides of the armchair. 'Goodness me, now where on earth did I put them?'

'They're on top of your head, Cordelia,' said Peggy.

'On my bed? They can't be. I was reading the paper earlier.'

Peggy placed the iron on the hob to heat it up again and then reached over to pluck the half-moon glasses from the mass of snowy white hair. 'They were on your head,' she said clearly.

'Oh, silly old Nan-Nan,' Cordelia chuckled to Daisy. 'She'll lose her head next, won't she? And then where would we be, eh?'

Peggy smiled. Cordelia was animated and totally absorbed with Daisy, and it was lovely to see how delighted they were in each other. Daisy's arrival had brought interest to Cordelia, and Peggy knew that she relished being the baby's Nan-Nan, even though they weren't related.

With a sigh of pleasure, she went back to her ironing. There was always a silver lining to the clouds, no matter how dark they were, and the war had brought new life to Cordelia. The comings and goings of the girls with their little dramas, their energy, laughter and lively music, had bucked her up no end – and being involved so closely with Daisy's care had confirmed to her that she was truly cherished and regarded as an intrinsic part of the family.

Peggy's heart was warmed at the thought, for Cordelia's own sons had emigrated to Canada many years ago, and until recently she'd had very little contact with them or their families. It was a blessing to Peggy that she was able to make Cordelia's later years happy and fulfilled.

Peggy's thoughts returned to the job in hand as she swept the hot iron over one of Ron's decent shirts (there were only two meriting this description). He seemed to be wearing his best ones more often – this was the second week they'd been in the wash – and she wondered if at last he'd turned over a new leaf and the days of dressing like a tramp were coming to an end. Perhaps Rosie had finally ordered him to smarten himself up when they were together – for he'd surprised them all at Beach View by actually going to a barber to get his hair cut and eyebrows trimmed – or perhaps he'd taken note of how neat and handsome Bertie Double-Barrelled looked every time he came round to see Cordelia, and had decided that a smart appearance was the way to Rosie's heart – and her bed. Either way, it was good he was taking a pride in himself, and Peggy rather hoped it lasted.

She carried on with the ironing as Cordelia turned the pages of the rag book and pointed out the different colours to Daisy, who was trying very hard to repeat the words. But Peggy's mind wasn't really focused on either Ron or Daisy, for an airgraph from Jim had arrived in the second post, and she was eager to see what he had to say.

She knew he was up near the tea plantations in the mountains of India and that he was in charge of a motor repair station which serviced American vehicles as well as the British ones. Thankfully, the camp didn't appear to be anywhere near the fierce fighting that was going on between the Americans and the Japanese, and she prayed fervently that it would stay that way.

Jim seemed, as usual, to have managed to kit himself out with what he considered to be the necessities of life – as well as taking on a stray pup he'd called Patch – and was set up comfortably in camp with servants to tend to his every need and native mechanics to do most of the work at the garage.

She smiled at the thought. He'd better not get too used to that state of affairs, or he'd have a nasty shock when he got home. The house needed decorating from top to bottom, the floors scraped back and revarnished, and there was a long list of repairs awaiting him. And it would be nice if he could buy a washing machine like the one Doris had – and an electric iron, perhaps even a proper toaster. It would make her chores much easier with so many people in the house, and give her more time to concentrate on him and Daisy.

It was all wishful thinking, really, and she gave a sigh that was laced with worry and sadness. Despite all his wheeling and dealing to make himself comfortable out there, she knew he was suffering from the awful heat and being plagued by the mosquitoes. It was a minor miracle he hadn't gone down with malaria like so many of the other men, but she suspected he had suffered from bouts of dysentery after eating all that strange food which probably hadn't been washed properly and was full of all sorts of bugs and creepy-crawlies.

Peggy's hand was a little unsteady as she set aside the iron and hung Ron's shirt on a hanger which she hooked over the back of a kitchen chair. Jim's continued absence was like a knife in her heart, and although she stumbled through the days and kept smiling no matter how low she felt, it was the nights that defeated her.

The bed felt so cold and empty without him lying beside her, and she missed the lovely Irish lilt to his voice and the way he could smile at her and make her feel like a girl again. She missed the lovemaking too – the intimacy of whispering in the darkness, of his hands on her skin and the drum of his heart against her ear as they...

'Hello, Peg. I hope I'm not interrupting?'

Peggy was snatched from her pleasantly disturbing daydream as Rosie Braithwaite came up the cellar steps and into the kitchen with Monty on his lead. 'Hello, Rosie,' she said, hoping her thoughts on Jim weren't revealed in her face. 'What can we do for you this afternoon?'

Monty and Queenie eyed one another suspiciously, and the cat hissed furiously then shot onto a higher shelf as Monty danced about, whining in frustration.

Rosie pulled Monty away from the sink and ordered him to sit down and behave. She laughed delightedly as the cat eyed them all imperiously from behind a saucepan before it lifted its tiny withered back leg and began to wash its bottom.

'I've come to tell you Mary's news,' Rosie said. She greeted Cordelia with a beaming smile and reached for her god-daughter. 'And to get a cuddle from my gorgeous Daisy.'

Cordelia looked slightly miffed as Daisy was unceremoniously plucked from her lap without so much as a by your leave, but as she was expected to share Daisy with all and sundry, she said nothing.

Rosie nuzzled Daisy's cheek, which made her giggle, and then gave her a soft kiss. 'She's so lovely, Peggy,' she said wistfully. 'You are lucky.'

'I do realise that,' Peggy replied as she put the kettle on, 'but she's not all sweetness and light, you know. Her temper tantrums can be quite appalling.'

'Surely not?' Rosie crooned. 'My sweet Daisy being naughty? I never heard of such a thing.'

Peggy could see that Daisy was getting a bit overexcited with all the attention and knew that there would be tears and a tantrum any minute, but she was loath to break up Rosie's happy moment, so she said nothing as she tidied away the pile of fresh ironing and hunted out cups and saucers, then spooned fresh tea into the old brown pot. She couldn't begrudge Rosie these precious times, for she knew how deeply her friend had longed to have a child of her own. But with her husband shut away in a lunatic asylum, and the law making it impossible for her to divorce him and marry again, her chances of that had been crushed.

There had been a time when Rosie had

88

planned to adopt her brother's illegitimate baby, but that too had come to nothing, and Peggy was well aware of how badly Rosie had suffered then. And yet, miraculously, her niece had come to Cliffehaven in search of the truth, and Rosie had been reunited with Mary for the first time since she'd held her as a tiny baby.

Peggy made the tea and put the pot on the table, leaving the fresh leaves to steep for a bit before she poured it out. It was a rare luxury to have fresh tea, and she meant to get all the flavour out of it. 'So, Rosie, what's been happening to Mary since she went back to Sussex?'

'She's working on the Bonifaces' farm and giving piano lessons at night.' Rosie put a squirming, grizzling Daisy carefully on the floor and encouraged her to take her wheeled horse for a turn round the kitchen. 'She's also started up a choir in the village – some of those land girls have really good voices, apparently, and she's hoping to enter them into a county competition.'

'Then I'm sure she'll be successful,' said Peggy comfortably. 'She's very gifted at music, is Mary. Look at the way she got everyone singing along in the Anchor, and how she encouraged Fran to show us what she could do on the violin.'

Rosie nodded a little impatiently. 'But there's more, Peg. Jack Boniface managed to get home on leave for a long weekend and they finally got officially engaged,' she said breathlessly.

'Oh, how lovely,' sighed Peggy, who did so love a good romance. 'He seemed such a nice lad, and they made a handsome couple.'

'They're planning on getting married on his

next leave, though goodness knows when that will be,' continued Rosie. 'The marines are being sent all over the world, to some of the worst fighting. I just hope to goodness he stays safe.'

There was a moment of silence between them and then Rosie visibly shook off her dark thoughts. 'But the really good news is she's planning to come down for a short visit in the summer before she goes off to teacher training college.'

Peggy saw the brightness in her friend's eyes and understood just how much this visit meant to her. She reached for her hand. 'Oh, Rosie, how lovely for you.'

'Yes, isn't it? She'll get to see what we've done with the spare room, and it will be just wonderful to spend some time with her.' She pulled a face. 'Although I suspect I'll have to be charitable and share her with you-know-who.'

Peggy knew about the years of bitterness that lay between Rosie and Mary's birth mother, but she was surprised that the two of them hadn't sorted out their differences by now. 'But you're getting on all right with her, aren't you? I thought you'd decided to let bygones be bygones.'

'We muddle through, but we'll never be as close as we once were,' Rosie replied. 'It's the loss of trust, you see, Peggy. Once that's gone...'

Peggy regarded her sharply and saw how she was twisting her fingers in her lap. 'What's the matter, Rosie? What's happened?'

Rosie stroked Monty's silky head as he rested his nose on her knees, then she lifted her chin and gave Peggy a dazzling smile that didn't quite reach her blue eyes. 'Take no notice, Peg. I'm just being silly, that's all.'

Peggy could see she wasn't being silly at all – and in fact was trying very hard to keep her emotions in check. 'If it's silly, then why not share it?'

'You'll think I'm very foolish,' Rosie muttered, 'but...'

Peggy waited.

'I thought Ron might be here,' Rosie blurted out.

Peggy frowned. 'He's off with Harvey somewhere and I'm not expecting him home until teatime. He's probably planning on calling in at the Anchor later – just as he does every afternoon. Why? Was there something you need to talk to him about?'

Rosie's lips trembled. 'That's just it, Peg. I haven't had the chance to see much of him lately, let alone talk to him. I'm beginning to think he's up to something.'

Peggy remembered the best shirts and Ron's very rare trip to the barber – and a tingle of unease threaded up her spine. 'He's probably busy with the Home Guard and all his other commitments,' she said quickly.

Rosie looked at her evenly. 'That hasn't stopped him before – so why now? He hasn't called in to help change the barrels, or stopped for more than a few minutes in the evenings before he shoots off again. He hasn't even come up for his usual cup of tea mid-afternoon – and when I do get the chance to question him about this odd behaviour, he just looks shifty and clams up.'

'Ron always looks shifty,' said Cordelia with a sniff. 'Nothing new in that.'

Peggy tried to make light of it despite her own gathering doubts. 'Cordelia's right,' she said. 'Ron isn't one to let any of us know what he's up to.'

'I know. But this time it's different.' Rosie squared her shoulders and met Peggy's gaze evenly. 'I think he's got another woman.'

Peggy didn't want to believe that, but the shirts, the haircut and his neglect of Rosie all seemed suspicious. She shrugged off this thought and decided to give Ron the benefit of the doubt. 'Rosie,' she said firmly, 'he loves you. He's loved you from the minute you took over the Anchor, and I'm positive he wouldn't dream of even looking at another woman.'

'No sensible woman would have him,' said Cordelia tersely. 'I do think you're making a fuss about nothing, Rosie.'

Rosie bit her lip. 'You're probably right, Cordelia, but as a woman you must know how it is. Something doesn't feel right, and I can sense that his thoughts are elsewhere even when he *is* with me.'

Peggy was certainly familiar with that feeling, for over the years she'd always known when Jim's head had been turned by a pretty face or a well-bolstered bosom. Luckily she'd always managed to nip it in the bud – but if Ron was straying... That was a different thing entirely and she hadn't a clue as to how she would deal with it.

Rosie lifted her chin and met Peggy's gaze almost defiantly. 'You know as well as I do that a woman's intuition about these things rarely fails her. And if I find out he's messing about, I'll have his guts for garters. And whoever the woman is, she'd better watch herself, because I'll claw the skin off her cheating face.'

Peggy had no doubt of it, for beneath that feminine, film siren appearance beat the heart of a steely, determined woman who would stand no nonsense from anyone – especially her man. If Ron had been straying – and it was looking quite likely that he was – then she didn't hold out much hope of him escaping Rosie's wrath. This was far more serious than any of his other escapades, and Irish blarney and twinkling charm were no match for a Rosie scorned.

'Oh, dear,' twittered Cordelia. 'Poor Ron. I almost feel sorry for him.'

Peggy saw the spark of anger in Rosie's eyes and quickly interrupted. 'I think we could all do with drinking this tea and having a fag,' she said briskly. 'You need to calm down, Rosie, and not let your imagination run away with you. Ron might be many things, but I really can't believe he'd do you wrong. We'll get to the bottom of this, but we'll do and say nothing before we have absolute proof that your suspicions are correct.'

'And if it's proved I was right?'

'Then he'll have you and me to deal with,' Peggy said flatly. 'And I don't much reckon his chances of getting out of *that* alive.'

The subject of this conversation was blissfully unaware of the impending storm clouds that were gathering around him as he sneaked out of the back door of the Crown that afternoon and hurried down the litter-strewn alley with Harvey. There was a spring in his step and he was feeling quite rejuvenated. Life was exciting and it just went to prove that although there might be snow on the roof, there was a furnace in the hearth, and a man of his age could still make his mark.

Gloria was a grand girl, with a quick mind and a ready smile – and having got to know her better over the past few weeks, he'd come to admire her hugely. The rest of the townsfolk in Cliffehaven might turn their noses up at her, but that brassy façade covered hidden depths, and in Ron's opinion, she was worth more than all of them put together.

Warmed by this thought, he reached the end of the alley. 'Stay low, Harvey,' he murmured, stilling the dog. 'There could be nosy parkers about.' He glanced up at the many windows that overlooked the narrow alleyway, but could see very little evidence that anyone was watching him, so he shot a quick look out into the street. The last thing he needed was to bump into anyone he knew.

The coast was clear, so he tucked his chin into the collar of his poacher's coat and pulled the brim of his cap low on his brow.

Harvey began to head for the Anchor, but Ron clicked his fingers and pointed in the other direction. Confused by this unusual behaviour, the dog cocked his head in puzzlement and then trotted along beside him as he strode up the hill.

'We could both do with some fresh air,' Ron muttered to him. 'And I need time to think, so get on with you, ye heathen beast.'

Despite his newly found energy and all the excitement his latest adventure had brought, Ron's happy mood was tinged with guilt over Rosie. He hadn't given her much time lately, and that was careless, for he was experienced enough in life and in the ways of women to realise that his unusual behaviour was making her suspicious.

In the rare moments when they had managed to exchange a few words, his mind had been somewhere else and he'd used his many home guard duties as an excuse for neglecting her – after all, he was a busy man and that had always been the way of things. However, lying to Rosie didn't sit easily with him, and he knew he had to get things back to their usual routine and Rosie mollified before her suspicions hardened and caused him real problems.

'But not today,' he muttered to himself. 'There's too many things on me mind today.'

Harvey raced on ahead, nose to the ground, tail windmilling in delight as they reached the lower slopes of the hills and he scented rabbits and voles in the long grass.

Ron tramped up the hill behind him, his thoughts whirling. He was playing a dangerous game in more ways than one, and it had been a nasty shock to bump into Stan the other week. It was that sort of surprise that could make everything swiftly unravel and cause untold complications. Yet Ron knew that his old friend could be trusted with a secret. After all, they'd both had them over the years, and the bond they'd forged in the trenches during the first shout was strong enough to withstand anything – even a suspicious Rosie.

As he reached the top of the cliffs he saw that the early mist had cleared and now the sky was duck-egg blue, the sun sparkling on the sea as gulls hovered and mewled overhead, and the light wind whispered through the trees. He reached into the pocket of his poacher's coat and pulled out his pipe, gazing at the town which spread out from the horseshoe bay.

He'd once thought he knew everything he needed to know about the people who lived there, but he'd since learned that beneath those many roofs lay innumerable secrets – some of no real importance, but others – like his – that had far-reaching consequences should they be revealed.

He filled his pipe and lit the tobacco, the smoke curling away on the breeze as he shook off the dark thoughts. Breathing in the salty air, he headed for the high wire-mesh fencing that surrounded the Cliffe estate. It was time to do a bit of poaching.

6

Following the distressing conversation with Rosie, Peggy monitored Ron's movements more closely over the next two weeks. Not that she could do much about it when he left the house, of course, but his long absences were usually explained by the rabbits and pigeons he brought back. However, she kept an eye on how he dressed, and looked out for other signs: the smell of perfume about him when he returned home late, or smudges of make-up on his collars, or if he'd suddenly taken to talking about anyone in particular. But Ron was his usual untidy self despite the haircut and eyebrow trim, and when he wore his best shirts, it was to go and see Rosie.

Peggy was delighted to report to Rosie that her suspicions had proved to be unfounded, and was very relieved when her friend decided to forgive him his minor lapse, for it seemed that Ron's old routine was re-established and harmony between them restored.

Peggy had accepted that Ron might have become frustrated and a bit put out by Rosie's refusal to commit to him, but she also knew him well enough to realise that if he *had* been playing about with another woman, he'd have faced up to the fact that it was over between him and Rosie and found a kindly way of telling her.

Even so, as she pushed the pram along Camden Road, her thoughts were still troubled by the disquieting suspicions that simply wouldn't go away despite all the evidence to the contrary. If, during his lapse, he had been seeing another woman, then he'd been very clever about it, for she hadn't heard a whisper of it in the town – and the local gossips could usually be relied upon to have seen or heard something they couldn't wait to pass on.

There again, Ron had been part of an elite force during the First World War, and was an expert in covert operations. He was a wily old so-and-so, and no one knew what he got up to on those nights when he didn't come home – or during those long daylight hours in which he said he was out on the hills – and there was something intangible about his demeanour recently that really niggled her. She couldn't identify what it was, but the difference was there, and it was unsettling.

She had thought about asking Stan if he knew anything, but had rapidly dismissed that idea. Ron and Stan were as thick as thieves and she knew from past experience that she'd get absolutely nothing from him – or from Fred the Fish or Alf the butcher – they were old comrades who'd survived the Somme, and their loyalty to Ron could not be shaken, however dire the threats.

Peggy gave a deep sigh of frustration as he turned into the High Street. She hated feeling this way about the man she'd always admired and loved – hated what it would do to her friend Rosie should her suspicions prove true after all. Her womanly instincts told her to heed those worrisome doubts, for Ron was clearly up to something. All she could do really was pray it had all been a storm in a teacup, that Ron hadn't been unfaithful, and if he had, that it was a moment of madness that he'd bitterly regretted and swiftly brought to an end.

She steered the pram round the long queue that was waiting outside the Home and Colonial general store. She had no need to join it today, because her brother-in-law, Ted Williams, who managed the shop, had already brought over two tins of fruit salad the night before, and they'd all enjoyed this treat with a fair dollop of tinned evaporated milk on top.

Acknowledging the greetings from the women in the queue, she hurried on. She was already late for her shift with the WVS at the town hall, and she'd get it in the neck from Doris, who was one of the local leading lights of this worthy institution and made it her business to let everyone know how very important she was.

At the thought of her older sister reading her the riot act and bossing her about for the rest of the day, Peggy hurried past the town hall and parked the pram outside the tobacconist's shop. She was out of cigarettes and she would need one with her cup of tea if she was to survive the afternoon.

A packet of Park Drive was tuppence ha'penny in this particular shop, whereas they were a ha'penny cheaper in Camden Road, but the extra cost was her own fault. She should have been concentrating when she walked past the shop and not worrying over Ron and Rosie.

It was as she came out of the tobacconist's and was putting the packet in her handbag that she saw Ron's retreating figure up ahead. He had Harvey with him as always, and was striding up the hill like a man on a mission. Intrigued, Peggy watched his progress, for it was just after two and he usually went to the Anchor to help Rosie with the barrels and crates – so what was he doing going in the opposite direction?

She lost sight of him as a group of soldiers and airmen poured out of the Crown and swarmed towards her, clearly having enjoyed a very liquid lunch. By the time they'd passed her, Ron and Harvey were nowhere in sight – which was odd, because she hadn't thought he'd been walking fast enough to make it over the humpbacked bridge in such a short time.

With all her senses on alert, she nudged the brake off and pushed the pram a little way up the High Street, wondering if he'd gone into a shop, or disappeared down one of the alleyways that threaded through the built-up streets of terraced houses which lay to the east of the main road and eventually would take him to Camden Road and the Anchor. But there was no sign of him still.

Having reached the Crown, she glanced through the heavily taped windows into the deserted, gloomy bar without really expecting to see him. Ron knew how Rosie felt about Gloria Stevens, and he wouldn't dare step one foot over her threshold – it was more than his life was worth.

With a sigh of frustration, she realised she was on a fool's errand, which had now made her very late for her WVS shift. She turned the pram and headed back towards the town hall, unaware that her every step was being watched by Ron from behind the curtains of Gloria's bedroom window.

It was late afternoon and Stan was tending his allotment, trying very hard to ignore the heartburn that had been plaguing him all day. He probably shouldn't have had that fried egg, potato and Spam for his lunch, but it had looked so appetising and he hadn't wanted to disappoint Ethel after she'd made such an effort to cook it for him.

He leaned on his hoe and regarded the neat rows of vegetables before silently admiring the roses he'd trained up the mellow brick wall. He had the best, most sheltered spot on the allotment, and his roses had won prizes at last year's annual fete. There were three months to go before this year's, and he was hoping to win again, but it was an ongoing battle to keep everything clear of greenfly, slugs, leaf rust and black spot.

Stan thudded his chest with his fist and gave a deep, satisfying belch which seemed to ease the acid burn in his throat. Feeling more cheerful, he winked at the bright-eyed robin which was watching his every move from the top of an overturned flower pot, and continued to hoe the weeds.

'I thought I'd find you here. Any chance of a cuppa and one of Ethel's buns?'

The robin fluttered off and Stan grinned as he straightened his back and eyed his old friend. 'I dare say I could manage that, Ron.' He patted Harvey and plodded towards his shed which was comfortably kitted out with everything a man might need for a bit of time away from work, women and war. He dragged out the two deck-chairs, lit the primus stove and placed the tin kettle on top before hunting out biscuits for Harvey and a rock cake for Ron.

Ron eyed him from beneath his brows. 'Not joining me in a bun?'

Stan shook his head and rapped his fist against his chest. 'Got a bit of indigestion, so I'm not that hungry.'

Ron's eyebrows shot up. 'Never known you to turn down food, Stan,' he said with a chuckle. 'You must be lovesick.' He sank into one of the deck-chairs and made short work of the rock bun while Harvey sat and gnawed on a hard dog biscuit.

Stan didn't reply, for although he was over the moon that Ethel and he were engaged, he was getting a bit concerned that he couldn't get rid of this indigestion. Ethel had suggested he go to see the doctor, but Stan thought it would be wasting the man's time – after all, flatulence never killed

101

anyone and the poor doctor was run ragged as it was with so many patients to deal with.

He made the tea in the old brown pot, hunted out two fairly clean tin mugs and plumped down next to Ron, the deckchair creaking under his weight. This was the first time he'd actually been alone with Ron since the day they'd bumped into one another at the Crown, and Stan could feel the unusual tension between them – it was almost as uncomfortable as the heartburn.

Ron seemed to feel it too, for he fidgeted in his chair and kept fiddling with his freshly lit pipe. 'Thanks for not saying anything about the other week,' he said eventually.

Stan regarded him as the many questions which had plagued him since churned in his mind. 'You can always rely on me, Ron. You know that.'

'How did you explain that bottle of champagne to Ethel?' Ron's blue eyes were twinkling.

Stan felt the deep blush suffuse his cheeks and he looked away. 'I hope you don't mind, but I told her you'd got it for me,' he admitted.

'Aye, to be sure she'd understand that, me old friend.'

They sat in silence as the robin dared to return to pluck a worm from the softened earth and Harvey went to investigate the possibility of more biscuits and titbits from the other gardeners. Stan wanted to ask Ron why he'd been at the Crown in the first place; if he was having a fling with Gloria – and what on earth possessed him to do such a thing when he already had the lovely Rosie. And yet, as one of Ron's oldest and closest friends, he was disinclined to pry unless Ron decided to enlighten him.

'Ach, Stan,' Ron sighed. 'To be sure 'tis a lovely day, so it is, and far too pleasant to be worrying about things that really don't concern you. Just keep the faith, me auld friend. Just keep the faith.'

Stan gave a wry smile. Ron could always read his thoughts, but he did wish he wouldn't talk in riddles. 'If by that you mean keep my mouth shut, then you've got it,' he replied. 'But if Rosie gets even a hint of what you're up to – and I can only guess what that is – then you're on your own. Ethel's enough of a handful, and I don't think I could withstand an onslaught from Rosie as well.'

Ron examined the burnt contents of his pipe and tapped them out onto the ground. 'Aye, I can understand that,' he murmured. 'But I'm thinking it's wee Peggy who must be minded. She's far too sharp for her own good.'

Stan was startled. 'Why? Has she said something?'

'Not yet,' Ron replied, hauling himself out of the deckchair, 'but I can tell she's suspicious, because she's been watching me like a hawk.'

'Then why not end it?' spluttered Stan. 'It's sheer madness to be carrying on with Gloria like that. You're bound to get caught, and then there will be hell to pay.'

Ron eased his cap low over his brow and grinned. 'Ach, to be sure, Stan, 'tis a bit of excitement, so it is, and I'll not be ending anything until I'm good and ready.'

Stan sat and watched as Ron strolled away to round up his dog and head for ... where? Beach View? The Crown, or Rosie and the Anchor? He shook his head in bemusement and felt a burst of admiration for his old pal. Ron was playing with fire, but if he could handle Gloria *and* Rosie at his age, then fair play to him. For himself, it was as much as he could do to keep up with Ethel.

7

April and Paula were deep in the sweltering confines of a motor gun boat's hull, struggling to unscrew a bolt that seemed determined not to budge. They'd oiled it, hit it, used every ounce of strength they possessed to try and turn it, but it was stuck fast, and it was with a sense of frustration that they had to accept it had defeated them.

'Now what?' April brushed her filthy hand over her forehead to clear the sweat, knowing she was probably leaving a great smear of grease behind, but not caring.

'I don't know,' sighed Paula, slumping against the hull. 'But if we don't get that loose, we can't finish the service – and those plugs definitely need changing.'

April could feel the sweat beading her top lip and she smeared it away. 'We'll give it one more go and if that fails, I suppose we'll have to get a man to do it,' she said wearily.

'If we do that we'll never hear the end of it,' muttered Paula, attacking the bolt with sturdy pliers.

'I know they're only teasing,' said April, 'but it does do their ego a lot of good when they have to help us poor, feeble women out.' She placed her hands over Paula's and they both tugged as hard as they could.

'Bloody thing,' muttered Paula, giving it a hefty whack with the pliers. 'Move, damn it. Bloody well move, will you?' she snarled.

'What seems to be the problem down here, sailors?'

Paula and April exchanged frustrated glances as the boatswain blocked out the light and came down into the hull to glare at them. He was a big man, as wide as he was tall, with a fierce black beard and bushy eyebrows. All the girls were wary of him, for he was inclined to roar his displeasure and loom over them.

'We can't get this bolt to shift, sir!' said April reluctantly.

The man rolled his eyes and gave an exasperated sigh. 'That's the problem with getting women to do a man's work,' he grumbled. 'Not enough muscle.'

He snatched the wrench from Paula and with two short twists had the bolt out. He dropped it into her hand and smirked. 'There,' he said. 'Wasn't so hard, was it?'

'Thank you, sir,' they replied in unison, although it was shaming how easily he'd managed it after they'd spent at least half an hour trying to shift the blasted thing.

'Get on with your work then,' he barked. 'We need this boat tonight – not in a week's time.'

April glanced at Paula and they quickly returned to the task in hand, both aware of him leaning against the bulkhead and watching their every move. It was a tight enough squeeze in here without his great body taking up so much room, and both of them knew that his critical eyes would miss nothing.

They did their best to ignore him and finished cleaning and changing the plugs, checked the wiring, the fuel lines and the level of oil, then bolted everything back in place. The sweat was running freely down their faces and soaking their hair and their overalls, but with him standing there smirking, it was a matter of pride to ignore the discomfort and get on with their job.

'All finished and ready for inspection, sir,' said April, wiping her filthy hands on an equally filthy rag.

He nodded and without a word went up the ladder to the wheelhouse.

April and Paula grabbed their gas-mask boxes, tool-bags and caps and swiftly followed him, eager to get away from the heat and the stink of oil and high-octane petrol fumes. The air on deck was clean and fresh and they both took great gulps of it as the bosun turned on the engine and listened to its steady burble.

'That's fine,' he said almost grudgingly before switching it off again. 'See you tomorrow.'

They saluted him and hurried up the ladder to the dock, eager to get washed and changed so they could have supper. It had been a long, tiring day, with countless interruptions by the Luftwaffe who seemed determined to swoop in at the most inconvenient moments and cause havoc, and they were starving.

April did her best to keep up with Paula, but

she was feeling a bit light-headed and sick after the stench and heat of that engine room, and the corset she'd taken to wearing to disguise her burgeoning stomach was almost unbearably tight.

'Are you all right?' Paula stopped to let her catch up.

April nodded as she pushed back her sweaty hair and caught her breath. 'I will be once I can get this corset off,' she replied. 'It feels as if it's cutting me in half.'

Paula slowed her pace as they continued towards their billet. 'It can't be doing you or the baby any good,' she murmured. 'What does the doctor say?'

'I don't wear it when I go to see him for my checkups,' April admitted. 'But everything's fine, really, and at least the morning sickness is now a thing of the past.'

'You won't be able to hide it much longer, though,' said Paula quietly as they approached HMS Firefly in the swiftly gathering gloom. 'Another few weeks and no corset on this earth will mask it.'

April was all too aware of that, and could only pray that her bump stayed small and neat and didn't swell up like a balloon for a while yet. 'It's a good thing we practically have to live in these,' she said, plucking at the baggy overalls. 'They hide everything, which is more than can be said for our uniform.'

They continued on in silence and were about to go through the front door when the sirens started to moan all through the city and the searchlights fizzed into life. 'Damn and blast,' muttered Paula. 'There goes supper, and I'm absolutely ravenous.'

107

April was hungry, sweaty and uncomfortable too, but she needed the lavatory more than food and a wash. 'I'll catch up with you,' she said, dashing indoors and racing to the downstairs loo as the other girls clattered down the stairs to the large, reinforced cellar which had once been the bar and hotel restaurant but now served as an emergency shelter.

She felt a good deal better as she emerged a few minutes later. The pressure on her bladder had eased and she'd used the opportunity to quickly loosen the sweat-soaked corset and have a delicious rub and scratch. She had no idea how her mother had survived all those years of wearing such a torturous garment, but it was sheer heaven to get the damn thing loose.

As she hurried through the main lounge she could see the searchlights weaving across the darkening sky and hear the drone of incoming aircraft above the shrieking sirens. Soon the big guns of the warships would boom out and the anti-aircraft guns would rattle off thousands of rounds, tracer fire stitching through the darkening sky as the brave boys from the RAF became embroiled in dogfights.

She hurried down the cellar steps, urged on by the petty officer who was impatient to close the reinforced door. The lights were dim within wire-mesh cages, the windows had been bricked up, and the only air came from a large vent which had been cut into the outside wall. It was a bleak, grim place even though the collection of old chairs and couches offered at least a bit of comfort during the long hours they'd had to spend in here.

There was a general moan about the no smoking, no alcohol rule, but there were books and magazines scattered about, a tea urn and a stock of biscuits and sandwiches which were a bit stale, but nevertheless, very welcome. The other drawback to being shut in down here for hours on end was the toilet facilities, for no matter how much they were scrubbed and disinfected the buckets behind the flimsy screens in the corner still stank, and April was not alone in avoiding them unless it was absolutely necessary.

She sank down beside Paula on the couch which had seen better days several decades before, and curled her arm around one of the moth-eaten cushions to camouflage the swell of her stomach which was more pronounced now the corset wasn't holding it in. She could feel the mysterious and rather wonderful flutter of the baby moving inside her and she lived with the fear that her subterfuge might be damaging it.

She struggled to resist the almost driving need to run her hand protectively over her bump, for she also had to contend with the absolute terror of being discovered. There had been an extremely tricky moment at the naval stores when she'd gone to buy a replacement skirt in a larger size. The girl had given her a long, hard look before handing one over, and April had made some stupid joke about having suddenly discovered a liking for beer which had brought about this necessity.

There had been other moments when some of the girls had noticed her fuller breasts, and had teased her about giving Hedy Lamarr a run for her money in the bosom department, and times when a remark was jokingly made about her putting on a bit of weight. From then on, April had become almost reclusive, spending her off duty hours in her cabin, and eating in the dining room after she knew most of the others had left for the night. It was exhausting having to be on her guard all the time, and there were instances when she longed to just own up and get the whole thing in the open. But she had very little money and not the least idea of what she would do once she was out of the navy, so she gritted her teeth and carried on.

'I'll get us a cuppa and a sandwich,' said Paula. 'You look all in.'

April smiled gratefully and closed her eyes as she nestled into the musty cushion. She could sleep for a week if only her worries would let her – but with the planes roaring overhead, the guns going off at sea and the crash and thump of bombs exploding, there was fat chance of any real rest tonight.

Paula returned with a mug of cocoa and a Spam sandwich that looked as if it had been made at least two days ago. 'Beggars can't be choosers,' she sighed, 'but I do wish the navy had a bit more imagination.'

April nodded her thanks, sipped the sweet cocoa and nibbled on the stale sandwich as the thunder of aircraft and the boom and rattle of guns impeded any further conversation. The walls trembled as a bomb exploded nearby and dust began to sift down from the cellar ceiling. The whine and zip of tracers mingled with the thud of flack and the whoosh of the pom-poms which April knew would be lighting up the sky and exposing the enemy bombers for the Allied gunners.

Another thud made the walls tremble and the ground shudder beneath their feet, but because they'd all experienced this before – and worse if they'd been caught out at sea – there were no cries of alarm, just a few sharp intakes of breath as everyone carried on reading, gossiping and drinking their tea. April burrowed deeper into the cushion as Paula went off to fetch another mug of tea and see if she could find a sandwich that was a bit more appetising.

April didn't hear the explosion – and wasn't aware that she'd been lifted from the couch as the blast ripped through the basement and dumped her unceremoniously on the other side of the cellar. She was unable to know that HMS Firefly was now no more than a lethal skeleton of toppling masonry which fell with inexorable purpose on those hidden in the cellar beneath it.

8

It was a relatively quiet night in Cliffehaven, and although the planes had been taking off and landing at Cliffe aerodrome on a regular basis, the noise they made was so familiar that no one really noticed it any more.

The atmosphere at Beach View was tranquil, and Peggy sat by the fire in her kitchen with the wireless turned down low for company. Daisy was asleep in her cot, Ron was off somewhere with the

Home Guard, the girls were at the pictures, and Cordelia had been taken to dinner at the Conservative Club by Bertie Double-Barrelled, who'd turned up looking very dapper in black tie with a yellow rosebud in his buttonhole.

Peggy sipped her tea, thinking how pleasant it was to have the house to herself for a while, and not to be interrupted by the sirens going off. These quiet moments would give her the chance to really relax and enjoy Jim's latest letters – and there had been a bonanza of five arriving today which she'd only managed to skim through earlier on.

She smiled fondly at Harvey and Queenie who were curled up together in front of the range fire, and then sifted through the collection of airgraphs and air letters to make sure she read them in the correct order. Some were almost two months old, while two of the airgraphs had been written less than ten days ago, which went to prove how efficient those girls were in the Kodak factories with their filming and censoring.

The air letters gave Jim much more space to write than the airgraphs, and accordingly, his handwriting sprawled across the thin blue paper. Ernie, his best pal, was recovering from yet another nasty bout of dysentery, and although Jim was suffering from a sore throat, a cold and a gippy tummy, he was muddling through. He'd found leeches on his legs that morning and on the puppy, Patch, that he'd taken on, but he'd burnt them off with a lighted cigarette and given him and the pup a good scrub in a bath of disinfectant.

The heat was almost unbearable at midday, but the work on the broken-down trucks continued, and he'd been sent further north to take over the running of another depot. The accommodation there had proved to be very basic, and he'd had to share with another officer who he hadn't thought much of, because he was a terrible snob and kept banging on about his days at Eton and Sandhurst.

He was finding the routine boring, but it had been enlivened a bit by an invitation to visit one of the tea plantations, which had turned out to be a rather lively occasion after sampling the man's stock of good Irish whiskey. There had also been a party of sorts laid on by his commanding officers which had involved the arrival of eight nurses from the nearby American hospital. The sight of white women had gone to some of the men's heads and the night had ended up with one of the majors trying to perform acrobatics while a young captain showed his prowess – or lack of it – at juggling empty bottles.

Peggy smiled at this and tried not to think about Jim dancing with the nurses, for it was too painful and she knew he'd have been the life and soul of the party. She finished the two flimsy airmail letters and took the airgraphs out of their brown envelopes.

They were small and Jim's writing was cramped, but she was delighted to read that he'd loved receiving all her letters, and those from Ron and Cordelia, and the rest of the family. They had helped to pass the time when the monsoon rains and the heat made it impossible to work, and he was longing for the war to end so he could come home to the clean sea winds of Cliffehaven.

There had been a large forest fire nearby, but no

one had been hurt, and so far, the Yanks were keeping the Japs well away from where Jim was based. The mosquitoes were still attacking in swarms, but at least his pal Ernie had now recovered and was back in camp. He and Jim had rigged up some decent electric lighting in their basha – bamboo hut – and had even managed to find a couple of old tin baths somewhere that the native servants would fill with hot water. Jim and Ernie had grown quite fond of bathing out of doors, and with a cold beer in their hands, they'd sit and gossip and watch the world go by in luxury.

Peggy finished the airgraphs, put them back in their envelopes and sat for a moment, staring into the fire. It was hard to imagine Jim in a jungle – harder still to believe that he was beginning to feel settled amidst the mosquitoes and natives. Yet she knew Jim would always make the best of any situation by commandeering the little luxuries in life, dodging the dirtiest and most difficult jobs and making sure he ate three square meals a day. It was simply not in his nature to volunteer for anything unless there was some personal benefit in it, and it looked as if that hadn't changed.

She placed the letters carefully on the mantelpiece beneath the coloured print of the King and Queen, and then dug her cigarettes out of her apron pocket. Resting back in the chair, she smoked her cigarette and closed her eyes. She supposed she ought to be doing some knitting or mending, but she was too tired. It had been a long, busy day. Doris had been an absolute pain in the neck all afternoon, and teatime had been disrupted by Queenie coming indoors with a field mouse in her mouth. Ron had dealt with it, Queenie had gone off in a huff and Cordelia had taken some time to pacify, for she didn't like any sort of rodent especially when they came into the house.

Peggy heard a key turn in the front door and glanced up at the clock, surprised to see it was only nine o'clock. 'Who on earth?'

'It's only me, dear,' said Cordelia. She came into the kitchen looking disgruntled.

'You're home very early,' said Peggy. 'And where's Bertie?'

Cordelia propped her walking stick against a kitchen chair and took off her gloves before struggling out of her overcoat to reveal her smartest black velvet dress. 'He had to rush off,' she said flatly. 'And I'm not best pleased about it, because I never got a chance to have dessert and coffee.'

Peggy could see that she was very put out, so bit back on a smile. Cordelia loved her puddings, and the Conservative Club was renowned for serving wonderful plum duffs and jam roly-polys. No wonder Bertie was in her bad books. 'Oh, dear. Was he not feeling well – or have you two fallen out again?'

'He was as fit as a fiddle,' Cordelia retorted as she poured tea into a cup. 'And I didn't argue when he said we had to leave – I was having a rotten time of it anyway. But if he does that sort of thing again I shall refuse any more of his dubious invitations.' She plumped down into the chair on the other side of the range and primly smoothed her dress over her knees.

Peggy felt a jolt of concern. 'Dubious? I thought

115

you were going to the Conservative Club – not some racy gambling den.'

Cordelia sipped her tea. 'Perhaps dubious was the wrong word,' she said. 'Unsatisfactory would be better.' She set the cup and saucer down and regarded Peggy evenly. 'He spent the first hour in a huddle with a group of his men friends, leaving me to converse with their wives, who were really quite awful. Doris would have loved it, because they did nothing but boast about their smart houses and friends, and their husbands' important positions in the town.'

'Oh, dear,' sighed Peggy. 'How awful for you.'

'I was bored rigid, so I made an excuse and went and sat in the powder room flicking through old magazines until the gong went for dinner.' Cordelia grimaced. 'No one had even noticed I'd gone, and I have to say I was quite tempted to get a taxi home and leave them to it.'

Peggy's eyes widened. 'Good heavens,' she breathed. 'You must have been very upset, and I don't blame you one little bit for wanting to leave. And here's me thinking what a gentleman he is. Does Bertie always carry on like that when he takes you out?'

Cordelia shook her head. 'He's a sociable sort, and usually very attentive. But since joining the Cliffehaven Gentlemen's Society, he's changed.'

Peggy frowned. 'I've never heard of the Cliffe-haven Gentlemen's Society.'

'You wouldn't have unless you move in certain circles,' said Cordelia with a sniff that denoted her disapproval. 'It's as secretive as the Masons – and probably just as daft – but Bertie thinks he's the

116

absolute bee's knees since he was invited to join it.'

'So what does this society stand for? Are they a charity linked to the Conservative Club?'

Cordelia shrugged, her lips pursed. 'I don't think they're affiliated to anything political, but I suppose it could be charitable. It's most likely just some silly men's club that gives them an excuse to eat and drink and stay out late at night without their women in tow. Their wives don't seem to know anything, and as I said before, it's all very exclusive.'

Peggy stubbed out her cigarette and threw the butt into the fire. 'However exclusive it might be, it's no excuse for treating you badly. Did Bertie explain why he had to bring you home so early before dashing off?'

'He'd forgotten there was a special meeting tonight,' Cordelia replied. 'He did apologise, but I could tell he was more interested in getting to that meeting than seeing me home safely, so I made him pay for my taxi.'

'He made you come home on your own in a taxi?' Peggy gasped. 'Good heavens, Cordelia, that's appalling bad manners.'

The fight seemed to go out of Cordelia and she shrugged. 'Better that than him driving like a lunatic and risking our lives to get me here so he wasn't late for his meeting. At least the taxi driver helped me up the steps to the door.'

Peggy patted her hand. 'I should give up on him altogether, dear,' she murmured. 'It seems he's not quite the gentleman we thought he was.'

'I agree. But it's a shame, because I really rather enjoyed our little drives out into the country and

117

the evenings playing bridge at the golf club. Bertie could be good company.'

She gave a wistful sigh and then looked back at Peggy with a twinkle in her eyes. 'I obviously don't fit in with his smart new set – and frankly, I wouldn't want to. But I tell you what, Peggy dear, they might think an awful lot of themselves, but my late husband wouldn't have approved of any of them. Nouveau, he would have called them, with more money than sense and absolutely no substance or class.'

Peggy was relieved that Cordelia seemed to be in a better mood. 'Oh dear. They do sound horrid.'

Cordelia gave a little snort of derision. 'The women were covered in flashy jewellery and expensive silks, and the men were little better in their brand new tuxedos with pearl studs in their shirts and vulgar cufflinks. My father always said you could tell a real gentleman by the age and cut of his dinner jacket – at least Bertie didn't let me down on that.'

Peggy had never moved within the sort of circles that called for tuxedos and flashy jewellery, and couldn't really understand why an old dinner jacket was better than a new one, but she let it pass. Cordelia had some old-fashioned ideas that didn't always make sense.

'Well, I'm glad you're feeling a bit mollified,' she said quietly. 'But I have to say, I am intrigued by this society Bertie has joined. It must be very new for me not to have heard about it. Did you recognise any of the men Bertie was talking to? Perhaps they might give us a clue as to what it's all about.'

'Simpkins the town clerk, Mr Eade, that ghastly

little solicitor, and Lord Cliffe's nephew. There were one or two others I recognised, but couldn't put a name to.'

'Lord Cliffe's nephew? I would have thought he had better things to do than hobnob with people like Eade and Simpkins.'

'There's no accounting for taste,' said Cordelia. 'And I never did like Jasper Cliffe anyway – far too pompous and pleased with himself – not at all like his uncle.'

'Lord Cliffe is a lovely man, I agree,' sighed Peggy 'and so approachable when it comes to doing good works in the town. It's a shame his nephew failed his medical into the services. A dose of army training would have done that wastrel the world of good.'

Cordelia's eyes widened. 'Oh, no dear, he didn't fail the medical. That was just an excuse so he could get a cushy desk job up in London.'

Peggy stared at her in utter amazement. 'I can scarcely believe it,' she gasped. 'And after all the wonderful work his uncle has done for the war effort...' She fell silent as her thoughts whirled. 'Eade's a slimy creep too. Do you think this society Bertie has joined is for that kind of man?'

Cordelia stared at her. 'I shouldn't think so for a minute,' she said stoutly. 'Bertie might be many things, but he's a patriot to the core and has the medals he won from the last war to prove it. As for Eade and Jasper, Bertie has always been very scathing about them and others like them – calls them dishonourable cowards for cheating enlistment.'

'But that didn't stop him from accepting the

119

society's invitation to join,' Peggy pointed out.

'That's as maybe. But I'm sure Bertie will give the two of them a very wide berth. After all, there are plenty of others in the society with whom he has more in common. I've seen them up at the golf club.'

'It's all very odd,' murmured Peggy.

'I shouldn't let it bother you, dear,' said Cordelia comfortably. She finished her cup of tea and wriggled out of the chair. 'Men join these things to make them feel important, and I suspect making money is at the root of it all.' She kissed Peggy's cheek. 'Now, I'm off to bed for an early night with my new library book. See you in the morning.'

Peggy made sure she negotiated the stairs safely and then returned to the kitchen where she sat and stared into the fire. Jasper Cliffe had always been a thorn in his uncle's side, with his gambling and rather fast set of friends – and she could only imagine the humiliation poor Lord Cliffe must be going through now it seemed to be common knowledge that his nephew was an immoral coward hiding behind a desk.

But why would any society actively recruit men like Jasper and Eade, who were considered social pariahs? What was it other than money and position that linked them to Simpkins and Bertie Double-Barrelled, who'd fought so bravely in the First War and were patriots to the core? Could it be about making even more money, as Cordelia suspected? And who were the other men involved?

Peggy had never trusted secretive societies. She finally gave up trying to figure it all out and decided to ask Ron about it in the morning.

9

April's eyes fluttered open to total darkness and air filled with dust and acrid smoke. She coughed and covered her mouth and nose with her hand, her eyes stinging, her sluggish thoughts struggling to identify where she was and what had happened.

As the moments passed and the strange, muffled silence was broken by a weak cry for help and whimpers of pain, she realised she was curled up – not on the couch, but on the concrete floor – and that the distant rumble was not enemy aircraft, but heavy-lifting machinery.

Dazed and disorientated, she coughed again and squeezed her eyes shut on the stinging dust that was drifting down on her. She tried to un-curl, but the movement sent a ferocious spear of agony from her wrist to her shoulder and into the back of her head. Gasping with pain and in rising panic, she cradled her arm against her chest for a moment and then tentatively explored her surroundings.

The terror of discovering that she was surrounded on all sides by shifting, groaning rubble and rafters made her heart hammer, and she had to battle to keep her wits about her and stay calm. One false move and everything would bury her. She felt the throb in her injured arm being echoed in her head as she forced herself to breathe slowly, find calm and think. HMS Firefly had been hit.

She and the others were trapped in the cellar. But the rescue services would come. Of course they would. It was just a matter of time.

And yet how much time did they have – and had the blast that had knocked her from the couch also destroyed the tiny living thing inside her? April waited anxiously to feel the flutter that would signal the baby's survival, her thoughts and emotions in turmoil. She didn't want it to be dead, but selfishly it would be an answer to all her problems if it was. And yet to wish harm on something that was innocent of blame was wicked and unforgivable, so it was with a deep sigh of genuine relief that she felt the baby move inside her.

She closed her eyes, the tears of remorse hot on her cheeks as she prayed for forgiveness and vowed she would never wish such a wicked thing again.

'April? April, is that you?'

'Paula?' April wiped back her tears and listened hard, for her friend's call had been close, but very faint. 'Paula? Where are you?'

'I'm here,' she said weakly from the other side of what felt like a huge fallen rafter. 'Help me, April. I'm frightened.'

April slid her good hand beneath it, searching for and finding her friend's fingers. 'Hold on to me, Paula. I can't move, but help will be here soon.'

Paula's grip was feeble. 'Are you all right?' she asked tremulously.

'Yes. I'm fine,' April said, despite the blinding headache and the awful stabs of pain shooting up her arm. She didn't like the sound of her friend's weak voice and could only pray that any injury she had suffered wasn't too serious. 'Keep talking to me, Paula,' she urged. 'You have to stay awake.'

'I'm so tired,' Paula sighed as they lay in the darkness, their fingers entwined beneath the rafter.

'Fight it, Paula. There'll be plenty of time to sleep once we're out of here.'

'I... I'm...' Paula fell silent.

April tried to squeeze her fingers but they were slippery and unresponsive. 'Wake up, Paula,' she said urgently. 'Paula? Paula?'

There was no reply, and April's concern deepened, but there was absolutely nothing she could do but murmur soothing words in the hope her friend would hear them.

April was getting cramp in her legs and the concrete floor was digging into her hip. She tried to ease into a different position, but with every small movement something shifted and sent great clouds of dust over her. But she was alive, and apart from her wrist and the headache, she seemed to have come through reasonably unscathed. And yet what of Paula and the others who were trapped down here with her?

She became aware of groans and whimpers and a few muttered prayers, and beneath the muffled roar of heavy machinery overhead she could hear the encouraging sound of the petty officer trying to boost morale with a rousing burst of 'God Save the King'.

There were a few takers for this show of bravado, but the voices petered out as the sound of drills and the shouts of men drifted down to them along with the thick dust. April could hear the debris shifting around her, the creak and groan of timbers under strain, and the drip, drip, drip of water hitting something metallic – probably a bit of guttering – and as it went on it seemed to resonate in her head like a ticking time bomb.

She continued to hold Paula's hand, but there was no answering movement of her fingers and her breathing sounded too rough and rapid. It was a miracle that any of them were alive, but the cries of those nearby were becoming weaker, and she began to wonder how long any of them would last if the men above them didn't get down here soon.

Her wrist felt as if it was on fire and the headache was making her feel sick. There were pinpricks of light darting before her eyes which felt like needles stabbing into her brain, her calf muscles were threatening to cramp, and her hip had gone numb against the unforgiving concrete floor. She kept a tight hold of Paula's fingers as she closed her eyes and tried to bury her nose in the collar of her shirt to avoid the dust which was thickening by the minute.

She had no idea of how long she'd been lying there in the darkness, the distant sounds of the men above drifting in and out of her consciousness. She was very thirsty, her tongue dry and rasping over her dusty lips, and her head felt as if it had been divided by a cleaver.

'Look out below!'

April cringed and curled into a tighter ball as debris clattered down and the dust rose in a great, choking wave.

'Nearly there!' shouted someone above her. 'Hold on, girls. We'll have you out in a tick.'

The man's shout revived the spirits, and the cries around April were suddenly stronger and full of hope – but there was still no response from Paula. 'Paula,' she urged. 'Paula, wake up. The men are coming. We'll be out of here very soon now.'

Paula gave a groan and April prayed the men would hurry. The shifting, creaking debris sounded louder now, and the drip of water had become a downpour, soaking her to the skin.

And then, suddenly, there was glorious light piercing the surrounding blackness, and a blast of fresh, salty air laced with rain. She blinked in its brilliance despite the agony in her head, and lifted her face as if to capture the heat of that light and taste the life-giving rainwater that came with it. 'They're here, Paula. They're here,' she said, gripping her friend's hand, trying desperately to get some sort of reaction from her. 'Come on, Paula, wake up. Please wake up.'

'Stay still, all of you,' said the man sternly from above. 'We have to move this lot slowly or it'll come down on top of you. Don't be alarmed, girls. We know what we're doing.'

The cries of the other survivors fell silent as bit by bit the heavy wooden rafters and lumps of concrete and brick were lifted away. The long shaft of the emergency light never wavered as the dark, elongated shadows of their rescuers moved eerily above them.

April finally realised how she'd been so lucky in surviving the blast, for one of the armchairs had been knocked sideways, and she'd landed within its sheltering, padded interior – it was indeed a miracle. The huge beam that separated her from

Paula had missed them both by inches, and was holding up great chunks of concrete and brick interlaced with lead guttering and bits of the staircase.

'Paula, open your eyes,' she said. 'They'll be here any minute now. You've got to hang on.'

Paula remained silent and April didn't want to imagine what had happened to her friend on the other side of that beam. She tried to quell her panic and turned her face again to the rain which was now teeming through the hole above her, feeling its clean, life-giving coolness on her skin and revelling in the taste of it on her lips.

'Give me a shout if you think you can walk,' shouted one of the firemen.

'Over here,' called the petty officer. 'But I've got three badly injured with me.'

Other cries came from all corners of the shelter. April shouted up, 'I'm all right, but my friend is injured and I can't get her to respond. She needs help, and quickly.'

It felt like a lifetime as, with aching slowness, their rescuers finally managed to get down to them on rope ladders. April watched as girls began to climb up the ladders while the medics carefully examined the wounded.

'Come on, love. Your turn next.'

April looked up at the brawny fireman and shook her head. 'I think my wrist is broken, and I want you to see to my friend first.'

'The medics will look after her,' he said, reaching for her good hand and gently drawing her to her feet. 'It's the bosun's chair for you, I think.'

'I'm not going anywhere until I know Paula's all right,' she said determinedly.

'That's not up to you, Wilton,' said the petty officer sternly. 'Do as you're told.'

Chastened, April bit down on any further argument and let the fireman help her over the rubble. She couldn't see Paula, who was hidden by the rafter and a great pile of broken bricks and concrete, but at least the men were starting to clear it away so the medic could get to her.

Her wrist was agony, making her feel quite faint, and her legs were cramping so badly she could barely walk.

The fireman lifted her into his arms and carried her the rest of the way to the bosun's chair. 'Hold on tight with your good hand,' he said kindly. 'Someone up top will look at that wrist.'

The chair swayed and twisted as it was hauled up through the gaping hole and April clung to the rope, desperately trying to control the swirling, debilitating nausea and the darkness in her head which threatened to overcome her. The rain was needle sharp and icy cold as strong hands steadied the chair and brought her safely to firm ground, but her legs refused to support her and she crumpled against the fireman in a dead faint.

When she next opened her eyes she discovered she was lying on a bed which was surrounded by curtains, her arm in a sling, her wrist tightly bandaged. It took a moment to gather her wits before she realised she must be in hospital, for she could hear hurrying feet on the other side of the curtain and the distant ringing of ambulance and fire-engine bells. She tried to remember how she'd got here, but everything was a blank from the moment that fireman had lifted her out of the bosun's chair.

'Paula,' she breathed. 'Where's Paula?' She sat up, fighting the dizziness and nausea this caused, pushed back the light blanket that was covering her and gasped in alarm. She'd been stripped of everything but her filthy underwear and was covered in scrapes, lumps and bruises. Her head swam as her gaze fell on the incriminating corset and the tattered remains of her sodden overalls which were lying on a chair. Her secret was out.

She froze momentarily, her thoughts spinning. Would the doctor tell her superiors? Was this the naval hospital or the Portsmouth General? If it was the latter, then she stood a chance of keeping her condition under wraps, for patient confidentiality was key. But if it was the naval hospital...

She pushed aside her own terrors and concentrated on finding Paula. She still felt light-headed and unsteady on her feet, and the sling was making it difficult to wrap the blanket around her, but it stood to reason Paula must be somewhere in this hospital, and she was determined to find her.

As she reached to draw back the curtain she came face to face with a harassed-looking doctor and hope fled. He was in a white coat, but the nurse beside him was in naval nursing uniform. 'I have to find Wren Paula Simms 99254,' she said quickly. 'Was she brought in here? How bad are her injuries?'

He looked down at her, his expression softening. 'I'm sorry, but the name isn't familiar. I'll get nurse to check for you, but we've had a lot of casualties tonight and some have had to go to other hospitals.'

As the nurse hurried off to check, he pressed April back onto the bed and closed the curtain. 'That wrist will need a plaster, but we're a bit busy right now as you can imagine, so I'm afraid you'll have to wait a bit,' he said. 'Other than that, you've been a very lucky sailor. The abrasions and bruises will heal quickly, and that lump on your head will go down soon enough.'

April waited, knowing what was coming and although dreading it, felt strangely relieved that her subterfuge was over. She saw his gaze drift to the discarded, filthy corset and then to the swell of her stomach which she hadn't quite covered with the blanket.

His grey eyes met her blue ones. 'Unfortunately there is nothing I can do about keeping that quiet,' he said. 'You know the rules, Wren Wilton.'

'But I'm still quite capable of working and doing my bit,' she protested. 'I'm only four months gone and in good health. It would be an awful waste of all that training and...' She fell silent beneath his unwavering gaze, knowing that all the protests in the world wouldn't save her now.

'The navy has rules for a reason, and now you must face up to the consequences,' he said sternly. 'Foolish girls like you should know better, and make use of the family planning clinics. It's what they're there for, for goodness' sake.'

April went scarlet and dipped her chin in shame as she pulled the blanket more closely around her body.

'I'll get the nurse to find you something to wear and then you can go to the fracture clinic and wait there until they're ready for you.' He turned on his heel, swished through the curtain and was gone.

April blinked back her tears, rattled by his ticking-off and his scorn, and ashamed that she had indeed been very foolish.

The nurse came back armed with clean overalls, a shirt, sweater, bell-bottoms and navy issue underwear. 'Your petty officer got stores to send them over for the casualties,' she explained, putting the neat pile on the bed. 'You won't be expected to pay for them as this is an emergency.'

'Did you find out what happened to Paula?'

The nurse shifted her gaze momentarily and then reached for April's hand. 'I'm sorry,' she murmured. 'But Wren Paula Simms died on the operating table a few minutes ago.'

April stared at her, unable to take in what she was hearing. 'No,' she breathed. 'No, that can't be right. She was talking to me while we were waiting to be rescued.'

'She was very badly injured,' said the nurse, perching on the bed beside her and squeezing April's hand. 'Both her legs were horribly crushed by the falling masonry, and there was some internal bleeding. The doctors here are marvellous and I know they did everything they could, but the blood loss was too great and she couldn't withstand the shock of such drastic surgery.'

April felt numbed by the sheer weight of loss. 'Are you saying they had to amputate both her legs?' she asked through her tears.

130

The nurse nodded. 'I'm so sorry I had to tell you such awful news after all you've just been through.' Her gaze flitted to April's midriff. 'And what you're about to go through. Life can be very hard sometimes, can't it?'

April let the tears flow freely as she nodded and thanked her, and once she'd left, pulling the curtains tightly together, she collapsed onto the pillows and sobbed her heart out. Paula had been her best friend, her staunchest ally and confidante – and now she was gone. She'd never hear her laughter again, never have her to share the joys of a soppy picture or the fun of a dance, or be able to share secrets and dreams and giggle over silly things.

As her tears slowly dried and it became clear that she was taking up a much needed bed, she began to get dressed. She wondered how her friend would have coped with having both legs amputated. The prosthetics were marvellous now and she'd seen many a man managing quite well with them. But it was different for a girl, especially a lively young one like Paula who loved dancing and sport, and hoped one day to get married and have lots of children. Would she have managed to overcome all the setbacks, and to see a bright future again?

'Yes, she would,' she whispered fervently. 'Paula would have snubbed her nose at all of it and soldiered on regardless, for she liked a challenge and wouldn't have let it defeat her.' She finished dressing, then collected the corset and tattered remains of her overall, and pulled back the curtains. She had her own challenges to face now, and she would meet them with the same determination and courage that Paula would expect of her.

10

Peggy had dreamt that Jim was having a bath in the jungle, with roaring lions and tigers and chattering monkeys surrounding him while the flames of a raging bushfire slowly encroached on the camp and girls in bright saris danced for him. It had been a disturbing, muddled dream, for he'd got out of the bath fully dressed in a dinner suit and black tie, and had begun to waltz a pretty nurse across a ballroom floor. She'd called out to him, but he hadn't heard her, and she'd woken to discover she was crying.

She was cross with herself for being so daft, and as Daisy was awake, decided to bath and feed her before the morning rush of breakfast and getting all the girls to work on time. There was no sign of Ron, and she suspected he'd left early to take Harvey and Monty for their morning run over the hills before breakfasting with Rosie. Peggy admired his stamina, for he'd come home very late last night and could only have had a couple of hours' sleep.

Once breakfast was over, the girls did the washing-up and tidied everything away, and Ivy hung out her bits of washing on the line before she scampered off to her job at the aeroplane factory.

Peggy knew she was blessed with her girls, for they helped around the house without being asked, and often kept Daisy amused so she could get on with the mending or relax over a cup of tea.

As Cordelia read the morning newspaper, Peggy looked out of the kitchen window and watched Queenie, who was sitting by the back wall transfixed by something in the grass. The only moving part of her was the occasional twitch at the end of her tail, and Peggy was fascinated by the length of time the kitten could keep so still and focused. She watched for a while, hoping Queenie hadn't found a vole or fledgling that had fallen from its nest – the mouse had been bad enough, but trying to trap a vole in the house would be almost impossible.

She gave up on Queenie when it was clear the kitten was biding her time, and sat down at the kitchen table to have a second cup of tea and a cigarette. Daisy was pushing her doll's pram around the room, and it was making a horrid squeaking sound which would drive everyone mad if those wheels weren't oiled. Peggy made a mental note to ask Ron to see to it.

Cordelia was looking much brighter this morning after her disappointment of the previous night, and Peggy wondered if she really would refuse any further invitations from Bertie. Peggy rather hoped she would, for Bertie had proved to be an utter cad, and no amount of posh dinners and drives out into the country could change that.

Peggy heard the slam of the back gate, swiftly followed by a scamper of paws up the concrete steps from the basement. Harvey charged into the room and delightedly nuzzled Daisy before trying to climb onto Peggy's lap to lick her face.

'Urrgh. Get down, for goodness' sake,' Peggy spluttered, shoving him away. 'You're filthy and you stink to high heaven.'

Ron came clumping up the steps and just managed to grab Harvey's collar before he gave Cordelia the same boisterous welcome. 'Get down, ye heathen beast,' he rumbled. 'Outside with you, you smelly eejit.'

Harvey hung his head and, with a look of utter despair and shame, slunk back down the steps with his tail between his legs.

'He's had a good roll in dead badger,' said Ron. 'I'll hose him down after I've had a cup of tea.'

Peggy wrinkled her nose. 'You could do with a hose down yourself.'

Ron sniffed his coat and then grimaced. 'Aye. I had a bit of a tussle with the old fella to get him away from the mess. I must have got some on me too.'

'You certainly did,' said Peggy, eyeing the smears on his poaching coat.

'Well, I'll have that cup of tea first, and perhaps a wee slice of toast.'

'Didn't you eat at Rosie's?' asked Peggy.

'She sent me off with a flea in my ear, so she did,' he said ruefully. 'Made me promise not to go back until me and Harvey were smelling sweeter – cheeky wee girl.' He bent down to pick up Daisy and give her a cuddle, but she didn't appreciate being in such close proximity to that filthy coat and wriggled furiously until he put her down again.

Peggy poured him a cup of tea, added a half-spoon of sugar and placed the sugar bowl out of his reach. Ron was inclined to over-sweeten his tea, and sugar was now a precious commodity.

He scowled at Peggy and stirred his tea with some vigour. 'Ach, to be sure, Peggy girl, 'tis a poor state of affairs when a man can't have three sugars in his tea.'

'It'll be even poorer when there's none left for the rest of the month,' she retorted, placing slices of bread on the hot plate. 'And you haven't exactly earned extra sugar this morning.'

'Well, that's where you're wrong,' he said triumphantly. He reached into one of the many inside pockets of his poaching coat, drew out a brace of pheasant and held them aloft.

'Shooting season finished three months ago,' said Peggy. 'Where and how did you get them?'

'I'm thinking they evaded the guns and that gamekeeper and escaped for the good fresh air and freedom of the hills.' His blue eyes twinkled as he laid the pheasants on the wooden draining board.

'You'll get arrested,' she said, trying to be stern.

'They were on common ground,' he said with all the dignity he could muster. 'I'll not be arrested by anyone.' He grinned and stroked the pretty feathers. 'Ach, to be sure, Peggy, the birds walked right into me hands, so they did. It would have been foolish not to wring their necks and bring them home for the pot.'

Peggy giggled and placed his toast in front of him. 'You've got an answer for everything, you old scallywag,' she teased. 'But you'd better not

135

leave them lying about for Queenie to get her teeth into.'

'I'll be hanging them in the shed for a wee while until they're ready for cooking, so don't fret yourself.'

He liberally spread margarine and home-made jam on his toast and looked across at Cordelia, who was making a show of not being impressed at Ron's prowess as a poacher by pretending to be immersed in her morning paper. 'I'll be betting they didn't have something as grand as pheasant at the Conservative Club last night, did they?'

Cordelia looked back at him from over her half-moon reading glasses. 'Certainly not. We had cod roe on toast followed by liver, bacon and onions. There was jam roly-poly too, although I never got to eat any of it,' she said tartly.

'Bertie was in a hurry to get to some special meeting of the Cliffehaven Gentlemen's Society,' said Peggy quickly and went on to tell him about Cordelia's upsetting evening. 'Have you heard of that society, Ron? It's a new one on me.'

Ron chewed on his toast before he replied. 'I can't say I'm familiar with it,' he said. 'To be sure, Cordelia, I'm thinking you should give Bertie his marching orders. That's no way to treat a woman of your advanced years.'

'It's not the way to treat a woman of any age,' said Peggy. 'He's an utter disgrace, and he won't be welcome here again, I can assure you.'

'And I'll have you know,' said Cordelia wasp-ishly, 'that I do not appreciate being called old – especially by someone like you, Ronan Reilly.'

'Aye, well, to be fair, Cordelia, you're no spring chicken, and it's probably time you stopped gadding about with the likes of Grantley-Adams.'

'I shall gad about as much as I want,' she retorted rather grandly. 'And with whomsoever I might choose to escort me. I'm sure Bertie will come round to apologise, and if he does, then I'm prepared to forgive him. As long as he doesn't expect me to encounter those ghastly people again. We were quite happy in each other's company before he got embroiled with that set.'

Ron finished the toast and sipped his tea, his gaze thoughtful as he regarded Cordelia over the rim of the cup. 'What was it about them that you didn't like, Cordelia?'

She shrugged. 'They were all far too pleased with themselves, and the women were rather fast, with their jewellery and questionable behaviour. Not my sort of people at all,' she added with a sniff of disdain.

Ron drank the last of his tea, poked his pipe in his mouth and shoved back his chair. 'If you want my advice, Cordelia, you'll give the lot of them a wide berth.'

'For once, Ron, I'm inclined to agree with you,' she said, and returned to her perusal of the morning paper.

Peggy was grateful to Ron, for although Cordelia rarely agreed with him on anything much, she did value his opinion in certain circumstances – and this seemed to be one of them. She could only hope that Bertie Grantley-Adams didn't show his face here any time soon, for if he did she would certainly give him a piece of her mind and show him the door. Yet she was sad for Cordelia. She had so little social life and few opportunities to have fun. It was a terrible shame that Bertie had turned out to be a complete rotter.

11

It was almost midday by the time April's arm had been plastered, and as she stood in the bustling entrance of the navy hospital, she wondered what she should do and where she should go. There was no sign of Petty Officer Rainsworth or any of the girls who'd been trapped in the basement with her and Paula, and with her arm in a plaster cast and the threat of dismissal hanging over her, there was little point in reporting for duty.

She looked out at the glistening streets, still wet from the earlier rain, and the scudding clouds which promised more to come. The weather matched her mood, for she was downhearted and grieving for Paula, and feeling very lost and alone, the weight of her troubles pressing on her narrow shoulders.

She dumped the tattered clothing in a nearby waste bin and slowly began to walk through the city streets, heading back to HMS Firefly because she couldn't think of anywhere else to go – and there just might be a chance she could retrieve some of her belongings from the wreckage. The navy-issue sweater and shirt were not much protection against the chilly wind, but at least she still had her sturdy boots to keep her feet dry.

Her thoughts meandered as she walked, drifting to memories of Paula and the close friendship they'd had – and on to Daniel who had betrayed her so utterly – and finally to the dreaded interview with her superior officer which would surely come within the next few hours.

She turned the last corner and stared in shock at the sight that greeted her. HMS Firefly was nothing more than a pile of smoking rubble, the line of terraced housing on either side blasted into extinction. There was a gaping hole in the road and both the pub and the two warehouses on the other side were nothing more than blackened shells.

April could smell the smoke still lingering in the air, could feel the particles of ash and soot falling softly onto her face as the firemen doused the last of the flames and the utility workers checked that the gas and electrics had been made safe. A group of soldiers were hunkered down around something beyond the ruins of the pub, and as she drew closer, she could see that at the bottom of the bomb crater lay a pool of oily, scummy water.

She stared at the great piles of rubble which had once been her billet, and it suddenly dawned on her that she'd lost everything, for even the clothes she wore belonged to the navy. The tears threatened again and she began to tremble. She'd never owned anything much in terms of value, but she had treasured the photograph of her father, the gold locket and chain he'd given her just before he'd died, and her one good overcoat. Now they were gone, destroyed for ever in the burnt-out remains of HMS Firefly. The tears ran down her face as she stood there, unaware that it had started to rain again.

'Stay back,' shouted a warden as he came running towards her. 'There's an unexploded bomb.'

She blinked and stared at him in dumb confusion.

'Didn't you see the signs?' he asked, taking her arm and roughly propelling her to the end of the road. She shook her head and his expression softened. 'It's all right, ducks,' he said. 'I can see you've had a bit of a nasty do – caught up in that lot, were you?' At her nod he continued, 'Why don't you go to the central office building? They'll help you there, and probably get you a nice cuppa at the same time.' He regarded her sympathetically. 'It looks as if you need it, ducks, if you don't mind me saying.'

April thanked him dully and began to tramp back the way she'd come. She had no choice but to do as he suggested, for she had no billet, no possessions, no money, identity papers or ration books – and soon she wouldn't even have a career.

The navy's central administration offices were housed in a forbidding red-brick building that had once been a workhouse and home for destitute sailors and their families. It was even grimmer inside, with battleship-grey paint on the walls and woodwork, cold flagstones on the floors, and windows so narrow they let in very little light.

April reluctantly climbed the steps and pushed open the heavy wooden door which creaked ominously. Her footsteps echoed as she walked along the dimly lit passageway towards the sound of rapid-fire typing and the chatter of voices.

'There you are,' said Petty Officer Rainsworth, stepping out from the door ahead and startling her. 'I wondered where you'd got to.'

'I had to get my arm seen to and there was a long wait,' she said, stumbling over the words.

The older woman's expression was kindly as she regarded her. 'You look like a drowned rat, Wilton. A cup of tea, I think, and a bit of a wash and brush-up before I take you in to see Chief Wren.'

April didn't have the strength or the will to argue, so she meekly followed the other woman down several corridors until they came to the washrooms.

'You'll find soap and towels in there, and I'll get one of the girls to bring you that tea. I'll come and collect you in half an hour. That should give you time to catch your breath.'

'Paula died on the operating table,' April blurted out. 'Has her father been informed?'

The petty officer nodded. 'The next of kin of all the deceased have been informed where possible.' She looked suddenly less efficient and rather downcast. 'We lost eight Wrens last night,' she said softly. 'You were one of the lucky ones.'

'That depends on how you look at things,' April replied, feeling the prick of tears again – and not wanting to shame herself any further, she pushed through the door into the washrooms.

It was bitterly cold in here, with nothing to soften the grey walls, stone floor and line of metal basins. She caught sight of her reflection in the large mirror above the basins and almost smiled, for her hair was plastered wetly to her head, she had a corker of a black eye on her bruised and battered face, and looked as bedraggled and wretched as a street urchin.

There were piles of clean towels and even a few decent-sized bars of utility soap, so April took one of each and stepped into a shower stall. Having stripped off, she turned on the water, which was hot and plentiful. Wary of getting her plaster wet, she awkwardly washed with one hand and used the soap to scrub the dirt from her hair.

The needle-sharp jets of water warmed and restored her, and after struggling to get dry and dressed again, she stepped out of the stall to discover that a mug of tea had been left for her on a bench alongside a plate of sandwiches.

April hadn't realised how hungry she was, and she sank onto the bench and wolfed down the sandwiches before sipping the scalding and very sweet tea – the one perk of being in the navy was the abundance of lovely brown sugar, supplied by an English company in Africa. Feeling much more able to face the chief Wren, she rubbed her hair dry and tried to tidy it with her fingers. The navy didn't provide brushes or combs, clearly expecting their personnel to possess their own.

She had just finished the mug of tea when the door opened and Petty Officer Rainsworth appeared. 'At least you look a bit more presentable,' she said. 'Come on, the chief Wren is waiting for you.'

April's heart was thudding as she followed the other woman down another long corridor. She could scarcely breathe as they came to a halt outside a door, and after a discreet tap, Petty Officer Rainsworth indicated she should go in.

Quaking with trepidation, April marched smartly into the room, saluted and gave her name, rank and number. She stood stiffly to attention and tried not to meet the woman's eye.

The chief Wren sat behind a polished desk on which lay a leather-edged blotter, a buff-coloured service record folder, a fancy silver inkwell and pen and a tortoiseshell-framed photograph of her husband – a rather stern rear admiral. She was an imposing woman in her late forties, with a no-nonsense expression and unfriendly blue eyes. Her uniform was immaculate and her hair had been pulled back from her hawkish face into a very tight bun. This was clearly not the sort of woman who would show clemency.

'Wren Wilton, you have been found guilty of breaking one of our most stringent rules. Therefore I have no option but to dismiss you from the service with immediate effect.'

'Please, ma'am,' she blurted out. 'I can still work for a while yet.'

The blue eyes became arctic as they bored into April. 'I did not give you permission to speak, Wilton.'

April flushed hotly and fixed her gaze on distant point over the woman's shoulder.

'You will take this chit to stores and they will provide you with civilian clothing, as circumstances have led to HMS Firefly being out of commission. You will then take this chit to the accounts department and collect wages owing to you, new identity papers and ration books. The navy is very

143

charitable, regardless of any unseemly behaviour by its personnel, and therefore will grant you a train ticket home and an extra month's pay to help you settle.'

'Thank you, Chief Wren. That's most generous.'

'I'm disappointed in you, Wilton. You had the makings of a first-class Wren, and I thought you had more sense than to get yourself into this unseemly mess. Dismissed.'

April took the chits, saluted again and left the room. She was still churning inside as she walked unsteadily down the deserted corridor towards the entrance hall, and she kept her gaze focused ahead of her determinedly, aware of the girls in the typing pool whispering behind her back and the glances of disapproval coming from the officers who watched her pass from their offices.

Closing the front door behind her, she stood for a moment to catch her breath and take gulps of fresh air in an attempt to steady herself. Her body was aching, the migraine was returning and her left eye was so swollen she could barely see through it. The only glimmer of light on this awful day was the fact that it had stopped raining, and the sun was trying to come out from behind the dark clouds.

She hurried towards the large naval stores, her teeth chattering with nerves at the thought of having to face her mother before the day was out. The last place she wanted to go was home, and she could only hope and pray that someone in accounts would take pity on her and give her a ticket to somewhere else. But where? There was no other family to turn to except for an uncle she'd only met once when she was a very small child, and she didn't even know if he was still alive.

She arrived at the store and handed over the chit in silence. The girl glanced at it, shot her a look of sympathy and then went off for several minutes before returning with an armful of clothes that had definitely seen better days.

'They've all been laundered after they were donated to the seaman's mission,' she said, 'but the underwear is new. You can change over there,' she added, indicating a curtained-off cubicle.

April dumped the clothes on the narrow bench and struggled one-handedly to strip off the overalls, the bell-bottom trousers, shirt and sweater for the very last time. Refusing to allow herself the luxury of self-pity, she unlaced the boots and tucked the socks inside them along with the service-issue bra and knickers.

The second-hand clothes had been of good quality once upon a time, and to her relief, she discovered that the underwear was indeed new, and by some miracle the bra actually fitted her. She pulled on the woollen skirt, the cotton blouse and knitted cardigan, fumbling awkwardly with the buttons, and then slipped on the plain black shoes. There were no stockings or socks and the shoes were a bit tight, so she suspected she'd end up with a blister before the day was out – which in the scheme of things hardly mattered.

The mackintosh was gabardine and apart from an amateurishly repaired tear in the lining, it didn't look bad at all. She struggled into it and covered her injured arm, leaving one sleeve dangling. She picked up the gloves and woollen scarf and then carried her navy-issue clothes through the curtain and laid them regretfully on the counter.

'I thought you could do with this,' said the girl, handing over a black umbrella. 'Someone left it behind, and there are at least a dozen others out the back.'

April was barely clinging on to her emotions in the light of such thoughtfulness. 'That's very kind, thank you,' she managed.

'It's rotten luck, Wilton. I hope things turn out all right for you.'

April nodded her thanks and headed for the door. She stepped outside, and after a moment of hesitation made her way to the accounts office.

It hadn't taken very long to sign the forms which would bring her naval career to an end, and to collect her ticket, new ration books and identity papers, and within the hour she was standing on the station platform waiting for the train that would take her to the cold comfort of a loveless home.

She breathed in the scent of the sea as she gazed out to the fleet of battleships that were anchored on the horizon, and the flotillas of MGBs and MTBs which were moored in the harbour. Other girls would be servicing them now and enjoying those heady rides across the choppy waters of the Solent – would they even notice that she and Paula were no longer amongst them?

Seagulls mewled and shrieked as they hovered and swooped against the leaden sky, and April could hear planes taking off from nearby and the rattle and clang of rigging against masts accompanying the shouts of sailors and the distant rumble of ships' heavy engines as they prepared to set sail.

She turned from the scene she'd come to love at the sound of the approaching train. Her navy days were over. It was now time to say goodbye to Portsmouth, and to the work she'd found so rewarding and fulfilling, and begin again.

April blinked back the tears and swallowed hard as she climbed aboard the train. She would have to dig deep to find the courage to face her mother and deal with whatever happened next. And although the prospect was daunting and would take every ounce of will to achieve, she was determined not to fail.

12

The train eventually arrived in Royal Tunbridge Wells, having been delayed several times by damage to the tracks caused by the previous night's enemy raid. April's headache hadn't improved despite the two aspirin a kindly lady had given her during the journey, and the bruising on her hip ached in competition with the throbbing pain in her left eye. She knew she looked a fright, and at first had shied away from the curious looks of the other passengers. Now she was so tired and dispirited, she didn't really care what they thought.

She stepped down from the train and followed

the long line of people to the gate where she handed over her ticket to the stationmaster. The entrance to the station was guarded by great stacks of sandbags, and the moment she stepped onto the pavement she was forcefully reminded that her home town had had its own share of bombing raids.

There were bomb craters where there had once been elegant houses and smart shops, and several roofs had been covered in tarpaulins to keep out the weather. Boarded-up windows and doors and ruined possessions lay abandoned in overgrown front gardens, and there was a sense of gloom as darkness fell and the rain blew down the hill on the wind.

April opened the umbrella, pulled up the collar of her mackintosh and crossed the road. She was heading for the narrow cobbled lanes that would take her to Rosemary Cottage. Tucked away in a tiny back lane, with whitewashed wattle and daub walls and a peg-tiled roof, it was a charming example of the period cottages which had once been a delightful attraction for the tourists who'd come to the historic town to take the waters from the famous spring.

There had been little damage to these alleyways and lanes and she slowed as the cottage came into view. Pausing, she regarded the small, heavily taped windows, the sturdy wooden front door and the steep steps leading up to it from the cobbles. Rosemary Cottage had been her home all her life and it looked as neat and fresh as ever despite the war. Mildred Wilton was clearly determined to keep up her high standards even in

148

these trying times.

April stood in the shelter of the umbrella as the rain pattered down, the memories of her childhood flooding back. There had been rare occasions of fun and laughter in that house when her father was alive, and April had had a glimmer of how good life could have been if only her mother had been less absorbed in herself. April had found an escape at school where she'd made friends and slowly learned that other families talked to one another, that other mothers were interested in their children and always ready to kiss and cuddle them. She'd envied her friends, and had basked in the reflected glow of their good fortune before returning to the brittle atmosphere of Rosemary Cottage for the holidays.

April's sigh was one of longing. It was at moments like this that she yearned to see her father again, to have him by her side as she faced her mother with this terrible thing she'd done. But would her father have understood? Would he have forgiven her and stood by her? She didn't know, for he'd been an old-fashioned man who rarely had very much to say for himself, let alone get emotional about things. Even so, it was a comfort to think that he might have done.

April heard the clock on the nearby church chime seven. The hat shop in the Pantiles would be closed now and her mother should be at home – there again, she could be at one of her Women's Institute or WVS meetings. Mildred was very community-minded when it suited her – and being an intrinsic part of such organisations gave her a certain kudos as well as the chance to rub shoulders with what she considered to be the right sort of people.

She wondered briefly if perhaps she should have telephoned to warn her she was coming, but then dismissed the idea. The reason for her being here was not something to be discussed on a telephone, and even if she'd said she was coming for a visit there was always the chance that Mildred would find some reason why it would be inconvenient.

Without allowing herself to dither any further, April climbed the steep stone steps and, although she had a door key, rapped the horseshoe-shaped knocker. Her pulse was racing and her mouth was dry as she heard the familiar tap, tap, tap of her mother's high-heeled shoes on the polished hall floor, and she took a trembling breath for courage.

The door opened and Mildred's welcoming smile faded into a stare of astonishment. 'What on earth are *you* doing here?'

'I've come home to recuperate,' she replied, taking in the freshly set hair, the immaculate make-up and the beautifully cut black skirt and jacket and cream silk blouse.

Mildred fingered the twin rows of pearls at her neck as her gaze trawled from April's battered face to her plastered arm. 'Yes, I can see you've been in a spot of bother,' she said distractedly. 'I suppose you'd better come in.'

April left the wet umbrella outside before she closed the front door behind her and followed her mother into the drawing room which over-looked the lane. The chintz covers on the chairs matched the curtains and there were fresh flowers in a cut-glass bowl on a side table where glasses and bottles had been laid out on a silver tray. The cushions were plumped and perched on their corners like soldiers along the couch and there was a welcoming fire in the hearth. 'This looks very cosy,' she said, unbuttoning her mackintosh. 'Are you expecting company?'

'I am, as it happens,' Mildred replied, glancing at the ornate gold clock on the marble mantelpiece. 'It's all a bit inconvenient really, April. I do wish you'd telephoned to warn me you were about to descend like this.'

April shrugged off the mackintosh and sank into the softness of the armchair closest to the fire. 'I didn't have the time,' she said as the warmth of the fire slowly thawed her cold hands and face, 'and you'd only have found some excuse to stop me from coming.'

'That's hardly fair,' Mildred retorted. She checked her appearance in the mirror above the mantelpiece and patted a strand of hair into place. 'You know how busy I am, April, and now I've had to take in two evacuees, things are even more difficult. Really, you have been rather thoughtless.'

April was stunned by her lack of care. 'Most mothers would have asked what happened to me, and welcomed me with open arms and comforting words. Thoughtlessness clearly runs in the family.'

Mildred's brown eyes narrowed momentarily – she clearly didn't appreciate April turning the tables on her. 'Of course I'm concerned,' she snapped. 'You just caught me at a bad time and I wasn't prepared, that's all.'

151

It was always a bad time, thought April sadly. 'Well, I'm here now, so can I stay for a while?'

'I suppose so.' Mildred reached for her cigarettes and lighter. 'It will be a bit of a squash, but the evacuees are in the third bedroom so your own room is free, and you can help about the house, which will be an enormous relief. I'm just not used to having to share my home, let alone with strangers, and I'm finding it frightfully trying.'

So much for a warm, caring welcome, April thought in despair. But at least she hasn't shown me the door. 'I'll do what I can to help, of course, but with my arm in a cast it might be a bit difficult.'

Mildred sat down and regarded her through the cigarette smoke. 'I have to say, April, you do look ghastly. Your eye – and those awful clothes. What on earth happened?'

April told her about the raid and being trapped under the house. 'Paula didn't make it, and I didn't have a chance to even say goodbye to her,' she finished brokenly.

'Oh, dear, poor you,' said Mildred, who was clearly giving scant attention to what April had been saying.

'Look, Mother, I realise you never really liked Paula, but she was my best friend and I miss her terribly.' April was swept by a sudden wave of giddiness which made the room swim. 'Actually, I don't feel at all well. Do you think I could have something to eat and drink, and perhaps an aspirin, before I go up to bed?'

Mildred fished in her handbag and passed over two pills before pouring a glass of water from the cut-glass jug on the side table. 'You're welcome to what you can find in the larder,' she replied. 'But there isn't very much as I haven't had time to stand in all those awful queues, and I don't trust Mrs Stavely with my ration book.' She saw April's frown. 'Mrs Stavely is my new evacuee from London, she came with her sister last week.'

April swallowed the tablets and finished the glass of water. She would have liked more, for she was very thirsty, but in the light of her mother's frosty welcome, she didn't feel inclined to just help herself.

Mildred's eyes narrowed. 'Why are you wearing those awful clothes? They look as if they've come from some jumble sale. I thought you Wrens had to be in uniform at all times?'

April felt a pang of dread and her heartbeat quickened. 'The clothes came from a seaman's charity because I lost everything in the raid,' she said hesitantly. 'And ... and...' She licked her lips and couldn't meet her mother's steady gaze. 'I'm not a Wren any more,' she finished quickly.

Mildred's gaze sharpened. 'Why on earth not? I thought you were very settled and enjoying your work.' She regarded her daughter suspiciously as April remained silent. 'You haven't been dismissed, have you?'

April took a deep breath. 'Yes,' she admitted. 'This afternoon.'

'I see,' Mildred said darkly. 'And why was that?'

April stared at her, transfixed by her glare, but still retaining the tiny spark of courage she needed to see this through. 'Because I broke the rules,' she replied.

Mildred stubbed out the cigarette and folded her arms, her lips forming a thin red line. 'You must have done something very serious to get thrown out at a time like this. What have you done, April?'

'Can we talk about this tomorrow?' she asked. 'Only I've got the most awful headache, I haven't eaten properly for over twenty-four hours, and I need to go to bed.'

'You'll do all that when I have a satisfactory answer out of you,' said Mildred, rising to her feet and looming over her. 'What did you do to get thrown out of the Wrens?'

April couldn't tell her. The words simply refused to come out even though they were echoing round and round in her head. She placed her hand over her stomach and looked up at her mother, silently pleading with her to understand.

'Good God,' breathed Mildred. 'You're pregnant, aren't you?'

April looked back at her through unshed tears, her continued silence confirming her mother's suspicions.

Mildred's slap resounded in the quiet room, leaving a searing impression on April's already bruised cheek and sending shock waves of pain into her aching head and swollen eye. She cupped her cheek and stifled a whimper of distress.

'You stupid, *stupid* girl,' Mildred shouted. 'How *could* you? How could you *do* this after everything I've done for you?'

As she raised her arm to slap her again, April jumped to her feet and grabbed her wrist. 'Hitting me won't solve anything,' she said flatly. 'I know I was stupid – and I don't need reminding of it. It's

154

done, and I've lost everything because of it.'

Mildred twisted her arm from April's grip. 'So you thought you could bring your shame home to me,' she snapped.

'Yes, I'm ashamed – of course I am. And believe me, Mother, I didn't want to come home and have to face you – but I had nowhere else to go, and no one to turn to. All I ask is for some understanding, or at least a bit of help. Or is that simply too much for you to comprehend?'

A flicker of something too fleeting to identify flashed in Mildred's eyes. 'I understand well enough that you've brought disgrace on both of us, and now you expect me to house and feed you and tell you it's all right. Well it isn't,' she rasped. 'You've been a fool; a stupid little fool.'

April's head was spinning and she sank back onto the couch. 'Don't you think I know that?' she said bitterly.

'It's a great pity you didn't consider the wisdom of your wanton ways before you jumped into some man's bed,' Mildred retorted. Her brown eyes flashed with fury. 'How far gone are you?'

'Four months.'

'Who's the father?'

April swallowed nervously. 'An American GI.'

'Good grief.' Mildred rolled her eyes and sank into a chair. 'Have you told him – made him face up to the responsibility and organised some sort of financial help?'

'He doesn't know,' April replied. 'Besides, he's been posted abroad and I don't have an address for him.'

Mildred reached for the cigarette box on the

155

low table. 'You don't have the sense you were born with, April,' she said crossly. 'A letter to the American army HQ in London would soon find him.'

April shook her head. 'He'll only deny it's his. And the army will protect him as I can't prove otherwise.'

Mildred's gaze was sharp as she lit a fresh cigarette and blew smoke out impatiently. 'I hope that doesn't mean you were spreading your favours about,' she said coldly. 'Because if that's the case, you can leave right this minute.'

'He was the only man I have ever slept with, and I was in love with him,' April retorted. 'How dare you suggest otherwise?'

Mildred gave an exasperated sigh. 'What a filthy, awful mess you've brought to my door. How on earth am I going to explain this to my friends and neighbours?' She blew another stream of smoke and tapped the cigarette agitatedly against the ashtray.

April's head was swimming, the pain and hunger making her feel quite faint. She huddled into the chair, utterly defeated. Her mother was thinking only of herself as usual – and as for any sympathy or understanding... Why on earth had she even considered it a possibility? However, it was time to try and mend fences, to pacify her mother and assure her that she was all too aware of how difficult the whole situation was for both of them.

'I'm deeply sorry I've brought such shame on you,' she said quietly, 'and of course I wouldn't expect you to let me stay once it becomes obvious that I'm pregnant. But if I could just stay for a few weeks until I can find a job and somewhere else to live, I would really appreciate it.'

'You certainly can't live here once you start showing,' said Mildred. 'As for staying in Tunbridge Wells, that's out of the question. I have a reputation to uphold in this town, as well as my business interests, and I will not allow you to destroy either.'

April's smile was wan. 'Don't worry Mother. I'll make certain your reputation isn't sullied in any way by having the baby well away from here. Once it's born it will be adopted, so you'll never have to see it or think of it again.'

'Well, at least you're showing some common sense at last,' said Mildred with a sniff. 'It would ruin both our lives if you actually kept it.' She regarded April coolly. 'Tell me about this American. Who was he, where did he come from – was he at least an officer?'

'He was a sergeant in a tank regiment, and his home was a ranch in South Carolina.'

'So, the family had money then? Even more reason to get him to pay for the situation he's left you in.'

'I don't think the family was rich, even though they had land,' said April carefully.

'I see. Well, you should still write to the American army people and try to get him to take some responsibility. Times are hard enough, and having you home again will stretch my budget to breaking point.'

'Father left you very comfortably off,' said April. 'I'm sure he wouldn't have begrudged me

157

some food and a bed.'

'That's as maybe, but with wartime restrictions, things are rather more difficult to come by.' Mildred checked the time on her gold watch. 'My friends are due to arrive in half an hour, so you'd better make yourself scarce.'

'I'll get something to eat and drink and go to bed,' said April, relieved that the badgering and dangerous questions had come to an end before things really got out of hand. She could imagine all too well what Mildred's reaction would be if she discovered that her baby was unlikely to have fair skin and blue eyes.

She fought the swirling in her head and got to her feet. 'Have a good evening, Mother,' she said quietly. 'I'll see you in the morning.'

13

Peggy was sitting by the range fire knitting some socks from the wool unravelled from an old sweater of Ron's that had seen better days at least a decade ago. The socks would go into one of the comfort boxes for the troops who were fighting in the colder climates, and which Peggy now spent most of her time packing during her shifts with the WVS.

She glanced across at Cordelia who was dozing over her tangled knitting, her spectacles askew on her nose. Poor Cordelia, she thought sadly. There had been no sign of Bertie today, and she knew that Cordelia had been hoping he'd come round to apologise. Yet there hadn't been a telephone call, or even a note, which to Peggy's mind just went to prove how badly they'd all misjudged him.

Queenie stretched out in front of the fire before curling back into a purring ball of fluff. She was getting sturdier, Peggy noticed, and her coat was gleaming, but that poor leg looked more withered than ever. Still, it seem to stop her getting into mischief, or cause her any pain, so she supposed it was best to just leave it alone.

The house was quiet, with Fran at the hospital, Ron at the Anchor and Ivy and Rita off with their young men at some fund-raising dance. Sarah was upstairs writing letters to her mother in Australia and to her sister Jane, who had left for goodness knows where to go and break codes or some such thing in great secrecy. Peggy wasn't entirely sure what Jane was doing, or even where she was living now, but she seemed to be enjoying it, because her letters had been jolly – albeit lacking in any real detail – and she appeared to be making friends.

Peggy gave a sigh, put down her knitting and rubbed her eyes. The light bulb was so weak she could barely see what she was doing, and it was straining her eyes to the point where she'd started wondering if she might need glasses. She gave up on the knitting, and was thinking about getting up to make a pot of tea when there was a knock at the back door.

'Cooee. Only me,' called Ethel. 'I hope we're not disturbing you?'

Queenie looked rather bored at the intrusion

and went back to sleep.

'Who's that?' mumbled Cordelia, her glasses falling into her lap as she was startled awake.

'It's Ethel and Stan with Ruby,' said Peggy, getting up to put the kettle on and greet them. 'Hello. This is a lovely surprise. Come in and get warm.'

They trooped in and kissed and hugged Peggy, then greeted Cordelia, who was still fuzzy with sleep, and shrugged off their coats and woollen scarves, still so necessary in the chill evenings. Ethel, for once, wasn't wearing a knotted scarf over her hair, but the minute she sat down she lit a fag and stuck it in the corner of her mouth, where it would stay until it was finished.

'We're sorry to barge in like this,' said Stan, putting his hat and a large tin on the table before plumping down on a kitchen chair. 'But we've got a couple of things we need to discuss with you and Cordelia.'

'Oh, dear,' said Peggy. 'That sounds a bit ominous.' She smiled at Ruby, who was looking a bit peaky. 'What's the matter, dear? You look as if you've lost a bob and found a tanner.'

Ruby promptly burst into tears and threw herself into Peggy's arms. 'It's Mike,' she sobbed. 'He's, he's...'

'Oh, no,' Peggy breathed, holding the girl tightly to her, the ready tears threatening.

'He ain't dead,' said Ethel in her no-nonsense way. 'The Canadian army's sending him up to some island in Scotland.'

Peggy's relief was immense, for she loved Ruby. She knew her well from the time Ruby had lived here at Beach View, and she also knew how much

160

the young Canadian meant to her. She gently eased the sobbing girl away from her and tenderly stroked back her tousled hair before cupping her face. 'He'll be all right up there,' she crooned, 'and when this horrid old war is over he'll be back to marry you, you'll see.'

Ruby sniffed and knuckled back her tears. 'I know,' she admitted. 'But it's ever such a long way, and who knows when this flamin' war will end? What if the army send him back to Canada? I couldn't bear it if that 'appened.'

'I told 'er to see if she could get permission to go up there after 'im,' said Ethel around the fag, which now had a tube of ash suspended from it. 'But Stan looked into it, and she ain't allowed to travel that far without a proper job waiting for 'er.' She grimaced. 'There ain't nothing but rocks, sheep and birds where 'e's going, so there's no chance.'

'Perhaps it's for the best,' Peggy soothed Ruby. 'You probably wouldn't get to see much of him, and you'd be very lonely up there without your mum and me and all your friends.'

'Yeah, I know.' Ruby sniffed and twisted the engagement ring on her finger. 'But it would've been worth it if I could've seen 'im now and again. It ain't fair,' she said crossly. 'I 'ate the army and Hitler and this bloody war, 'cos all they do is muck everything up!'

'My thoughts exactly,' said Peggy, 'but there's nothing we can do about it but soldier on. Why don't we have a nice cuppa to cheer ourselves up?'

Ruby nodded and Ethel patted her hand. 'It

ain't easy for no one,' she said gruffly. 'Especially the young 'uns. Flamin' Hitler. I'd like to knock 'is bleedin' block off and no mistake.'

Stan opened the tin he'd brought to reveal Ethel's famous rock buns. 'The army could do with more Ethels,' he said proudly. 'When she gets her dander up, she can be a holy terror.'

'I certainly wouldn't want to upset her,' said Cordelia with a wry smile. 'But there are times I wish I could be as fierce. There are certain people – mentioning no names – that could do with a good dose of Ethel's forthrightness.'

Ethel took the fag out of her mouth, delicately knocked off the ash with the tip of her little finger into the ashtray and then stuck it back between her lips. 'Blimey, love, you say the word and I'll put 'em straight, never you mind. Can't have people upsetting a lovely lady like you, can we?'

'I doubt you'll get the chance, Ethel,' Cordelia replied with a grimace, 'but I'll bear it in mind.'

Peggy caught Ethel's questioning look. 'It's a long story,' she said quietly. 'And best left until another time.' She poured out the tea and sat down. 'So, you two, how're the wedding plans going? Set a date yet?'

'We didn't see the point in having a long engagement,' said Stan, passing the tin of buns round. 'So we thought we'd get hitched in June.'

'Oh, how lovely,' sighed Peggy. 'I do so love a wedding.'

'We've been to see the vicar, and he can do it on Saturday the seventeenth,' said Ethel. 'So you'd better dust off yer 'at, Peg. It's gunna be a grand knees-up and no mistake.'

'Which brings us to the reason for our visit,' said Stan. He wiped the crumbs from his mouth and reached for a second bun. 'As long as this war lasts, and I'm kept on at the station, I'll have to live in the railway cottage. So when Ethel and me get married, she'll be moving in there.'

'We was wondering, Cordelia,' said Ethel, 'if you'd mind if Ruby 'ad a friend come and live with 'er in the bungalow. There ain't the room at the cottage for three of us, and I don't like the thought of 'er being on 'er own.'

'Of course I don't mind,' said Cordelia. 'The rent brings in a nice little income, and I'm pleased the bungalow is being used and looked after so well.'

'That's all right then,' said Ethel with a sigh of relief. 'Only I were worried you might not want no stranger moving in there.'

Cordelia looked at Ruby. 'Did you have anyone in mind, dear?'

'Dotty Fairclough. She works with me and Ivy at the aeroplane factory. Ever so nice, she is, and particular about keeping things clean and tidy. She's in a hostel at the moment and can't wait to get out, and is quite happy to pay her share of the rent.'

'Bring her round so I can meet her,' said Cordelia. 'But I'm sure that if she's a friend of yours then she'll suit very well.'

'Thanks, Cordelia. You're a diamond,' Ruby said, giving her a kiss on the cheek.

Peggy smiled indulgently as Ruby relaxed and sipped her tea. 'So, Stan. Where are you having the reception? I understand the Crown has a big function room and Gloria lays out a grand spread,' she teased.

Stan went puce and Ethel bristled. 'Don't talk to me about that woman,' she snapped. 'No better than she should be – and from what I've 'eard, it ain't only a grand spread she lays out!'

'Ethel, love,' murmured Stan. 'That's not nice. Gloria isn't all that bad.'

Her eyebrows shot up and she took the fag out of her mouth. 'And 'ow do you know that, Stanley Dawkins?'

'Because I've lived in this town all my life, and know more about the people who live in it than anyone bar Ron, Alf and Fred, of course,' he added quickly. 'Show a little kindness, love. She's just lost her only son, and things aren't easy for her.'

Ethel stubbed out the remains of her cigarette and folded her arms. 'I speak as I find, Stan – always 'ave, and always will. Speaking of which, 'ave you written to that sister of yours to tell 'er about our wedding? Gawd knows, neither of us 'ave much family to speak of, so it's only right she should be sent an invite.'

'I doubt she'll come,' Stan said. 'We've had no contact for years, and getting here could be difficult with all the travelling restrictions.'

'You won't know 'til you try,' she said firmly.

Stan gave a great sigh. 'I bow to your greater wisdom, my pet, and will write to her as soon as I get home.'

14

April had been living at Rosemary Cottage for almost a week when she received a reply from Paula's father, thanking her for her letter of condolence and the flowers she'd sent for the funeral. He'd clearly been devastated by his daughter's death, and had been deeply touched by the many letters and cards he'd received from her friends. He expressed regret that April had been unable to attend the funeral because of travel restrictions, but wrote that it had been a quiet service in the local church and she was now at rest with her mother in the graveyard.

April had carefully placed the letter between the pages of the photograph album in which their friendship had been recorded in a series of black-and-white snapshots, and vowed that one day she would make the journey to that tiny village and say goodbye to her friend properly.

For now, she had other, more pressing needs to worry about, for although she'd been to the job centre and the housing people, no one seemed to want to hire a pregnant girl with a broken arm, or rent her a room when she had perfectly good accommodation at home. She had run out of options, for her mother refused to contemplate the idea of her staying here until the baby was born, and April was in real dread of what the future might hold.

It was Easter Sunday and for the first time since the start of the war all the church bells were ringing. She sat on the window seat and leaned out to listen to the joyful sound and feel the warmth of the spring sun on her face. The swelling around her eye had gone down and although the bruising was still visible, at least the pain had gone from her face and hip. And yet it was the deep ache inside that tormented her, for Daniel's betrayal, her dismissal from the WRNS, Paula's death, and her mother's lack of welcome were variations of abandonment and she felt horribly alone and vulnerable.

She sat there until the last melodic peal of bells fell silent and then began to get dressed for the day. Mildred hadn't pursued her questions over the baby's father, or badgered April about contacting the American army to get him to help financially, for which she was very thankful. She knew she was on her own in this, and was determined to find some way of coping, but she did wish the atmosphere between her and her mother wasn't quite so cool, for it would have been an enormous help to be able to really talk to her and learn what was in store as far as having this baby was concerned.

With a deep sigh of regret, April stood sideways on to the full-length mirror and ran her hand over the swell of her stomach. She was almost five months pregnant and the day was fast approaching when she would no longer be able to hide the fact. Time was rushing by and yet she was in limbo, unable to plan for the future, or think beyond where on earth she could go until her baby was born. And once it was – what then? Returning home was not an option, for Mildred would no doubt make things difficult by constantly reminding her of the shame she'd brought to her door.

'And how will I feel after giving you away?' she murmured to the mound of her stomach. 'It's easy now to think about handing you over – you're not a real person and I won't let myself think about loving you. But once you're here and I see you – what then?' She plumped down on the bed, the questions whirling in her head, the answers out of reach until that long-off moment came.

She was startled from her dark thoughts by the sound of the front door slamming. Peeking out of the bedroom window she saw Mrs Stavely and her sister hurrying down the cobbled lane towards the Sunday market. They'd proved to be chatty and full of fun when Mildred wasn't about, but cowed and almost silent when she was. April felt sorry for them being so far from home and knowing they were unwelcome, and had done her best to help them feel more at home, by making tea and offering to help them find their way around the town.

She finished dressing, struggling a bit to do up the second-hand skirt that only a week before had fitted her perfectly. She desperately needed more clothes, but they cost money and lots of clothing coupons, and as she had very little of either, she'd just have to sew some elastic into the waistband and hope it wouldn't show beneath the blouse and cardigan.

Having made the bed and tidied the room, she

went down the narrow stairs and into the kitchen, where Mildred was going through the post that had arrived the previous day.

'Good morning,' April said with determined brightness. 'Wasn't it lovely to hear the church bells again?'

'Yes, very nice,' Mildred replied, concentrating on a letter.

April poured a cup of tea from the pot on the table and sipped it while her toast was browning.

Mildred set the letter aside. 'As I haven't heard to the contrary, I'm assuming you still haven't managed to find work or accommodation? Are you sure you've tried absolutely everywhere?'

'Of course I have,' April replied flatly. She sat down at the table and smeared some of the horrid margarine on the hot toast. 'But the minute the accommodation people hear that I'm living with you, they refuse to help, and when I tell employers that I'm pregnant, they show me the door.'

'Then you should learn to be economical with the truth,' said Mildred crossly. 'Really, April, you can be very dense at times – rather like your father.'

'Daddy wasn't dense,' she retorted. 'He just liked to be honest – as do I. What's the point of finding a job and a room to rent if in a month or two I'll be back on the streets?' She suddenly didn't feel at all hungry and pushed the toast away. 'The only option I have left is a hostel or one of those awful homes for single mothers.' She regarded her mother across the table. 'Unless you let me stay here.'

'I have a better idea,' said Mildred. She picked

up the letter she'd been reading. 'This is from my brother. He's getting married in mid-June and suggests that if we accept his invitation he can arrange for us to stay with a friend of his – a Mrs Reilly, who owns some sort of boarding house.'

'I don't see how that's any help,' said April. 'I'll have to leave here long before June.'

'I'm sure Stan can persuade Mrs Reilly to take you in sooner than that,' said Mildred. 'He's a rather soft, sentimental man, who would never turn you away. I don't know why I didn't think of him earlier.'

'The last time I saw Uncle Stan I was about four – which I believe was the last time you saw him too. I hardly remember him, and it would be incredibly rude to just turn up on his doorstep and expect him to help.'

Mildred waved the objections away. 'Stan is a great believer in doing the right thing,' she said dismissively. 'I grant you, your arrival might prove a little awkward, but if this Mrs Reilly has a boarding house, then I'm sure she'll take you in if the money's right.'

April regarded her steadily. 'You seem to forget that I have no money.'

'The government pays those taking in evacuees, and I'm willing to add to that if it will get you settled and out of my hair.'

Stung by this, April squared her shoulders and met her mother's cool gaze. 'How very generous of you. And what if Mrs Reilly doesn't want to take me on in my condition – or has no rooms to let?'

The hand waved again to negate her objections.

'You're just playing devil's advocate,' Mildred retorted. 'Everyone needs a bit of extra money at times like these, and I'm sure Mrs Reilly is no exception. She takes in evacuees and all sorts according to Stan, so a pregnant girl will hardly be a bother, especially if she's paying over the odds on rent.'

April felt a tremor of despair as she stared at her mother. 'Why do you hate me so?' she asked. 'What did I ever do to you that stopped you from loving me?'

Mildred met her gaze briefly and then concentrated on her brother's letter. 'This is not the time to get emotional, April, or go into things you simply wouldn't understand.'

'Why not? We're alone in the house, and once I leave here, I doubt I'll ever come back. I would have thought it was the perfect opportunity to clear the air.'

'Don't be ridiculous,' her, mother said impatiently. 'You're attempting to make something out of nothing as usual. Really, April, you can be very trying at times – picking away at things just like your blessed father used to do.'

April made no comment as it would serve no purpose, but she wished wholeheartedly that Mildred would respect her father's memory and not use it to put her down all the time.

Mildred set the letters aside and clasped her hands on the table, her gaze drifting to some spot beyond April's shoulder. 'There are other more important things to focus on. You'll need some decent clothing to take with you – that skirt is far too tight and the rest of it is very shabby. I can't have you turning up at Stan's looking like that on top of everything else. He'll think we're living in reduced circumstances, and I do have my pride, you know.'

April snorted softly with derision.

Mildred carried on as if she hadn't heard. 'I'll also sort out your travel permit and a train ticket to Cliffehaven. You'll have to barter with this Mrs Reilly over any extra – there's only so much in my bank account that I can spare over the next four months. After that you'll have to sort things out for yourself.'

'And when are you planning for me to leave?'

'As soon as the travel permit and ticket are arranged. I suggest you telephone Mrs Reilly and book yourself in for the end of the week. Everything should be through by then.' She glanced across at April. 'I also suggest you tell everyone you're engaged and that your fiancé was sent abroad before you could arrange a wedding. It would be pointless to pretend you were married – your identity papers and so on will prove otherwise.'

April nodded, for it made sense. 'Will you be coming down for Stan's wedding?'

'I really don't have the time or the inclination,' Mildred said brusquely. 'My brother and I have never been close, and I'm sure the invitation was sent more out of duty than anything. But you can make my excuses when you see him. He's evidently still working at Cliffehaven station.'

April felt a chill of foreboding as she watched her mother push away from the table and gather up her jacket, gas-mask box and handbag. An

171

invitation sent out of duty was one thing, turning up in need was quite another.

Mildred pushed the letter across the table. 'Make that telephone call and then write to Stan to let him know you're on your way,' she said, slipping on her jacket. 'I have to go and do a stocktake, and then I'm out to lunch with friends. I don't know what time I will be back.'

The front door slammed behind her and the house fell silent. April burst into tears. She had been effectively abandoned to an uncle she could barely remember and some woman she'd never heard of. She sobbed with distress, longing for someone to care – to tell her it would be all right and that she was no longer alone. But the only company she had was the steady ticking of the kitchen clock.

15

Ron was used to ducking and diving and keeping his business to himself, but things had escalated to the point where he was beginning to find life very awkward indeed. Rosie was being unusually demanding of late, expecting him to help in the bar over the Easter weekend, and it had been the devil's own job to persuade her that he had other commitments which he couldn't possibly ignore. It helped being part of the Home Guard, of course, for there were always practice manoeuvres and arms training to attend, and nights away were easily explained. But how to get out of afternoon tea with Rosie without making her suspicious – that was the rub, and although he hated lying to her, it was a necessary evil he couldn't avoid.

He stomped out of the scullery that morning with Harvey racing on ahead of him and began to tramp up the narrow alleyway towards the hills. Peggy was still giving him funny looks because he'd refused to tell her where he disappeared to several nights a month, but as he was on special duty at the highly secret arms and supply dump hidden deep underground within the hills, he'd had to say it was just night training, or fire-watch duty.

And then there was Gloria – lovely Gloria, whose presence in his already hectic routine had turned everything upside down. All in all, he wasn't too happy at the moment, for the women in his life were causing him all sorts of trouble, and there seemed to be no way out of it.

Harvey had shot off to investigate something in a clump of gorse, and he was about to follow him when he heard a soft mewl behind him. Turning, he saw Queenie streaking up the hill behind him.

'Go back home,' he said sternly.

Queenie ignored him and Harvey dashed back to see what all the fuss was about. He sniffed the cat and gave it a lick, then barked and ran in excited circles. Queenie sat down and eyed him imperiously for a moment and then carried on tiptoeing through the grass towards Ron.

'Ach, ye fool animal. Go back, Queenie. This is no place for a wee cat.'

Queenie shot past him and scampered about in

173

pursuit of Harvey, who seemed to think the whole thing was terrific fun.

Ron could only see her tail above the grass as she darted about, chasing a fly, and he gave a great sigh of exasperation. 'Now what?' he muttered. He decided not to take the cat back to Beach View – it would cost too much time – something of which he had little to spare. He would just keep an eye on her, and next time he'd make sure she was shut indoors when he came for his walks. Peggy would have his guts for garters if Queenie got lost or injured. It seemed that his life was plagued by strong-willed females who took not a jot of notice of anything he might say.

He kept an eye on Queenie, who bounced about after Harvey rather like Tigger from the children's books. He noted that Harvey was constantly running back to check on her, and he fervently hoped that nothing would frighten her and send her into hiding – which would mean having to spend hours looking for her. He checked his watch. He was due at the Crown in just over an hour, so he'd have to keep the walk short.

Lighting his pipe, he strolled through the long grass and admired the scenery. It was the first day of May, and although there was still a mist shrouding Cliffehaven, it promised to be a lovely day. His mood lightened as the fresh air restored him. The news on the wireless was all good, with the Axis forces all but defeated in North Africa and the Americans ousting the Japs from vast areas of the Pacific. His son Jim seemed to be relatively safe and distanced from any fighting in India, as was his elder son, Frank, who was serving out his call-

174

up as a storeman on a military base in the Midlands. Frank would soon be of an age when he was no longer eligible for the services, but Ron suspected he'd continue to do his bit after being demobbed by joining the Home Guard.

He continued walking, his thoughts turning to Gloria and the Crown. He'd have to be extra careful today, for Rosie had arranged for her barmaids to take over this lunchtime and was meeting Peggy and Cordelia in town to treat themselves to a meal at the new British Restaurant which had just opened up in one of the abandoned shops in the High Street.

Such restaurants had sprung up all over England, and as they offered three courses of non-rationed food for the princely sum of ninepence, they were excellent value and therefore very popular. Ron wouldn't have minded trying it out for himself, but as it was, he'd have to make do with whatever was left over from the meeting in Gloria's function room. Not that this was any hardship, for Gloria always laid on a good spread.

He checked his watch again and whistled to Harvey, who came galloping towards him, tongue lolling, ears flapping, with Queenie bouncing along some way behind him.

Ron shook his head. He'd thought he'd seen it all – but a cat coming for a walk and answering to a whistle? He wouldn't have believed it if he hadn't seen it. He patted the dog and shooed him in the direction of home and then waited for Queenie to catch up.

'To be sure, you wee scamp, those three legs are doing a grand job, so they are,' he said, reaching down to scoop up a panting Queenie. Her little heart was thudding and her fur was soaked with dew from the grass. 'But I'm thinking they could do with a bit of a rest now.'

Queenie purred as he gently placed her in one of the deep pockets of his poacher's coat and headed for home.

As he shut the back gate behind him, Peggy came running out of the scullery. 'I've lost Queenie,' she said, on the verge of tears. 'I've looked everywhere and called and called, but there's no sign of her.'

Ron grinned, carefully lifted the purring bundle from his pocket and placed her in Peggy's arms. 'She came for a walk with me and Harvey,' he said. 'But there's no harm done.'

Peggy's eyes widened in astonishment. 'A walk? You took the *cat* for a walk?'

'Ach, to be sure, it was her idea, not mine,' he said defensively. 'I was halfway to Tamarisk Bay before I realised she was following us.' He beamed with pride. 'But she came when I whistled, which is more than Harvey ever does.'

Peggy rubbed her face against the soft, rather damp black fur. 'Thank goodness you didn't lose her,' she breathed. 'I couldn't bear it if something happened to her.'

She looked back at Ron and caught him surreptitiously checking his watch. 'Don't tell me you're off somewhere yet again, Ron, because I've got a list of things that need doing today.'

Ron started backing towards the gate in preparation for a quick getaway. 'Sorry, Peggy girl, but I'm needed elsewhere all afternoon. You enjoy

176

your lunch.' He slammed the gate behind him and shot off with Harvey in close pursuit before she could question him any further.

I'm getting too old for these shenanigans, he thought as he made his way through the back streets that would eventually lead to the yard behind the Crown. But there was an undeniable spring in his step as he turned the final corner and saw Gloria waiting for him by the back door. He might be getting on a bit – some might even say he was past it – but as long as there was fire in his belly he wouldn't give up on living life to the full.

'I don't know what you're up to, Ronan Reilly,' Peggy muttered. 'But I'll find out. You see if I don't.' She carried Queenie indoors and dried and fed her before turning her attention to Cordelia, who was looking very smart in a navy dress and jacket and a white straw hat.

'Are you going to be warm enough in that?'

Cordelia frowned. 'Of course it's not corn in my hat. Really, Peggy, you should go and have your eyes tested.'

'I was just asking if you would be warm enough in that dress and coat,' she repeated rather more loudly. 'It's a bit chilly out still.'

'We're going in a boat? You're right,' Cordelia said with a sniff. 'Of course that would be silly.'

'Cordelia, dear, do turn up your hearing aid,' Peggy said.

She fiddled with it. 'It is up, and there's no need to shout, Peggy. I'm not that deaf, you know.'

'Not that you'd notice,' muttered Peggy. 'I'm

going up to see to the spare room,' she said clearly. 'The new girl will be arriving this afternoon and I want the poor little thing to feel comfortable and welcome.'

Cordelia was still fiddling with her hearing aid; making it screech quite horribly until she was satisfied she could hear properly. 'It comes to something when a girl in the family way has to live with strangers,' she said. 'Doesn't she have any parents or in-laws who could have taken her in?'

'I did ask when she telephoned.' Peggy collected up the basket of cleaning materials from beneath the sink. 'But she just said there was no one, and when she had to leave her present place a friend of a friend suggested she rang me.'

'Poor little mite,' muttered Cordelia. 'I wonder why she had to leave where she is?'

Peggy shrugged. 'I don't know, but she's obviously desperate for somewhere to stay, and that's all that concerns me. She even offered me extra money, poor lamb. But she'll find a safe haven here, never you mind.'

'None safer than with you, Peggy,' said Cordelia fondly. 'She's a lucky girl to have been given your number.'

Peggy chewed her lip. 'I wonder who gave it to her? I don't know anyone in Tunbridge Wells and I've certainly never been there.' She shrugged off this minor niggle and checked on Daisy, who'd fallen asleep in her playpen, then hurried upstairs.

The single room was on the first floor, just along from Cordelia's double, the bathroom and lavatory. As the girl was pregnant it seemed sensible to

178

have her close to the facilities as Peggy remembered what it was like when she'd been expecting Daisy – running to the lav every five minutes, she'd been.

She had put fresh linen on the bed the night before, and now she cleaned the windows, dusted the furniture and gave the bare floorboards a good wipe-over with a damp cloth, her thoughts troubled. April Wilton had sounded like an educated sort of girl on the telephone and clearly not short of a bob or two if she was offering to pay extra to live here, so why couldn't she have stayed where she was? She'd definitely been holding something back during their rather short telephone conversation, but not wanting to probe too deeply, Peggy had accepted that she had nowhere permanent to live, the baby's father was serving abroad and she didn't seem to have anyone to care for her. No doubt she'd find out the whole story once the girl had settled in.

Checking again that her sister Doreen hadn't left anything in the drawers or wardrobe, Peggy made sure there were plenty of hangers and that fresh paper lined the drawers. Tweaking the bedspread straight, she plumped the pillows so they looked inviting and then, after one final check, closed the door. April was due to arrive on the four o'clock train, and Peggy was aiming to be there to meet her. She just hoped it wouldn't be delayed as so many trains were these days, for it would put her evening routine right out of kilter.

She quickly checked the bathroom, pleased to see that the girls had cleaned the bath and run a mop over the floor, and not left wet towels everywhere like Ron was in the habit of doing. She then went into the large double room shared by Ivy and Rita, took one look at the chaos of clothes strewn everywhere, the unmade beds and the clutter on every flat surface, and shut the door. It was what she'd expected really, but she'd have to have a word with them, for as cheeky and lovable as they were, she didn't approve of them living in such a pigsty.

She went downstairs and into her bedroom off the hall to get changed into something a bit more respectable. Peeling off her wrap-round pinafore and the cotton dress she always wore to do her housework in, she took off her headscarf and tidied her hair. She was looking forward to her lunch out, for it was a rare treat and she'd heard that the food in these British Restaurants was very good as well as being cheap.

She pulled on a tweed skirt and pale lavender-coloured sweater and cardigan, all of which were hand-me-downs from her older sister Doris. They'd hardly been worn, but Doris changed her wardrobe so often there weren't enough days in the year for her to wear everything more than a couple of times, and Peggy was grateful to have her discarded clothes and shoes. She pushed her feet into her second-best pair of shoes – they were marginally more comfortable to walk in than her best ones – and then clipped on her earrings and put on her blue felt hat. It was a bit shabby, but it didn't matter – most things were shabby now, what with making do and mending, the rationing and the paltry amount of clothing coupons to be had.

Daisy was waking up and demanding a drink and something to eat, so Peggy got her out of the playpen and handed her a rusk to keep her occupied while she watered down some of the orange juice the government provided each week for small children. Once Daisy's demands had been met, Peggy put on her little hat and coat and buckled her shoes. She would soon need some new ones, she noticed, so there would have to be another trip to Clarks to get her properly fitted now she was on the point of really finding her feet.

Peggy carried Daisy on her hip as she helped Cordelia navigate the cellar steps, and once Daisy was strapped into the pram, she shut the back door and they set off. The pace was deliberately slow for Cordelia's sake, but with the warm weather arriving, it seemed her old joints were easing up and she was quite sprightly today.

Rosie was just emerging from the Anchor as they approached, looking as glamorous as ever in a short navy blue skirt, white blouse and light-weight three-quarter length coat, her feet shod in two-tone navy and white high-heeled shoes. Her hair had been freshly washed and set beneath the rather fetching hat, and her blue eyes sparkled with fun.

'Hello, darlings,' she said warmly as she kissed them both and made a huge fuss of Daisy. 'What a lovely day – perfect for lunch out with friends.' She chuckled. 'I feel as if I'm playing truant by taking the day off.'

'You deserve it, Rosie,' said Peggy. 'You work far too hard and it's time you had a bit of fun.'

They ambled along the pavement, chattering

about the war news, the weather and the latest scandal that was doing the rounds, and then stopped to say hello to Rita, who was hosing down one of the fire engines. They continued in this fashion as they slowly wandered up the High Street, stopping now and again to discuss the very uninteresting shop windows and the ugliness of the utility clothing that was the only available thing to buy.

'I know we're supposed to feel patriotic by wearing those awfully dull things,' sighed Rosie. 'But you'd have thought a bit of colour wouldn't go amiss. After all, grey, brown and black are hardly uplifting, are they?'

Peggy agreed rather distractedly and let Cordelia continue the discussion as she watched Ron emerge from one of the council offices, deep in conversation with a man she didn't recognise. Whatever the topic was, it looked very serious, and as the conversation came to an end, they shook hands and went their separate ways; Ron ducking into a side alley with Harvey at his heels, and the other man coming down the hill towards them.

'Are you all right, Peggy?' Rosie frowned with concern.

Peggy quickly gathered her wits. 'Just daydreaming of pretty clothes and proper stockings,' she said, still darting glances at the man approaching them and hoping to goodness that Ron wouldn't suddenly emerge into the High Street again and thereby cause trouble between him and Rosie.

The stranger was tall and she guessed about forty or so, with a sturdy figure and a rather fine handlebar moustache. Dressed in a good suit, with polished shoes and a smart black bowler hat, he carried a briefcase and tightly furled black umbrella, and looked as if he'd just stepped out from a tailor's shop window in London.

'I say, no wonder you're distracted,' whispered Rosie as the man raised his hat to them and smiled before going on down the hill. 'He's rather attractive, don't you think? I wonder who he is?'

'I have no idea,' Peggy replied thoughtfully as all three of them turned to watch his progress. 'But he's not local, that's for sure.'

'He's a dish,' sighed Rosie.

'You should both remember you have men of your own,' said Cordelia briskly, 'and not behave like silly girls.'

Peggy and Rosie exchanged glances and stifled their giggles. 'It doesn't hurt to admire a good-looking man,' said Rosie. 'After all, Cordelia, you were watching him too, and I saw that glint in your eye as he passed.'

Cordelia gave a sniff. 'If you ask me, he's far too attractive for his own good – and what's a man like that doing here in the first place? I bet he's up to some sort of mischief.'

'It *is* unusual to see a man of his age out of uniform,' mused Rosie. She grinned impishly at Peggy. 'Perhaps Cordelia's right and he's a spy from MI5, or one of those Fifth Columnists the newspapers have been banging on about.'

Peggy laughed. 'Cliffehaven is hardly a hotbed of spies and Nazi sympathisers. He's probably just dressed up to meet some lucky lady for lunch.' She gave a sigh of longing for the days when Jim had taken her out, and then perked up again. 'Talking of lunch,' she said. 'It's time we had ours. I'm starving.'

16

Mildred was dressed and ready to leave to open her hat shop by the time April came downstairs in her newly purchased second-hand dress, coat, hat and shoes, and carrying the suitcase which contained yet more bargains her mother had brought home from the WVS clothing centre several days before.

'The shop is very busy at the moment,' she said as she pulled on butter-soft leather gloves and checked her appearance in the mirror above the hall table. 'So I'm sure you'll understand why I can't hang about and go with you to the station.'

'Of course, Mother,' April replied. 'It isn't as if we might never see each other again, is it?'

Mildred eyed her sharply. 'You're hardly a child any more,' she replied tartly. 'And I do not appreciate your sarcasm after all I've done to help you.' She picked up a small box from the hall table. 'You'd better have this,' she said. 'Your father gave it to me years ago and I have no use for it.'

April opened the box to discover a gold ring set with a small single sapphire of the deepest blue. 'But it's lovely,' she breathed. 'Why have you never worn it?'

Mildred shrugged. 'I'm not particularly fond of

184

sapphires, and that one's so small it was hardly worth the effort of wearing it. But it'll do for you – after all, you *are* supposed to be engaged.'

Stung by her words and the careless way she'd dismissed her father's beautiful gift, April slipped the delicate ring on her finger. At least she had something to remind her of her father and, unlike her mother, she would appreciate it and take very great care of it.

Mildred leaned forward and almost brushed April's cheek with a fleeting, frosty kiss. 'Take care, and write to me when...' She darted a glance towards the kitchen where the two evacuees were having their breakfast. 'You know when,' she said agitatedly. 'Now, I really do have to rush.'

April stood in the hall as the front door closed and she heard her mother's high-heeled shoes tapping on the concrete steps and then along the cobbles. Mildred had obviously considered she'd done enough to rid herself of an unfortunate embarrassment and now the object of this burden was out of sight, she was probably already out of mind, and Mildred could carry on as if nothing had happened.

April glanced towards the kitchen and the sounds of chinking crockery and murmured conversation. The evacuees were naturally curious about the cool relationship between her and her mother and had probably realised quite quickly that there was little love lost on either side. As they were nice women and she didn't want to lie to them when they asked the awkward questions she knew they wanted answers to, she picked up her case and quietly let herself out of the front door.

Clicking it shut behind her, she slowly went down the steps and, without looking back, headed for the station. Her train wasn't due for another two hours, but she couldn't bear to remain in that house a moment longer, so she planned to put her case in the left-luggage office and go for a walk in the park, perhaps buy a cup of tea in the café by the bandstand and then find a sunny spot to while away the time.

The sun was still hidden behind the many roof-tops and it was chilly in the shadows, but the sky was a pale blue, promising a fine day. April gripped the handle of the case she'd unearthed from the accumulation of junk in the attic, and walked slowly through the familiar streets, wondering if indeed she ever would return home again. It was unlikely, she accepted sadly, for there was nothing for her here.

Having handed her case in and checked that her train was due to arrive on time, April wandered around the town for a bit and then went into the Grosvenor recreation ground in search of a cup of tea. Time seemed to move very slowly as she sat in the British Restaurant which had been opened on the site of the old bandstand, and watched the children playing on the grass nearby while she drank her tea and admired how the early May sun glinted on the little ring.

At last there was only half an hour to go before her journey began, and with a sigh of relief she made for the railway station. Once she'd collected her case and handed over her ticket and travel permit to be clipped, she found the ladies' waiting room, where someone had lit a fire in the hearth to chase away the evening chill, and even provided some out-of-date magazines.

There was no one about except for the station-master who was sweeping the platform, so April put the case down, settled on one of the rather uncomfortable benches and opened the news-paper she'd found on the seat. It was yesterday's, but that didn't matter.

The train was eventually delayed by almost an hour and she'd read the paper from cover to cover and had started on the cryptic crossword by the time it chuffed into the station. Folding the paper neatly into her mackintosh pocket so she could finish the crossword during the journey, she put the straps of her gas-mask box over her shoulder and picked up her case to join the throng waiting impatiently on the platform.

Despite the crush, April managed to get a window seat. She put her case and gas mask in the luggage rack above her head, loosened the belt of her mackintosh and left it draped over her shoulders as she sat down. She'd become used to doing everything one-handed, but the plaster was getting very grubby and the sling was fraying quite badly.

She watched the activity on the platform as the stationmaster organised the porter and the guard stood stoically, waiting to blow his whistle and wave his flag. The train was obviously a popular one, for almost every seat was taken, and a group of young servicemen had filled most of the space in the connecting corridor.

She caught sight of her reflection in the window and quickly looked away. Her eyes were too large and sad in her pale face, the remnants of her bruises still evident on her jaw and cheekbones, and she knew that if she didn't keep a tight rein on her emotions she would simply disintegrate into a sobbing, self-pitying heap.

Blinking hard, she squared her shoulders, determined not to weaken. She'd been through so much these past weeks she could certainly manage to get to Cliffehaven without falling apart at the seams. She looked out of the window again, fleetingly wondering if her mother might have changed her mind and come to see her off. But the platform was empty and she became cross with herself for even allowing this foolish thought to enter her head.

Steam and smoke billowed along the now deserted platform as the guard blew his whistle and the train's wheels began to slowly turn. The driver responded with a blast from the train and the great iron wheels got up speed. They passed the end of the platform and began to chuff their way between high embankments which were dotted with spring flowers of yellow and white with the occasional wild hyacinth daring to show through.

April took the newspaper out of her pocket, but the words blurred and she found she'd taken in nothing as she stared at the crossword, her thoughts scattering. Mrs Reilly had sounded nice on the telephone, and hadn't been at all fazed by the fact April was unmarried and pregnant. Of course April had had to bend the truth a bit about a fiancé being in the army abroad, even though she hadn't really wanted to start out on a lie, but maybe, if Mrs Reilly turned out to be as nice as she'd sounded, she'd tell her the truth.

And yet, however nice she was, she might not be quite so accommodating when she discovered April was having what people now called a 'khaki baby'. It seemed she hadn't been the only girl to fall for one of the coloured GIs, and she'd heard awful tales about girls being thrown out of their homes, of babies being abandoned, and men coming home on leave to find living proof that their wives had been unfaithful.

April took a shallow breath and stared out at the passing scenery as she twisted the ring round her finger. It was too late for regrets, what was done was done. She'd simply have to face what happened next and deal with it, no matter how difficult it might be.

Her thoughts moved on to her Uncle Stan. She had vague memories of a big, jolly man who'd swung her about and made her giggle, and who'd tucked her up in bed at night and read her stories until she fell asleep. She'd had no idea why they'd gone down to visit him all those years ago. Mildred had simply said that he'd lost his wife, and April couldn't understand why he didn't go and look for her. She knew better now, of course, and felt rather sad that he'd been alone for so long. Quite why Mildred hadn't stayed in touch with him was a mystery, for he'd seemed to be a lovely, caring man.

She continued to gaze out of the window as the train chugged and puffed its way through the out-skirts of Tunbridge Wells and into the countryside. Her childhood memories of that visit were few and rather muddled, but she'd retained the impression of a cosy cottage right near the railway lines and a lovely garden full of flowers and fruit trees and vegetables. And of course she remembered the sea, and how Stan had rolled up his trouser legs and held her hand as they'd paddled in the icy water.

April's smile was soft at this memory, for it was the only time she'd been to the seaside, and she'd prattled away to her father about it all on her return, begging him to take her again. But his busy solicitor's practice hadn't left any time for holidays, just the odd day out once he'd bought a car – and because he was a nervous driver, they never went very far, and certainly not to East-bourne or Brighton, the latter being considered far too racy for a family outing.

The train came to a halt and panted patiently by the platform as people got off and luggage was quickly stored in the guard's van. April's thoughts wandered, speculating on how accurate her memories of Cliffehaven were, and how much it might have changed after all these years. If Tunbridge Wells was anything to go by it was probably unrecognisable, but she hoped something of her childhood had been left the same.

As for Uncle Stan, he would be in his mid to late sixties now, and although he should have retired, the war had meant he'd had to carry on his duties at the station. Did his little railway cottage still exist? Was he still as jolly as she remembered – and what was the woman like who was about to become his wife?

She had no way of knowing, for she'd suffered enough rejections these past months and her courage had failed her when it had come to writing him a letter. In the end, she'd decided she would move into Beach View with Mrs Reilly and get to know more about him before she revealed who she was. That way, she wouldn't be taking a leap in the dark.

17

The British Restaurant was basic, with mismatched chairs, and tables covered in rather faded oilcloth. The walls were unadorned, although they had been recently distempered, and the floorboards had been stripped and waxed to a gleam. Their waitress was a jolly, middle-aged woman who used to work at the Grand Hotel before it was smashed to smithereens during a bombing raid, and the menus were handwritten in pencil so they could be used repeatedly. The cutlery was cheap but serviceable, and there was a pot of flowers on each table to cheer things up, with proper linen table napkins which were very posh considering the rest of the place.

Despite the lack of ambience and the cheap prices, lunch had not been a disappointment. They'd had a rich tomato soup, a very tasty shepherd's pie and sliced bottled pear with custard. Daisy had been very well behaved and there hadn't been too much of her lunch on the floor beneath the high chair when she'd finished.

Peggy was feeling relaxed and rather sleepy as

they dawdled over cups of tea and Daisy became engrossed in a picture book the waitress had found for her. She couldn't remember the last time she'd gone out to lunch – or had a meal prepared for her – and it was absolute bliss not to have to worry about the washing-up. She smothered a yawn, thinking how lovely it would be to go home and have a bit of a snooze before she had to go to the station to meet April.

'Peggy? Peggy, are you with us, or off in dreamland?'

She shook her head to clear the fog of drowsiness and shot Rosie a smile. 'Sorry, I was miles away. I'm not used to eating so well at this time of day, and I almost nodded off.'

'It's a sign of getting old,' said Cordelia darkly. 'I drop off when I least expect it, and it's awfully confusing to suddenly wake up and not know what day it is.'

'I wish I had the time to sleep during the day,' sighed Rosie. 'There's always something to be done even after I've locked the pub doors.'

Peggy looked at her watch and was startled to discover that it was almost two and the restaurant was about to close until the evening. 'We'd better head back,' she said, stubbing out her cigarette. 'I've got things to do before I meet the train.' She cleaned Daisy's face with the linen napkin, tidied up around the high chair as best she could and then pulled on her coat.

They left the friendly waitress a generous tip, promised to come again, and then slowly headed towards home in the lovely spring sunshine.

Having said goodbye to Rosie at the door to the

Anchor, Peggy and Cordelia ambled on to Beach View to discover there was no sign of Ron or Harvey. Cordelia shed her hat and coat and promptly fell asleep in her favourite armchair while Peggy checked on the vegetable stew she'd left in the range's slow oven.

Once the potatoes were peeled and the table set ready for later, she glanced up at the clock on the mantelpiece and quickly deposited Daisy on her potty. Praising her warmly, she emptied the potty in the outside lav and plonked her back in the pram. She left a note for Cordelia to tell her where she'd gone, checked that Queenie was happily asleep on Ron's crumpled bed and then headed back into town.

She didn't follow her usual route along Camden Road, but went up the hill and turned into the labyrinth of narrow streets which would finally emerge about halfway up the High Street. She didn't know these streets very well despite the fact she'd lived in Cliffehaven all her life, for she'd never really had cause to use them, but today she was curious to see where Ron might have ended up when he'd disappeared earlier.

It had occurred to her as she'd been peeling the potatoes that Ron had disappeared down a similar side street a week or so before, and she was intrigued enough by his odd behaviour – and his continued absence from home – to want to explore.

She pushed the pram along the quiet residential streets, noting the surprising number of twittens that ran between the houses, and seemed to end in high fences or someone's back yard. At this

193

thought she felt a chill of foreboding, and using her infallible sense of direction, headed down one of the alleyways that she knew would eventually lead to the High Street and the back yard of the Crown.

She weaved the pram around the weeds and rutted puddles and avoided the wind-blown rubbish that had gathered in the long grass at the base of the fences until she reached the sharp dog-leg and came to an abrupt halt. The Crown stood before her in all its shabby glory, the big back yard almost filled with empty crates and beer barrels, the tall gates standing open.

She stared hard at the sets of doggy paw-prints and large human ones that went from the muddy puddle by the gate to the back door. They could have been anyone's, of course, but with her suspicions already aroused, she came to the conclusion that they had to be Ron and Harvey's.

She gritted her teeth and looked up at the windows, dreading what she might see, but the sun was shining on them, making it impossible to see anything beyond the heavy taping and partially closed curtains. Furious with Ron and with herself for allowing her curiosity and suspicions to bring her here in the first place, she followed the dog-leg and within moments had reached the High Street.

The doubts began to crowd in. Was this where he'd disappeared to the other week? And was it the same alley he'd shot down this morning?

She looked down the High Street to get her bearings in relation to the restaurant – and then to the tobacconist's. It could very well have been, for she remembered how she'd lost sight of him that first time when the crowd of young servicemen had come pouring out of the pub – and today, he'd crossed the road from those nearby offices and done a disappearing trick again. And yet there was another alleyway a bit further down, and a second just beyond the pub. Was she making too much of it all? Were her suspicions leading her astray and making her jump to conclusions?

'Oh, Ron,' she sighed. 'I do so hope I've got it all wrong.'

Daisy clapped her hands and started shouting at the seagull which was sitting on a nearby lamppost, so Peggy quickly pushed the pram up the hill and headed for the station. It was all very worrying, and she could only hope that her imagination was indeed playing tricks on her – that Ron's meeting with that man had been above board – and that he wasn't involved with Gloria Stevens in any way.

She tried to tell herself that it could easily have been a different alleyway – that she'd been too far away to pinpoint the exact spot where he'd disappeared – and that Ron had more scruples than to get mixed up with a woman like Gloria. However, the doubts and suspicions lingered and cast a shadow over what had been a lovely day, and she knew she wouldn't rest until she got to the truth.

'I'll have a word with him later,' she said to Daisy as they went over the humpbacked bridge. 'Perhaps if I can find out who that man was it will make things clearer.' Having decided on a plan she felt marginally easier, and turned her attention to Stan, who was watering his spring vegetable in the tubs he'd lined up at the back of the platform.

'Hello, Stan. How's tricks?'

'All the better for seeing you, Peggy,' he replied, his ruddy face breaking into a beaming smile. 'What can I do for you today, then?'

'I'm meeting someone off the four o'clock train.'

He immediately looked downcast. 'Sorry, Peg. It's been delayed by more than an hour. Some trouble with the signals further west, I think.'

Peggy chewed her lip. 'What a nuisance,' she said irritably. 'I can't really hang about for an hour, but then neither can I come back. Daisy has to have her tea and her bath and all the girls will be coming home, and Cordelia's exhausted after being out today, so I can't leave Daisy with her and—'

'Peggy, Peggy, love, don't fret yourself,' he soothed. 'I'll be here until the last train, and am perfectly capable of steering whoever it is to Beach View.'

'She's just a young girl, Stan, and I promised to be here when she arrived. I can't just abandon her – not in her condition.'

Stan's bushy brows lifted. 'Condition? You mean she's...'

Peggy realised in horror that she'd been indiscreet. 'No, Stan,' she said hastily. 'She's been in a nasty bombing raid and is feeling rather fragile. I get the feeling she's been through the mill, what with nowhere to live and her fiancé abroad with the army.'

'I tell you what, Peg. I'm expecting my Ethel to

come down after her shift at the factory. She could hang on here and walk the girl to yours if that would help.'

Peggy dithered. 'It's very kind of you, Stan, but I don't want to put either of you to any trouble, and a promise is a promise, after all. Ron's bound to be home soon, so he can look after Daisy for me.' She shot him a radiant smile before turning the pram around. 'I'll be back as soon as I can, so if the train comes in earlier than expected, keep her here.'

She began to walk away when Stan shouted after her. 'What's her name?'

'April,' she replied over her shoulder.

'Right-oh. I'll keep an eye out for her, never you mind.'

As the train pulled into Cliffehaven station, April twisted the ring on her finger and could only hope that it would deflect the awkward questions people were bound to ask once her condition began to show. Yet, disliking the subterfuge and having to live a lie, she silently berated herself to buck up her ideas and get on with it.

She dragged the case down from the luggage rack and made her way along the corridor to the door. She was the last passenger off, and she walked slowly along the platform, taking these few moments to study the man who was chatting to a couple of housewives while he took their tickets.

It was definitely Uncle Stan, for he was just as she remembered him – if a good deal stouter, older and redder in the face. He was certainly as jolly, for his smile was beaming and his laughter hearty as he exchanged a joke with the women. She paused at the back of the straggling queue waiting to hand in their tickets, listening to his voice and trying to find anything about him which reminded her of her mother.

There were almost twenty years between them – another sister had died before Mildred had been born – and the only things they seemed to have in common were their brown eyes and dark hair. Stan was tall, well over six feet and, to put it politely, rather sturdy; whereas Mildred was as thin as a sparrow and would barely have reached his chest. They certainly didn't share the same sense of humour and joy in life, she thought wistfully, for she'd never heard her mother laugh as wholeheartedly or seen her relaxed and naturally interested in what other people had to say.

'Hello, dear,' he said, his dark eyes regarding her intently. 'You wouldn't happen to be April, would you?'

'Well, yes,' she stuttered. 'But how...?'

'It's no mystery,' he said and smiled. 'Peggy Reilly told me you were coming to stay, and because she's been held up, she asked me to keep an eye out for you.' He held out a meaty hand. 'The name's Stan, by the way.'

April's fingers were smothered in a warm, gentle grip. 'Nice to meet you, Stan.'

'Nice to meet you too. Funny, isn't it, but I've got a niece called April, and she'd be about your age now.'

'That's nice,' she murmured, having been caught on the hop by this declaration. They stood there in

198

a rather awkward silence until April found her voice again. 'Perhaps if you showed me how to get to Mrs Reilly's it would save her the trip?' she suggested.

Stan shook his head. 'Peggy was very definite that I keep you here until she arrived to fetch you home.' His gaze trawled over her bruised face down to the plaster cast and sling. 'My Ethel's making a pot of tea at the cottage, and there's a fresh batch of scones just waiting to be eaten. So why don't I take that case, and we can wait for Peggy in comfort?'

'That's really kind of you,' April replied. 'But I don't want to put anyone to any bother.'

'It's no bother,' he boomed. 'Goodness me, my Ethel always makes tea at this time of day, and we can't have you sitting about on a draughty platform, can we?' Without further ado, he took the case from her and led the way to the cottage.

As April followed him down the short path to the front door the memories flooded back. The vegetable plot had overtaken the flower beds, but the fruit trees were snowy with blossom and the old lean-to still looked as if it was about to collapse. The warm, welcoming gloom beyond the front door held the remembered scents of oil lamps, wood fires and baking, the lantern lights flickering over the highly polished brass pans that hung over the range where a wiry little woman was briskly whisking something in a bowl.

'And this,' said Stan proudly, 'is my Ethel.'

'Hello, love. You must be April.' She wiped her hands down her wrap-round pinafore and took the fag out of her mouth without spilling the length of ash at the end of it. 'I 'ope yer 'ungry, 'cos I've made a lovely batch of scones, and there's real jam and cream to go with them, an' all.'

April smiled and shook her hand. 'It's very kind of you,' she stammered. 'I hope you didn't go to all this trouble because of me.'

'Nah, I feed my Stan a spot of tea at this time every day when I ain't up the factory,' she said matter-of-factly. 'Now, you sit down, love, and put yer feet up. You look fair worn out, if you don't mind me saying.' She picked up the sleepy ginger cat which hung limply over her arm like a fur stole and patted the fat cushions of the fireside chair in enticement.

April was warmed, not only by the lovely atmosphere of the cottage she remembered with such affection, but by the genuine welcome. To them she was a stranger, someone who was stranded for a while, and would eventually pass through – how very different it was to the cold formality of home.

She sat down and wrestled to get her coat off. Ethel dropped the stoic cat on the hearthrug where it turned in several tight circles before going back to sleep. She fussed around April, took her coat and hung it up on the back of the door and then ordered Stan to pour the tea and sort out plates while she prepared the scones.

April watched them as they worked in harmony in that tiny, old-fashioned kitchen. Ethel clearly wore the trousers in their relationship, but Stan seemed not to mind – in fact he was quietly glowing with happiness – and although Ethel had to be about twenty years younger than him, April could see the genuine adoration in her eyes every time she looked up at him.

As for the room, it was redolent with memories of sitting by this ancient range listening to Stan reading her a story, or playing with her dolls under the narrow table that had been jammed tightly beneath the window. And of how at night, sleepy and warm in Stan's arms, he'd carried her up those narrow stairs to tuck her up into the little bed which had been placed next to her mother's beneath the eaves to read her a story.

'This is a lovely cottage,' April said dreamily as the warmth of the fire started to chase away the chill of the long, drawn-out journey.

'We like it,' said Ethel, placing a jug of thick cream on the table, 'although it could do with a bit of modernising to make it easier to run.' She shot April a bright smile. 'Me and Stan are getting married in June, so we'll live 'ere until the war ends and 'e can retire.'

She threw the butt of her cigarette into the range fire. 'It's a shame, really,' she continued, ''cos the railway won't let us live 'ere once that 'appens, and we sort'a got used to the old place. Stan's lived 'ere since he were a boy, you know.'

April did know this, but feigned surprise. 'Really?'

'Oh yeah,' said Ethel, doling out whipped cream onto the scones. 'He were born upstairs, him and his two sisters. His dad was stationmaster then, and when Stan got back from the trenches after the first shout, 'e took over with Barbara.' Ethel leaned closer. 'That were Stan's wife what died a long time ago,' she murmured confidentially.

'I really don't think young April needs to know

201

my family history,' said Stan cheerfully. 'Give her time to enjoy that scone and catch her breath, my love.'

'But I'm finding it fascinating,' said April truthfully. She bit into the scone and closed her eyes in pleasure. It was as light as a feather, with real butter, the raspberry jam sweet, and the cream thickly rich. Such luxury during wartime was unknown, and she suspected Ethel was the canny sort who could source such wonderful things regardless of whether they were legal or not.

Savouring every last crumb, she ate it all and then sighed. 'That was the very best scone I've ever had,' she murmured. 'What a wonderful treat, and how very kind of you to give me such a warm welcome.'

Ethel went pink and tried not to show how pleased she was at this praise by shrugging off the compliment, while Stan helped himself to a second scone. 'Aye, my Ethel's a grand little cook,' he said, munching happily and dropping crumbs down his uniform jacket.

Ethel offered April another scone, which was very tempting, but she doubted she could finish a second one.

'They are a bit rich, I grant you,' said Ethel. 'Tell yer what, I'll bag the rest up and you and the others can 'ave them after yer tea.' She grinned. 'Cordelia and them girls love my scones, and so does Ron. I can guarantee there won't be a crumb left.'

Stan must have seen April's look of confusion. 'Ron is Peggy Reilly's father-in-law,' he explained. 'Cordelia has been a lodger for many years, and is

202

getting on a bit now, and then there are the four girls who live there – all lovely, hard-working lasses it's a joy to be with,' he added comfortably.

'Soppy old so-and-so,' Ethel teased with a nudge of her elbow into his side. 'I swear to God, April, he's like a father to them girls – my Ruby and all. Always listening to their tales and giving them a packet of sweets or something from his allotment. Spoils 'em rotten, he does – but they do love 'im.'

April could believe that about Stan, and she suspected Ethel was just as caring in her rather gruff way. 'So, how did you two meet?' she asked, intrigued by this odd couple who seemed to suit each other so well.

'My girl Ruby come down 'ere to live with Peggy,' said Ethel, lighting another fag and sticking it in the corner of her mouth. 'She were 'aving a bit of trouble back in the Smoke, yer see, and needed to get away.'

Stan cleared his throat and shot her a warning glance.

Ethel seemed to realise this was a sign that she was babbling on again. 'Anyway,' she continued, 'to cut a long story short, I come down a few months later, met Stan who'd been keeping an eye out for my gel, and that were it. We none of us looked back after that, did we, Stan?'

He shook his head and looked rather smug. 'It was the luckiest day of my life when Ethel came off that train,' he sighed.

'How lovely for both of you,' April said warmly. She caught their exchange of loving smiles and silently prayed that she too might find someone she could love like that and who would love her back.

'You'll be all right with Peggy,' said Ethel as she poured out a second cup of tea for them all. 'She's a diamond, is Peg, and nothing's too much trouble.' Her bright brown eyes darted over April's face and arm. 'Looks like you've been through the wars a bit. What 'appened, love? Air raid, was it?'

April nodded, suddenly wary of revealing too much about herself.

'Yeah,' sighed Ethel. 'We 'ad a right do 'ere, an' all. The factories took a direct hit, and we was all lucky the bleedin' place didn't go up like a rocket, what with all that ammo in the munitions.' She cocked her head. 'And what about your family, love? Are they from around 'ere?'

'There's only my mother, and she's not living locally,' April said firmly in a bid to stop the questioning.

Ethel's gaze fell on the sapphire ring. 'Yer bloke's away, then?'

April twisted the ring round her finger. 'He's fighting abroad with the army somewhere,' she murmured, ashamed of having to lie to these lovely people, and feeling very uncomfortable in the light of Ethel's curiosity which no doubt would not be satisfied with such a brief answer.

Peggy had arrived back at Beach View to find the place in chaos. Ron had clearly forgotten to shut the shed door properly, and Queenie had found the pheasants he'd hung in there and was in a frenzy of excitement with her trophies. There were bits of bird and feather all over the back garden,

Harvey was rolling luxuriously in the stinking carcasses, and Cordelia was having hysterics.

Peggy grabbed Queenie's scruff and quickly shut her in Ron's basement bedroom, where she yowled and scratched in fury to be let out. Then she snatched up the length of rope that was tied to a hook outside the back door and threaded it through Harvey's collar. 'You should have known better,' she scolded.

Harvey immediately slumped down as if the weight of the evil world was on his shoulders, his amber eyes looking up at her in contrition.

'And it's no good you looking at me like that,' she snapped. 'You're a bad, bad dog.' With that, she went back into the basement and tried to calm Cordelia. 'I know it isn't a pretty sight,' she said. 'But the birds were already dead and they didn't feel anything.'

'It's the blood and feathers everywhere,' Cordelia spluttered. 'I can't stand them, really I can't. How could dear little Queenie *do* that? And as for Harvey rolling about in it all...' She shuddered as the tears streamed down her face.

'Unfortunately it's in a cat's nature to mess with birds,' soothed Peggy above the cat's yowling and Harvey's whimpers. 'But it's all right, Cordelia. I'll clean up the mess after I've made you a lovely cup of tea. How about that?'

'That would be nice,' she said, dabbing her eyes with her handkerchief. 'Oh, dear, Peggy, I'm so sorry,' she sobbed. 'I heard the noise, but by the time I got down the steps it was too late to do anything.'

'It's not your fault, Cordelia. Ron should have

205

secured the shed door properly,' Peggy replied grimly as Harvey howled piteously and Queenie took up the protest from behind Ron's bedroom door.

Daisy decided she didn't like Cordelia crying, the animals complaining or her mother getting cross with everyone, so she began to wail. Her little face reddened as she bawled, waved her fists about and kicked off her blankets so they fell in the gore on the doorstep.

'Oh, for pity's sake,' muttered Peggy, 'that's all I need.' She left Daisy to her tantrum, helped Cordelia up the stone steps to the kitchen and settled her at the table before she went back down to get Daisy out of her pram.

'Stop that,' she said firmly as Daisy kicked and fought against her. 'Stop it at once, or I'll put you to bed and shut the door on you.'

Whether it was her tone of voice, the determined look on her face, or the threat of something that had happened to her before, Daisy's tantrum petered out into hiccups and the odd fat tear rolling down her little face.

'That's better,' said Peggy, carrying her up the steps and putting her on the floor by her wheeled horse. 'Now you play with that while I make tea, check on the stew and go and clean up that mess.'

Order was restored eventually, but there was still no sign of Ron, and Harvey was howling fit to bust outside the back door. Thankfully, it seemed Queenie had finally given up on her protests, and Peggy suspected she was sleeping off her feast of filched pheasant on Ron's bed.

With Cordelia happily sipping her tea and keeping an eye on Daisy, Peggy went down the steps and turned the hose on Harvey to wash away the muck and feathers from his coat. Once this was achieved, she gingerly wrapped the chewed remains of the birds in newspaper and shut them firmly in the shed for Ron to deal with when he put in an appearance. Filling a tin bucket with soapy water, she gave the back step a good scrubbing, then tipped the dirty water into Ron's garden butt.

Feeling very put-upon and out of sorts, Peggy let Harvey free, checked on Queenie who was indeed curled up and fast asleep on Ron's bed, and then went up to the kitchen for a well-deserved fag and a sit-down.

She regarded Harvey who was warily keeping an eye on her as he lay in front of the range, and gave a sigh. Every day was a struggle without having to cope with cats and dogs and blasted pheasants, but she supposed she'd laugh about it once she'd calmed down. Life at Beach View could never be described as boring, that was for sure.

'What are all those feathers doing floating about my vegetable plot?' Ron ambled into the kitchen minutes later, tracking dirty footprints across her clean linoleum.

'For goodness' sake, Ron, get those boots off and clean up after yourself,' Peggy snapped. 'I have quite enough to do without having to run about after you.'

His wayward brows shot up and his eyes widened in surprise at her unusual sharpness. 'What's bitten you?'

'I'd give you a list if I had a week to read it out to you,' she said tartly, and went on to tell him about the chaos she'd come home to. 'So I'm leaving you in charge while I'm out collecting April,' she finished, stubbing out her cigarette. 'And woe betide you if you let that stew burn or the potatoes boil dry.'

'To be sure, Peggy girl, ye're not in the best of moods today, are you?' he grumbled. 'And here's me thinking you'd be all relaxed and happy after your lunch out.'

'Are you surprised?' She finished the cup of tea and reached, for her coat. 'There are things we need to talk about, Ron,' she said quietly. 'So don't make any plans to go out tonight.'

'But I–'

'But nothing,' she snapped, thoroughly fed up with everyone. 'You'll stay here for once and no excuses. Do you hear me?'

'Aye, and I should think half the street can too,' he muttered.

Peggy glanced up at the clock. If the train had come in as expected, then April would already have been at the station for half an hour. She pulled on her coat, grabbed her handbag and gas mask, and ran down the cellar steps to fetch her bicycle. It would be quicker than walking, and she was so fired up over everything, she certainly had the energy to tackle the steep High Street.

Ron stood in the doorway and watched her departure with a sense of foreboding. Peggy was on her high horse, and that usually spelled trouble.

But he suspected she had more on her mind than pheasants, and because he was already feeling guilty about his recent escapades, he mentally prepared himself to face her accusations. Life could be very difficult at times, he thought woefully as he returned to the kitchen, especially when women got involved.

An awkward silence had fallen between them as April refused to be coaxed into revealing more about herself, and she breathed a sigh of relief when the door opened and a small, bustling woman in her forties came bursting into the cottage.

'So sorry I'm late, but we had a right to-do at home and I had to sort it out.' She took in the tea things at a glance and smiled at April. 'Hello, dear. I'm Peggy Reilly, and I see you've been right royally entertained by my friends. I must say, I could do with a cuppa myself after cycling up that blessed hill.'

'It's nice to meet you, Mrs Reilly,' said a rather taken aback April. Mrs Reilly wasn't at all what she'd expected – for she was so energetic and pretty, and a far cry from the landladies much lampooned by comedians.

'You must call me Peggy,' she said as she shed her coat and gloves and plumped herself down by the table. 'I'm not one for formalities, as these two will tell you.' She took the cup of tea from Ethel and sipped it gratefully. 'Oh, that's better,' she sighed.

'I made scones for you to take 'ome,' said Ethel. 'I expect you already got the tea on the go, so you can 'ave them after.'

Peggy turned to April. 'Ethel's trying her best to fatten everybody up,' she said cheerfully. 'Anyone would think there wasn't a war on.'

She made them all laugh as she told them about the cat and the pheasants, and then finished her tea. 'Come on, dear, we'd better let these good people get on, and make our way home. I've left Ron and Cordelia in charge of Daisy, and goodness knows what sort of chaos I'll find. If it's anything like last time, there'll be ructions, and no mistake.'

Ethel fetched April's coat. The cat stirred from sleep and promptly jumped up into the warm chair April had just vacated, and Peggy took the cake tin from Ethel which held the quickly prepared, delicious jam and cream scones.

'Thank you so much for everything,' said April as Stan tied her case firmly to the back of Peggy's bike, and Ethel watched them from the doorway.

'Glad to help,' he said. 'Now you make sure you come and visit me and Ethel whenever the mood takes you. I can show you round my garden and the allotment, and tell you stories about the folk of Cliffehaven and what they get up to.'

'He's nothing but an old gossip,' said Peggy fondly. 'But his stories are definitely worth listening to.' She kissed him and Ethel and then pushed her bike down the short path. 'It's not too far to walk,' she said once they were out of earshot of their hosts. 'You're not too tired, are you, after that long journey?'

'I'm fine, really, and Stan and Ethel were such lovely company, I already feel quite at home.'

Peggy paused as they reached the other side of the humpbacked bridge. 'They're the salt of the earth,' she said, 'and I so hope you'll be happy here with me. Beach View might not be a palace, but I like to think it's homely, and that any girl who stays with me will be cared for as if she was my own.'

The tears pricked and April had to blink them away. The kindness of strangers had touched her heart. They'd made her welcome and offered sanctuary – and yet she was betraying all that by keeping the truth hidden. She looked at Peggy, the words trembling on her lips, the need to begin this new life with a clean slate suddenly very important.

'It's all right, dear,' murmured Peggy as she patted April's cheek. 'I can tell you've been having a hard time of it recently, but that's at an end now. You'll be safe with me, and we'll look after you for as long as you need.'

April was so deeply touched by this that she threw caution to the wind and gave her a hug. 'Thank you, thank you,' she breathed. 'You have no idea what this means to me.'

Peggy hugged her back. 'Oh, I think I do, dear,' she murmured. She drew back from the embrace, her eyes suspiciously bright. 'Now, come on, it's late and the others will be waiting for their tea.'

'She's a nice little lass, isn't she?' said Stan as he closed the door and followed Ethel back into the main room.

'She seems pleasant enough,' said Ethel, clearing away the plates and starting on the washing-up.

211

'But I reckon there's more to 'er than meets the eye, Stan, and so I wouldn't get carried away too quick, like you usually do.'

'That's not like you, Et,' he said with a frown. 'You've always been very supportive when it comes to girls like that.'

Ethel plunged her hands into the hot soapy water. 'I'm not saying she don't deserve a bit of 'elp, it's clear she's been through it and then some. I'm just saying that I reckon she's 'iding something under all that posh voice and pretty smile.'

Stan decided Ethel was just being fanciful, so didn't pursue this. 'She reminds me a bit of Mildred when she was that age,' he mused as he reached for the tea towel to help with the drying-up. 'Although they've got different colouring, and there's something softer and far more vulnerable in April than there ever was in my sister – there is something about her...'

'Soppy old git,' she said fondly. 'A sob story and a pair of blue eyes never fail to touch you, do they?' She glanced at the cup he was mangling in the tea towel and her tone sharpened. 'Watch what yer doing, Stan, them cups are the good ones.'

Stan concentrated harder on drying his mother's precious china as Ethel briskly finished the washing-up and carried the bowl outside to empty it into the butt which he used to water his garden. Despite Ethel's rather surprising opinion of April, he'd liked her – felt sorry for her in fact. He knew a troubled, lonely girl when he saw one, but he was also curious as to why she was troubled, and how it was she'd ended up in Cliffehaven with Peggy. He mulled this over and came to the conclusion that perhaps Peggy's earlier slip of the tongue had held more truth than he'd realised. Perhaps she really was in the family way? He decided not to share this thought with Ethel, for she could be a bit of a stickler when it came to things like that, and was already prepared not to like the girl.

'And I'll tell you something else, Stanley Dawkins,' said Ethel as she returned from the garden with a bowlful of freshly picked vegetables. 'That girl will be trouble. You mark my words.'

Stan felt very uneasy. 'Why do you say that?' he asked carefully.

Ethel dumped the bowl in the sink and reached for a sharp paring knife. 'A woman's intuition, Stanley. That's what.'

Stan tried to laugh this off. 'You and your in-tuition. It'll get you into hot water one day, my pet.' To distract her, he nuzzled her neck, which made her giggle, then he reached for his coat. 'The next train's due, but I'll not be long, and then we can settle down to a lovely cosy evening.'

Holding a potato in one hand and the knife in the other, she turned and kissed him. 'You can mock, Stan, but a woman's intuition is rarely wrong. You wait. You'll see I was right about that gel.'

Stan shrugged on his coat and went out into the gathering darkness, utterly bemused by Ethel's ability to get straight to things others simply couldn't see – but then he'd be the first to admit that he never had understood women and their odd ways.

18

April could smell the sea as Peggy pushed the bike and they walked down the High Street, but there was nothing about the town that looked familiar, which was rather disappointing. She hoped that in a better light, she might find some remnants of her childhood memories.

'That's the fire station where Rita works as a driver and mechanic,' said Peggy as they turned into Camden Road. 'She's one of my evacuees, and has lived in Cliffehaven all her life.' She went on to give April a potted history of how Rita had been bombed out after her father had been called up, and how she'd been raising money for a second Cliffehaven Spitfire by organising motor-cycle races at the old dirt track.

'This is Cliffehaven General,' she said rather unnecessarily as they reached the wide entrance to the hospital where the ambulances and Red Cross trucks were lined up. 'My little Fran works there as a nurse in the theatre. A lovely girl, she is, too, though she can be a bit fiery at times. It's all that red hair and Irish blood,' she added with a giggle. 'Goes off like a firework, she does. But it's never over anything serious, and soon blows over.

'And that's the uniform factory,' she said, barely pausing for breath as she pointed out the ugly red-brick building that sprawled the width of an entire block. 'A couple of my girls have worked there in the past, and Mr Goldman seems to be a fair employer.' She glanced across at April. 'Have you thought about work at all?'

April nodded. 'I need to find a job, certainly, but I've never worked in a factory and haven't a clue about sewing. Besides, with this plaster cast, I doubt I'd be much use at anything.'

'Yes, it will certainly hamper you. When's it due to be taken off?'

'In another four weeks, and I can't wait. It makes me itch.'

Peggy smiled with understanding. 'What sort of job were you doing before?'

'I did a secretarial course after school, and then I joined the WRNS, servicing and maintaining boat engines.'

Peggy came to an abrupt halt. 'Goodness me, how exciting. In that case, I'm sure we can find you something with those sorts of skills. I'll have a word round and see what there is. Best to get these things organised in advance, so when you're rid of that plaster, you'll be all set.'

Peggy's enthusiasm was heartening, but April felt she had to point out one drawback. 'It might be difficult to persuade anyone to take me on in my condition, even though I'm sure I can work perfectly well for another few months.'

'Just how far gone are you, dear?'

'Five months, but I'm very well and perfectly capable of earning my keep.' April put her hand on Peggy's arm. 'Talking of which, I meant what I said about paying extra. I do have the money set aside.'

'The government pays me once you've been registered as an evacuee,' said Peggy, 'and that's the going rate. Keep the money, April, you're going to need it in the coming months – especially once your baby's born.'

April said nothing as they continued walking. If she was to keep up the pretence of being engaged, then it was hardly appropriate to tell this lovely woman that she would have the baby adopted as soon as she could.

'You'll have to be registered with the doctor, of course,' said Peggy. 'And be booked in to see the midwife. She'll sort you out a bed at the hospital when it's time, but it's important you have proper check-ups and receive all the vitamins and such that you're entitled to.'

She patted April's arm. 'Don't look so worried, dear. My Daisy is less than eighteen months old, so I'm up with all the latest rigmarole when it comes to expecting. You leave it all to me.'

'Ethel was right,' said April softly. 'You really are a diamond, aren't you?'

'Get away with you. I'm only doing what any other mother hen would do when her chicks need help.' As they walked on, Peggy pointed out the bomb site where the school used to be. 'All my children went there, and Anne taught the little ones.' She carried on, telling April all about her scattered family.

April could hear the tremor in her voice as she talked about her loved ones, and she knew then that behind that sweet smile there was a breaking heart, which only served to make her like her more.

Peggy continued to point out places of interest as they walked along Camden Road. 'These are our local shops. You'll have to register your ration books there, and that's the Anchor – Ron's home from home where the love of his life, Rosie Braithwaite, lives.'

April heard the catch in her voice. 'What is it, Peggy? Don't you approve of their romance?'

Peggy shook her head, sniffed and seemed to make an effort to pull herself together. 'It's the best thing for both of them, if only a certain person could see that,' she said firmly. 'Take no notice of me, April. I've just had a very long and rather fraught day.'

'Oh, dear,' sighed April. 'And my arriving so late probably hasn't helped at all. I should have been firm with Stan and made my own way here.'

'Nonsense,' said Peggy. She wheeled the bike up the hill and turned into a rather rutted back alley. 'I couldn't possibly have let you walk alone in a strange town with so many drunken servicemen roaming about in the blackout. What would your mother think?'

April noted the bright curiosity in her brown eyes and realised she couldn't continue to lie to her. 'I doubt my mother would be particularly concerned,' she said evenly. 'We've never been close.'

'Oh, dear,' sighed Peggy. 'That's an awful shame when there's so much trouble in the world.' The curiosity was back in her eyes. 'Is that why you're here? Wouldn't she let you stay with her?'

'Something like that,' murmured April, unwilling to go into detail.

Peggy must have noted her reluctance to add anything further, for she shot her a warm smile and then pushed the bike through the gate and leaned it against the back wall. 'Well, here it is,' she said, taking in the house and garden with an expansive sweep of her arm. 'Home sweet home, warts and all.' She plucked the tin of scones from the basket. 'Let's get you inside so you can meet the others before we have our tea.'

April took her case from the back of the bike and followed Peggy into what looked like a basement scullery. She could hear the murmur of voices and the tramp of feet overhead, and began to feel nervous about meeting another set of strangers.

A great brindled, leggy dog hurtled down the stone steps and she cowered back to protect her arm as it tried to leap up and lick her face.

'To be sure, wee girl, Harvey will do you no harm,' said the scruffy man who came down the steps in his stocking feet to grab the dog's collar. 'Will ye sit, ye heathen beast, and not be a nuisance?'

'This is my father-in-law, Ron,' said Peggy. 'You'll get used to him and Harvey soon enough – the pair of them are rogues and as scruffy and disobedient as each other.'

April nodded to Ron and tentatively put out her hand to pat the dog's head. She was rewarded with twinkling blue eyes from Ron and an enthusiastic squirm and lick from Harvey.

'Welcome to Beach View,' said Ron, taking charge of her case. 'Now I'll take this up to your room and then I'll be off on fire-watch.'

'But I told you–'

'Now, Peggy,' he forestalled her. 'There's a war on, and I can't be letting the side down by not turning up for me watch, can I?'

April noted how Peggy's lips thinned at this and wondered fleetingly why she was cross with him. He seemed affable enough, even though he looked like a tramp, but there was definitely a naughty gleam in his eyes, so it probably wasn't anything too serious.

They followed Ron and Harvey up the concrete steps and walked into a shabby, badly lit kitchen that was warmed by a glowing fire in the range, the aroma of cooking, and a happy atmosphere. A small black cat was sitting on a shelf by the stone sink, bright eyes watching everything rather imperiously; Harvey had slumped down in front of the range and a little girl was pushing a toy horse about the floor. April felt a stab of anxiety as she realised everyone was looking at her, but as they were smiling, she told herself not to be so feeble and smiled back.

'This is April,' said Peggy. She shed her coat and gloves and made the introductions as Ron returned to the kitchen to pull on a long coat which seemed to have lots of pockets.

April discovered that Fran did indeed possess an abundance of curly auburn hair and a bright smile that lit up her amazing green eyes. Rita and Ivy were like two peas in a pod, both small and dark-haired with impish grins and a rather odd taste in clothing, and Sarah was tall and slim and very elegant by contrast. Daisy looked up at her from the floor, her dark curls in a tangle, her sweet little face smeared with what looked like

219

coal and jam.

'Oh, Ron,' sighed Peggy, cleaning the child's face with a damp flannel. 'I told you not to let her get into the anthracite.'

'Ach, to be sure, the wee girl must have done it when me back was turned,' he said airily.

'She's not the only one to get into mischief, Ronan Reilly,' she retorted darkly.

Ron's eyebrows twitched. 'Why, what have you been up to, Peggy girl?'

Peggy glared at him and he hastily shoved his feet into wellingtons and disappeared down the steps and out of the back door with Harvey close behind him.

Peggy sighed in exasperation and then continued her introductions as an elderly woman came into the kitchen. 'This is Cordelia,' she said fondly. 'She's been part of the family for many years and I'm sure you'll come to love her just as much as we all do.'

April smiled at the tiny, birdlike woman who was beaming up at her and they shook hands. 'It's lovely to meet you all,' she said to the room in general. 'I'm sorry I'm so late, but the train was delayed and took ages.'

Cordelia frowned. 'I know it would be lovely to have meat on your plate, dear, but I'm afraid it's only vegetable stew again tonight.' She shrugged. 'But we do have cabbages and grain, although I can't see why you'd want it.'

Now it was April's turn to be puzzled. She heard the girls giggling and looked to Peggy for an explanation.

'I'm afraid you'll have to get used to Cordelia's

funny ways,' Peggy said. 'She forgets to turn her hearing aid up and doesn't always hear things correctly.' She shook her head as April was about to repeat what she said. 'I wouldn't bother, dear, she'll only get even more muddled.'

April nodded and smiled at Cordelia, and then took off her coat and hung it on the hook behind the door. Turning back towards the table she caught Fran looking at her midriff and felt the colour rising in her face.

Fran chuckled. 'Sorry, April, but Peggy didn't tell us you're expecting. What are you, four, five months gone?'

'It's due in September,' she replied, sitting down quickly at the table.

'Oh, how lovely,' twittered Cordelia, who'd obviously turned up her hearing aid. 'Another little baby in the house. You must be so excited, dear.'

'More nervous than excited,' admitted April, feeling horribly exposed and awkward at being the centre of attention. 'I've never had one before.'

'Ach, you're not to be worrying yourself,' said Fran. 'I'll keep an eye on you and make sure you get the best care, and once it's here, you'll have all of us watching over you both. It can't be easy being on your own at a time like this.'

April felt hemmed in and longed to escape as the other girls plied her with questions about her non-existent fiancé, how they'd met, where he was, and what had happened to forestall their wedding plans.

'Leave the poor girl be,' said Peggy rather sharply. 'Can't you see you're overwhelming her with all your questions, and she's barely caught

221

her breath, let alone got a decent meal inside her. Hush now, and get on with your tea.'

April caught her eye in gratitude and then dipped her head so no one could see just how close she was to bursting into tears. She'd never known such warmth and affection, and she was riddled with guilt that she couldn't be honest with them for fear of them rejecting her. Yet it seemed that in this house of strangers, in the glow of their genuine interest and kindliness, she had – for now, at least – found sanctuary.

With the delicious supper over, and the scones devoured with relish, all the girls helped wash up and clear away while Peggy settled Daisy for the night in her bedroom off the hall. Cordelia sat down to listen to the wireless with Queenie purring in her lap, and Fran reluctantly left the house to go on night shift at the nearby hospital. Sarah disappeared upstairs to write letters, Ivy shot off to meet her boyfriend Andy at the Anchor and Rita was using the last of the daylight to tinker with the engine of her motorbike.

April sipped from her cup of tea as she leaned against the back wall and watched the other girl's nimble fingers adjusting plugs and wires. 'Where did you learn to do that?'

'My dad taught me,' Rita replied, wrestling with a recalcitrant screw. 'We rebuilt this old bike together, you know. He had a garage, you see, and for as long as I can remember, I used to sit and watch him servicing and repairing engines. I suppose it's only natural that I picked up something along the way.' She looked up at April and grinned. 'What about you? I understand you were in the Wrens.'

'They taught me the basics so I could strip down and service the engines in motor gun boats and motor torpedo boats, but I wouldn't know where to start on something like that.'

Rita nodded and continued to battle with the screw until she had it loosened. 'It must have been great fun in the Wrens,' she said. 'I wanted to go into the WAAFs originally. A pal of mine's flying Spitfires now, and I've ended up driving fire engines.'

'Yes, I loved my time there, but why didn't you go into the WAAFs?'

'It's a long story.' Rita explained how she'd had to look after the English wife of her Italian neighbour when he and their son had been interned, and how she'd been offered the job at the fire station, and much to her surprise had learned to love it.

'I wouldn't swap my job for anything now,' she said. 'It's exciting and a bit scary at times, but they're a good bunch at the station and I feel I'm really doing something worthwhile.'

April nodded with understanding. That was how she'd felt until the navy had kicked her out. 'I know Fran's a nurse, but what about the other girls?' she asked.

Rita replaced the plugs and started to check the wiring. 'Ivy works up at the factory that makes bits of plane, and Sarah works for the Women's Timber Corps in their office on the Cliffe estate.'

'So you're all doing your bit while I'm hanging about doing nothing,' sighed April. 'And I really need to do something, Rita, because I feel such a fraud. There's nothing physically wrong with me apart from this broken wrist, and I'm sure I could find something.'

'There's always voluntary work,' Rita said. 'But of course that doesn't pay. I'll have a word with my boss John Hicks and see if he needs help in the office or something.'

'Thanks, Rita, that would be kind.'

Rita grinned up at her. 'You remind me of Kitty, who used to live here for a bit,' she said. 'She talked posh too and was always impatient to be out and about doing something despite the fact she'd lost a leg.'

April listened as Rita told her the uplifting story of Kitty Pargeter, marvelling at how the girl had overcome her disability and returned to flying with the Air Transport Auxiliary.

'She's married now and her husband's a Spit-fire pilot up at Cliffe aerodrome, where my chap Matt is flying bombers, and Peggy's son-in-law is the Wing Commander.' She finished the service and wiped her dirty hands on a scrap of old towelling. 'Right, that's me done. I'm off to the Anchor for a beer. Want to come with me?'

April shook her head. 'Maybe another night. I'm tired after a long day and need to get some sleep after that filling meal.'

Rita grinned. 'Peggy's lovely, isn't she? You'll be all right here, April, and I wouldn't be at all surprised if Peggy asked you to stay after your baby's born. She fusses over us like a mother hen, and I can't see her turning you away until the end of the war when your chap can come home and look after you himself.'

April couldn't reply to this for the lump in her throat, so she just smiled and waved as Rita left for the pub.

'There you are,' said Peggy when she returned to the kitchen to find that Cordelia had nodded off in her fireside chair. 'You and Rita getting to know one another, were you?'

At April's nod she shot her a beaming smile. 'I'm not surprised. You're about the same age and she's a sweet girl, even though she's an untidy imp and dresses like a boy most of the time in that awful First World War flying jacket.' She replenished the kettle and put it on the hob. 'Would you like some more tea? Or cocoa? You need lots of milk to help build you up now.'

'Actually, Peggy, I'm really tired. Would you mind if I went to bed?'

'Of course not, dear. What was I thinking of? Come on, I'll show you your room and where everything is, then you can settle in and get all the rest you need.'

April was shown the dining room which had been virtually abandoned since the war had begun and the rationing of coal had made it impractical to light two fires, and then they went up the stairs to the first landing. She noted that the carpet was threadbare in places, the paint on the woodwork cracked and yellowed with age and the wallpaper was coming loose where damp had got in. It was a far cry from her mother's immaculate house, but that didn't matter a jot, for the atmosphere and the homeliness made up for everything else.

'Cordelia is in there next to the toilet and the

bathroom,' said Peggy, 'and Rita and Ivy are sharing the big double at the front of the house. Fran and Sarah are upstairs. I've put you in here because it's cosy and close to the lav.' She grinned. 'I remember how it was when I was expecting Daisy.'

Peggy opened the door and switched on the light. Blackout curtains were tightly drawn beneath pretty chintz ones that matched the bedspread, there was a lovely smell of beeswax coming from the polished furniture and the pillows looked hugely inviting. There was a bedside chest with a night light and a stack of well-thumbed paperback books sitting on it, and on the floor was a handmade rag rug of many colours. An amateurish painting depicting what she recognised as Cliffehaven promenade hung on one wall, and there was a small posy of spring flowers in a vase on top of the chest of drawers.

'It's really lovely, Peggy. Thank you so much,' she managed.

Peggy patted her cheek. 'You settle in, dear, and I'll see you in the morning.'

April sank onto the bed as Peggy quietly closed the door. She could hear old wood creaking and the gurgle of water through pipes, but the blankets beneath her fingers were soft, the sheets and pillowcases crisp and smelling of fresh air and sunshine. She kicked off her shoes and went to turn off the light so she could look out of the window.

It was almost dark now, the last of the light merely pale streaks of grey in the gathering gloom above the rooftops of the surrounding houses, but as she opened the window she could hear the sea hissing on shingle and the sleepy cries of the few gulls that still floated overhead, and smell the salty tang on the air, and the scent of warmed earth from the vegetable garden at the back of the house.

She stood there lost in thought, remembering Paula, the grief raw as she struggled to accept the swiftness of her departure and the sheer weight of pain that the past weeks had dealt her. She took a shuddering breath, determined to stay positive and hopeful that her new start amongst these people who seemed so welcoming would help and encourage her to look forward and learn to trust again. And yet, by the very nature of her deceit, she was already building barriers between them.

Impatient with her ever-circling and conflicting thoughts, she closed the window and drew the blackouts tightly across it, then switched on the bedside light and began to unpack. Tomorrow she would explore the town, register with a doctor, the billeting people and the local shops and then try and find a job. It would be a new day – the first of her new life – and she was determined to make the very best of the opportunity to start again.

Peggy was still sitting in her kitchen long after she'd helped Cordelia to bed. The cat had abandoned her lap for the dubious comfort of Ron's bed, and the girls had finally settled down to sleep after their night out. The wireless was playing chamber music softly in the background as she knitted yet another pair of socks for the comfort boxes. It was late and she was exhausted after yet another long day, but she was deter-

227

mined to catch Ron when he came in.

As she knitted and listened to the lovely music, her thoughts wandered to April. The girl reminded her a bit of Kitty Pargeter in her looks and the way she spoke, but she certainly didn't seem to have Kitty's fighting spirit – in fact she looked rather defeated and almost afraid of her own shadow. It was to be expected, she supposed; being on her own and pregnant, her young chap away fighting and her mother obviously not caring what happened to her. She'd also had to give up her job in the Wrens, which must have been an awful blow, and now, here she was, adrift and probably feeling very alone.

Poor little lost girl, so young and in need of love and care. It was shocking how some mothers could simply abandon their children to strangers when all they really needed was love and warmth and someone to rely upon. But she'll be all right here, Peggy thought firmly. I'll see she's looked after, and the girls will rally round as they always do, bless them.

Peggy sighed. There were too many lonely people in the world, bereft of family and everything they'd once known because of this blasted war. And she knew from experience that loneliness could be even harder when surrounded by people – for there had been times recently that she'd been in a crowded room when suddenly the longing for Jim and her children had swept over her in a great wave and she'd felt so very isolated, even though she'd carried on smiling and pretending everything was all right.

She put her knitting aside and gazed up at the

photographs lining the mantelpiece. There was Jim looking so darkly handsome in his uniform, his eyes glinting with a secret message just for her; and Cissy in her WAAF uniform, arm in arm with her young American pilot; and Anne with her baby Emily and little Rose Margaret, sitting at the farmhouse window down in Somerset. And her boys, Bob and Charlie, larking about in the back garden before she'd had to send them away. Only God knew how that had broken her heart, and she could only pray to Him that the war ended before Bob was called up – he would be sixteen in a matter of months and was already almost as tall as his father.

She blinked and brushed away her tears, still trying to come to terms with the fact that her family was scattered to the four winds. All she could do was carry on believing they'd all make it through safely to pick up the threads of their lives together again – and continue to protect and nurture the girls who'd come to Beach View in search of shelter.

This applied especially to April. If the war hadn't ended by the time her baby arrived, then she'd be more than welcome to stay until her young man came home. A girl and her baby would be no burden, and Daisy could probably do with being taken down a peg or two and made to share. She was in danger of becoming spoilt.

Peggy stared into the meagre fire, her thoughts going over April's arrival at Beach View. She didn't like to admit it, even to herself, but there was something about the girl that didn't quite feel right, but try as she might, she simply couldn't put a finger on it. Perhaps she was just tired after that long, interrupted and frustrating journey, and overwhelmed by having to meet so many people at once and answer their questions. But there had been a definite reluctance to discuss her fiancé even in the vaguest of terms, and Peggy wondered why.

'Now, Peggy, stop that,' she said sternly. 'The poor girl has enough to contend with without you poking and prying into what isn't any of your business.'

'Talking to yourself again, I see,' rumbled Ron as he came into the kitchen with Harvey. 'It's the first sign of madness, Peg. You should be careful.'

Peggy packed her knitting away and went to make a fresh pot of tea while he fed Harvey. 'I'm halfway round the bend already,' she said, 'trying to keep tabs on everyone and sorting out their mischief.'

He raised his bushy eyebrows. 'Oh aye? And what mischief would that be then?'

She stirred the leaves in the pot and left them to mash while she hunted out cups and the last of the rather stale biscuits. 'The mischief that some people get up to when they think no one's looking,' she said, plumping down on the chair beside him.

Ron poured out their tea and passed her cup across. 'You're talking in riddles, Peggy girl. Why don't you just tell me straight what's eating you?'

It was all the opening she needed. 'Who was that man you were talking to this lunchtime?'

'A government official who was asking the way to the town hall,' he replied, his gaze steadily meeting hers. 'Nice chap. Turns out I knew his uncle.'

'And what would a government official want with our town hall?'

He shrugged. 'To be sure it was no business of mine, so I didn't ask.'

'He looked very smart, not like most of the inspectors we get.'

'He's young and keen and probably feels he needs to make a good impression, I expect.' Ron sipped his tea and gave Harvey half the soggy biscuit. 'I don't know why you're so suspicious,' he said. 'It's not as if our meeting was clandestine.'

'Wasn't it?' she countered. 'You both came out of that office building together and were talking very seriously before you went your separate ways.' She folded her arms, her gaze steady, determined to get a straight answer out of him.

He gave a deep sigh, dunked the remains of the biscuit in the tea and popped it in his mouth. 'I was in the office trying to persuade the powers that be to give us more rifles and ammunition for the Home Guard. We met in the lift, so of course we talked – it would have been rude not to.'

She supposed she had to accept his explanation, but she still didn't quite believe that was all there was to it. 'It seemed to be a very serious conversation you were having,' she probed.

'Ach, Peggy, we were just two strangers passing the time of day.'

It hadn't looked like that to her, but she let it pass for now. 'So, what's down that alleyway you keep disappearing into? The one by the Crown?'

He grinned back at her. 'It's a short cut to

Camden Road,' he replied.

'It also leads to the back yard of the Crown,' she retorted.

'Aye, so it does. And what of it?'

Peggy saw the teasing glitter in his eyes and realised he wouldn't tell her anything he didn't want to, no matter how much she badgered him. 'Are you messing about with Gloria Stevens?' she asked baldly.

He chuckled and shook his head. 'You can think what you like, Peggy darlin', but I'll not be satisfying that awful curiosity of yours tonight, or any other night for that matter.' The smile slipped a fraction and there was an unusual, slightly disturbing edge to his voice. 'Just know that what I get up to is *my* business and it would be unwise for anyone to meddle in it – and that includes you, Peggy Reilly.'

Peggy tried to hold his gaze, but was the first to look away. 'Right,' she managed. 'If you say so, Ron.'

He nodded, finished his tea and pushed back from the table. 'Aye, I do that. Loose lips sink ships, remember.'

Peggy had absolutely no idea what he was talking about, but his expression brooked no further argument so she nodded.

He leaned towards her. 'You have to trust me, Peggy,' he said more gently. 'And keep that tongue still.' He clicked his fingers at Harvey and they went down the cellar steps to his bedroom, the kitchen door closing quietly behind them.

Peggy's hand was unsteady as she lit a cigarette and sat there in the silence. Whatever Ron was up to, he meant to keep it to himself, and she felt horribly uneasy about the whole thing. Was he carrying on with Gloria? He hadn't denied it. And yet, if he was, then perhaps, after realising she was suspicious, he would bring an end to it. Jim had always backed away the moment she'd let him know she was aware of his latest distraction – but this was Ron, and she really had no right to question his behaviour.

She finally stubbed out the cigarette, dampened down the fire for the night and switched off the light. However, as she lay in her bed and stared up at the flickering shadows cast by the night light, she was still fretting.

19

April woke early and used the bathroom before the rest of the house had begun to stir. Returning to her room, she got dressed and then pulled back the blackouts and curtains and opened the window to breathe in the salty air and listen to the waves sighing over the shingle.

It was the first week of May and although the early morning sun had yet to reach the back garden where the dew glistened, the sky was an eggshell blue, promising fine weather. She leaned on the windowsill to enjoy the vista of surrounding houses and the distant hills lined with trees, feeling much more positive about things. She'd slept surprisingly well considering the emotional turmoil she'd been through, and was ready to face this new day with optimism.

She eventually turned away from the window and regarded the room which already felt far more homely than the one back in Rosemary Cottage. She'd stowed her suitcase above the wardrobe where she'd hung her few second-hand clothes, and placed the photograph album she'd brought with her on top of the dresser alongside the vase of early blooms. There was a photograph of her father, and another of Paula that she'd found in the album, propped against the vase, and she'd laid out the rather fancy hairbrush and comb set she'd discovered in a box in her mother's attic on the kidney-shaped dressing table. She didn't have much, but it was all she needed.

The house was slowly coming to life, the sound of footsteps overhead and on the stairs telling her that the other girls were preparing to have their breakfast and go to work. She swiftly made the bed, smoothed the pretty counterpane over it and then checked her appearance in the dressing-table mirror.

She still looked pale, but the bruising was very faint, and there were no longer any shadows under her eyes. The straight black skirt had an elasticated waist, so it was comfortable, and the shirt and cardigan were loose enough to cover her pregnancy. She slipped her feet into the rather clumpy black shoes, tied the laces and then opened the door.

'Good morning, dear,' trilled Cordelia from her own bedroom door. 'My goodness, you look as if you've had a good sleep.'

'I did, thank you, Mrs Finch.'

Bright blue eyes twinkled up at her. 'My girls all call me Grandma,' she said. 'And I hope you will too, dear. Now, could I just get you to help me balance down these stairs, I'm always a bit unsteady first thing in the morning when I have so much to carry down.'

April realised she was laden with a knitting bag, a gas-mask box, a handbag and walking stick. She took charge of the handbag and box by hooking their straps over her shoulder, tucked the knitting bag under her arm and then took Cordelia's soft, gnarled hand. Making certain she was holding tight to the banisters, they slowly descended.

'These stairs must be a bit of a trial for you,' she said as they finally reached the hallway.

'Not at all, dear,' Cordelia said. 'I only use them twice a day – and if I've forgotten something, one of the girls will always run up and get it for me.' She chuckled as she headed for the kitchen. 'There are some advantages to being old, as you will no doubt discover one day, and with so many willing young legs able to run about after me, I'm treated like a queen.'

April smiled as she followed her. Cordelia certainly seemed to enjoy her regal status, and she couldn't blame her, for who wouldn't revel in being cherished?

Peggy turned from the cooking range as they entered the room and shot them both a warm smile. 'Good morning,' she said brightly. 'It's going to be a lovely day by the look of it, and the chickens have come up trumps, so we've all got an egg this morning.'

April smiled back and settled Cordelia at the

235

table, placing her bags and things by the fireside chair. She returned the greetings from the girls who were already tucking into their boiled egg, bread and tea, and gave a shy smile to Ron who was slathering margarine onto a doorstep-sized slice of wheatmeal toast. Queenie was lapping at a saucer of milk while Harvey was sitting eagle-eyed by the table waiting for someone to notice he needed a tit-bit or three to supplement his own breakfast and get him through the morning.

'Sit down, dear,' said Peggy. 'And eat that before it gets cold.'

April slid into the empty chair next to Cordelia and eagerly tucked into the bowl of porridge.

'I put the top of the milk on it,' said Peggy. 'I don't know what the navy was feeding you, but it certainly wasn't enough by the look of you.' She patted April's shoulder. 'I'll soon put some meat on those little bones, don't you worry.'

April blushed as she chuckled. 'I've always been skinny, and I doubt that'll change.'

'You don't want to be taking any notice of Peggy,' rumbled Ron. 'She's as bad as Stan's Ethel when it comes to trying to fatten us all up. Though how she does it on the ridiculous rations we all have to put up with, I don't know.'

Peggy placed a boiled egg and a slice of toast in front of April and whipped away her empty bowl. 'Ethel has the advantage of being friendly with the girls in the factory canteen and the land girls up at Cliffe,' she said. 'Isn't it about time you managed to use that Irish charm of yours to get me a bit of extra butter, or cheese?'

He eyed her from beneath his brows. 'I got you

pork a couple of months ago,' he reminded her.

'Yes, it was lovely and I'm very grateful, but it caused a lot of trouble with Doris, remember?'

'Aye, well, your sister would have an argument with herself, given half the chance,' he retorted. 'Now I'll be off to fetch Monty. The ferrets need exercise, so maybe I'll be coming home with a rabbit or two.'

'If you happen to spot a couple of pheasants who look as if they're about to climb into your pockets, ignore them, will you?' she said drily. 'They're too much bother.'

Ron gave a great, weary sigh and pulled on his poaching coat. 'To be sure I'm surrounded by women who are never satisfied,' he grumbled good-naturedly. 'I'll see if Lord Cliffe's salmon are more obliging.'

'Don't you dare,' warned Peggy sharply. 'That gamekeeper's got your measure, and if he catches you near the salmon ponds you'll be in jail before you can blink.'

'*If* he catches me.' Ron winked and clumped down the steps to the basement.

April saw that Peggy wasn't at all happy with her father-in-law's rather liberal attitude to poaching and gamekeepers, but as it was clearly something he did on a frequent basis, she supposed Peggy had become inured to it.

'He's an old scallywag,' said Cordelia, 'and one of these days he will get caught. But the pot would have been empty many a time without his poaching, so we all keep our fingers crossed and just hope he's as clever as he thinks he is.'

April giggled and then tucked into the boiled

237

egg. She was going to enjoy living here.

One by one the girls washed their plates and left for work, cheerfully wishing her good luck on finding a job. Peggy cleaned Daisy's face and lifted her out of the high chair so she could toddle about with her doll's pram. She topped up the teacups and then set about writing a list.

'I've got shopping to do, so I'll come with you this morning. I'll need to register you with the billeting people and show you the way around the town.' She smiled across at April. 'I don't want you getting lost on your first day.'

'I'm sure I could manage to find my way around if you have lots to do,' April said. 'I really don't want to be a bother.'

'You're no bother,' Peggy replied, 'and I like showing off my town, even if it is looking a bit ragged at the edges now.'

April smiled at her and finished her egg on the last bit of toast just as the rattle of the letterbox heralded the arrival of the morning's post. She watched Peggy rush out into the hall and return with quite a stack of letters which she was swiftly sifting through.

'There's one for you from Canada,' she said to Cordelia, 'two for Rita – from her father by the look of the writing, one for Fran – probably her mother writing from Ireland, and several for Sarah, which includes an air letter from her mother in Australia.'

She put aside the letters and ran her hands over the airgraphs. 'And I've got two from Jim,' she said softly, 'but I'll read them later when I've got a spare minute.'

'Tell me what you need me to do so you can read them now,' urged April. 'I can see how much you're longing to.'

Peggy regarded her for a long moment, her eyes suspiciously bright. 'Thank you, dear, that's kind – and don't fret, I'm sure your young man will write as soon as he knows where to reach you.'

April nodded and dredged up a reassuring smile. 'I'm sure he will, yes,' she murmured. She pushed away from the table and began to clear the last of the dishes. 'I'll do these while you enjoy your letters.'

Peggy eagerly tore open the brown envelope and devoured the cramped writing. Jim had been moved again to another camp further north, and his friend Ernie was also with him. They'd taken Patch along and loaded up their truck with all the comforts of their previous billet because they didn't know what conditions they'd find at such an outpost.

It turned out the basha – bamboo hut – was all but falling down, the rush thatch rotting from the heat and the monsoon rains, and alive with fleas and creepy-crawlies. There was a fast-flowing river running close to camp which meant the mosquitoes weren't quite so bothersome, but there was now the danger of frequent flooding as the rainwater came off the mountains to swell the river. With the help of the natives, they'd built another basha on firmer, flat ground well away from the river, and had then had to set to and repair the machine shops which were in a terribly dilapidated state.

Jim was furious to discover that the local mechanics were untrained, couldn't speak a word of English and actually hardly knew one end of a Studebaker from the other. He complained to his superior officer, which got him nowhere, and had to roll up his sleeves and start to educate his mechanics as quickly as possible, because the workload was so great it would have been impossible for him and Ernie to get through it on their own.

The bright side of all this was the nearby tea plantation where the Scottish owner was so bored with his own company that he insisted Jim and Ernie visited him each night for what he called 'tiffin' and a jolly good feast served rather grandly by numerous servants. These sessions involved a great deal of home-made hooch, which Jim was convinced would have him blind before the war was over, or at the very least rot his guts.

He still had the portable stove he'd 'won' from a man who was in Signals, and they supplemented their diet with frequent fry-ups consisting of bully beef, eggs and tins of the Americans' baked beans. The basha now had twin bathtubs, electric light, fans and comfortable beds, and he and Ernie had educated the native servants in the proper way to look after His Majesty's soldiers, so all in all, it wasn't too bad.

He loved her and missed her intensely, and although it was wonderful to get everyone's letters and cards, and the snapshots Peggy had sent, they couldn't make up for the fact that they were parted by an ocean. He hoped she was coping and signed as always, SWALK – sealed with a loving kiss.

Peggy smiled softly as she put the airgraphs back in their envelopes and carried them into her bedroom where she placed them almost reverently in the shoe box. There was quite a stack of them now – proof, if she needed it, that Jim had been away far too long.

She took off her apron and headscarf and tidied her hair before pulling on her overcoat. Life went on, regardless of which side of the ocean they were, and if she stopped to think about it for too long, she'd just get depressed and be of no use to anyone.

She returned to the kitchen to find Cordelia occupied with her letter from Canada, and April briskly scrubbing the stone sink while Daisy played with her doll. 'You won't get the stains out of that,' Peggy said ruefully. 'Goodness knows I've been scrubbing it for years and no amount of bleach or elbow grease will shift it. Come on, leave that and fetch your things. We have a lot to get through this morning, and we could both do with making the most of this lovely day.'

As April hurried out of the room to fetch her coat and gas-mask box, Peggy explained to Cordelia where they were going.

'She's a nice girl, isn't she?' said Cordelia. 'But it's a great shame she's in the family way without a wedding ring on her finger.' She gave a deep sigh. 'I don't know what this world is coming to, and I have to admit that I find it rather shocking, but then I'm old-fashioned, I suppose.'

'She needs a home and someone to look after her.' Peggy cleaned Daisy's hands and face and sat her on the potty. 'She's only just nineteen,

241

Cordelia – almost a baby herself.'

'Mature enough to do what she did,' said Cordelia briskly. 'It's a great pity neither of them showed some self-restraint.' Her rather fierce expression softened. 'But in times of war people do things in haste that they are forced to repent at leisure, and I agree that we must all rally round and do our best for her seeing as how her mother has abandoned her to strangers and her young man is away fighting for king and country.'

She peered at Peggy over her half-moon glasses. 'Another waif to take under your wing, Peggy. Just mind you don't overdo things. You have enough on your plate as it is.'

'I'll cope,' she said airily. 'But I'd appreciate your support.'

Cordelia's eyes widened. 'You have it, Peggy, of course you do. I'm surprised you ever doubted it.'

Peggy praised Daisy for using the potty, emptied it in the outside lav and got her dressed for their journey into town. 'Ron is a bit reluctant about me taking her in now he knows the situation,' she said quietly. 'I do hope he'll put aside his prejudice and warm to her.'

'You leave Ron to me,' said Cordelia. 'I've got his measure and know how to handle him.'

Peggy very much doubted that. Ron could be strangely old-fashioned at times, but in the light of his current shenanigans, he was hardly in the best position to cast aspersions on poor little April. He would need careful handling, and she could only hope that his soft-heartedness would overcome his reluctance.

April came into the kitchen dressed for the outdoors, her hair brushed to a shine, and with just a hint of make-up to hide the faded bruises. 'I'm ready when you are,' she said brightly.

Peggy finished dressing Daisy and kissed Cordelia goodbye. 'We might be some time, so don't fret. And Ron should be back soon to keep you company. I've left a list on the table of things I want him to do. Please make sure he does at least some of them.'

'Don't you worry, dear. I'll soon sort him out.'

Peggy rolled her eyes skyward and picked up Daisy. 'Let's get going, April. Half the morning's gone already.'

They left Cordelia contentedly reading her newspaper, and headed for Camden Road. April was introduced to Alf the butcher and Fred the fishmonger and regaled with some of the exploits they and Ron had been involved in over the years. They continued on down Camden Road to the bakery and ironmonger's, and then paused for a moment to wave to Rita, who was under a fire engine doing something with an oil can.

The day was bright and breezy, the salty air coming from a sparkling sea. April would have liked to go down to the promenade to see if there were any reminders of those halcyon days of childhood, but Peggy turned up the hill towards the town hall and council offices.

'We'll register you with the billeting people first,' she said. 'Then we'll pop into the labour exchange and sign you on. You never know, there may be something you can do, even with your arm in plaster. It'll probably be something menial up at the factory estate, mind you.'

'Anything will be better than idling about,' said April. 'I'm used to keeping busy, and at least I'd feel I'm contributing to the war effort, even if it just means making cups of tea in the canteen.'

They reached the council offices and Peggy parked the pram by the piles of sandbags, telling the young lad from the Home Guard to keep an eye on Daisy, then led the way inside.

April was glad to have Peggy beside her as she answered all the questions and filled in the seemingly endless forms to be registered as an evacuee.

They emerged from the office to find Daisy was being entertained by the boy with a game of pat-a-cake. Having thanked him warmly, Peggy pushed the pram across the street.

'I'll rummage through my cupboards and collect up the baby clothes Daisy can no longer get into,' she said as they walked along the pavement. 'I know I've given some away already, but you'll need to start collecting all the little things your baby will need. These things can't be left to the last minute, you know.'

'That's very kind of you, Peggy, but—'

'But nothing,' she replied briskly. 'They're only sitting there going to waste, and I can't think of anyone I'd rather give them to.' She parked the pram once again, checked that Daisy was keeping warm and led the way into the labour exchange. 'Oh, Lord,' she sighed. 'Look at the queue. We could be here for hours.'

'I tell you what, Peggy. Why don't you leave me here and go and do the rest of your shopping. If

I've not finished by then, go home. I can find my own way back.'

'Well, if you're sure,' she replied hesitantly. 'I do have a lot of shopping to do, and I promised to pop in and see Ted this morning...'

'I'll be fine, really.'

'Very well,' she said reluctantly. 'But I'll pop in again later to show you the way to the doctor's. It's best to register today while we're both in town.'

April nodded and smiled her thanks before turning back into the crowded room. What did she do now? She'd never been in such a place before and hadn't the first idea of what was expected of her. She eyed the shuffling queue at the far counter and then looked at the people stoically waiting on the hard chairs.

'You look a bit lost,' said the cheerful girl at the back of the straggling queue who was holding a baby swaddled out of sight in a white blanket. 'First time, is it?'

April nodded. 'What's the procedure?'

'Well, you've got to queue up here and sign in. Then you sit down over there and wait for your name to be called.' She grimaced as she rocked the baby in her arms and regarded the crowded room. 'It could be a while, but then this place is always busy.'

'Oh, well, I've got all day,' said April.

'You might need it,' the girl replied with an impish grin. She shuffled forward and the baby began to whimper. 'Oh, crumbs,' she sighed. 'He's waking up, and he's bound to cause a fuss because he's teething.'

245

April smiled as the girl drew back the blankets to reveal a great shock of curly black hair and a little red face screwed up in readiness to howl his displeasure – but it was the lack of a wedding ring on the girl's finger that caught her eye.

The girl caught April staring, and her expression became defiant. 'His name's James Elroy,' she said. 'After his father – though neither of us have seen hide nor hair of him since I fell pregnant and the American army shipped him out.'

'He's beautiful,' April said truthfully as she gazed at the squirming infant who was slowly becoming mollified by his mother's embrace.

'Not at two in the morning, he isn't,' the girl said wryly. 'He wakes everyone, and my landlady is getting fed up with it.' She reached the head of the queue, signed her name in the large book on the counter and waited for April to do the same before hurrying to find two empty seats next to one another.

'My name's Shirley, by the way,' she said. 'Shirley Ryan.'

'April Wilton. Have you always lived in Cliffehaven?'

Shirley gave a wry smile and shook her head. 'My home was a small village in Hampshire until I fell for this one.' She kissed the baby's cheek and propped him over her shoulder to distract him from his grizzling. 'Small villages harbour small minds, and when you're the daughter of a parish councillor who produces a baby without the benefit of a wedding ring, life can become impossible. My father threw me out, but my mother found me a place here and stays in touch. It seemed easier somehow to just stay on here once James Elroy was born.'

April knew exactly how Shirley must have felt about that. 'So your father hasn't relented then?'

Shirley's smile faltered. 'He made it plain he wanted nothing to do with me unless I had him adopted.' She nuzzled the baby's cheek. 'But I just couldn't do it, could I, precious boy?' she crooned. 'You're far too gorgeous to give away, aren't you?' She blushed as she met April's amused gaze. 'Silly, I know, but I do adore him.'

'It's not surprising,' murmured April. 'He is very sweet. But isn't it difficult, trying to cope with him on your own? How on earth do you manage to work and look after him?'

'Sometimes it's very hard,' Shirley confessed. 'But he's worth it, even if I do have to work strange hours and put up with sly looks and snooty tutting.' She grinned. 'It seems I'm a scandal, and no better than I should be, but actually I've realised it's only the naïve girls who get caught – the more knowing and flighty ones know how to protect themselves.' She gave a regretful sigh. 'I did love his father, you know. Thought we'd be together always. How stupid is that?'

April knew exactly how stupid it was, but she didn't know Shirley well enough to share her own experiences. 'How are you going to be able to carry on working and look after the baby with no one to help you?' she asked.

Shirley's eyes were suspiciously bright. 'You're the first person to ask me that,' she said softly. 'Most just leave me to get on with things and couldn't care a fig.' She blinked rapidly and shot

247

April a watery smile. 'I'm hoping to get a place at Goldman's uniform factory. Mrs Goldman has set up a crèche for working mothers, and although the cost will come out of my wages, it's not a lot and will be worth it to know he's being looked after properly.'

'I didn't realise employers did that sort of thing,' said April.

'Well, they've had to now there's a war on,' Shirley replied. 'It's all hands on deck, isn't it, and girls want to do their bit even if they do have little ones. Besides, I need the money – Mother can't always help me out with Father breathing down her neck over every penny of her housekeeping.' She shrugged. 'You don't get anything free in this world, so you've got to get on and make the best of things, haven't you?'

Shirley cocked her head as her name was called. 'That's me. It's been lovely talking to you, April. Could we meet up again, do you think?'

April saw the wistfulness in her expression and knew they were both in need of a friend. 'Yes, I'd like that very much. Tomorrow, perhaps, if neither of us has a job to go to?'

Shirley waved her hand at the woman who was calling out her name. 'Yes, I'm coming,' she shouted back. She hitched the baby more comfortably over her shoulder and turned back to April. 'Tomorrow, midday at the kiosk down on the seafront,' she said quickly before she hurried off.

April watched her go to one of the four counters and sit down. She seemed such a pleasant girl, and clearly from a good background. How strange it was that they should meet so fortuitously, and have so much in common – even though Shirley had yet to know that. April admired her enormously, for she hadn't hidden away from the world, but had faced up to her responsibilities with great optimism and against all odds. She had kept her baby and was making a new life for herself down here, far from family and friends.

April sat and thought about that, and wondered if she'd ever have the courage to do such a thing, for it would mean sacrificing so much, and surely a baby would be better off with two adoptive parents who could afford to look after it properly?

'April Wilton. Desk three.'

Snatched from her thoughts, April glanced out of the window. There was no sign of Peggy, so she nervously approached the stern-looking woman behind the desk.

Without preamble she was asked her name, home address, billet address, age and previous work experience. There was a tricky moment when she had to reveal she'd left the Wrens, but she managed to gloss over it by citing a crisis in the family that had since been resolved.

She had to show her identity card and the letter confirming her billet with Peggy, which had so recently been signed by the clerk at the council offices, and give a short resumé of her skills and experience in the workplace. Even as she talked, she realised she had very little to offer – and hadn't yet revealed she was expecting. Thankfully, that question had not been asked.

'Your injured arm will make it almost impossible to place you,' the woman said. 'But I will

249

add your name to my list, and when you've fully recovered, you must come in again.'

'Is there nothing I could do in the meantime? I've got quite adept at using one hand, and I'm sure I could sweep a floor or answer telephones.'

The woman looked down her rather long nose and took a deep breath before she reluctantly sifted through the large box of index cards. She pulled one out and examined it thoughtfully. 'I do have a vacancy on the telephone exchange. It's to provide cover while the usual telephonist is recovering from a bereavement.' The pale blue gaze settled on April. 'Mrs Downes is expected to return to work in four weeks, and so the job isn't permanent.'

'But that's marvellous,' said April. 'My plaster cast is due to be removed about then, and I'll be able to take up a more permanent post elsewhere.'

'You'll have to be properly trained to begin with,' the woman said sternly. 'Running the exchange isn't as easy as you might think.'

April didn't care how difficult it might prove. It was a job. She'd had some brief experience on an exchange at the secretarial college, and she was a quick learner. 'I'll do it,' she said eagerly.

The woman eyed her for a long moment and then reluctantly filled in the card. 'I doubt very much if you'll be able to manage,' she said, 'but at least you show willingness to do something. You'll find the telephone exchange in the small building at the back of the town hall. Miss Gardener is in charge, and she has asked that any candidate should present themselves there at three in the afternoon when she has finished her shift.'

'Have there been any other candidates?' April asked breathlessly.

The woman sniffed. 'Only one, but she was most unsuitable. Take this card and be prompt. Miss Gardener does not approve of tardiness.'

'Thank you. Thank you very much.'

April took the card and left the counter. She shot a quick look around the room, hoping to spot Shirley, but there was no sign of her and Peggy was outside preparing to park the pram, so she hurried out to tell her the good news.

'What marvellous luck,' said Peggy. 'It's almost as if the job was made for you. And you'll get on with Vera Gardener once you accept that her bark's worse than her bite. She was headmistress at the local girls' school years ago, and can come across as being a bit bossy.'

'I went to an all girls' school where the head-mistress was a terrible old dragon, so she won't faze me. But my experience on the exchange at the secretarial college probably won't help me much as it was very small. I saw the one down in Portsmouth and that was simply vast. What if this one's the same and I keep cutting people off, or putting them through to the wrong number?'

Peggy chuckled. 'I doubt it's that big. Cliffe-haven doesn't have that many telephones, but I'm sure you're bright enough to pick it up quickly, and Vera will keep a close eye on you to begin with. Now we really must get you signed on at the doctor's before he closes for lunch.'

'I met a nice girl in the exchange,' April said, her spirits high as they went down the hill. 'Her name's Shirley Ryan and she's hoping to get a job at Goldman's because they've started up a crèche there for working mothers.'

'I can't say I know the girl,' said Peggy. 'She must be new to the town. But I'm glad you're feeling more positive about things, April – it means you're beginning to settle. As for the crèche, that was Rachel Goldman's idea. She's a strong supporter of working mothers and raised a good deal of money to set the whole thing up and provide safe care for the little ones.'

April found she was smiling as they turned off the High Street into a quiet crescent of stately Victorian villas overlooking a small park. She had the chance of a job, and had met a girl she felt sure she'd get along with very well – but above all she had Peggy, and she thanked her lucky stars that she'd fallen on her feet here in Cliffehaven.

The doctor's surgery proved to be a double villa with a wide turning circle at the front. The brass plaque was barely visible beneath the tangled branches of wisteria and clambering roses, and neatly planted flower beds edged a freshly cut lawn at the side. Facing the park and almost surrounded by trees, it was the sort of house which promised security and quiet efficiency.

Peggy plucked Daisy out of the pram because she'd started to grizzle with boredom. 'Old Doctor Sayer retired last year,' said Peggy, 'but his son's very nice, and so is the new chap he's taken on. Doctor Bradford was injured in Egypt and his poor face is a terrible mess, but he's easy to get along with once you can get past that.'

She shot April a naughty grin. 'Just watch out for Eunice Beecham, the receptionist. She's just got engaged to young Doctor Sayer, and is frightfully pleased with herself. She's been after him for years and gave my poor Julie a terrible runaround when she worked here as a midwife.'

'I'm assuming Julie was one of your girls?' asked April with some amusement. 'Is there any institution in this town that hasn't employed someone from Beach View?'

Peggy laughed. 'One or two,' she admitted. 'But I've got most of them covered one way or another.'

April followed her into a large square hall that smelled of beeswax and disinfectant. The floor was laid with black and white tiles, the walls were half panelled, and there was a very large chandelier hanging from the ornate ceiling. Three doors led from this imposing hall and Peggy led the way through one of them into what was clearly a waiting room and reception.

The girl behind the desk looked frighteningly efficient and was immaculately groomed. This must be Doctor Sayer's fiancée, the dreaded Eunice Beecham, April realised, taking in the perfectly made-up face and the rather superior expression.

'We've come to register April,' said Peggy. 'She's just arrived in Cliffehaven and is living with me at Beach View.'

'Doctor Sayer isn't taking on any more patients at the moment,' said the snooty Eunice after giving April a calculating once-over. 'She will have to be registered with Doctor Bradford. Does she have a letter from her own doctor?'

'No, I do not,' said April, who didn't appreciate being talked about as if she wasn't present. 'But

253

I'm happy to be registered with Doctor Bradford, and would like to make an appointment to see him as soon as possible.'

A fiercely plucked blonde eyebrow was lifted and blue eyes regarded her coolly. 'Doctor Bradford is a very busy man. Is it urgent?'

'No,' April admitted. 'But it is important I see him sooner rather than later.'

Eunice made sure they saw the large diamond engagement ring on her finger as she handed over a form to be filled in, demanded to see April's identity card and then turned the pages of her appointment book. 'He can see you at the end of the week during evening surgery at seven o'clock.'

April handed back the form she'd filled in and gave her a bright smile. 'Thank you, I look forward to meeting him.'

'Hello, Peggy. Nothing wrong, I hope?'

April turned to see a tall, well-built man in his thirties smiling back at them. Dressed in a lightweight tweed suit and polished brown brogues, he instantly exuded a sense of reliability.

'Hello, Doctor Sayer. No, I'm all tickety-boo. We're just registering April with the practice. She's my latest girl, you know.'

'I'm delighted to meet you, April.' His handshake was warm and firm, his smile lighting up deep brown eyes. 'Look, I have half an hour before the children's clinic. Why don't you pop into my surgery now and we can have a chat?'

'I've registered her with Doctor Bradford,' Eunice piped up. 'She's booked in to see him at the end of the week.'

'Oh, well, I'm sure he won't mind. He's very

254

busy at the moment and it seems silly for April to have to wait when I can just as well do the preliminaries.' He stood back and indicated she should go through into his consulting room.

April glanced at the clock, then turned to Peggy. 'You go home, Peggy. You've already wasted half the morning on me, and I can easily find my way round from here.'

'Well, if you're sure.'

'I am.' She smiled at her and then followed the doctor into his surgery, all too aware that Eunice was glaring daggers at her back.

20

Peggy had just pushed the pram into the scullery and turned on the copper boiler to heat the water when she heard voices upstairs. Frowning, she gathered up Daisy and climbed the concrete steps to discover Bertram Grantley-Adams sitting in her kitchen, sipping tea and chatting away to Cordelia as if he owned the place. Cordelia was looking rather flushed, and Peggy immediately wondered if it was from pleasure, fury or embarrassment.

'Hello, Bertram,' she said coolly as she divested Daisy of her outdoor clothes and let her totter about the floor. 'To what do we owe this dubious pleasure?'

Bertram leaped to his feet. 'I have come to apologise most sincerely,' he said. 'My behaviour was unforgivable towards dear Cordelia, and I hope that you will receive this small token as a sign of my heartfelt remorse.'

Peggy eyed the beautiful bouquet of early roses which mirrored the bunch already in a vase on the table. It seemed he was determined to ingratiate himself into the house again – but it would take more than a bunch of flowers to do that.

'Very nice, I'm sure,' she said stiffly, laying them carefully on the draining board. 'But you've left it rather late to come round with apologies and flowers, haven't you?'

'Yes, I know.' He hung his head. 'But I was taken ill later that night when I so shamefully mistreated Cordelia, and have only just been released from hospital.'

'I'm sorry to hear you were so incapacitated that you couldn't even write a note, or make a telephone call to Cordelia to apologise,' Peggy said briskly.

Bertram slumped into the chair, his face suddenly rather pale. 'I'm afraid I was rather,' he replied solemnly. 'They put me into the isolation ward because I had a return of the malaria I contracted during my time in Africa. Ghastly thing does rear its ugly head now and again, and quite knocks me senseless.'

'Oh, I see,' said a chastened Peggy, who only now noticed he'd lost weight and looked very drawn and pale.

'He's apologised so beautifully,' chirped Cordelia. 'The poor man has really suffered quite an appalling attack, so don't be cross with him, Peggy.'

Peggy realised she couldn't really carry on defending Cordelia's honour when she clearly didn't want her to. 'As long as there is no recurrence of your behaviour that night, then I'm prepared to welcome you back to Beach View,' she said stiffly. 'But if you ever put that silly society above Cordelia's comfort again, you'll have me to deal with.'

He looked contrite. 'You have my assurance that it will not happen again, dear lady.'

'I'm glad to hear it,' she replied, still not quite forgiving him. 'Now, if you'll excuse me, I have Daisy to attend to and a pile of washing to get through.'

April left the surgery comforted by the fact that although he possessed poor taste in women, if Eunice was anything to go by, Doctor Sayer proved to be understanding and not judgemental. He'd asked questions about the baby's father and hadn't even raised an eyebrow at her answers, then had examined her, prescribed iron tablets to combat her anaemia, and filled in all the forms so she would receive the extra milk and rations to supplement her diet.

He'd also made arrangements for her to see the midwife, and took time to discuss the options open to her once the baby was born. April was enormously relieved that these important things had finally been dealt with in a kindly manner, for her experience at the clinic in Portsmouth had not encouraged her to talk about anything in the light of the doctor's brusque disapproval. After he'd listened and advised, they came to an agreement that an appointment should be made to meet a Miss Franklyn from the Church of England Adoption Society early the following week.

April walked slowly down to the seafront, going over the day's events. Was she doing the right thing by having her baby adopted? After all, she reasoned silently, Shirley seemed to be managing, and if factories were offering nursery facilities to working mothers, then surely she too could cope?

But did she want to be saddled with a baby that would command all her attention and radically change her life – to be reminded every day of Daniel and the way he'd betrayed her? Was she brave enough to snub her nose at a world that would shun her, and give up any hope of marriage? Certainly, no decent man would want to take her on with a brown baby in tow.

Her head ached with it all and her previous high spirits had ebbed by the time she sat down on a promenade bench to watch the sea and the swooping, raucous gulls. If only Paula was still alive she could talk it over with her and try to make sense of it all – but there was no Paula, and although she suspected Peggy might be the perfect person to confide in, there was no guarantee that she'd forgive her deceit and continue to support her once she knew the truth. The colour bar that existed so clearly in America was also becoming apparent to her here, for although the black GIs were welcomed as part of the Allied forces, and given freedom they'd never experienced before, it was quite another thing for a girl to sleep with one and then present the proof to a world that simply wasn't ready for it.

April took a deep breath of the fresh air and lifted her face to the weak sun. She had to accept she was on her own, and there was little point in driving herself mad by going over everything in endless circles, for it solved nothing. She must learn to deal with this calmly and sensibly, take each day as it came, look after her health and be guided by the doctor and the woman from the adoption society who had experience in such things.

She sat with her eyes closed, the sun warm on her face, the sounds of the gulls and the waves slowly bringing her an inner calm which strengthened her resolve to face the future and make the best of what lay ahead.

Feeling a little better about things, she opened her eyes and really took in her surroundings. She marvelled that although there were barbed-wire and gun emplacements strung along the promenade and the lovely pier was no more than a ruined skeleton, Cliffehaven seafront hadn't really changed. The white cliffs still towered over the beach to the east, the tumbling grassy hills to the west still huddled over that end of the promenade, and the sea still rattled over the shingle as it dragged it back and forth.

It was almost as if she could hear the fairground music that had once come from the carousel at the end of the pier, and the laughter and chatter of people enjoying their seaside holiday as the aroma of toffee apples and candyfloss vied with the delicious smell of vinegary fish and chips wrapped in newspaper.

The thought made her hungry, and noting that it was almost two o'clock, she made her way to the Lilac Tearooms which was opposite the hospital, and enjoyed a round of cheese on toast accompanied by home-made pickles, and a small pot of tea. Feeling refreshed and more optimistic, she tidied herself up in the small powder room and set off for the telephone exchange.

The enormous town hall overshadowed the square red-brick building behind it, and as April approached it from the narrow alleyway she shivered in the sudden drop in temperature. There was nothing to alleviate the ugliness of this utilitarian building, for the doors and window frames had been painted a sickly corporation green, a huge telegraph pole strung with numerous wires towered above it, and not a blade of grass or bright wild flower softened the austere concrete courtyard at the front.

She hitched the strap of her gas-mask box over her shoulder, adjusted her sling and then rapped on the door. Her heart was thudding in the most ridiculous manner as she waited, but it was important she got this job, and she just hoped to goodness that Miss Gardener proved to be as pleasant as Peggy seemed to think she was.

'It's no good you standing out here,' said the plump woman who was panting her way towards her. 'Miss Gardener won't leave the switchboard until I take over.'

'Oh. I didn't realise,' stammered April.

Curious watery blue eyes trawled April from head to toe as lips were pursed and a bulging handbag was tucked more firmly between sturdy arm and thrusting bosom.

'I suppose you're here about the job,' she said. At April's nod, she gave a sniff. 'Then you're

260

wasting your time,' she said bluntly. 'You can't possibly manage the exchange like that.' Her gaze fell on the plaster cast. 'Besides, my niece is coming later, and she has experience.'

This was something of a shock as the woman from the labour exchange had said nothing about a second candidate. 'Well, I'm here now, so I'd like to give it a go all the same,' April said firmly.

'Not from around here, are you?' The woman's expression was hostile. 'These sorts of jobs are best for locals to do, and my niece has lived here all her life.'

'Your niece is not getting the job, Bertha, so you can stop bullying that girl and get in here to start your shift. You're three minutes late as it is.'

They turned to see a tall, thin woman standing in the doorway. Everything about her was grey, from her rigidly permed hair, to her low-waisted loose dress, thick lisle stockings and sensible shoes. A pair of wire-framed glasses hung from a silver chain around her neck and her long, pale face was devoid of make-up.

'But I was held up because she was here,' Bertha blustered.

The steely gaze remained fixed upon her until she'd edged over the doorstep and disappeared into the gloomy interior. It was then turned on April.

'Are you the girl they sent from the labour exchange?'

'Yes, Miss Gardener.'

The gaze slipped momentarily to the sling before fixing back on April's face. 'You'd better come in then, although I doubt you'll be suitable

261

with that arm,' she said, turning on her heel.

April's old headmistress had been a dragon, but Miss Gardener was frightening enough to turn water to stone. April felt as if she'd regressed to five years old as she followed her into the building and closed the door behind her, wondering how on earth Peggy could ever have imagined that they would get on with one another. Miss Gardener had to be seventy if she was a day, and she clearly regarded everyone as children to be bossed about and kept in order.

'In here.' The command was imperious as the woman strode into a room off the narrow hall.

April suddenly saw the funny side of things and had to fight back a fit of giggles. She and Paula had spent many an hour waiting in the hall to be reprimanded by Miss Gosforth, their headmistress. As frightened as they'd been, they hadn't managed to keep from giggling, and the longer they'd had to wait outside that door, the worse it got – and this interlude with Miss Gardener had brought it all back.

She stepped into the room to find it was actually quite cosy, and served as a sitting room as well as a basic kitchen. There was a small cooking range, two sagging couches, a table, two chairs and a stone sink with a wooden draining board and highly polished brass taps. On the rug in front of the range fire lay a vastly overweight bulldog which grunted and snorted and dribbled in its sleep.

'That's Winston,' said Mrs Gardener. 'He's getting on a bit now, so sleeps most of the time. He doesn't appreciate strangers patting him.'

April couldn't think why anyone would want to

touch the dog, for it was the most unattractive animal she'd ever seen.

Miss Gardener sat down on one of the hard kitchen chairs and indicated that April should do the same. 'Tell me about yourself,' she said.

It was very warm in the room and there was a foul, lingering odour that April couldn't identify, but suspected it came from Winston. She loosened her coat and left it draped over her shoulders as she gave an edited resumé of her home life and education, and her short time with the WRNS.

'A fine institution,' the woman said with a solemn nod. 'It was a shame you had to leave due to a family crisis. Will you be returning to the service once your arm is healed?'

'My family commitments make that impossible,' she said smoothly. 'Which is why I'm looking for something in the civilian sector.'

'And what makes you think that managing a telephone exchange will suit you?'

April sat forward on the chair, eager to emphasise her keenness to have the job. 'I have had a little experience of working in the small telephone exchange at secretarial college. I realise that the post is only available for a few weeks,' she said earnestly, 'but I'm quick to pick things up and am willing to work hard.'

The steely gaze appraised her. 'You'd need to be quite dextrous with only one good hand, and I do have another candidate coming tomorrow.'

'That other lady's niece?'

'Not on my watch,' Miss Gardener replied with a delicate shudder. 'That girl is far too flighty at the best of times, and is positively unreliable as her short interlude here last year proved.'

'I'd like to be given a chance to at least try and see if it's possible to work here,' April pressed.

Miss Gardener was about to reply when a soft hiss came from the other side of the room accompanied by a grunt. Both were swiftly followed by the most appalling stench.

'Don't mind that,' Miss Gardener said airily. 'It's only Winston relaxing, and if you prove capable of the task of running the exchange, you'll soon get used to it.' She crossed the room to pat the dog and feed it a bit of chocolate.

Winston farted again as he shifted to gobble a second sweet.

The smell was making April feel quite sick, and she doubted she'd ever get used to it. She tried holding her breath, but that only made it worse, and she didn't have a handkerchief to put over her nose. She tried to breathe through her mouth, but the taste was even worse than the smell and she felt her stomach churn.

Miss Gardener made cooing noises to the revolting animal and rubbed his fat belly until he'd settled back to sleep. Satisfied that Winston was comfortable, she turned back to April. 'Come on then. I'll show you the exchange and you can watch Bertha for a while to get some idea of what the job entails. But let me warn you, Miss Wilton, I do not stand for gossiping on the line, over-familiarity with our customers, or any form of eavesdropping. There's a war on, and in an emergency, the lines must be kept free.'

April was only too pleased to leave the room and she hurried after Miss Gardener into the hall. Unfortunately the smell seemed to have been absorbed in her clothes and skin and she could have sworn it followed her down the corridor and into the main room.

The exchange was larger than the one at the college and took up most of one wall, but it didn't appear too daunting, for the set-up looked the same. The large main board consisted of neatly aligned, numbered slots into which Bertha was plugging coloured leads from a panel fixed to a desk in front of her. This panel also contained brass switches and dials, and when someone called the exchange a light went on over one of the numbered slots and was accompanied by a low buzz. Bertha wore a pair of headphones which were attached to a mouthpiece that sat neatly on the swell of her large bosom, the wires from it dangling to what April knew would be a series of plugs beneath the panel.

Miss Gardener ignored Bertha's glower. 'Our service is available twenty-four hours,' she said proudly. 'There are very few private telephones in Cliffehaven, but of course our businesses and administration offices see it as a lifeline to the outside world, and in these troubled times it is also a vital means of communication for the Allied services.'

She indicated that April should take the spare chair over to Bertha, who clearly resented this intrusion but didn't quite have the nerve to say so.

April sat down just as a call came through.

Bertha put on a plummy telephone voice that was nothing like her natural local burr and put the caller through to the number they'd requested.

'I'll leave you to it for an hour and then I shall supervise you when you take over,' said Miss Gardener. 'Winston needs some fresh air and to stretch his legs.'

'He isn't the only one,' grumbled Bertha when Miss Gardener left and the coast was clear. 'That dog stinks the place out.'

April giggled, relieved that Bertha seemed to be thawing towards her. 'Do you think she even notices?'

'It would be hard not to,' she said flatly, and then concentrated on a flurry of calls coming in.

When the rush was over she turned in her swivel chair and regarded April with open dislike. 'I've been working here for eight years and I've seen girls like you before,' she said sourly. 'Miss Gardener might like the fact you went to a posh school and talk la-di-da, but I know your type. You won't last a week.'

April met her disapproving glare and refused to be cowed. 'Well, we'll just have to see about that, won't we?' she said coolly. 'And by the way, you've got a caller waiting on line four, and number fifteen has hung up.'

The woman reddened, and in her rush to amend her negligence managed to cut off the caller and had to ring him back.

April sat back and watched her fumbling, calm in the knowledge that given a chance to find her way round the switchboard, she'd be quite capable of doing this job – even with one hand.

The Anchor's doors were shut for the afternoon and it was warm and cosy in Rosie's upstairs rooms. Harvey and his pup, Monty, were sprawled in a shaft of sunlight streaming through the window, and Ron and Rosie were having a cuddle on the couch following their late lunch.

'You're being very grumpy, Ron,' Rosie complained. She pushed away from him and began to stack their dirty dishes on the low table in front of the couch. 'Whatever's the matter with you today?'

'Ach, Rosie, me darlin', I'm feeling me age, so I am,' he grumbled.

Her blue eyes widened in surprise. 'You? Never,' she said, brushing his bristled cheek with her lips. 'Come on,' she coaxed softly in his ear, 'tell me what's really wrong.'

He slid his arm round her trim waist and pulled her back to his side. 'There are things I can't tell you, Rosie – you just have to trust me on that. But what with one thing and another, I feel a bit beleaguered at the moment.'

'Why? What's happened?'

He squeezed her closer and kissed her passionately. 'Women,' he said when he finally came up for air.

Rosie was immediately on alert and pushed away from him. 'Women? What women?'

'Ach, to be sure, not that sort of woman,' he blustered. 'I'm talking about the ones at Beach View. Cordelia's decided to forgive Bertie Double-Barrelled, which will only lead to complications. He's out with her now in his car, no doubt charming her into believing he's God's gift and filling her head with nonsense.'

Rosie regarded him squarely. 'Ron, it's you who's talking nonsense. Why shouldn't Cordelia make up with Bertie? He might be a little fulsome in his flattery, but he seems harmless enough, and at least he gives her the chance to get out and about.'

'Aye, he does that, but there are things about that man...' He fell silent and fiddled with his pipe. 'He's not suitable for Cordelia, that's all I'm saying,' he finished rather lamely.

'Why ever not?'

Ron took his time to fill his pipe. 'I'm just concerned about Cordelia,' he said. 'She's flattered by his attentions, and he's already proved to be unreliable. Look what happened when he left her high and dry at the Conservative Club that time.'

'You're a real old softy, aren't you?' she teased.

'Hmph. I just like to look after my own, that's all, and despite her age, Cordelia can be very naïve at times.'

'Well, I think it's marvellous that she's found someone to escort her to dinners and bridge parties. She must get awfully bored sitting around at Beach View.' She lightly kissed his lips and patted his cheek. 'Don't worry so much, Ron. With you watching over her, she won't come to any harm.'

He sat there in silence, puffing on his pipe, his thoughts unreadable.

'You said women,' Rosie reminded him. 'Who else has upset you?'

He gave a deep sigh and tamped down the smouldering tobacco with a calloused finger. 'It's the new girl, April,' he confessed.

'I've yet to meet her, of course, but Peggy said she sounded like a nice girl when they spoke on the telephone.' She smiled at him. 'Good heavens, Ron, she's only just arrived, how on earth could she possibly have upset you?'

'It turns out she's in the family way,' he muttered. 'Something Peggy decided to keep to herself until the girl was already in the house.'

Rosie nodded. 'Peggy did actually tell me after the girl had telephoned – in strict confidence, of course. I really don't see why you should be so concerned, Ron.'

'She's not married, Rosie, that's what concerns me.' He glowered at the sleeping dogs. 'It's not right, Rosie. Not right at all, and I don't want the other girls getting ideas.'

Rosie chuckled. 'I hardly think they'll all rush out and get pregnant just to keep April company. They're all far too sensible. Besides, Peggy said she was engaged to be married. It's hardly April's fault the army sent her chap off somewhere before they could have the wedding ceremony.'

'I'm not convinced about any of it,' he muttered. 'Why wouldn't her mother keep her at home, and where is this chap's family? Surely they wouldn't just abandon her like this without a valid reason?'

'It's really none of our business, Ron,' she said firmly. 'We don't know the girl's background, or anything about her chap's circumstances, and I have to confess that I'm a bit shocked by your attitude. I never suspected you were a prude and hidebound by old-fashioned ideas.'

'You make me sound like a churchgoing maiden aunt,' he complained.

'Well, you're acting like one,' she countered.

'Whatever her story, the poor girl clearly needs support. She's amongst strangers, Ron, and is looking to you and Peggy and the rest of the girls to help her through what can only be a very trying and distressing time.'

'So you think I should just accept her story and carry on as if none of it bothers me?' He shook his head. 'I don't know if I can do that, Rosie, not while I suspect she's not telling us the whole truth.'

Rosie folded her arms and regarded him squarely. 'Well, you're hardly in a position to do anything else, are you?' she said flatly. 'As for the truth – you've been a stranger to that for all the years I've known you. It's a bit late to set yourself up as a paragon of virtue, when I've lost count of the times you've tried to get me into bed without the presence of your wedding ring on my finger.'

He reddened and refused to look at her. 'Aye, well, that's different,' he mumbled.

'No, it isn't. It's human nature, Ron, and you can't blame the young ones for breaking all those old rules when the future is so uncertain. And in my experience, it's the innocent ones that get caught – not the flighty ones – so think on, Ron, and give the girl the benefit of the doubt.'

He looked at her rather shamefacedly. 'I'm an old fool, aren't I?'

'Yes, but you're my old fool, and I love you despite everything.' She wound her arms round his neck and kissed him hard before letting him go again and becoming businesslike. 'Let's have another cup of tea, and then we can talk about more important things – like the outfit I'm plan-

270

ning to wear to Stan and Ethel's wedding.'

Bertha had jealously guarded her switchboard during the hour they were alone, but April had taken careful note of all she did, and was feeling fairly confident by the time Miss Gardener returned from her dog-walking.

'You may go and make us some tea while I sit with April,' Miss Gardener said imperiously. 'Use the leaves I've left to dry in the saucer, there's still plenty of flavour in them.'

Bertha pushed back from the exchange and removed the headphones with a distinct lack of grace.

Miss Gardener waited until she'd clumped out of the room and then closed the door behind her. 'It's regretful that Bertha has yet to learn some manners,' she said coolly, 'but she is an excellent telephonist and you'd do well to learn from her.'

April took Bertha's place, settled the rather unpleasantly warm headphones over her ears and adjusted the mouthpiece to suit her smaller bosom. She was suddenly very nervous, for although the board was familiar, she was all too aware of Miss Gardener watching her like a hawk.

The click of a light above number eighteen told her a call was coming in and she hesitated momentarily before connecting and asking the caller which number they wanted. Four calls later, she felt a little more relaxed, and by the time Bertha had returned with a tray of teacups, she was managing without being prompted by Miss Gardener.

'You did very well,' Miss Gardener said some

time later as April swapped places with Bertha, who was clearly disgruntled by the whole episode. 'Come with me into the other room, and I'll discuss your hours and the rate of pay the Post Office provides.'

April gathered up her coat and gas-mask box and reluctantly followed her into the other room where Winston was shuffling about on his bottom.

'Poor Winston,' crooned Miss Gardener. 'He's a martyr to worms – nasty things. The vet's pills don't seem to work at all.'

April doubted that giving a dog chocolate was much help either, but she said nothing and tried to concentrate on Miss Gardener's long list of rules and regulations as the dog continued to shuffle and squirm.

She finally made her escape and took a deep, refreshing breath of the cold air outside before she headed back to Beach View to tell Peggy her good news.

Peggy and Fran had finished preparing the evening meal by the time April arrived back at Beach View, and Peggy could see instantly that April was in a celebratory mood. 'You got the job?' she said, smiling.

'I start tomorrow at eight in the morning until three in the afternoon, which is when Bertha takes over. Miss Gardener lives on the premises, so she's there to answer any calls during the night.'

'Ach, to be sure, that's brilliant,' said Fran. 'I'm so glad you've found something. How did you manage with your bad arm?'

'I can still use those fingers, so it wasn't too

difficult at all,' April said. She shed her coat and gas-mask box and hung them on the back of the door.

Peggy dished out some of the stew for Fran, who was about to go on night shift at the hospital. 'How did you get on with Vera Gardener?'

April grinned. 'She's definitely still a head-mistress, but she seems fair. It's Bertha who's taken umbrage, because she wanted her niece to have the job.'

'Bertha's always been a rather disagreeable woman,' said Peggy. 'Take no notice of her, dear. That niece of hers probably doesn't want the job anyway. She's a lazy piece.'

'I got that impression from Miss Gardener.' April poured tea into a cup and added a few drops of milk. 'But you didn't warn me about Winston, and the awful smells he makes,' she teased. 'Was that deliberate?'

'Oh, lawks, I forgot all about him,' gasped Peggy. 'I'm sorry, April, I was under the impression he'd died years ago, otherwise I'd have said something.' She regarded her, keenly. 'Was it really bad?'

'I thought I was going to be ill at one point,' April confessed, 'but thankfully the exchange is in a different room so I can close the door on him.' She sipped the tea and gave a sigh. 'He won't last much longer if she keeps stuffing him with choco-late and sweet biscuits.'

'Chocolate?' gasped Fran. 'She feeds a dog chocolate? But that's criminal when there's so little of it in the shops.' She finished the bowl of stew and rolled her eyes. 'Honest to God, some people

273

need their heads testing.'

April agreed, but said nothing as she drank her tea and watched Daisy playing with her dolls in front of the fire.

Fran drew on her cape and gloves and picked up her gas-mask box and handbag. 'I'll see you tomorrow,' she said cheerfully. 'Don't worry if I'm back later than usual, though. Robert's wangled time off and he's treating me to lunch in a country pub.'

As Fran ran down the steps and slammed the back door behind her, Peggy lit a cigarette and glanced up at the clock. Explaining to April about Bertie Double-Barrelled, she gave a sigh. 'He's taken Cordelia out for the afternoon in his car, and I suspect he'll treat her to supper somewhere. I do hope he's learned his lesson and will treat her properly from now on.'

April nodded distractedly, for her thoughts were on other things. 'Do you think I should have told Miss Gardener I'm expecting?'

Peggy shook her head. 'You're only there for four weeks, and it's not likely to affect the smooth working of the exchange, so I'd keep it to yourself, dear. Not that it's anything to be ashamed of, mind,' she added hastily. 'But Vera's old-fashioned and...' She shrugged. 'Well, it's not really any of her business, is it?'

April nodded and finished her cup of tea. 'I'd planned to meet Shirley Ryan down at the seafront kiosk tomorrow, but I won't be able to make it now I've got the job, which is a shame because I thought she was a very nice girl.'

'She might have found work at Goldman's,'

said Peggy. 'In which case neither of you will be there. Is there a way to get a message to her?'

'I don't know where she lives,' April admitted. 'But I don't like the idea of her hanging about waiting for me. She'll think I've changed my mind about meeting her.'

'I tell you what,' said Peggy. 'I've got my turn at the WVS tomorrow and I'll finish at about noon. Why don't I take a stroll down and see if she's there? You never know, she might not have turned up either if she has a job to go to.'

'Oh, Peggy, would you? But–'

'It's no bother,' she said airily. 'And if she isn't there, I'll leave a note with Mabel who runs the kiosk and ask her to pass on your telephone number and address should Shirley turn up there another day.' She smiled and patted April's arm. 'There, see. There's always a way to sort out these things. But you'd better give me a description of Shirley so that I can recognise her.'

'She's my height and very pretty, with brown curly hair and hazel eyes, and a baby boy who is about six months old. I hadn't got around to telling her that I was expecting,' April added quickly. 'We didn't really have time to do more than realise we got on well.'

Peggy felt a rush of pleasure that April had found someone her own age that she could relate to. 'Oh, how lovely. No wonder you two hit it off, and of course I won't breathe a word about your baby – that's for you to do.' She stubbed out her cigarette as the sound of Rita's motorbike rent the stillness. 'Write that note and leave it all with me, dear. Now I really do have to get on with everyone's tea.'

275

April helped Peggy by setting the table, and as the girls returned home and congratulated her on her job, she felt a glow of happiness at being at the heart of this lovely home. Yet despite their warmth and friendship, she couldn't help but wonder how Peggy would react when she discovered the baby was illegitimate. It could change everything.

21

The bombing campaign over Germany was still very much ongoing, and although everyone at Beach View had become inured to the sound of the planes taking off from Cliffe and mostly ignored them, they still reacted swiftly when the sirens went off.

April was fast asleep when the high-pitched whine alerted her to an enemy raid, and she quickly pulled on her dressing gown, grabbed her ID papers and the precious photographs and hurried downstairs to the kitchen where Harvey was howling at the shrieks of the sirens that were now going off all over town.

There was clearly a smooth routine for such events. April was handed the box of essentials and Cordelia was escorted by Ron down the garden path, while Peggy wrapped Daisy against the cold night.

They all trooped out as the sirens reached their ear-splitting pitch and the searchlights began to quarter the sky in search of enemy aircraft. Ron closed the door of the Anderson shelter, plunging them into darkness, and April shivered at the memories of her incarceration in the hotel cellar on the night Paula and seven of her colleagues had been killed.

Peggy lit the lamp that hung from the ceiling and as the pale glow illuminated the dank, cramped space, April forced herself to relax. She was as safe here as anywhere and actually it was a relief to know that she was above ground, for the thought of being buried alive again was enough to give her nightmares.

As Ron cradled Daisy in his arms, Sarah made sure that a sleepy Cordelia was secure in the deck-chair that had been wedged into a corner. Surrounded by pillows to keep her from sliding out, Cordelia promptly went back to sleep, undeterred by the awful noise of the aircraft because she'd turned off her hearing aid.

Peggy took the box from April and made tea on the small camping stove. Harvey had stopped howling now that the sirens had gone silent, but the sound of the dogfights continued overhead. Rita tried to snatch a bit of sleep, even so, huddled in her fleece-lined First World War flying jacket and thick trousers. She would have to go to the fire station once the raid was over to check if she was needed. Sarah was wrapped in a thick dressing gown, with trousers pulled over her pyjamas; Ivy was bundled in a blanket and woolly hat; and Ron was in his poacher's coat, the kitten tucked in one of the pockets while Harvey snored at his feet.

April sipped her tea, aware that Ron was watching her, his expression more puzzled than hostile, but it made her feel uneasy all the same, for she suspected that he didn't really approve of her or her situation, and so she was relieved when he closed his eyes and tried to settle down to sleep. She'd heard from Peggy that Ron and Stan were very close friends, and she accepted that Ron was of an older generation who frowned on girls like her. Would her Uncle Stan feel the same way?

The sound of heavy-bellied bombers made the walls vibrate and the ground shudder beneath their feet, and April looked up, wondering fearfully if Cliffehaven was to be tonight's target.

'They'll probably be targeting the airfield,' shouted Sarah above the thunder of engines and the boom and clatter of Cliffehaven's guns. 'Let's just hope to goodness all our planes are in the air by now.'

The distant thuds and crumps seemed to bear this out, but April was still finding it difficult not to remember that awful night back in Portsmouth.

'It ain't nice, is it?' asked Ivy, pulling the blanket more tightly over her shoulders. 'We 'ad a bomb hit our factory, and I were trapped for bleedin' hours down there. Lost one of me mates that night,' she added sadly, 'and it's still 'ard to forget how frightened I were every time Jerry comes over.'

'I'm sorry you're both finding it all such an ordeal,' said Peggy. 'It can't be easy after what happened to you.' She reached out and took the girls' hands. 'Perhaps you'd find it would help if you talked about it?'

'Nah, you're all right,' said Ivy stoically. 'Your

Doreen made it easier, and I've done all the talking I want.'

'And you, April? How do you feel?'

'Jumpy,' she admitted with a ragged smile. 'But I'd like to talk about Paula. She was my best friend, and like Ivy, this brings it all back.'

Hesitantly, April began to tell the others about Paula and how they'd met. She remembered the funny things that had happened to them both at school and during their time in the WRNS, and as the memories crowded in, she felt a wave of sadness wash over her. It was when she told them about the bombing raid that had killed her best friend, that April realised she was crying. 'I miss her so much,' she said, wiping away the tears. 'She was such a good friend, and I still can hardly believe I'll never see her again.'

A gnarled, warm hand momentarily covered her fingers. 'She'll always be with you, wee girl,' said Ron gruffly. 'The dead stay with us in our hearts and minds for as long as we still draw breath, and although I'm not a religious man, I like to think we'll be together again at the last trumpet call.'

April nodded, grateful for his kind words, and suspecting he'd lost loved ones during both wars. 'Thank you, Ron. That thought is comforting.'

'Aye, well, for now we have to concentrate on the living and do all we can to see this damned war at an end,' he said fiercely. 'This is no world to bring a new life into.'

April placed her hand protectively over the mound of her stomach as a particularly loud explosion shook the ground beneath her. It certainly wasn't, but her baby would be born, war or

279

not, and there wasn't much she could do about it.

Tactfully, Peggy changed the subject, and began to discuss what everyone would be wearing to Stan's wedding, which was now only a matter of weeks away.

'Are you all going?' asked April in surprise.

'Stan has been Ron's friend since the Stone Age,' said Rita with a teasing light in her eyes as she glanced across at Ron, 'and I've known him since I was a kid. He's helped all of us girls at one time or another, and as far as we're concerned, he's part of the family.'

'I'm sure he'll invite you too,' said Peggy comfortably. 'He wouldn't want to leave you out now he and Ethel have taken such a shine to you.' She smiled with affection. 'Stan's like that – a good man with a big heart.'

April smiled back, hoping this proved to be true.

The all-clear didn't go for another hour, and when they emerged from the Anderson shelter they discovered it was dawn. Yawning and stretching to ease the aches and pains of sitting on a hard bench all night, they trooped indoors, eager to get some warmth into their stiff muscles and frozen toes and fingers.

Cordelia was feeling quite sprightly, for she'd slept through the whole thing and was looking forward to her breakfast. Peggy bathed and dressed Daisy, while Ron checked on his ferrets and fed the dog and cat. Rita shot off to the fire station and the others got dressed for the day before they started to prepare breakfast.

Rita returned within half an hour to report that although the airfield had suffered a lot of damage, Cliffehaven itself seemed to have escaped. 'My boss said that by the sound of it most of the planes were airborne by the time Jerry arrived, but the admin buildings, machine shops and some of the Nissen huts have been wiped out.' Her little face was pinched with anxiety. 'I just hope to goodness Matt and the others are all right.'

Peggy put her hand over her mouth, her eyes wide with fear as she thought of her daughter Cissy and her son-in-law Martin. 'Did John Hicks have any idea of the number of casualties?'

Rita shook her head, her eyes dull with anxiety. 'Sorry, Aunt Peg, the fireman up at the airfield just told him there were some casualties amongst the mechanics when the repair shop was hit. There was nothing about the rest of the personnel.'

'Oh, Lord,' Peggy groaned tearfully. 'It could be hours before anyone can get through to me. This damned war is driving me mad with all its uncertainties and the endless wait to hear anything.'

'I'm sure Martin or Cissy will ring you as soon as they can,' soothed Sarah. 'But if I hear anything up at the Cliffe estate, I'll ring you immediately.'

'You are a dear,' sniffed Peggy. 'Thank you.'

Sarah pulled on her coat and beret. 'I'd better get a move on, or I'll be late,' she said. 'Try not to worry, both of you. I'm sure everyone is fine.'

Peggy watched her run down the steps, as lithe and graceful as a dancer despite the unflattering jodhpurs, dark green coat and heavy walking shoes. She had almost an hour's walk over the hills to get to the estate, and she did it cheerfully each day no matter what the weather.

'I'd better be off an' all,' said Ivy, hoisting the straps of her overalls over her shoulders and pulling on the coat she'd made out of a picnic blanket. She gave Rita a consoling hug, and then shot a grin at April. 'Good luck for today, and I'm looking forward to 'earing 'ow you got on with that smelly dog.'

'I expect you're feeling a bit nervous about your first day, aren't you?' asked Rita, who was now shovelling down the hot, welcome porridge as if her life depended upon it.

April nodded. 'Miss Gardener makes me nervous when she watches me, so I'm hoping she'll mostly just leave me to it.'

'I'll make you some sandwiches and a flask of tea for your lunch,' said Peggy as she spooned porridge into Daisy's mouth. She was trying hard to concentrate on the present and stifle her fears over Cissy and the others. 'I doubt Vera will provide anything, and it will save you having to go into the other room with Winston.'

April smiled at her gratefully and glanced at the clock. 'I have to go too,' she said apologetically. 'It would be very bad form to turn up late on my first day.' She washed up her breakfast things and shot upstairs to clean her teeth and prepare for the day. On her return to the kitchen she found it deserted but for Peggy, Cordelia and Daisy.

'They've all left for work and Ron's taken Harvey for his morning walk,' explained Peggy. 'I'm hoping he'll go as far as the airfield today to see if he can get any word about my daughter and son-in-law. Though I doubt he'll be let anywhere near the place. Security is very tight up there.'

She handed April a string bag containing a packet of sandwiches and a thermos. 'You have a good day, dear, and don't mind me. I'm a bit inclined to fret about everything and it usually comes to nothing.'

'I might hear something over the telephone line,' said April. 'And although I'm not allowed to repeat anything I hear, I'm sure that if it's relevant, I can get word to you somehow.'

'That is sweet of you, but I don't want you getting into trouble – especially on your very first day.'

April smiled at her and patted her arm. 'I won't,' she assured her.

'Now you're not to worry about your little friend Shirley. I'll see she gets your note one way or another.'

'April's hair isn't curly,' protested Cordelia from the other end of the table where she'd spread out the morning paper. 'And I can't see how you could possibly know that she looks like her mother. You've never set eyes on the woman.'

Peggy and April exchanged amused glances. Cordelia had forgotten to turn her hearing aid back on after her night in the shelter.

April kissed Peggy's cheek and then, armed with the string bag and gas-mask box, hurried down the steps and out of the back door. It was still early, but the sky was pearly with streaks of blue appearing between the small white fluffy clouds, promising a fine day. She took a deep breath of the lovely clean air. She was looking forward to getting stuck in on her new job, and she set off quickly for

283

the telephone exchange building.

Peggy watched her go from the kitchen window and then, trying to take her mind off Cissy and Martin, she got on with her day. First she saw to Daisy, cleaning her face of porridge before sitting her on the floor with a colouring book and her dolls. Then she put a few drops of milk in a saucer for Queenie, who was winding herself around her legs and mewing. Queenie was getting very demanding, but her fur was sleek, her eyes bright and her curiosity and energy unbounding, so Peggy didn't begrudge her a bit of milk now and again.

She tackled the last of the washing-up and then scrubbed the table and the kitchen floor, repeatedly looking at the clock, urging the telephone to ring. But it stayed stubbornly silent, and in the end she couldn't resist going into the hall to check that the receiver hadn't been left off the hook or the line disconnected for some reason.

'Number, please.'

'Sorry, April. I was just making sure the telephone line was in order.'

'I've heard nothing this end either,' she said quietly.

'No news is good news, I suppose,' sighed Peggy and hung up.

She went back into the kitchen to tackle the nappies that were soaking in a bucket under the sink. Thankfully, Daisy was almost potty trained, although she still couldn't get through the night without a nappy, and there was the occasional accident, but it did make life easier not to have so much washing to do every day.

With the nappies flapping on the washing line and the hall floor washed down, it was time to head off for the town hall and her session with the WVS. She made sure Cordelia had everything she needed, then dragged on her coat, glancing once again at the clock and cursing the new rules which forbade her to ring Martin's office up at the airfield. It was all so frustrating she could scream.

The raucous shrill made her jump and then she was racing into the hall and snatching up the receiver. 'Hello?' she said breathlessly.

'Mum? It's Cissy. We're all fine up here, so you're not to worry. I'm sorry I haven't called before this, but it's been chaotic.'

'Oh, darling, I'm so relieved. I've been going through agonies not knowing what's going on.'

'We were hit quite badly,' said Cissy, 'and we lost a couple of mechanics in the first wave.' She paused and her voice wavered as she spoke again. 'Tragically, we also lost two bomber crews when their planes were hit as they tried to take off – and a Polish pilot bought it when his Spitfire crash-landed right on top of the admin block. But Martin, Matt and all the boys you've met are all right, and Martin says he'll try to come over to see you when time allows.'

'That would be wonderful,' sighed Peggy. 'And Rita will be very relieved to hear that Matt has come through. Oh, Cissy, I can't begin to tell you how worried we've all been.'

'I know, Mum,' she said solemnly. 'It's a horrid business all round, especially when we lose our boys like this. Look, I have to go. I'll try and come for a visit, but you know how things are…'

'Of course I do, and thank you, darling, for ringing.' Peggy put down the receiver and sank into the hall chair, the tears streaming down her face. The relief was immense, but the fear went on day after day, and she didn't know how much longer she'd be able to bear living with it. Damn Hitler, damn the Luftwaffe and damn, damn, damn this bloody war to hell and back.

She eventually got her emotions under control and lifted the receiver. 'April, could you put me through to the fire station, dear? Everyone's safe up at Cliffe, and I have to tell Rita so she doesn't worry all day.'

'I'm so glad,' said April. 'Putting you through.'

Peggy had spent the rest of the morning in the large main room of the town hall helping to pack the comfort boxes for the troops. In her rare spare moments, she glanced towards the window that overlooked the telephone exchange building, wondering if April was coping all right, and whether she was enjoying the work. She'd sounded very competent earlier, her well-modulated voice so much more pleasant than Bertha's strangled vowels, so she was hopeful that Vera Gardener might keep her on should Lucinda Downes decide not to return to Cliffehaven, but to stay with her widowed mother in Devon.

It was almost midday and Peggy was counting the minutes until she could leave the confines of the noisy, busy hall for the fresh air of the seafront and a refreshing cup of tea. She was busy taping up a box when she was nudged by her neighbour's sharp elbow. 'Stand by your beds,' she murmured. 'Your sister's just arrived.'

Peggy's spirits plummeted. Doris was the last person she wanted to see this morning, but as there was no way of avoiding her, she plastered on a smile and prepared for battle.

'Margaret, there you are,' Doris said, striding towards her in her immaculately tailored dark green uniform, looking as if she'd just stepped out of a beauty parlour. 'I'm going to need you to stay on for an extra hour today. I have a meeting with the WVS committee.'

Being called Margaret always set her teeth on edge, and Doris's bossy attitude merely made it worse. 'No can do, Doris,' she replied. 'I have to be somewhere at twelve.'

'I'm sure it's not as important as my meeting with the committee,' Doris said dismissively, 'and I need someone to take charge during my absence.'

'I'm sure Edna would be delighted to fill in for you,' said Peggy, glancing across to another table. Edna was always keen to volunteer for things in the faint hope she'd be elevated to the committee.

'I'm sure she would,' said Doris coldly, 'but I'm not asking her, I'm asking you.'

'And I've already said I can't do it,' she replied firmly.

'I can't imagine what could *possibly* be more important than holding the fort here. Really, Margaret, it's a pretty poor show when I can't rely on my sister in my hour of need.'

'If you'd asked me yesterday, then I would have agreed to do it,' said Peggy, starting to fill another

287

box. 'But I've made arrangements which I'm not willing to cancel. Ask Edna.'

Doris glared at her and took a deep breath, clearly trying hard to contain her impatience. 'You do very little towards the war effort, Margaret,' she hissed, 'other than a few hours helping out here. I really do think it's time you got your priorities right.'

Peggy's hand stilled. She dropped the socks into the box and glared back at her sister, seething at her accusation. 'How *dare* you accuse me of doing nothing,' she said furiously, 'when you swan about in your car needlessly using petrol, turn up here when you feel like it to do nothing but boss people about, and resent having evacuees move in with you? It's you who's got their priorities wrong.'

Becoming aware that they had an interested audience, she leaned forward and lowered her voice. 'I'm not doing it, Doris, and if you were more organised, you would have sorted this out earlier.'

'It's a last-minute meeting,' Doris retorted. 'I only learned about it an hour ago.'

Peggy wondered if that was because Doris was being excluded by the snooty clique of women that made up the committees in Cliffehaven. Hearing about her impending divorce and the scandal over her husband Ted's affair with the woman on the fish counter, they had probably closed ranks. 'That's hardly my problem,' she replied. 'And I'm not willing to change my plans just to suit you. It isn't as if you'd do the same for me, is it?'

'Of course I would,' Doris blustered.

And pigs might fly, thought Peggy sourly. 'Then perhaps you'd like to babysit Daisy for the afternoon of Stan's wedding? That would be a terrific help.'

Doris went pink and fumbled in her lovely leather handbag for her diary. She flicked through the pages. 'I'm sorry,' she said without a hint of real chagrin, 'but I have a Women's Institute meeting to address that afternoon.'

Peggy knew for a fact it was the day before the wedding, but didn't even bother to argue. 'What a shame,' she murmured.

'Another time, perhaps,' said Doris, tucking the diary away and fastening her handbag. She looked round the room, her glare making their audience suddenly concentrate harder on their various tasks. She gave an exasperated sigh and turned on her heel. 'Edna,' she called across to another table. 'Edna, my dear, I need to have a quiet word.'

Peggy shot an amused glance at the women on either side of her and finished packing the box. Doris was a pain in the neck and wound her up like a clock, but she could certainly liven up a tedious morning.

Her shift was finally over, and she collected Daisy from the playroom where she and the other small children had been kept amused by a retired Norland Nanny who never seemed to lose her patience or her cheerful smile. Peggy didn't know how she managed it, for the noise was awful, the place was in chaos, and it seemed there was always a baby crying or an argument to settle.

She bumped the pram down the steps past the young Home Guardsman who stood watch by the high piles of sandbags, and set off down the High Street towards the promenade. She could do with a nice cup of tea, a cigarette and a sit-down after spending the morning on her feet without much chance of catching her breath.

The wooden kiosk was three times the size of Ron's garden shed, and it had been fitted out with a basic kitchen and a couple of tables and chairs, and outside, beneath a blue and white striped awning, were more tables and chairs so that Mabel's customers could enjoy the fresh air and sea views while they drank their tea. The place was deserted, so Peggy parked the pram and went in to order a pot of tea and some cordial for Daisy.

Mabel was a chatty woman in her early fifties who liked to be kept up with the local gossip as she doled out tea and sympathy as well as dubious homespun advice to anyone who would listen. Her husband and two sons were in the army, while her daughter worked as an observer up at the Fort where Peggy's nephew Anthony was involved in some highly secret carry-on for the MOD.

Peggy knew better than to gossip about anything with Mabel, for although she was pleasant enough to your face, she liked nothing better than to spread salacious rumours and stick the knife in if someone upset her.

'It's a nice surprise seeing you, Peggy,' she said as she filled the pot from the huge urn behind the counter. 'I can't remember the last time you popped in. Meeting someone, are you?'

Peggy saw the inquisitiveness in those grey eyes and shook her head. 'I need a cuppa before I walk home and start all over again,' she said.

'How's life at Beach View these days? I hear you've got a new girl.'

'That's right. She started at the telephone exchange this morning.' Before Mabel could ply her with endless questions, Peggy took the laden tray and carried it outside. She set it down on a table, plucked Daisy from her pram and let her toddle about for a moment, ever mindful of the rolls of barbed wire that were strung between the promenade and the mined beach.

She took off her headscarf and shook out her dark curls, enjoying the sun on her face after the hours spent in the gloom of the town hall. Daisy staggered towards her and gripped her knees, so she lifted her up and sat her on her lap so she could orchestrate the delivery of cordial straight into her mouth and not down her clean clothes.

The manoeuvre wasn't entirely successful and Peggy was dabbing at the splashes on Daisy's coat when a girl arrived pushing a pram. Her interest was sparked immediately, for she fitted April's description of Shirley. Aware that Mabel's ears were probably flapping, she smiled at her and said nothing as she parked the pram to one side of the kiosk and ordered a pot of tea and a Spam sandwich.

As the girl emerged from the kiosk with her tray, Peggy smiled again. 'Lovely day, isn't it?' she said. 'Perfect for sitting out with a nice cuppa.'

The girl gave her an uncertain smile.

'Why don't you join me, dear?' said Peggy. 'There's plenty of room and it seems silly not to share a table when there's only the two of us.'

She hesitated, glancing quickly over her shoulder at Mabel before putting the tray down and checking on the baby which was hidden deep within the pram. Without drawing the pram to the table, she left it in the lee of the kiosk and sat down with a shy smile. 'Shirley Ryan,' she said, shaking Peggy's hand.

Peggy thought it was a bit odd that Shirley seemed reluctant to draw the pram closer, but she smiled and introduced herself and Daisy.

Shirley smiled at Daisy and then poured out the tea. She glanced down the promenade, and then turned back to Peggy. 'I'm supposed to be meeting someone,' she said, 'but it looks as if she isn't coming.'

'April asked me to give you this,' Peggy said quietly as she handed over the note. 'She's got a job at the telephone exchange and couldn't make it this morning. But I know she'd love to meet you another time.' She gestured towards the note. 'Our address and telephone number will be in there.'

'Oh, how kind. Thank you.' The note was swiftly read and then tucked carefully away in the depths of a cheap handbag. 'I don't know if she told you, but we met at the labour exchange.'

Peggy nodded and smiled. 'Did you manage to get a job at Goldman's?'

'Yes. I start as a machinist at the end of the week. They couldn't take James Elroy before then, you see.'

It was an unusual name, and Peggy suspected it might be American. When she noted the lack of a wedding ring, her natural curiosity was roused. 'Don't you have anyone else to look after him while you work?'

The girl blushed and avoided her gaze. 'Not

292

really.' She bit into the sandwich as if to preclude any further discussion on the matter, and although she shot Peggy a tentative smile now and again, Peggy could tell she was uneasy.

'April's on her own too,' she said, hoping to draw her out a little. 'And I think she's feeling a little lost being so far from home, so it's lovely that you've met.'

'Yes. She seems very nice,' Shirley murmured.

'Have you been in Cliffehaven long?' Peggy persisted.

'Just over a year.'

It was clear to Peggy that Shirley Ryan was not a talker, but perhaps that was because she was shy and unwed. She was also very young, and probably reluctant to say much to Peggy who was, after all, a complete stranger.

A grizzle came from the pram which soon turned into loud protest, and Shirley shot to her feet to see to her baby. Lifting him out of the pram, she laid him over her shoulder and rubbed his back before reaching into a bag and pulling out a bottle of thin juice.

'My goodness, he's got a good pair of lungs,' said Peggy. 'Bless him. Is he teething?'

Shirley nodded and drew the baby from her shoulder to her lap, her gaze constantly darting towards a watchful Mabel.

'What a lot of lovely dark hair,' Peggy said in delight. 'He is a bonny baby. How old is he?'

'Six months and three weeks,' said Shirley proudly. 'He's usually very good when I take him out, but he's suffering with his teeth, poor little love.'

Daisy climbed off Peggy's lap to get a closer look at the baby, and Peggy felt a tug of remorse for her initial disapproval. Shirley clearly adored him, so what did it matter if there was no ring on his mother's finger?

She watched as Daisy took the baby's hand and tried in her babyish way to soothe him, but he was having none of it. 'Would you like me to try and quieten him?' she offered. 'I find that sometimes a stranger's face can soothe.'

Shirley was about to hand him over when Mabel came out of the kiosk, arms folded beneath her large bosom, her expression hostile as she looked at the girl and her baby. 'I thought I recognised you,' she said flatly. 'I've told you before that I won't have your sort here, so sling your hook.'

Peggy gasped, appalled that Mabel could be so rude and unkind. 'She's not doing any harm,' she retorted, 'and I don't like your attitude, Mabel.'

'Like it or lump it,' said Mabel, who was clearly out of sorts. 'I don't want her kind in here frightening off my customers with her illegitimate brat.'

'There's only me and I'm enjoying her company,' snapped Peggy. 'And what proof have you that the baby's illegitimate? You need to hold your tongue, Mabel.'

'Really, Mrs Reilly, it's all right. We'll go.'

'Not until you've finished what you've paid for,' said Peggy firmly. 'As for you, Mabel Wilkins, you should be ashamed of yourself.'

Mabel folded her arms and glared. 'It's my kiosk and I have the right to say who I serve. Unmarried girls with babies have no business here. They should be locked away out of sight of decent people.'

Peggy felt like smacking that smug fat face, but just managed to resist. 'In that case you can refund the cost of her sandwich and tea and we'll be on our way.'

Mabel looked for a moment as if she was going to argue, but something in Peggy's expression must have warned her not to dare. She stomped back into the kiosk, opened the till and then stomped back, slamming the money on the table in front of Shirley. 'You're nothing but a slut and I don't want to see you or that brat again.'

Peggy gathered up Daisy, thoroughly riled by Mabel's disgusting behaviour. 'I'm sure you'll see neither of us again,' she snapped. 'And I can promise you, Mabel, that I'll make sure that all the right-thinking people in this town will give your kiosk a wide berth from now on.'

She turned to a distressed Shirley. 'Come on, dear, we'll have our cup of tea at my place and leave this sour-faced, vicious old trout to her own devices.'

Shirley gathered up the money and, with shaking hands, strapped the baby back in the pram. 'Please don't feel you have to, Mrs Reilly,' she stammered as they turned their backs on Mabel and her kiosk. 'I should be used to this by now, and really, I shall be fine in a minute.'

'I'm sure you will, but the offer was a genuine one and I really think it would be better all round if we went to Beach View and you had time to catch your breath.'

Shirley hesitated momentarily and then shook her head. 'It's really kind of you, and I do appreciate your support, but I have things to do back home.' Her tears were close to falling as she looked at Peggy. 'Do you think April will still want to be my friend?'

Peggy's soft heart went out to her. She was so young and vulnerable, and she wished she could just give her a cuddle and reassure her that not everyone thought like Mabel. She resisted and squeezed her hand instead. 'I'm sure she will,' she said softly. 'And you must come and see me at Beach View. You'll be made welcome there, I assure you.'

Shirley nodded, blinking away her tears, then hurried off.

Peggy watched until she was out of sight, wondering how often she'd had to put up with such disgusting abuse. It made her feel ashamed that such vile prejudice should rear its ugly head in her beloved town, but she was unfortunately all too aware that behind the closed doors and among the gossiping busybodies, it had always been there – just less blatant.

She finished strapping Daisy into the pram and began the long walk home, her natural tendency to protect and nurture battling with the moral influences that had moulded and shaped her since childhood.

It was only as she arrived back at Beach View that her heart won the battle. The world had changed, the morality of that bygone age had shifted and blurred, and although she couldn't wholeheartedly approve of girls like Shirley, she knew what it was to be young – to need someone to cling to in times of war – and how easy it was to let things go too far. She was certainly in no position to judge or condemn, for Anne had been born seven months after her marriage to Jim. At the end of the day, they were all sinners, and in these perilous times surely the true way to peace was to open one's heart and learn to be more tolerant and forgiving?

22

April had quickly felt at home working at the exchange, and if it hadn't been for the awful dog, she might have enjoyed it even more. However, Miss Gardener didn't approve of her closing the door while she was working, and Winston had waddled in and sniffed at her legs before shuffling his bottom on the floor and waddling out again, leaving his awful odour behind him. April had opened the window to get rid of it, but Miss Gardener didn't like open windows in case Winston caught a chill, so April had to put up with it.

She thanked Miss Gardener for helping her with a complicated overseas call and headed outside to take in great deep breaths of glorious fresh air. It was just after three and Bertha had now taken over. Unfortunately she was still out of sorts, and had barely managed a gruff hello, but April didn't mind – it wasn't as if she was the sort of woman she wanted to be friendly with anyway.

She came out of the deep shadows that lay behind the town hall and slowly walked up the hill to see if Stan was at the station, and had a few minutes to chat. It was time to get to know him a bit better.

'Hello, dear,' he boomed as he set aside his watering can and eased his back. 'I'm just watering my few bits of spring veg. They seem to like it here on the platform.'

'Hello, Stan. I hope you don't mind me turning up like this, but you did say–'

'And I meant it,' he replied. 'You and the girls from Beach View are always welcome. Now, I think a cup of tea is called for – and one of Ethel's famous rock buns.' He led the way into the Nissen hut and set the tin kettle on the primus stove. 'How are you settling in?'

'Very well,' she replied, and went on to tell him about her job, the lovely warm way everyone at Beach View had welcomed her, and her hopes for a new friendship with Shirley.

Stan raised an eyebrow. 'Shirley's in need of friends,' he said thoughtfully. 'The poor lass has a lot to contend with, but be careful, April, there are some in this town who are quick to condemn, and your friendship might lead to some unpleasant-ness.'

April felt a twinge of unease. 'Because she's not married?'

'Aye,' he said on a sigh. 'It's a sad situation all round.'

April's discomfort increased, for his gentle warn-ing was a clear message that although he felt sorry for Shirley, he didn't actually approve of her.

Before she could probe further, he visibly brightened and changed the subject. 'Peggy is a

298

wonderful woman,' he said, pouring the boiling water into the teapot and giving the tea leaves a vigorous stir. 'You've fallen on your feet there. But how did you hear about Beach View?'

April thought quickly. 'Someone recommended it to my mother,' she said, sticking as closely to the truth as she could. 'And yes, I know I'm very lucky.'

'Let's take our tea out to the platform and enjoy this sunshine,' he said. 'You grab the tin of buns, and I'll bring the tray.'

She followed him out to the platform where they made themselves comfortable on the wooden bench which had once had a brass plaque announcing the name of the town screwed onto the back. The war meant that every signpost, noticeboard and plaque had to be taken down so any invading force wouldn't be able to find their way, which also led to some confusion for innocent visitors to the town.

April decided to keep the conversation light and friendly, and not pursue the subject of Shirley. 'Not long until your wedding,' she said as they sipped their tea and enjoyed the bright afternoon sun. 'I expect Ethel's getting very excited.'

'She's in a terrible panic,' he said with a soft chuckle. 'She's had a dress and jacket made by a friend and now she's not sure she likes them – and then there's a problem with what shoes to wear, and which hat and gloves, and should she carry a bouquet.' He gave a contented sigh. 'My Ethel would look good in a grain sack, but weddings have a strange effect on women, and it's all fuss and to-do. I'm keeping well out of it.'

He didn't look too hard done by, thought April in amusement. She bit into the delicious rock bun and savoured the crystallised sugar on the top and the juicy raisins inside.

'I hope you're coming to the wedding, April. We've asked everyone else at Beach View, and we'd hate the thought of leaving you out of things.'

'That's very kind, Stan, but please don't feel you have to invite me. You don't really know me, and it's a very personal day for you and Ethel.'

'I insist,' he said, brushing crumbs from his straining waistcoat. 'Neither of us has got much family to speak of, and we regard Peggy and everyone at Beach View as the closest thing.' He sipped his tea and stared down the deserted railway lines. 'I did send an invite to my sister, but I haven't heard back. I was rather hoping she might find the time to come and visit again as it's such a special occasion.'

'I'm sorry to hear that,' murmured April, embarrassed that neither she nor her mother had replied to his letter. 'Did you two have a falling-out?'

'Not really,' he replied. 'We just didn't see eye to eye on something when she came down here after Barbara died, and we haven't been in touch since.'

He reached for a second bun and munched it thoughtfully. 'Mildred was always one for bearing grudges, and didn't take kindly to my advice. She's driven, you see, forever searching for something better, and I suspect she was frustrated that she didn't always get it – especially after...'

He fell silent and April waited on tenterhooks while he finished eating the bun.

Stan swallowed the last morsel, his expression sad. 'She had some sorrows and difficult decisions to make, but that was no excuse...' He heaved a sigh and dredged up a smile. 'You don't want to hear all about things like that,' he said. 'Far too depressing on such a lovely day.'

April did want to hear about her mother's sorrows and difficult decisions, and the reason behind her falling-out with Stan, but of course she couldn't make Stan tell her – not until he knew she was Mildred's daughter. She decided to change the subject as it seemed to be upsetting the old man. 'Let's talk about the wedding instead,' she said. 'Will you be having a reception?'

'Oh, yes. We both agreed on that. You can't have a wedding without a knees-up, and my Ethel loves a grand do. We'll be having it at the Anchor – Rosie puts on a lovely spread, and she'll get in extra beer and so on, so there's no danger of anyone going thirsty.'

'Rationing doesn't help when it comes to such things, does it? I suppose you'll have to have one of those cardboard cakes.'

'Not on your life,' he protested. 'My Ethel's got the cook up at the factory canteen to do her a proper one, with icing and fruit and even a bit of decoration.

She's managed to wangle coupons from everyone so she has enough flour and such, so it should be a real humdinger.'

April smiled. 'Goodness. Your Ethel is resourceful, isn't she?'

'She certainly is,' he said proudly. He pulled the watch from his waistcoat pocket and checked the time. 'The four-fifteen will be in soon, just time to have the last bun and finish our tea.'

They shared the last rock cake and chatted about Ron doing best man duties and Ethel's Ruby taking on the role of bridesmaid. 'Hopefully it will help her cheer up a bit,' said Stan. 'The poor lass is feeling very low because her young man has been sent up to the wilds of Scotland. They've only recently got engaged, and who knows when they'll see one another again – it certainly won't be before this war's over.'

April had yet to meet Ruby and therefore couldn't really add much to the conversation, but it was clear that Stan loved the girl as if she was his own, and this made her warm even more to him.

When the last morsel of bun was devoured and the teapot had run dry, April thanked him and picked up the tray. 'I'll put this in the ticket office and then get back to Beach View to help Peggy with the evening meal,' she said. 'It's been lovely talking to you, Stan.'

'You be sure to come again,' he said heartily. 'And perhaps next time I'll show you round my allotment.'

April returned the tea things to the Nissen hut and headed home, her thoughts troubled by the possibility that even if their friendship flourished, he would find it very hard to accept her situation and perhaps, despite his open-heartedness, even then turn his back on her.

And yet she was intrigued by what he'd said about her mother. Mildred had always been tight-lipped about her personal life, and if she was harbouring some deep secret from her past, that might explain her reluctance to talk openly. But could it also explain her coldness towards her daughter and husband?

April thought about it long and hard as she walked back to Beach View, and came to the conclusion that everyone had secrets – it was just that some never came to light, and she really had no business to delve into her mother's private life.

The curtains had been closely drawn across the bay window overlooking the High Street, but the diffused light gave a warm hue to the flowery wallpaper and the frilly pink and white counterpane on the enormous, ornate brass bed which wouldn't have looked amiss in a bordello. The light gleamed on the mirror above the dressing table where silver-backed hairbrushes and cut-glass bowls glowed against the highly polished mahogany, and illuminated the flattering black-and-white studio portrait of Gloria which must have been taken two decades previously.

Ron gave a sigh as he pulled on his coat, for this would be his last visit, and he was going to miss coming here. He shot a rueful grin at Gloria who was perched on the side of the bed. 'Ach, to be sure, things will not be the same from now on,' he sighed. 'But it's over, Gloria, and I'll not be back.'

She brushed a lock of hair from her face and regarded him sadly. 'Are you sure I can't tempt you to stay?'

He shook his head. 'You know I can't, Gloria.'

She slid off the bed, cupped his face with her hands and softly kissed his lips. 'It's been fun,

Ron,' she murmured, 'and I'm going to miss your visits. Rosie's a lucky woman.'

Ron wasn't too sure about that, for loving him meant that Rosie had a great deal to contend with – and if she only knew the half of it, she'd run a mile.

He turned away from Gloria and headed down the stairs to the main bar where Harvey was sprawled in front of the dying fire. 'Come on, ye heathen beast, we've things to do and people to see.'

Gloria had followed him down the stairs and was now unbolting the back door. 'Don't forget me entirely, Ron,' she said quietly.

'To be sure I could never forget you, Gloria Stevens,' he said fondly. He winked, pulled on his cap and stepped out into the back yard of the Crown. 'Just remember this is between ourselves and keep those lovely lips sealed.'

She grinned back at him. 'You can count on that,' she promised and then blew him a kiss before she shut the door and bolted it again.

Ron walked briskly into the alleyway and closed the large gates before heading along the narrow paths to his next destination. His mood was thoughtful, tinged with sadness that the adventure was over, and yet enormously relieved that they'd managed to keep it secret. Gloria was a remarkable woman, and if circumstances had been different, he might have taken her up on her offer – but they both knew deep down that the excitement and intrigue wouldn't last, however much they might have wanted it to.

Harvey padded along beside him, stopping only

to water a lamppost or garden wall as Ron ambled down the street of unremarkable terraced houses. Ron drew to a halt at the gate of number nineteen. He was exactly on time, and was expected. He glanced up and down the deserted street then quickly strode up the path. His rap of the knocker was answered almost immediately and with Harvey following him closely, he slipped inside.

As it was such a lovely spring day the back door was open and the kitchen window had been flung wide to make the most of the fresh air, diffusing the heat of the range fire, which had to be kept alight for cooking. Peggy was helping Cordelia prepare the vegetables for the evening meal. She'd spent most of the afternoon fretting over whether or not to forewarn Cordelia that April's new friend was an unmarried mother. It could be very awkward if the girl came to visit, for although Cordelia was the kindest, sweetest person, she did hold certain very old-fashioned ideas, and Peggy didn't want either of them getting upset.

'I met April's new friend at lunchtime,' she said as they peeled the potatoes and carrots. 'Her name's Shirley, and she has the most enchanting baby boy.'

'That's nice, dear. Do you want these carrots sliced or chopped into fingers?'

Peggy looked in alarm at the very sharp knife in Cordelia's unsteady hand and had visions of little fingers going into the pot alongside the carrots. 'I'll do those,' she said hastily. 'You carry on with the potato peeler.'

Cordelia gave her a wry look and handed over

305

the knife. 'You were saying about April's friend,' she murmured.

'It's good she's got a baby, don't you think?' Peggy said carefully. 'It gives them something else in common along with their age and circumstances.'

'That depends on the baby,' said Cordelia. 'If it does nothing but screech and make a fuss, it will probably put April right off the idea – though it's rather late in the day to have second thoughts,' she added with a touch of asperity.

Peggy finished the carrots and covered them in cold water, unsure how to proceed with this tricky conversation.

'You say circumstances,' muttered Cordelia, pausing in the act of peeling. 'Does that mean she's not married either?'

Peggy nodded. 'But she's a lovely girl, well spoken and polite and clearly a very doting mother.'

Cordelia dropped the potato and peeler into the bowl of water and regarded Peggy steadily for a moment. 'I'm sure she is, but I don't think you should condone that sort of behaviour by encouraging this friendship, Peggy. One unmarried mother in the house is enough – two is just asking for trouble. You'll get us all a bad name.'

'She and April are just young girls, Cordelia,' she replied calmly. 'Young girls who've made a life-changing mistake and are doing their best to cope with all that entails. I rather admire them actually,' she said defiantly, 'especially Shirley.'

'Why?' Cordelia's expression was suddenly wary.

Peggy took her hand and met her gaze solemnly.

306

'Shirley isn't engaged to be married, Cordelia. In fact I suspect she's been abandoned by her baby's father and is doing her very best to raise him on her own. And today I witnessed the appalling way people treat her because of it. It made me ashamed, Cordelia. Ashamed of my own initial disapproval, and ashamed of the people in this town who see that baby and condemn him for something of which he's entirely innocent.'

Cordelia met Peggy's gaze squarely as Peggy related what had happened at the kiosk. 'I was always brought up to believe that people – especially young women – should conduct themselves with unimpeachable honour,' she said softly. 'And I'm too old and set in my ways to change my opinions. But I'm horrified that some in this town are openly vilifying her.'

She withdrew her hand from Peggy's and stared out of the window. 'The same thing happened during the last war,' she murmured, 'and although it was rather shocking to see white girls with their black babies, I couldn't understand why people thought they had the right to pass judgement on others when their own failings should have been seen too. And yet you're telling me it's still going on.' She sighed deeply and turned back to face Peggy. 'Clearly the lessons of the past haven't been heeded.'

'Shirley's baby isn't black, Cordelia.'

'Well, I suppose that's something to be grateful for.'

'And surely it's better to show some compassion regardless of what colour a baby is? They are young, foolish girls, yes, but who are we to punish them? If the girls are to be friends, then Shirley and her baby will be welcome here at Beach View, and that's an end to it.'

'You're letting your soft heart rule your head, Peggy,' Cordelia chided softly. 'Doing such a thing will only cause a lot of gossip and ill-will against you.'

Peggy tossed her head. 'Perhaps amongst the prejudiced, like Doris and that horrid Mabel, but I wouldn't give tuppence for their opinions anyway.'

'You might if it damaged your reputation, and that of the other girls living here,' said Cordelia. She looked back at Peggy, her expression solemn. 'How would you feel if your Cissy came home with a baby?'

'I'd be mortified,' she admitted.

'There you are then.'

Peggy shook her head. 'I'd be mortified that she'd been silly enough to get herself into trouble. But that wouldn't stop me loving and supporting her – even if the baby turned out to be sky-blue pink with yellow spots,' she said firmly.

'And Jim?'

'He'd feel the same way,' she replied defiantly, though she had a fair idea that Jim would rant and rave and threaten all sorts before he came to his senses and accepted what had happened.

'Then I hope neither of you are faced with such a predicament,' said Cordelia drily. 'It's all very well defending such girls, but it's a very different matter when it involves one of your own.'

'We'd face it together – as a family,' retorted Peggy boldly, aware that Ron might not co-operate in any such thing without a good deal of persuasion and nagging. 'We're not the sort of parents to abandon our children when they need us most.'

'Like April's mother, you mean?'

Peggy stared at her. 'You don't think...? You can't mean...? Surely not, Cordelia?'

Cordelia shrugged. 'The situation with April is unclear, I grant you, but she's taken up with this Shirley – could it be because they have rather more in common than we supposed?'

Peggy's thoughts were in a whirl. April had revealed very little about her mysterious and absent fiancé, and was just as secretive about her relationship with her mother and the reason behind her coming here to live. The girl was definitely hiding something – could it be that Cordelia was right?

She struggled to dispel the doubts that clamoured. 'We mustn't let our imaginations run away with us, Cordelia,' she said firmly. 'April seems to be a very pleasant, well-brought-up girl who's feeling a bit lost and needs a friend. We must trust that she will prove to be what she claims to be and let her choose her pals regardless of who they are.'

Cordelia sniffed and returned to peeling the potatoes. 'The world's gone mad,' she muttered. 'Everything was different when I was that age. One knew the rules, knew how to conduct oneself – and would never have dreamt of flouting society in that way.'

Peggy could see her point even though she didn't fully agree with it. 'Things have indeed changed,' she said thoughtfully. 'And, in my opinion, not for the better either. Yet, surely such prejudice has no

309

place here when a war is being fought against the subjugation of those born into different faiths and cultures – and who don't fit into what society deems to be acceptable?'

'As admirable as it is to want a more forgiving world, I still advise caution, Peggy.'

'I'll keep that in mind, Cordelia.' Peggy reached for a saucepan, her thoughts still on Shirley and her baby, and the disgusting way Mabel had treated them. She probably couldn't expect Cordelia to change her thinking, for she'd been born in a different time and a very different world, but witnessing Mabel's assault earlier had made her realise that should the same fate befall any of her girls she would do her very best to offer love and support. She just hoped and prayed that she wouldn't be called upon to prove it.

April stood on the back step by the open door. She'd heard every word of the conversation in the kitchen, and although she dreaded the thought, she knew it was time to tell the truth. It would be a relief in a way, for she'd never found lying easy, and the burden of her secret was weighing heavier each day.

She took a deep breath for courage, hoisted the strap of her gas-mask box firmly over her shoulder and went up the steps. Peggy and Cordelia turned to smile at her, but she could sense their unease, and their suspicion that she must have heard at least some of what they'd said. 'Peggy, Cordelia,' she said nervously. 'There's something I need to tell you.'

They both paled, and Cordelia sank into a

nearby chair. 'You heard,' she stated.

April nodded. 'And you were right, Cordelia. Shirley and I have a great deal in common, because my baby's father abandoned me too.'

'Oh, lawks,' breathed Peggy, sinking into the kitchen chair beside Cordelia. 'But why all the pretence, April? Couldn't you trust me enough to tell me the truth?'

April dumped her gas-mask box over the back of the chair and sat down at the table. Her pulse was racing and she was finding it hard to breathe. 'I'm so, so sorry I lied to you before, but you see there's something else, and I don't know how to tell you.'

Peggy's gaze remained steady as she reached out and grasped April's hand. 'Trust me, April,' she said softly. 'Whatever it is, I promise not to cause a fuss.'

April gripped her fingers, praying that she'd understand and perhaps even forgive her for being so deceitful. 'My baby's father was an American,' she began hesitantly, 'and he came from the South.' The tension was almost unbearable as the two women waited for her to continue. 'Daniel Clement was a light-skinned Negro,' she finished in a rush.

Cordelia went very pale and Peggy tightened her grip on April's fingers. 'Oh, my dear,' she breathed. 'No wonder you were so reluctant to confide in me.'

'It's not something to be proud of,' April admitted on the verge of tears, 'and of course I didn't know how you'd react.' She looked into Peggy's eyes and saw understanding and kindness there, so continued. 'I wanted to tell you, really I did, but I was terrified you'd throw me out, and I was desperate to stay.'

'Oh, April,' Peggy sighed. 'I'd never have done that.'

'Of course she wouldn't,' said Cordelia brusquely.

'But I didn't know you, Peggy, and although you seemed happy enough to give me a room in your home knowing I was pregnant, it was quite another thing to reveal that my baby's father was a black GI.'

'Those Americans have a good deal to answer for,' said Cordelia with some asperity. 'Unfortunately you aren't the first silly girl to be lured in by their dubious charms – and I very much doubt you'll be the last.'

April sensed her disapproval and it made her feel very uncomfortable. She regarded them both, realising they were finding this hard to take in. 'I'm so sorry,' she whispered, the tears blinding her, 'and I'll quite understand if you want me to leave. I'm sure they'll have a spare bed at the hostel.'

'You're not going anywhere,' said Peggy firmly. 'You're part of the family now, and as such, I will not abandon you to some filthy, overcrowded hostel.' She pushed back from the table and gathered April to her. 'This is your home for as long as you want, April. All I ask is that you never lie to me again.'

April sank into her embrace and held her tight, overwhelmed by Peggy's love and understanding. 'I promise,' she murmured.

Peggy stepped back and softly smoothed April's hair back from her face before giving her a handkerchief. 'Dry your eyes, dear, and once we've had a nice cup of tea, we can talk about what we do from now on.'

April cleaned her face, then glanced at Cordelia, who still looked rather shell-shocked by it all, and took a shuddering breath. 'You're so kind, Peggy, but won't my staying here cause trouble?'

'It's bound to cause a flurry or two,' said Peggy candidly, 'but it won't last – not if I have anything to do with it. I've seen enough today to make me realise that a stand has to be made against prejudice and ill-will, and I'm blowed if I'll let it come into this house.'

'What's got you all fired up, Peggy girl?' Ron came into the kitchen and plumped down in a chair as Harvey enthusiastically greeted everyone. He glanced from Peggy to April and then to Cordelia. 'I see there's trouble afoot,' he muttered. 'Come on, out with it.'

April shivered with apprehension, for Ron was made of sterner stuff than Peggy and she already suspected he didn't approve of her. Was he about to throw her out?

'Well, I'll tell you what the trouble is, Ron,' Peggy said flatly as she put the teapot on the table, sat down and told him about her run-in with Mabel.

April listened in stunned silence. The thought that Shirley had routinely been abused in such a way was appalling, but what was even more terrifying was the realisation that it could happen to her if the truth got out about Daniel's brown baby.

313

Peggy seemed to read her thoughts, for she squeezed her shoulder and shot her a supportive smile before turning back to a stony-faced Ron. 'The reason behind that nasty little story is that it also concerns our April,' she said.

The heavy brows lowered as the bright blue eyes settled warily on April. 'Oh, aye? And how's that?'

'She's also been abandoned by her baby's father, but unlike Shirley's little one, hers will be born brown-skinned,' said Peggy evenly.

Ron's brows shot up as he stared at Peggy. 'Brown?' he rasped.

'That's right,' said Peggy, 'and if you don't like the idea, then you'll just have to lump it, because she's staying here for as long as she wants.'

His frown deepened. 'So my opinions are not to be counted,' he rumbled.

'You can have your say, Ron,' said Peggy, 'but it won't make any difference.'

'I've warned her of the consequences, Ron,' said Cordelia querulously, 'but you know what Peggy's like once she gets the bit between her teeth.'

'Aye, all too well,' he replied. 'And what about you, Cordelia? How do you feel?'

'Sad that April's got herself into such a situation,' she said, her gaze drifting to April. 'I can only imagine how frightened and alone she must feel – but I honestly can't condone any of it.'

April pushed away from the table. 'I'm sorry, so sorry to cause such trouble. It's the last thing I wanted after you've all been so kind. I'll go and pack.'

'You'll be doing no such thing,' said Ron sternly. 'You'll sit back down, and tell us the truth. All of it, mind – right from the start.'

April hesitated, then after an encouraging nod and smile from Peggy, sat down. She steeled herself to face his stern gaze and told him everything from her first meeting with Daniel to the moment her mother had forced her to leave home.

'I wasn't brave enough to admit to Mother that I was having a brown baby,' she said finally. 'That would just have made things even worse and solved nothing.' Falling silent, she realised that the weight of her secrets and lies had lifted and she felt suddenly more able to cope with whatever came next.

'Oh, April, you poor girl,' sighed Peggy tearfully. 'How could any mother treat her daughter like that?'

April was watching Ron closely, waiting for his reaction. 'She's always been distant, so it was hardly surprising,' she murmured.

Cordelia, who'd remained silent throughout, shook her head and dabbed at her eyes. 'Some women shouldn't have children,' she said. 'But to be fair, April, it must have come as an awful shock to her.'

April dragged her gaze from Ron, who was still mulling everything over. 'Yes, it did, and although we've never been close, I felt terrible at having let her down so badly.'

Ron clattered the cup in the saucer and began to fiddle with his pipe. 'To be sure, wee girl, that's a sad story, and unfortunately it's one that's been repeated ever since the foreign troops came over in the Great War.'

April met his penetrating gaze in dread.

'I'm not condoning what you've done, but I'll not be punishing you for it by showing you the door,' he continued. 'To be sure you have a big enough burden to shoulder, and I'll not be the one to make it heavier.'

April breathed more easily. 'Thank you, Mr Reilly. You can never know how very grateful I am for your understanding.'

His expression softened. 'You'd better call me Ron, seeing as you're part of the family now. I'm not a man to stand on ceremony. But there is one thing that puzzles me,' he continued. 'Why choose to come to Cliffehaven of all places?'

April smiled. 'I came here as a child with my mother to stay with her brother. He's still living here, but I've yet to pluck up the courage to tell him who I am and why I've come.'

'So you've met him – talked to him – and he doesn't know who you are?' asked Ron.

April nodded.

'I can't say I approve of such subterfuge, but I suppose it's better not to jump in with both feet until you know what you've got to face.' His bright blue eyes regarded her thoughtfully. 'Who is this uncle? Perhaps I know him.'

'It's Stan Dawkins, the stationmaster.'

Ron chuckled as Peggy and Cordelia gasped. 'Well, I'll be blowed,' he said. 'I've known Stan man and boy – even knew his sister before she left for bigger and better things in London.' His eyes glinted with humour. 'So, Mildred Dawkins is your mother, eh? Well, well, well. That explains a great deal. It doesn't sound as if she's changed much – always did think quite highly of herself and her position in the world – rather like Peggy's sister, Doris.'

'But Stan has the softest heart and would never turn you away,' said Peggy.

'But I didn't know that for certain,' April replied. 'And I've had enough rejections over the past few months to last me a lifetime. I thought it best to get to know him first before I said anything.'

Ron nodded. 'Aye. That sort of news will be hard to swallow, even for Stan.'

April looked down at her tightly clasped hands. 'I saw him earlier and told him about meeting Shirley, and although he spoke kindly of her, I could tell he didn't really approve.' She took a deep breath. 'And then, of course, there's Ethel, and I have no idea how she'll take my news.'

'Aye, lass, you're wise to be cautious,' said Ron. 'Ethel's got a sharp tongue at the best of times and isn't fearful of calling a spade a shovel and speaking her mind.'

April nodded. 'I guessed as much when I met her,' she admitted. 'Now I'm not sure what to do.'

Ron finished lighting his pipe and threw the match into the tin ashtray he'd pinched from the Fishermen's Club. 'That, of course, is up to you, but if you want my advice, you should tell Stan the truth – and the sooner you do it, the better.'

'But surely I should wait until after the wedding? I would hate to cause ructions at such a sensitive time, especially if Ethel has strong ideas about such things.'

317

'Stan's a great believer in family ties,' said Ron. 'He was very hurt that Mildred didn't stay in touch after she'd visited with you all those years ago. And I know for a fact that those few days you spent here are something Stan has always treasured. I'm sure he'll manage to win Ethel round.'

'I don't think April should say anything until after the wedding,' said Peggy. 'Ethel is already tense and worked up over the arrangements, and something like this could just tip her over the edge.'

'I'm inclined to agree with you, Peggy,' said April. 'But you know Ethel better than I do. How do you think she'll react?'

'I really have no idea,' Peggy confessed. 'She can be brittle at times and as Ron said, is the possessor of a sharp tongue which she's not afraid of using. She was born and raised in the East End of London where there's a real mix of races and cultures, but how she feels about that, I don't know.'

Ron tamped down the tobacco in his pipe. 'I'll sound out Stan and see how the land lies – but not to worry, April, your secret's safe with me.'

'With all of us,' said Peggy firmly. 'The girls can be trusted to keep it all within these walls – but of course it won't be so easy once that little one is born.'

'Doctor Sayer and I have already made an appointment with the adoption people for next week,' said April. 'The baby won't be in Cliffehaven long enough to cause any scandal.'

'Oh, my dear, are you sure?'

'Yes, Peggy. Absolutely positive.'

'It's probably for the best,' murmured Cordelia.

'A baby needs two parents to love and nurture it and give it all the things a struggling single mother simply can't provide – especially with the added pressures from people like Mabel.'

'My thoughts exactly, Cordelia,' April replied softly.

'You might feel differently once it's born,' said Peggy. 'The bond between a mother and her baby is the strongest in the world – which was what made Shirley keep her baby.'

April shook her head. 'I've made up my mind, Peggy. It will be adopted, and that's an end to it.'

Peggy didn't look convinced, but she didn't press her point. 'I think we should tell the girls after tea,' she said instead. 'Do you want me to do it, April?'

She was warmed by her thoughtfulness, but shook her head. 'That's lovely of you to offer, Peggy, but I think that's my responsibility, don't you?'

'Aye,' said Ron. 'It is, but we'll be here to support you.'

The girls returned home from work to enjoy their evening meal, and in the lull that fell as they drank their tea afterwards, April took a deep breath and told them everything.

There was a mixed reaction following the initial shocked silence. Sarah, who'd been born and raised amongst the expats in Singapore, found it very hard to accept what April had done, for in her world, that racial line was very rarely crossed – and if it was, the perpetrators were shunned by society. It was clear that she and her great-aunt,

319

Cordelia, were of like minds, but as it was April and she'd become part of the household, they were willing to gloss over what she'd done and support her.

Rita and Ivy were almost casual in their acceptance that these things happened in wartime, and that she'd been very unlucky to be caught. Fran had agreed with them, even though her strict Catholic upbringing frowned upon such things, for she'd witnessed the same prejudices back in sectarian Ireland and had learned to accept during her nursing career that human nature didn't always stick to the rules.

As Ron nodded and Peggy squeezed her hand in support, April became tearful. She felt blessed to have found a home here amongst people who were willing to set aside their doubts and welcome her into the fold. Her secret would be safe within the walls of Beach View.

23

Shirley had telephoned April the following day, and over the next week they met up when their work shifts allowed – but they avoided the kiosk on the seafront. Shirley was nothing like Paula, but April suspected she would have approved of the friendship, for it was strengthened by their shared experience, and they both benefited from having someone to talk to whom they could trust.

Shirley hadn't been at all fazed by the fact

April's baby would be dark-skinned, and April discovered that she was a good listener, so freely discussed her fears and doubts over what she should do once her baby was born. The others at Beach View were being very supportive, but Shirley was the only one who really understood what she was going through and April was hugely thankful that fate had brought them together.

They were sharing a picnic lunch in Havelock Gardens, enjoying the warmth of the May sunshine while James slept peacefully in his pram and the birds sang from the branches of the surrounding trees. April had worked an earlier shift this morning to accommodate her appointment with the adoption agency, and Shirley had a day off from the factory, so they were making the most of the lovely weather.

'What time's your appointment, April?'

'Two-thirty. And I'm still not sure if I'm doing the right thing.'

Shirley grasped her hand. 'Only you can really decide what to do,' she said quietly. 'So don't let them steamroller you into signing anything until you're absolutely sure.' She gave April an encouraging smile. 'Would you like me to come with you?'

'Peggy's meeting me there, but thanks for the offer, Shirley.' She gave a deep sigh. 'I suppose it's best to get things organised now, but I won't really know how I'll feel until the baby's born.'

'That's the hardest part. Once you've held it, you're lost. They made me look after James for the ten days I was in hospital, and after that it would have been like ripping out my heart to hand him over.' Her expression was solemn. 'If you really want yours to be adopted, then my advice is to have nothing to do with it. Leave the hospital straight away, refuse to see it and sign the papers there and then. You'll be feeling weepy, but that's natural because your system's all mucked up, but according to all the leaflets it will pass.'

April nodded and regarded the rows of vegetables that had been planted amongst the few surviving rose trees. 'At least you have your mother on your side,' she murmured. 'I haven't heard from mine even though I've written to her twice.'

'Mum has been brilliant despite the fact she's terrified of Father finding out she's still in touch and sending me the occasional postal order. She's hoping to come down for a couple of days while he's inspecting factories in the Midlands, and I'm really looking forward to seeing her. The last visit was just for a few hours after James was born.'

Shirley visibly brightened. 'It was lovely to see her cuddling him and making a fuss of him, and I'm sure that if only she could persuade Father to unbend and accept what's happened they'd both be much happier. After all, James is their only grandchild.'

'It must be very hard for your mother.'

Shirley nodded. 'It is. She's torn between wanting to be with me and James and having to placate Father. She hates going behind his back, but she has no other choice if she wants to support me.' With a deep sigh, Shirley adjusted the light blanket over her sleeping baby. 'I'm their only child, and if I'd stopped to think how much anguish it would cause for everyone I wouldn't have been so utterly stupid and let my heart rule my head. It wasn't as if I was that naïve – I knew how babies were made, for goodness' sake.'

'We both did,' said April ruefully. 'And yet, here we are.' She looked at her watch and began to pack up their picnic 'I'd better get going. I don't want to keep Peggy waiting.'

'I'll walk with you as far as the High Street. There's a stack of nappies to wash, and my room needs a thorough clean. Mrs Jackson, my land-lady, is very particular about tidiness, and as she's been good enough to give me a room in her house, I don't want to upset her.'

They strolled out of the small park and walked up the hill towards the ruins of the old church on the corner. 'Good luck, April. I'll be thinking of you.'

'Thanks, Shirley. I'll let you know how I got on tomorrow after work.'

April watched her push the pram a bit further up the hill before turning into a side street towards her billet, which was a single room in a large house overlooking the recreation ground. Shirley counted herself lucky that she had managed to get any accommodation at all and therefore put up with Mrs Jackson's constant nagging for fear of being shown the door – and April knew how unsettling it was for her new friend to always be on tenterhooks.

Thinking about her friend's situation merely sharpened her resolve to have her own baby adopted. Life was difficult enough for Shirley; how much worse would it be if her baby had been black?

April shivered. She adjusted her coat over her bandaged arm, then headed up the High Street towards the imposing and rather forbidding council building where the Church of England Adoption Society had its office. She was doing the right thing – of course she was.

Peggy was already waiting for her and chatting to the young Home Guardsman who was standing looking very bored by the enormous piles of sandbags which protected the façade of the building. She caught sight of April and gave her a warm smile.

'I managed to persuade Rita and Ivy to look after Daisy for a couple of hours,' she said. 'They're going to take her to the playground and buy her an ice cream, which will no doubt end up down her front – but at least we'll be able to fully concentrate without her.'

'It's really kind of you to come with me,' said April.

'Not at all,' said Peggy airily. 'I couldn't possibly let you go through this on your own, and two pairs of ears are better than one – we're bound to get bogged down in all sorts of details and not take in half of it.' Her gaze was penetrating as she took April's hand. 'Are you all right, dear? Only you look very pale.'

April nodded, determined to remain calm and focused. 'I'm fine, really. Let's just get this over and done with, shall we?'

'Just remember that you're not alone, April. I'm here and will support you the best I can, and Evelyn Franklyn is a wise old bird after all the years she's been doing this, so you've no worries there.'

April followed Peggy up the concrete steps and into a vast, echoing hall that was tiled in red and dark blue and panelled with dark oak. Peggy gave April an encouraging smile before they headed up the sweeping staircase to the first-floor landing. Stretching into the distance on either side was what looked like an endless corridor of highly polished doors, each sporting the name of the department that was being run from behind it.

April followed Peggy along the line, their footfalls muffled by the deep red carpet as the portraits of past mayors and town councillors stared down at them from the panelled walls. It was as daunting as she'd expected, and April's pulse was beginning to quicken.

Peggy came to a halt. 'Take a deep breath, dear, and just remember that it's your decision in the end. No one can force you to do anything you don't want to do.'

April took the deep breath, but it didn't help much, and as Peggy knocked and pushed open the door, she wondered just how fast her heart could beat before it gave out altogether.

The office was much larger than she'd imagined, with long windows overlooking the High Street, an imposing mahogany reception desk and several comfortable chairs placed round a low table on which was a stack of well-thumbed magazines and newspapers.

'My name's April Wilton, and I have an appointment with Miss Franklyn,' she said breathlessly to the little grey-haired woman who seemed dwarfed by the enormous desk.

'If you'd like to take a seat, Miss Franklyn will

be with you shortly.'

They sat side by side on the sagging couch and Peggy reached for her hand. 'They have a good system here,' she said quietly. 'You come in this door, then into her office, and from there you go out through another door much further down the corridor. That way no one bumps into anyone. Discretion is key here, and they're very good at it.'

April regarded her with some surprise. 'But how do you know so much about it, Peggy?'

'I have a friend who came here a long time ago in the hope of adopting her brother's baby,' she replied. 'That sadly didn't work out, but by the look of things, this place hasn't changed much over the eighteen years.'

The far door opened and a pleasant-faced woman stepped into the room. She was wearing a sprigged cotton blouse and cream skirt beneath a pink cardigan, her greying hair was neatly brushed back into waves from her lightly made-up face, and the only jewellery she wore was a pretty brooch. 'Do come in. I'm sorry you were kept waiting,' she said in a mellow voice.

They followed her into the room to find that it wasn't furnished as an office at all, but was more like a comfortable drawing room. There were chintz-covered chairs surrounding a low table on which stood a carafe of water and glasses; there were pretty pictures of country scenes on the wall, and a huge vase of flowers stood on the desk that had been discreetly placed beneath the long window.

'Make yourselves comfortable,' said Miss Franklyn. She waited until they were seated and then looked at Peggy. 'It's nice to see you again, Peggy, although of course the circumstances are a little unusual. Are you related to Miss Wilton?'

Peggy smiled back. 'April's my evacuee, Evelyn. I'm here to lend her some support.'

Evelyn Franklyn chuckled. 'Still the mother hen, I'm delighted to see.'

She turned to April and picked up the notebook and fountain pen from the table between them. 'There's no need to be nervous, dear,' she said calmly. 'Anything said in this room goes no further – and nothing you may say will shock me. I've been doing this for almost forty years, and I very much doubt I haven't heard it all before.'

She smiled and settled back in the chair, the pen poised over the notebook. 'Why don't you begin by telling me about yourself?'

April's qualms were eased as the older woman's gentle voice led her through her family history, education and work experience. It was only when Miss Franklyn began asking questions about Daniel that she faltered. 'I really know very little about him,' she confessed. 'He proved to be a liar and a cheat, so I can't really say for sure if anything he told me was true apart from the fact he eventually revealed that he had a wife and children back in America.'

'That's not unusual,' Evelyn replied calmly. 'Just tell me what you think you know.'

April conjured up an image of Daniel and described his dark, honey-coloured skin, black hair and gold-flecked eyes. 'He said his mother was a native Indian and his father was a light-skinned African whose roots went back to the days of slavery. Judging by his bone structure and colour, I can assume that that at least was true,' she finished lamely.

'I know this is upsetting for you, but we need to know as much as possible so we can place your baby with the right people,' Evelyn said, pouring a glass of water for April from the carafe on the table. 'Were there any serious medical problems, do you know?'

April shook her head and Evelyn turned a page in her notebook before she began to question April about her health and that of her family.

'My father had no siblings and his parents were very elderly by the time I was born. Father died of a heart attack when I was little, and it was thought to have been caused by his experiences in the trenches during the first war.' April paused to gather her thoughts.

'Mother has an older brother who's in good health, but they did have a sister who died when she was a baby. I don't know why that was,' she finished lamely.

Silence fell as Evelyn wrote in her notebook before setting it aside and replacing the cap on her fountain pen. 'Are you fully committed to having your baby adopted, April? Because once the final papers are signed, you will never be permitted access to its records or be able to trace it.'

'I realise that,' she replied, 'but I think it would be best for the baby to have two parents who really want him – or her – and who will be able to provide a proper home. I've seen enough to know that life would be a real struggle for both of us if I didn't go through with this, and I don't

328

think that's fair on the baby, do you?'

'Have you talked this over with your mother?'

'I wanted to, but she made it very clear she had no interest in me or the baby.' April clasped her hands tightly in her lap and regarded the other woman evenly. 'I've discussed it with Peggy and my friend Shirley, who decided to keep her baby and weather the storm of disapproval even though it seems relentless. But I seem to go round in endless circles trying to decide what to do for the best. What's your advice, Miss Franklyn?'

'Your circumstances are not unusual, April, and some girls have taken the very brave step of keeping their brown babies. But you seem to be aware of the prejudice and unpleasantness this can cause,' she added with a sigh, 'and no matter how much the mothers love their babies, without support from family members, life becomes almost impossible for them. In many cases this results in older children being put into care – and they are much harder to place with adoptive parents. In my opinion, your child would fare better by being placed with a family already in a mixed marriage.'

'Are there such people willing to adopt a brown baby?' asked April tentatively.

'There are,' Miss Franklyn replied carefully, 'but they are in the minority, April.'

'Yes, I see,' she murmured. 'And what if no one wants my baby? What will happen to it?'

'There are foster homes and orphanages which will take your baby and look after it until a suitable family is found. The Church of England Adoption Agency prides itself on making sure that no child is placed with the wrong parents.'

April looked at Peggy for reassurance. 'What do you think, Peggy?'

'I think you should sign the first batch of documents to get the ball rolling,' she replied as she took her hand and held it tightly. 'That way, the Agency can start to look for the right people, so that when your little one is born, there will be someone there waiting to take him in.'

April nodded and turned back to Evelyn. 'If I sign these papers now, will that mean I can't change my mind later?'

Evelyn leaned forward and patted her knee. 'It's as Peggy said, it will merely start the search for suitable parents. Applicants have to be vetted very carefully, their homes inspected, their characters and medical history looked into, along with their lifestyle, habits and religion. This all takes time, April, so the sooner you sign these, the sooner we can begin.' She discreetly placed a form on the table between them.

April looked at the heading on that form, and suddenly everything came into sharp focus. This was real, so real that it made her heart skip a beat as all the doubts and fears returned.

She read every word and looked back at Evelyn. 'You promise I'm not signing my baby away with this?'

Evelyn's smile was soft. 'This is the first document of three. You will sign the second nearer to the birth to give us permission to present your baby to the adoptive parents, but they will have no right to keep the baby until the third document is signed six weeks after the birth. Only after that will you be relinquishing all your rights to your child.'

It all sounded horribly cold and callous, but feeling reassured that she was merely getting things started, and not giving up her baby even before it was born, April signed.

Evelyn nodded her thanks and carefully placed the document in a beige cardboard folder. 'I will telephone you at Peggy's when it's time to sign the second document,' she said. 'Now that things are on a more official standing, your doctor will keep me informed of your progress, and nearer the time, we'll meet again.'

She gathered up her notebook and pen and stood to indicate that the interview was over. 'If there are any questions you wish to ask then make a list and we can go through them then.' She pointed to the door on the other side of the room. 'If you go through there you won't have to go back into the waiting room, where I do believe I have my next appointment waiting,' she said quietly.

April shook her hand and headed for the door as Peggy said goodbye to Evelyn and hurried after her.

They walked in silence along the corridor and down the sweeping staircase to the entrance hall where April drew to a halt. 'What have I done, Peggy?' she managed through gathering tears.

'You've given some childless couple real hope that they will soon have a lovely baby to love and cherish and raise as their own,' she said softly before drawing April into her arms. 'It's a wondrous gift, April, and they will bless you for it.'

April sniffed back her tears and returned Peggy's hug before searching in her coat pocket for a handkerchief. 'I don't know how to feel at the moment,' she admitted. 'One minute I feel that I'm doing the right thing – the next I think I must be very wicked to give my baby away. It's not its fault – any of this – but mine. And yet he's the one being punished.'

'Now you're just getting worked up,' said Peggy firmly. 'Come on, dry your eyes and think properly, April. You're doing the best thing, really you are, and at times like these we have to remain clear-headed and practical – not get maudlin and over-sentimental. That baby will be loved and cared for, so it's no punishment – and you, well, you're still young and have the rest of your life ahead of you. It's a harsh lesson, April, but now you need to learn by it and do the best you can for you and that baby.'

April knew she was right, but the awful weight of guilt simply refused to leave her – and she wondered then if it ever would.

Despite his outward support of April during the past week, Ron had struggled to accept the situation, for like Fran, his upbringing in Ireland had been a strict one, the moral code adhered to through dire threats of hell fire from the priests and the intransigent opinions of society in general. This might be a different world – a world once more plunged into a war that brought uncertainty with every hour – but surely it was no excuse for turning from the lessons that had been drummed into them since childhood, for, to him at least, they were more important than ever.

He plodded along the undulating hills, his thoughts churning. Rosie had been correct when she'd said he was hardly the right person to judge anyone. He was a sinner, and an unrepentant one at that, but April's dilemma worried him on several levels.

Her arrival at Beach View had stirred things up and although, on the face of it, everyone seemed happy to support her, Ron knew there was a deep unease in Cordelia and Sarah, which caused some tension. Even his darling Peggy was struggling despite her determined smile, for he'd noted the worry in her eyes every time Shirley came to the house with her baby, and knew that the tittle-tattle had already started in the town – no doubt fanned by that sour-faced bitch Mabel.

And then there was his oldest and dearest friend, Stan, who was blissfully unaware that his blossoming friendship with April would soon force him to face an unpalatable truth, which could cause a huge amount of trouble for him, and for Ethel.

He reached the brow of the hill and looked back to check that Queenie hadn't been left too far behind – the damned cat still insisted upon accompanying him on these walks and managed somehow to evade all attempts to shut her indoors.

On seeing her fluffy tail waving above the grass, he breathed a sigh of relief and then turned to admire the view of the sparkling sea beyond the jutting white cliffs. It was the tail end of May and in three weeks' time Stan and Ethel would be getting married. Ron was glad the girl had taken Peggy's advice not to say anything until after the celebrations, for his old pal deserved to enjoy his special day before the proverbial hit the fan – but he wasn't too sure he wanted to be around when it did. Ethel could be a ticking time bomb.

He settled down on a tussock of grass while Harvey and Monty raced about like hooligans in search of something to hunt. He lit his pipe and waited for the now familiar sound of Queenie's miaow, and when he heard it, he gave a soft grunt.

'Damn fool cat,' he muttered affectionately as she insinuated herself against his legs. 'It seems I'm outnumbered by females with minds of their own and no regard for the opinions of a man who suffers terrible from the moving shrapnel.'

Queenie purred loudly, rubbing her cheek against his hand, and then settled down in a patch of sunlight to stretch luxuriously. Her tail fanned out behind her as she yawned and cleaned her pink paws before going into a doze, fluffy ears twitching at the slightest sound.

Ron contentedly smoked his pipe, watching the seabirds hover and swoop above the shore, and the tide begin to turn, bringing the waves further up the shingle at each roll. May had seen a turn in the tide of war too. Ron thought back over the developments of recent months. Despite the terrible toll of lost young lives, the Allied air forces had achieved great victories in the Mediterranean as well as in the heavy bombing campaign over Dortmund, Düsseldorf and Essen in Germany. With further air attacks on southern Italy and Sardinia, and growing support for the Allies in Argentina, it seemed that Germany was at last losing its grip, and that Italy could very soon change sides.

There had been retaliations, of course, with devastating raids on Torquay and Eastbourne, and accounts of utter brutality in Poland against the Jews in their ghettos. It seemed Hitler was determined to wipe them from the face of the earth, and there were appalling stories coming out of Europe about concentration camps and forced labour. And yet the breaching of those German dams in the Ruhr by Barnes Wallis's amazing bouncing bombs was a triumph of ingenuity and skill, and the thought that Peggy's younger sister Doreen might have played a very small part in that gave him an enormous sense of pride.

Ron looked at his watch, then scooped up a supine Queenie and gently placed her in one of his larger coat pockets where she settled back to sleep for the ride home. Since being spayed she'd put on weight and was now quite a large, glossy cat; queen of Beach View and all she surveyed and the undoubted nemesis of any other feline that dared encroach on her domain. She'd decided to accept Monty's presence – under sufferance, as he and Harvey came as a pair – but she didn't allow any liberty taking, and if his nose got too inquisitive, it would receive a right royal battering from those needle-sharp claws.

Ron strolled back down the hill and along to the Anchor, to return Monty to his home. Back at Beach View, he found the house deserted. Now he remembered that Cordelia had gone out with Bertram, and Peggy was with April at the adoption agency. He grimaced at the thought, his soft old heart going out to the girl. 'To be sure,' he muttered as he poured some milk in a saucer for

Queenie, ''tis a hard lesson for one so young. This world can be very cruel.'

He watched Queenie lap at the milk while Harvey gobbled down some biscuits and water, and then left them to sleep off their walk in the basement. Closing the back door firmly behind him, he set off for Stan's allotment. He'd promised to help him do a bit of hoeing, and it would provide the perfect opportunity to sound him out about his and Ethel's views on mixed-race babies.

Stan wasn't feeling too clever this afternoon. He'd been troubled with indigestion throughout the night and as the day had gone on, the heartburn had become even worse. He slumped into the deckchair outside his shed and stared morosely at his allotment as he swallowed the chalky antacid straight from the bottle.

It was the third bottle he'd gone through in a week, and the regularity and gathering strength of these attacks was finally starting to worry him. He couldn't afford to be ill, not with the wedding only three weeks away, and it was no good the doctor telling him to cut down on rich food and fried breakfasts – Ethel would think he didn't appreciate her cooking.

He gave a deep sigh and watched the friendly robin hopping about amongst his early vegetables. Ethel was a marvellous cook who managed to magic up things other people could only dream about during this time of shortages and strict rationing, and he was easily tempted, for he'd always loved his food, and it was a pleasure to have

336

a woman cooking for him again.

'Hello, Stan. What's this? Sitting down on the job?'

'Just resting for a minute, Ron.'

'Getting too much for you, is it?' teased Ron as he plumped down in the other deckchair. 'Get us a cup of tea then, and tell me what you want doing – although it all looks fairly shipshape to me.'

Stan set the kettle on the primus stove. 'April and Ruby came over to help yesterday,' he confided. 'Did a lovely job of weeding and burning the rubbish, too, and it was good to see how well they got on.'

'They're about the same age, and now Mike's been sent up to the wilds of some Scottish Isle, Ruby needs a pal to take her out of things,' said Ron comfortably.

Ethel appeared around the corner of the shed dressed in her working overalls and knotted headscarf, the usual fag stuck in the corner of her mouth. 'I'm sure your April's a pleasant enough girl,' she said. 'But I don't want my Ruby mixing with the likes of that Shirley.'

'Shirley's a nice girl,' protested Stan.

'*Nice* girls don't have babies without an 'usband in tow,' she retorted sharply. 'Are you making tea, Stan? Me mouth's as dry as a duck's arse after working in that factory all day.'

Stan smiled and kissed her cheek. 'Just waiting for the kettle to boil, my little flower. Why don't you sit down and relax?'

'I ain't got time to relax,' she said, gathering up scattered flower pots and setting them in neat

337

stacks by the shed wall. 'What with me 'aving to 'ave me dress taken in again, and Rosie to see about the last-minute arrangements, there ain't enough time to breathe, let alone sit down.'

Stan smothered a soft burp and wished he could sneak another few drops of his medicine, for the heartburn was making him feel decidedly sick.

Ethel looked at him sharply. 'You don't look right, Stan. You got indigestion again?'

'Just a touch, but nothing for you to worry your pretty head about,' he said lightly.

He made the tea and gave it a good stir in the pot before leaving it to draw and then nipped into the shed while Ethel was talking to Ron to have a surreptitious slug of his indigestion mixture. He could hear their conversation through the shed wall, and it made him feel uneasy, for Ethel was inclined to say things he didn't always approve of – and she was at it again now.

'Look, Ron,' said Ethel, 'I don't mean to be unkind, but your April needs to be careful who she mixes with. That Shirley's no better than she should be, and 'anging about with 'er ain't gunna do April's reputation no good. The gossip's already started, you know.'

'We've had that chat among the family,' said Ron calmly, 'and we decided we like her and her little boy, so if April wants to be her friend, then why not?'

'That's up to you, o' course, but where I come from gels know better than to get in the family way.'

'I think you're exaggerating, Ethel,' drawled Ron. 'Girls and boys are the same the world over, and accidents happen – even in the East End.'

'Not in my neck of the woods, they don't,' retorted Ethel. 'They wouldn't bleedin' dare. If some girl in our family went that way she'd be thrashed by her dad and thrown out on the streets. We don't 'old with that sort of carry-on.'

'That sounds very harsh, Ethel,' protested Stan, emerging from the shed. He poured the tea.

'Yeah, it might to a soft old sod like you, Stan, but the fear of God and a beating from yer dad is usually enough to keep the gels on the straight and narrow.' She flicked the ash off her cigarette and stuck it back in her mouth with a grimace. 'Course, there's some what won't be deterred by nothing, but at least we ain't got khaki babies down 'ere in Cliffehaven – yet.'

'A baby's a baby regardless of their colour,' said Stan mildly, 'and innocent of any sin their parents might have committed. I really do think you should be a bit more charitable, my darling.'

'I speak as I find, Stan. The world's gone to 'ell in an 'andcart, and I ain't afraid to say so.'

Stan didn't agree with Ethel – and by the look on Ron's face, neither did he – but he wasn't about to continue the argument, for he knew he'd only come off the worse for wear and he was feeling lousy enough already. He decided to change the subject.

'I hope you've got your best suit all sorted for the wedding,' he said to Ron.

'Aye, but there's time enough yet to be worrying about such things.' Ron regarded him from beneath brows that had become unruly again. 'Have you been to the doctor about that indigestion,

Stan? Only you don't look right.'

Stan nodded. 'He gave me something for it. I didn't sleep well last night, that's all – worrying over all the wedding arrangements and wondering if my replacement on the railway for the day is up to the job. He's been retired for fifteen years and his eyesight isn't much good. I just hope he can cope.'

'The railway people wouldn't have employed him if he couldn't cope,' said Ron. He slurped down the last of his tea and got to his feet. 'Well, if you don't need me to do anything, I'd better get back home.'

'Thanks anyway, Ron. See you for dominoes later on. And don't be late.'

'Will we be planning a wee drink or three before the wedding, Stan? You can't be getting hitched without a drop or two inside you, and I'd be failing in me best man duties otherwise.'

'We'll have a couple at the Anchor on the night before – but I don't want a late one, Ron, or to be waking up with a blinding hangover.'

'I'll sort something out with the others then,' he replied cheerfully, 'and warn Rosie she'll need to get some more beer in.'

'You mind you don't get 'im 'alf cut and staggering,' warned Ethel. 'I want 'im sober and in one piece at the church.'

Ron nodded to her briefly, pulled on his cap and ambled off, his thoughts churning over Ethel's diatribe. It had left an unpleasant taste in his mouth. If Ethel should ever discover the truth about poor little April's baby, it could destroy Stan's happiness and wreck any chance of reconciliation with his niece. After today, it was more important than ever to keep April's secret safe.

April was aware that everyone knew where she and Peggy had been today, and as she was feeling particularly low, she was grateful that none of them badgered her with questions. She didn't have much appetite either, but with a war on and rations becoming tighter every week, she knew better than to waste any of her supper, so she forced it down and tried to look as if she was enjoying it. However, as the chatter went on around her she was isolated by her thoughts and the implications of those papers she'd signed this afternoon.

'Just leave it, love,' murmured Peggy. 'I can see you don't really want it.'

'But it's such a waste.'

Peggy shook her head. 'Nothing goes to waste when Harvey's about.' She patted her hand and gave her an encouraging smile. 'Everything will sort itself out, April, you'll see,' she said quietly beneath the excited chatter around the table.

April made a stoic effort to dredge up a smile and tune in to the conversation around her, which had now turned to Stan's wedding and the clothes the girls had been sewing ever since they'd received their invitations. Like everyone else during this war, they'd had to make do with what they could find, and the four girls had managed to cobble together something special for the, occasion out of what they had in their various cupboards. As April listened, she realised she had nothing remotely suitable to wear, and would be

341

in her sixth month of pregnancy by then. It would probably be best if she stayed at home that day.

'I found something in my wardrobe that will be perfect for you,' said Peggy as if she'd read April's thoughts. 'It's a navy dress and jacket that my sister Doris passed down to me and that I've never had the chance to wear. It was always a bit big for me, you see, and although I meant to take it in and alter it, I never had the time.'

'I don't know if I should go to the wedding at all,' April said hesitantly. 'I'll probably be the size of a barrage balloon by then anyway.'

Peggy smiled. 'I doubt it,' she murmured. 'You're not half the size I was when I was five months gone with Daisy, and you don't want to miss out on Stan's wedding, surely?'

'I do feel I ought to go. There should be someone from the family, but...'

Peggy pushed back from the table. 'That's settled, then. Come on, let's see how that outfit looks on you.'

'Are you sure you don't mind lending it to me?'

Peggy laughed. 'I wouldn't have offered it if I wasn't.'

April followed Peggy into her bedroom, where Daisy was snuggled in her cot on the brink of sleep, her thumb in her mouth, the silky end of the light blanket clasped in her tiny fist as a comforter. The sight of the sleeping child stirred disturbing emotions in April and she determinedly looked away to watch Peggy unhook a hanger from the wardrobe door.

'Take it upstairs and try it on,' she whispered, 'and if it's all right, then come and show us. If not, I'm sure one of us can sort something out.'

April closed her bedroom door and took a quavering breath to steady herself before she slid the linen cover from the dress and jacket. The navy blue reminded her sharply of her time in the WRNS, but she refused to let that put her off, for the linen was of good quality, the cut and stitching immaculate and the jacket very smart with white piping and pretty silver buttons.

She stripped off the skirt and blouse that through necessity had become her uniform over the past week, eased off the sling, and stepped into the dress. The silky lining was cool against her skin, the hem reaching to just below her knee. She struggled a bit to thread her plastered arm through the armhole and then had an awful tussle with the buttons at the back. She gave up, and set aside the narrow white belt that came with the dress. It would merely emphasise her thickened waist and rounded stomach.

Slipping on the black pumps she'd bought the day before with her first wages, she pulled on the three-quarter-length jacket, and regarded her reflection in the dressing-table mirror with a critical eye. The dress was loose enough to hide her bump and the jacket draped perfectly as an added layer of camouflage. The colour was flattering, and all in all, she didn't actually look too bad.

Despite all that had happened today, she felt a flutter of pleasure, for this would be her first social event since she'd been thrown out of the navy, and because it would be Stan's wedding day, it made it even more special.

She went down to the kitchen and twirled in

the doorway to a chorus of praise. 'I just hope it will still fit in three weeks' time,' she said, blushing, 'and someone will have to do me up on the day. I can't reach the buttons with one hand.'

'Don't worry,' said Peggy, 'I'll help with those if your plaster cast isn't off by then.'

'I have a hat that will look just right with that,' said Cordelia from her armchair. 'I'll put it in your room when I go up to bed.'

'Oh, thank you, Cordelia, that's very kind.'

'I've got some fake pearl earrings you can borrow,' said Ivy, 'and a necklace. They were only cheap, but they look quite posh.'

'And I've got a small black clutch bag I brought over from Singapore,' said Sarah, looking up from the book she was reading. 'You're welcome to borrow it for the day, if you'd like.'

'I'll do your hair,' piped up Fran, 'and help with your make-up. We've got to make a real effort for Stan on his special day.'

April regarded them all with the deepest affection and once again thanked her lucky stars that she'd found such a warm and loving home in her hour of need.

24

A week had passed since Ron had quietly confided in Peggy about Ethel's rather shocking attitude to unmarried mothers and khaki babies, and she'd been fretting about it ever since. They'd decided that as the baby would be adopted and April had agreed not to tell Stan about her pregnancy or who she was until after the wedding, it was probably best not to say anything to April just yet.

However, Peggy knew that April was struggling with the knowledge that she'd taken the first step towards giving her baby away. Fran had noticed it too, and they'd done their best to listen and comfort her when things became overwhelming. The fact that Stan was also a sympathetic listener and that April had taken to seeing him most days was very worrying. The girl was clearly on edge with having to keep their relationship a secret, and Stan was very persuasive when it came to winkling out the truth of what ailed those he cared about. Peggy began to feel she was walking on eggshells, for the whole situation could erupt at any moment, and she didn't have the first idea of how to handle the fallout.

The tension had become so great that she decided she needed to escape it all. That Friday morning she would do something she would never have contemplated before: she was going to leave Daisy with Ron and attend her first Women's Institute meeting.

The WI was something she'd managed to avoid until now, for she had little in common with the snooty women who ran the Cliffehaven branch, and she usually had better things to do than sit in on lectures about how to make jam – which was on a par with teaching your grandmother to suck eggs – but today she needed her mind taken off all her worries, and to spend some time out of the house.

In the draughty drill hall, the speaker was burbling on about how to make sure that only the very best fruit should be picked for jam, and how to ensure that the jars were thoroughly sterilised before using them. Since Peggy had been making jam for as long as she could remember, she tuned out of the speech and surreptitiously regarded the women surrounding her. They were mostly middle-aged, with some very elderly ones nodding off in their chairs, waiting for the lecture to come to an end so they could have their cup of tea and a slice of cake.

The chairwoman was Marjorie Gardener, the spinster sister of Vera who ran the telephone exchange, and although she was a pleasant woman most of the time, she too had once been a schoolmistress and old habits clearly died hard, for she was inclined to be rather bossy and hectoring when determined to get her own way.

Peggy's gaze trawled the room. Lady Chumley, or 'Lady Chump Chop', as everyone at Beach View called her, was in the front row, wearing a very expensive hat and a mink wrap to ensure that everyone knew how important and rich she was. Beside her were the equally overdressed cronies who formed her special clique – they were well-to-do women who did a vast amount of fund-raising for good causes, but rather spoiled the charitable aspect by boasting about it to all and sundry.

They were also the women who'd shunned poor old Doris when Ted caused a scandal by having an affair with the woman who worked on the fish counter in the Home and Colonial Store. There had been a slight easing in their frostiness when it

346

was thought Ted might return home to Doris, but that had fizzled out when Ted refused to do any such a thing and gave Doris all the evidence she would need to file for divorce. Their decree nisi was due any day.

Vera Gardener was on the far side of the room, sitting next to Clarice Hughes, who'd once taught games at the same school and now lived with her cat in a rather nice maisonette situated in the maze of streets behind the town hall. Peggy had always suspected that Vera and Clarice were more than just friends, but as it was none of her business what went on behind closed doors, she didn't give it much thought. The rest of the women were ordinary, decent folk who kept the home fires burning while their husbands and children were doing their bit, and Peggy recognised most of them, for they'd been locals all their lives.

She tuned back in to the lecture when sugar was mentioned, and perked up considerably as it was announced that the WI had been granted extra rations of the stuff to help them make their jam and cakes so they could raise more money by selling their produce. Now, that was worth coming for. She didn't mind a bit of extra jam-making and baking if she could keep some of it for herself.

Marjorie Gardener thanked the speaker and everyone politely applauded. This woke the elderly ladies, stirring them into a rush for the tea table. There was a bit of a scrum and Peggy waited patiently for her turn in the disorderly queue, hoping there would be enough Victoria sponge to go round.

'Is it always like this?' she asked Vera, who'd come to stand beside her.

'Unfortunately the sight of cake stirs the most gentle of souls,' she replied. 'But as there is always enough to go round, it's all rather pointless.'

Peggy was relieved to see she wasn't accompanied by her revolting dog – no doubt poor April was having to look after it until Bertha took over. She'd finally reached the table and had helped herself to a lovely slice of cake and a cup of tea when Vera stilled her hand.

'I'd like a quiet word,' she murmured. 'Now, if you don't mind.'

'Oh, dear, there's nothing wrong, is there?'

Vera remained tight-lipped as she indicated they should sit away from the others. Filled with trepidation, Peggy perched on the very edge of the wooden chair, the teacup rattling in the saucer. 'Whatever is it, Vera?' she muttered nervously.

'It's about April,' she replied, her thin lips barely moving. 'I'm rather concerned, and I thought you might be able to clear things up.'

Peggy played for time by sipping the very hot, milky tea and then placing the cup on a nearby chair. 'Concerned?' she hedged. 'Isn't she doing her job properly?'

'She's extremely efficient,' said Vera, 'and if Mrs Downes wasn't due to return in two weeks' time I would have had very little hesitation in asking her to stay on.'

Peggy had a nasty feeling she knew where this was going, but said nothing in the faint hope she was wrong.

Vera leaned closer, her voice barely above a murmur. 'I'm not blind, Peggy. Neither am I stupid. The girl is in a certain condition, isn't she?'

'It's not really up to me to discuss April,' babbled Peggy. 'And as she'll only be with you for another couple of weeks, I hardly see how it matters one way or the other.'

Vera pursed her lips. 'Your defence is admirable, but it does confirm my suspicions,' she said solemnly. Her grey eyes regarded Peggy with perhaps a hint of regret. 'I cannot condone such things, Peggy. I have my standards – as does the Post Office. If my employers were to discover that one of their telephonists was, shall we say, in an interesting condition and unmarried, it could cause the most frightful fuss and jeopardise everything.'

'They won't know if you don't tell them,' said Peggy hopefully.

Vera held her gaze for a long moment and Peggy began to feel like a recalcitrant child, caught in her glare of disapproval.

'I have been placed in a very awkward position, Peggy.'

'Yes, I can see that,' she stuttered. 'And I'm very sorry. But please let her stay, Vera, it's so very important to her.'

Vera's frosty expression softened. 'Your caring nature is a credit to you, Peggy, and I'm not a teller of tales. Unfortunately, Bertha is an entirely different kettle of fish. She has taken a dislike to April for some unfathomable reason, and with her sharp eyes and vicious tongue, I can see only trouble ahead.'

'But you can't dismiss April because of Bertha,'

gasped Peggy. 'It wouldn't be fair.'

There was another long silence as Vera thought about this, and Peggy waited on tenterhooks.

'I'm not an unkind person,' Vera murmured finally, 'and although I don't approve of her circumstances, I do value April as an employee.'

'So?' Peggy was holding her breath.

'I won't dismiss her unless I absolutely have to,' Vera said on a sigh. 'But be warned, Peggy. If Bertha says anything, I will have no other option.'

Peggy let out the breath she'd been holding. She'd always suspected Vera was a fair and down-to-earth woman behind that rather bossy façade. 'Thank you, Vera,' she said warmly. 'I do appreciate how difficult things are for you, and I want you to know that April and I are extremely grateful for your understanding and kindness.'

'There's no need to get fulsome, Peggy,' she replied with the ghost of a smile. 'April is a foolish girl who should have known better. But I do sympathise with her plight – people can be far too judgemental, and don't always know the true facts before they rush in with their condemnations and spread vile gossip.'

Peggy saw a fleeting dart of pain in those grey eyes and wondered if Vera and Clarice had suffered from gossip and innuendo, and came to the conclusion that they probably had. 'It's always the same, war or not,' she sighed. 'I do wish more people would look at the mess the world is in and learn to embrace a gentler, more understanding view on things.'

'That's unlikely,' Vera replied. 'There will always be gossips and nosy parkers to stir up trouble.' She

350

set aside the cup and saucer and became brisk. 'To that end, I have come up with a plan.'

'What sort of plan?'

'It's clear that April and Bertha must be kept apart, and although it will mean changing shifts round, which April might find a bit inconvenient, it's the only way forward.' She folded her hands primly in her lap. 'Would April be prepared to do the very early morning shift from five until one-thirty? Then I could take over until Bertha comes in at three-thirty.'

'I'm sure she wouldn't mind if it meant keeping her job,' said Peggy. 'But won't that make things awfully difficult for you?'

'Not at all. I don't sleep well at the best of times, and there are rarely any calls during the night unless there's a flap on up at Cliffe aerodrome.'

Peggy smiled. 'Then I'll have a word with April tonight.'

Vera nodded and slipped on her overcoat. 'Get her to telephone me this evening after eight o'clock, and we'll organise things for tomorrow. Better to start straight away, I think.' She gathered up her handbag and gas-mask box. 'Now I must be away. Clarice and I are going to the matinee at the cinema. They're showing *Casablanca.*'

Peggy watched her stride away and then lit a cigarette to go with her cooling tea. Vera had been very understanding considering her age and reputation for being a stickler for correct behaviour – and if it wasn't for that beastly busybody Bertha, they would never have had to have that awkward conversation. Now poor little April, who already had enough on her plate, must face the fact that her secret was out and for the next two weeks she'd be working the most unsociable of hours.

Peggy mulled everything over, stubbed out her cigarette and wrapped the untouched slice of cake in a paper napkin to take home. She returned her cup and saucer to the tea table and quickly left the hall before she got roped into doing the washing-up.

Shirley was working at the factory until late today, so April strolled up to the station to see Stan once her shift was over. A cup of tea and a biscuit would go down well after being shut in the exchange with smelly old Winston all morning, and she needed to stretch her legs and breathe fresh air.

Afternoon tea with Stan had become a bit of a ritual, and she was looking forward to quietly talking with him and helping him care for his vegetables and flowers. It was so peaceful up there on the allotment, and it was very easy to imagine that they weren't at war when the sun shone, the birds sang, and the scent of the roses drifted in the air.

'Wotcha, April.' Ruby stuck the garden fork into the ground, eased her back and brushed her hand across her sweaty face, leaving a smear of dirt.

April grinned back. 'Hello, Ruby. Looks like you've been busy.'

She dragged the knotted scarf from her head and used it to wipe her hot face. 'I've weeded and hoed until I'm fair worn out,' she said, stuffing the scarf in her overall pocket and shaking out her dark hair. 'Now I gotta get washed and be off to work. Mum and me are on the late shift now until next weekend.'

'Oh, that's a shame. I was hoping we could have a cuppa together.'

Ruby's smile was rueful. 'Yeah, I'm sorry too, but I got wages to earn so I can save up for me bottom drawer.'

'Have you heard from Mike?'

Ruby nodded as she washed her hands under the standpipe. 'He's bored rotten, poor ducks. There ain't nothing up there but sea birds, rocks and fish. But the other blokes are a good bunch by the sound of it, the locals are friendly, and the whisky never seems to run out, so I don't really know why he's moaning.'

She dried her hands on her overalls and lit a fag. 'If you're wondering where Stan's got to, he's due back any minute from the doctor's.'

'Why? What's the matter with him?' April asked in alarm.

Ruby shrugged. 'Dunno, do I? But I suspect it's 'is indigestion. I keep telling Mum to lay off the rich food and fry-ups, but she won't listen.'

'Perhaps if the doctor told her what it was doing to him, she might,' said April.

'You know Mum,' Ruby said with a shrug. 'Well, I'll be off, see you tomorrow.'

April returned her cheery wave and set about making a fresh pot of tea for Stan when he got back. She hunted out the tin of biscuits, and while she waited for the kettle to boil, she sat in the deckchair and enjoyed the calm and warmth of this early June day.

His booming voice broke the silence as he greeted his fellow allotment holders, and before

April could stir the tea in the pot he'd made his way through the vegetable patches to his shed. 'Hello, dear,' he said with a jolly smile. 'I see you've got the kettle on. That's a good girl.'

'Ruby had to get to work,' she said as she let the tea stew for a while, 'so you'll just have to put up with me for a bit.'

'That's no hardship.' He sank into the other deck-chair and took off his cap. 'In fact, it's a pleasure to have you to myself for a change.'

April poured the tea and added just a few grains of sugar for Stan, mindful of his ever-expanding girth. 'Ruby said you went to the doctor's,' she said, sitting beside him.

'The old indigestion was playing up, so I thought it was time to sort it out once and for all,' he replied airily. He sipped the tea and grimaced. 'I suppose I'm going to have to get used to no sugar in my tea from now on,' he muttered dolefully. 'In fact the doc says I've got to cut down on all the things I like if I want to stay alive. Proper put the wind up me, it did.'

'Then you must do as he says,' she urged him. 'You and Ethel are about to start a new life together, and think how awful it would be for her if anything happened to you.'

He gave a deep sigh. 'Yes, I know, you don't have to read me the riot act – the doc's already done that.'

His brown eyes regarded her solemnly. 'It's Ethel I'm worried about, though. She loves to cook, and enjoys putting on a spread for me.'

'Ethel would rather have you by her side for years to come, and as long as you explain clearly what the doctor has said, I'm certain she'll do all she can to help you.'

Stan nodded, sipped his tea and then looked back at her. 'And what about you, April? Who's going to look after you once that baby's born?'

April felt the heat suffuse her face and she couldn't look at him. 'How did you know?' she whispered.

'I've got eyes in my head, April love, and have just been waiting for you to say something.' He put his large hand over her fingers. 'I know a troubled girl when I see one, April, and it seems to me that you need to lighten that burden.'

His hand was comforting, but still she couldn't look at him. She wanted desperately to confide in him, but she felt so ashamed of her lies and subterfuge that she didn't know where to begin. 'Everyone at Beach View knows,' she admitted softly, 'so I have had someone to talk to.'

'That's good. I've always been a great believer in sharing troubles.'

April swallowed hard and finally found the courage to meet his gaze. 'Stan, there's something I have to tell you. I don't know if it's the right time to do it, or whether it will change things between us – but I can't keep it to myself any longer.'

'There's no fiancé, is there?' he said gently.

She shook her head. 'No. But that's not all,' she murmured. 'I've lied to you, Stan, and for that I am truly, truly sorry.'

He frowned and looked back at her, his hand still tightly clasping hers. 'Then it's best we clear the air, don't you think?'

She saw no condemnation in his eyes, merely

355

kindliness, and she knew then that she could trust him. 'When I came to Cliffehaven, it was because my mother's brother had written to her and suggested we stay with Peggy over his wedding celebrations.'

Stan's eyes widened and he leaned back in the chair and stared at her for a moment. Then he chuckled and finally burst out laughing.

'So you're not cross?' she stammered.

He mopped his eyes with a large handkerchief. 'Cross? How could I be when you've made me the happiest man alive?' He struggled out of the chair and pulled her into his arms. 'Oh, April. Why didn't you tell me straight off? You must have known I would never turn my back on you.'

'I couldn't,' she admitted, emerging from his bear hug close to tears. 'I didn't know if you'd changed or what your circumstances were – and how you'd react to the fact that I'm unmarried and pregnant.'

'Oh, you poor child,' he groaned. 'What a terrible burden you've been carrying.' He wrapped his arms around her and held her close. 'But it's all right now,' he murmured. 'Everything will be all right now you've got your Uncle Stan to look after you.'

April clung to him as her tears soaked through his uniform jacket and shirt. She felt as if she'd come home at last – that she'd found someone who truly cared for her, and who would be an intrinsic part of her life from now on.

They reluctantly drew apart, feeling a bit foolish about the emotional reunion which had no doubt been witnessed by everyone on the allotment.

Stan chucked her under the chin and grinned broadly. 'Let's drink our tea and get to know one another properly. If I'm to be that baby's great-uncle, then I have a lot of catching up to do.'

'Oh, Stan,' she said on a sigh. 'I won't be keeping the baby.'

'Why ever not? That baby's a part of my family, and although it might cause a bit of a stir with Ethel, it belongs with us – just as you do. No baby will be given away, not while I have breath in my body.'

April burst into tears again, sank into the deck-chair and covered her face with her hands. 'It's not that simple,' she sobbed.

He ran his hand over her head and gently drew her towards him. 'Then you'd better tell me why that is,' he said softly.

'My baby ... my baby will be brown,' she said in a rush as her tears flowed.

He was silent for a long moment and she didn't dare look at him for fear of seeing disgust on his face.

Stan cleared his throat and tightened his grip on her shoulder. 'Well, that could put the cat amongst the pigeons, certainly,' he breathed. 'But that baby's still part of our family, and come hell or high water, I'm determined you should keep it.'

April stared at him in wonder and rising hope. 'But what about the scandal it will cause? And then there's Ethel to consider. She'd have to agree to such a thing.'

Stan nodded thoughtfully. 'Good point – about Ethel, I mean – I couldn't care less about the scandal.'

'But *she* might, Stan – and you have to think how keeping the baby will affect all of us. This is a small town, and girls like me are routinely shunned and abused – look at how Shirley's been treated. Think how very much worse it will be when people realise my baby's brown.'

'Aye, I hadn't thought of that.' Stan fell silent, his gaze fixed on a distant point at the end of the allotment.

April's soaring hopes slowly dwindled as common sense took over. It would have been wonderful to keep her baby, to nurture and raise it in a loving home with her Uncle Stan's support – but he or she would forever bear the stigma of illegitimacy, and his colour would set him apart.

She took a shuddering breath and reached for Stan's hand. 'I would love to keep my baby,' she said softly, 'but it would be selfish to do such a thing. My baby deserves to have two loving parents who are experienced in this world where colour and differences matter so much, and who can give him a solid identity without the stresses of being raised in a white family.'

Stan sniffed back his tears but remained silent.

She squeezed his fingers. 'It's not an easy decision, Stan – in fact it's the hardest thing I've ever had to do – but adoption is the right way forward.'

His eyes were red as he turned to look at her. 'You might feel very differently when it's born,' he managed gruffly.

April nodded. 'But I have to think what's best for him. It's the only way.'

He looked down at their clasped hands and

then regarded her tearfully. 'You'll have to be very brave,' he rasped.

She took a shuddering breath. 'I know, but as long as I have you to turn to, we can get through it together.'

He patted her cheek. 'You have my promise on that, April.'

She kissed his cheek and they sat there in silence for a long moment, absorbing all that had happened and coming to terms with it. She turned to him eventually. 'What will you tell Ethel?'

He sighed deeply and slumped back into the chair. 'I will tell her that you're my niece and that you're pregnant. As you seem so determined to have the baby adopted, there's no reason to go into any further detail.'

April regarded him steadily, wondering if his reluctance to tell Ethel everything had something to do with her view on illegitimate brown babies. Suspecting this might be the case, she didn't probe. The poor man had had enough for one day. 'Then that's what we'll do,' she said softly.

The relief in his expression proved she'd been right, and as he gave her a watery smile and squeezed her fingers, her heart went out to him. He was a lovely, gentle man, and she felt blessed that she'd found him again.

The telephone rang just as Peggy was mashing the potatoes to go over the shepherd's pie. Leaving the task to Rita, she hurried into the hall and got to the receiver seconds before Ron.

'It's me, April. I'm ringing from the station.'

Peggy frowned. 'What are you doing there?'

'Uncle Stan and I have had a long talk about everything and he's asked me to stay on and share his supper as Ethel's on late shift. I should be home by nine, but don't worry if I'm not – we have a lot to catch up on,' she continued breathlessly.

Peggy's heart raced and she exchanged glances with Ron as she gripped the receiver. 'Did you tell him everything?'

April was clearly aware that Bertha was probably listening in. 'Yes,' she replied shortly.

'And Ethel's at work, you say?'

April was quick on the uptake. 'Yes, and that's all taken care of, Peggy. I'll explain when I get home.'

Peggy was hugely relieved to hear that, but she had other things on her mind. 'There's something I must tell you,' she said urgently. 'It's nothing bad, I promise, but it is important. Could you make sure you're not too late?'

There was silence at the other end, but Peggy could have sworn she could hear a second person breathing down the line. 'Just be home by nine,' she said firmly. 'That's all I can tell you at the moment.' She was about to disconnect the call when she changed her mind. 'And I'm delighted everything has worked out with Stan. See you later.'

She replaced the receiver and turned to Ron. Their eyes met and in that silent, tense moment they shared one thought. Was Stan capable of keeping such an important secret from Ethel?

25

April had tried to thank Vera for being so kind, but the older woman had merely told her she'd been a silly girl to get into such a dilemma, and that no more should be said about it. The early mornings hadn't proved to be too onerous, and as her time at the exchange was drawing to an end, April was simply grateful to still have a job. As for Bertha, their paths no longer crossed, and any suspicions she might have harboured had been nipped in the bud by Vera's clever planning.

The two weeks had flown since that emotional meeting with Stan, and although Ethel had made it patently clear that she didn't approve of April's subterfuge or her pregnancy, it seemed she was more concerned with Stan's health. Great changes had been wrought at mealtimes since Ethel had put him on a strict diet, and Stan tried to put a cheerful face on things, but April could tell that he was utterly miserable, and suspected he sneaked a biscuit or two while on his allotment.

Lucinda Downes had returned to Cliffehaven so it was April's final day at the exchange. It was one of mixed emotions for she would miss coming here each day; miss having something important to do – and even miss Vera Gardener. And yet her plaster cast was due to be taken off today and there was Stan's wedding to look forward to tomorrow.

A caller came on the line, and as she connected him, Vera came into the room carrying a tea tray. 'I thought you should have something before you go to the hospital,' she said. 'The tea they have in there is like dishwater.'

April thanked her and they sipped the tea in silence until April had to disconnect a call and then put another through. She smiled at Vera as her last few minutes at the exchange ticked away. 'It will feel strange not coming in any more. I won't know what to do with myself all day.'

'I expect Peggy will find something to keep you occupied,' said Vera. 'But it'll be so much easier for you once that plaster is off.' Her smile was unusually warm. 'It's good timing too, what with your Uncle Stan's wedding tomorrow.'

April smiled back at her. She wasn't such a bad old stick once you got to know her. 'It seems Stan's told everyone that I'm his niece.'

'You're family and he loves you,' she said matter-of-factly. 'And for Stan, family's the important thing. Everything else can take care of itself.'

April finished the tea, took one last call and removed the headphones. She knew Miss Gardener wouldn't appreciate any emotional sort of farewell, so stuck out her hand. 'Thank you again for everything, Miss Gardener. I really appreciate all that you've done for me.'

The older woman warmly shook her hand. 'Goodbye, April, and good luck.' Before April could reply she'd taken her place before the board and was settling the headphones about her ears. 'Just make sure you close the front door securely. I don't want Winston to get out.'

April pulled on her cardigan and headed for the door. Winston eyed her balefully from the front room, and she closed the door firmly on him and sighed. Her working days were over until the baby was born, and after that... She shook her head and strode away from the exchange, determined to face whatever fate had in store for her with courage.

Peggy's day had been filled with chores, and she was grateful to Ron for taking Daisy out, as it meant she could really get on. She'd scrubbed out the bathroom and kitchen, put fresh linen on the beds and even cleaned the windows, for there was something about a lovely June day that energised her and made her want her home to sparkle.

She nodded with satisfaction as she squeezed out the mop, for the hall tiles looked lovely when they were clean, and then carried the bucket out to Ron's water butt.

'For goodness' sake, Peggy,' said Cordelia from the depths of her deckchair, 'sit down and draw breath. You've been on the go all day.'

'I've still got Daisy's outfit to iron, and then there's tea to organise, and the button to sew back on my skirt which I meant to do last night,' she replied, emptying the bucket and stowing it with the mop in the scullery.

'You'll run yourself ragged and be in no state for tomorrow,' said Cordelia sternly.

'I'll be fine. It's Ron I'm worried about.' Peggy plumped down on the doorstep and lit a well-earned fag. 'If he and the others consume as much beer as they usually do on such occasions, we'll have him rolling home at dawn, and dead to the world until lunchtime.'

'Then you'd better make sure he has something hearty to line his stomach before he goes out.'

'Mmm. I just hope Stan doesn't go overboard after doing so well on Ethel's diet. It would be a shame after she's worked so hard to get him well.'

'I'm sure one night off the wagon won't hurt him,' said Cordelia. 'Ethel will soon bring him into line again.'

They both looked up at the sound of the latch on the back gate and saw April waving her hands in the air. 'Look,' she called in delight, 'no plaster.'

'How does it feel?' asked Peggy once she and Cordelia had inspected the slightly pale and withered arm.

April laughed. 'Rather strange, as if my arm's so light it will just float away.'

Peggy smiled and patted her cheek. 'It's lovely to see you so cheerful, dear, but now I must get on with putting the final touches to our tea.'

'I'll help you,' April replied quickly and they went up the steps into the kitchen, leaving Cordelia to bask in the late afternoon sunshine.

Ron stumped home soon after, and Peggy's concern over lining his stomach was eased by the fact that he'd treated himself and Daisy to fish, chips, peas and pickled onions at the local British Restaurant. He'd washed it down with three cups of tea and four slices of bread and margarine, and was ready for anything – which in itself was rather worrying, for Peggy knew Ethel didn't want Stan arriving at the church hungover and looking like death warmed up. Peggy and April got on with making a pie with the scraps of fish Ron had managed to buy from Fred that morning, and once they'd topped it with a generous layer of mashed potato, it was placed in the slow oven to cook through.

'I'll look after Daisy for you if you want to go to Ethel's party,' said April as they joined Cordelia in the garden for a cup of tea and watched Daisy playing in the old bathtub Ron had converted into a sandpit.

'I'm not going to that,' Peggy replied. 'It's for the factory girls, really, and not my cup of tea.' She smiled at April. 'But thanks for the offer, dear. I might take it up another time.'

'Please do,' she replied earnestly. 'You've done so much for me and I want to repay you somehow.'

'There's no need for that,' murmured Peggy. 'I do what I do out of love, and don't expect anything in return.'

As April took the tea things into the kitchen Peggy sat in the last of the sunshine and mulled over all that had happened in the past few weeks. The confirmation that Ethel could be downright nasty when it came to girls like April and Shirley hadn't come as too much of a shock, for Peggy had long suspected Ethel was that way inclined. Thankfully, Stan had managed to keep his mouth shut, but Peggy was concerned by his blindness to Ethel's faults, and his willingness to sweep any unpleasantness under the carpet and pretend it didn't exist.

She shifted in the deckchair, her thoughts making her restless. Stan was a loving, open-hearted man who was simply trying to protect those he loved, but keeping secrets from Ethel – especially such momentous ones – was not the best way to begin a marriage.

She finished her cigarette and crushed it beneath her shoe. Ethel had become very frosty where April was concerned, despite the fact that Stan was clearly delighted to have his niece back in his life and wanted them all to live in harmony. Her whole attitude had grated on Peggy, to the point where she simply couldn't go to that party tonight and laugh and talk and pretend that everything was all right. And yet it was the knowledge that Stan was probably making the biggest mistake of his life that really upset her, and she was dreading tomorrow's wedding.

'That tickles,' giggled April as she stood on the kitchen chair the next morning.

Fran continued to draw a pencil line down the back of her leg. 'To be sure, April, it will be worth it. But you must keep still.'

April endured her attentions and then gratefully clambered off the chair. The other girls were still waiting for the gravy browning solution to dry on their legs, and they were standing about the kitchen in their dressing gowns with their hair in rollers, rifling through each other's make-up bags in the faint hope they might find the end of a lipstick or a bit of eye shadow and mascara. Rationing meant that make-up was in short supply and cost lots of coupons, so everyone was in the same boat.

'Have you got any beetroot, Peggy?' asked Ivy.

Peggy looked up from where she was ironing Ron's best shirt. 'Beetroot? Whatever for?'

'It's a brilliant substitute for lipstick,' Ivy replied with a giggle. 'And if you're really clever, you can even use it as rouge.'

'Well, I've heard it all now,' said Cordelia, having admired her newly stained legs. 'When I was a girl we used to use strawberries or raspberries to give our lips a bit of colour. Lipstick was very frowned upon, you know.'

The girls giggled and teased her while Peggy hunted out a jar of beetroot she'd preserved the previous year. 'Just don't spill it,' she warned. 'I'll never get the stains out.'

April was relaxed and happy amid the bustle and chatter. It reminded her of her days in Portsmouth when everyone was getting ready for a party. She experienced a momentary pang of sadness as she thought of Paula and then determinedly focused on the present. This was her Uncle Stan's wedding day, and nothing must be allowed to spoil it. She would even attempt to soften Ethel's attitude towards her, though going by the way she'd been these past couple of weeks, she suspected it might be a lost cause.

Stan opened his eyes and groggily took in the familiar rafters and plasterwork of his bedroom ceiling. At least he'd made it home last night, he thought gratefully, but he did wish he hadn't drunk quite so much. It was the whisky chasers Rosie had provided at the end of the rowdy evening that had done the damage and now there was an entire band of drummers marching in his head.

He rolled over and struggled to focus on the bedside clock. When he saw that it was almost eleven, he threw back the bedclothes and leaped to his feet. He swayed alarmingly as the room spun and his head pounded, and he sank back down again until he felt steadier.

Dragging on his dressing gown and gingerly making his way down the narrow staircase, he tottered outside to find his day replacement sitting on a garden chair being closely watched by the cat as he ate what looked like a marmalade sandwich. 'You should be on the platform waiting for the eleven o'clock,' he said to the elderly man, whose eyes looked huge behind the very thick lenses of his spectacles.

'And you should be having a wash and shave and preparing for your wedding,' he replied with a wry smile. He studied Stan from head to foot as he munched his sandwich. 'It strikes me someone had a real skinful last night.'

'Yes, well, a man doesn't get wed every day,' Stan muttered. 'Ethel would kill me if she saw me now.'

'I can't say I'd blame her,' he muttered, wrapping the rest of his sandwiches in newspaper and stuffing them in the pocket of the oversized uniform jacket. 'You leave the trains to me and concentrate on how you're going to get through the rest of the day alive,' he said gruffly before plodding down the path to the station.

Stan ran trembling fingers through his hair, yawned expansively and turned back into his kitchen, almost tripping over the cat as it shot past him. There didn't seem to be any recurrence of his indigestion, which was a blessing, but his head was still pounding. 'A cup of tea and a couple of aspirin will soon sort me out,' he muttered.

He silenced the cat's strident demands by filling its bowl and then set about trying to sober up. Turning on the cold tap, he ducked his head and gasped as the icy water hammered down. He shook his head and dried it vigorously with a kitchen towel and then made a pot of tea. Leaving it to brew a bit while he used the outside lav he then cleaned his teeth in the kitchen sink and gargled with a peppermint-flavoured mouthwash in the hope it might sweeten his breath and unfur his tongue. Feeling a little better, he sat down to enjoy his tea and mull over the night before – or at least what he could remember of it.

Rosie had laid on a terrific spread at the Anchor, no doubt helped by Ethel having raided the factory canteen kitchen, and Stan had well and truly broken his diet. Ron had rounded up all his old pals, including Chalky White, Fred the Fish and Alf the butcher, and they'd supped their beers and reminisced with stories of their youth, the parts they'd played in the last war, and all the adventures they'd had since. Fran had come in to play a few Irish jigs with the help of some of the visiting servicemen, and there had been a great deal of laughter and a feeling of warm comradeship as they'd competed at darts, dominoes and shove-ha'penny in their favourite corner by the inglenook.

Stan smiled at the memory despite his headache. It had been a grand do, but he was certainly paying for it this morning.

Ron was feeling surprisingly sprightly considering he hadn't got to bed until after two this morning, and had certainly drunk his share of the beer and whisky. He'd risen at five and taken Harvey for a walk – the cat decided she was not going out at that silly time of the morning – and after a brisk walk over the hills, had returned home and cooked himself a large breakfast of egg, Spam and fried bread, followed by a gallon of tea and a stack of toast.

The house was in chaos as six females dashed about, bickered over whose turn it was in the bathroom, and who'd pinched the last of the hairspray, so he and the animals had taken themselves off to the peace and quiet of the basement bedroom, glad to be out of it all.

Ron brushed back his thick, greying hair, smoothed his shaggy brows down with a wet finger, and regarded his reflection in the fly-spotted dressing-table mirror he'd balanced on his chest of drawers. Peggy had pressed his suit and tie and he was wearing a freshly ironed white shirt. His shoes had been polished to a shine, but unfortunately he couldn't find a matching pair of socks, but as black was very similar to dark blue, he didn't think anyone would notice.

He winked at his reflection. 'Ach, to be sure you're still a fine figure of a man, so y'are,' he said. 'The ladies had better watch out today.'

Queenie paused mid-wash of her glossy coat and eyed him with disdain, and Harvey snorted as if he didn't approve of Ron's showboating.

'You'll be minding the house today,' Ron informed Harvey sternly. 'Weddings are no place for a fine fellow like you.' He grabbed his freshly brushed dark blue fedora – it was actually Jim's, but as he was in India, he'd surely not mind him borrowing it – and hurried upstairs to the kitchen.

'I'll be off to Stan's,' he said to Peggy who was wrestling Daisy into her best dress while she threw a tantrum. 'We'll see you at the church.' Before Peggy had time to reply or think up some sort of job for him to do, he ordered Harvey to stay in the kitchen and firmly closed the scullery door behind him.

Upon his arrival at the stationmaster's cottage, he didn't bother to knock, but strode straight in. There was no sign of Stan, although the teapot and china on the draining board revealed that he'd made it out of bed at some point this morning. 'Stan! Stan, where are you?'

'Up here trying to get these blasted buttons done up,' he yelled back.

Ron plodded up the stairs to find Stan out of breath and red-faced as he stood in the middle of the room in his shirtsleeves, his best suit trousers at half-mast. 'To be sure that's not a pretty sight at this time of day, Stan, my old friend,' he muttered, taking in the glaring white underpants and equally white thighs.

'I thought they'd fit now I've lost almost half a stone,' he moaned. 'What am I going to do, Ron?'

Ron hauled up the trousers and tried to get them to meet beneath the overhang of Stan's belly, but it was patently clear he was not going to get those fly buttons done up. 'I'll hold onto the waist and you do up the ones you can,' he suggested.

Stan struggled and fumbled, but he couldn't

get more than one button done up.

Ron eyed the situation and thought for a moment. 'Have you got any elastic, and some safety pins?'

Stan was sweating from the effort of trying to hold in his stomach and do up the buttons. 'If I have, they'll be in Barbara's sewing box,' he gasped, tilting his chin towards the top of the wardrobe.

Ron stood on a stool and after fumbling about for a bit located the sewing box. He rifled through it, and found a length of broad knicker elastic and a handful of rusting safety pins. 'Right,' he said, advancing on Stan, 'I'll fasten the elastic to the waistband with some of these pins, and use the others to try and keep you decent at the front.'

'You're a real pal, Ron,' sighed Stan.

'Aye, to be sure, Stanley Dawkins,' he muttered through a mouthful of safety pins, 'it's only a real pal who'd be willing to be on his knees pinning flies together when good drinking time is being wasted.'

'Watch what you're doing down there,' warned Stan in alarm as Ron wielded scissors and pins.

'If you stood still it would be easier,' grunted Ron. 'To be sure, Stan me old pal, 'tis a good thing these trousers have broad seams, so it is.' Having pinned the elastic firmly to the outer edges of the chasm left in the waistband by Stan's stomach, Ron folded open the seams of the fly so it covered the white expanse of his underwear and began to pin them firmly together. When he'd finished, he rested back on his heels to survey the result.

'How does it look, Ron?'

The trousers now had more metal in them than an armoured tank, but it all seemed to be holding, and luckily Stan's stomach masked the makeshift repairs. 'You'll pass muster as long as you don't eat anything or go for a pee,' he replied. 'And whatever you do, don't sit down too quickly. You'll put too much strain on that lot and risk getting stabbed if the pins give out.'

Stan hitched his braces over his shoulder and gingerly tested the trousers out by doing a few gentle knee bends. 'Thanks, Ron. I wish I'd tried them on when Ethel told me to, and then I wouldn't have this worry. It's no wonder my indigestion is playing up again.'

Ron made no comment, for he suspected it had more to do with the lashings of beer and the mound of Rosie's delicious food he'd got through the previous night than worries over his attire. He waited for Stan to slip on his suit jacket – which mercifully fitted as long as he didn't try and fasten the buttons – then followed him down the stairs.

Dipping into his own suit jacket he held out a brandy flask. 'Take a sip of this,' he advised. 'It'll settle your stomach and put hairs on your chest.'

Stan grimaced and shook his head. 'I had enough booze to sink a battleship last night, Ron. That would be a step too far.' He reached over to the vase on the window sill and plucked out the two perfect red rosebuds he'd picked the previous day.

With the rosebuds safely pinned into their button-holes the two old friends grinned at one another and awkwardly embraced. 'Thanks for getting me home last night,' muttered Stan. 'I'd never have made it on my own.'

'Ach, get away with you. That's what friends are for.' Ron regarded Stan with affection and could only hope that his old pal wasn't about to make a terrible mistake by getting himself hitched to Ethel. Deciding Stan was old enough and ugly enough to know his own mind, he gave him a hearty slap on the shoulder. 'Ready?'

'As ready as I'll ever be,' he replied, his nervous fingers running over the phalanx of safety pins.

'Then let's be off. Don't want to keep your bride waiting, do we?'

Stan put on his best black hat and chuckled. 'No fear.'

They left the cottage and set off at a comfortable pace for the church. It was just past one, so even if there was a malfunction with the pins they'd still have plenty of time until the service at two-fifteen.

'Are you nervous?' asked Ron as they ambled past the children's playground.

'No. Ethel's the one for me, and I can't wait to marry her.'

'I wish it was that easy for Rosie and me,' Ron said dolefully. 'But perhaps, one day, you'll get the chance to be my best man.'

'I'd be honoured,' Stan replied and then drew to a halt. 'I want to say how much I value your friendship, Ron, and how very grateful I am for all you and Peggy have done for my little April. She's going to find the next few months tough going, but I know you'll watch out for her.'

Ron felt a bit embarrassed and shrugged. 'No need to get soppy, Stan. She's one of us now, and we'll do right by her.' He glanced across at his friend. 'You've done very well to keep things to yourself regarding the baby's colour,' he said solemnly. 'So don't get carried away with the wedding and such and spoil everything, will you?'

'I know when to keep my mouth shut, Ron – there's too much at stake to get careless. I just wish Ethel would accept her. It would make life so much easier,' Stan sighed.

'She'll come round eventually,' soothed Ron, although he had grave doubts about that. Ethel was not the sort of woman to suddenly change her mind about anything.

They walked on and soon came to the rather ugly Victorian church which stood amid the surrounding houses in a bleak plot of land that had been concreted over. There was no churchyard or lychgate, merely a grey stone memorial to the dead from the first war which was adorned with a single and very weathered wreath.

They shook hands and chatted to their friends who were standing round the side of the church away from prying eyes so they could smoke and pass round brandy flasks. Ron saw Peggy, Cordelia and the girls talking to Bertie as Daisy tottered about between their legs, and he nudged Stan. 'Your April looks well in that outfit Peggy lent her. She's a pretty girl, Stan, much like her mother was at that age.'

'Thankfully she's nothing like her mother,' rumbled Stan, who'd succumbed to a drop or three of brandy to bolster his courage. 'And once all this is done and dusted, I shall be telephoning my sister and giving her a piece of my mind.'

Ron was about to reply when the vicar appeared and the guests began to filter into the cold, gloomy church. 'How are you holding up, Stan?' he asked, shaking his hand. 'I hear you had quite a night of it at the Anchor.'

'I'm fine,' he insisted, anxiously running his fingers over the safety pins before hurriedly drawing his jacket over his stomach. 'But I'll feel a whole lot better once Ethel gets here.'

The vicar muttered platitudes and gently eased him towards the church door as the organist played something soothing and the guests found somewhere to sit and gossip while they waited for the ceremony to begin.

Ron gripped Stan's arm and firmly steered him towards the front pew. He was concerned that his old friend was sweating quite heavily and his breathing had become ragged. 'Are you all right, Stan?' he asked quietly.

'The nerves have got to me at last,' he confessed. 'I think I'll have another nip of brandy, if you don't mind.'

Ron wasn't convinced that more brandy would help. 'Sorry, Stan, the flask's empty after Chalky took his last nip,' he fibbed.

'Never mind,' he replied, smiling fondly back at April and the other girls who'd slid into the pew behind them, 'I don't really need it.'

Ron turned round to greet Peggy and Cordelia, who were just sitting down with Daisy between them, and as he looked at all the women in his life he felt blessed. They were a grand bunch, and the prettiest in the church.

He was distracted by a hubbub at the back of the church which was swiftly followed by a great crashing of chords as the organist began to fumble her inexpert way through the wedding march. 'This is it, Stan,' he muttered as they stood. 'There's no escape now unless it's through the vestry.'

Stan looked a bit green around the gills and shot him a sickly smile. 'I couldn't run even if I wanted to.'

Ron steered him towards the vicar who was standing by the altar steps, and although he could feel Stan trembling, his colour was a mite better and a quick glance confirmed that the elastic and pins were holding.

Ethel made a regal entrance on the arm of the rather handsome Fred Gough – an older man who'd retired some years ago from the RAF and was now in charge of maintenance on the factory estate. She wore a pale blue silk dress and coat she'd had made from a purloined parachute which had been dyed to match her satin shoes. Her little veiled hat was a darker shade of blue and she carried a posy of roses gleaned from Stan's allotment. Ron nodded in approval for Ethel had a terrific pair of legs and certainly scrubbed up well.

He glanced at Stan, who was watching her progress down the aisle with unashamed adoration, and breathed a sigh of relief that he seemed to have recovered from whatever had ailed him momentarily, and would get through the service.

Ruby shot Ron a naughty grin as she followed her mother up the aisle, and Ron noted that she too was looking very fetching in what had clearly once been a ball gown of stiff, pale pink taffeta which had been cleverly converted into a most attractive knee-length day dress that Rosie would have loved to own. The outfit was enhanced by a jaunty straw hat decorated with flowers and she carried a posy of Stan's roses.

Ron rarely set foot in a church these days unless it was for something like this, and he was grateful that the service didn't drag on for too long. The happy couple took their vows; he managed not to lose the ring or drop it as he handed it to Stan, and then the congregation sang 'All Things Bright and Beautiful' while the register was signed. Before he knew it, there was another crashing of chords and he was walking beside Ruby as the wedding party made their triumphant way back down the aisle.

The church bells rang out joyously, and the happy couple posed for photographs on the church steps. Peggy and Cordelia, who always loved a good cry at weddings, dried their eyes and happily chattered to the other guests as Daisy tottered back and forth to gather up bits of confetti and try to eat them.

Ron took himself off to a quiet corner to enjoy his pipe and let them get on with it, thankful that his Heath Robinson attempt to keep Stanley decent for the day was still holding together. He wished Rosie could have come, for occasions like this weren't the same without her at his side, but she would be busy at the Anchor making sure everything was prepared for the afternoon reception, and he would see her soon enough.

Doris had refused to lend Stan her car for the occasion and Bertram's was in the garage being repaired after he'd run into a lamppost in the blackout. Peggy's car had been put into storage for the duration, and as hard as he'd tried, Ron couldn't get hold of any tyres to replace the old ones which had been chewed by mice and were as flat as pancakes. Having no other option, and thankful that it was a lovely fine day, everyone set off to walk the short distance to the Anchor.

Ron waited until everyone had left and then quickly ducked home to collect Harvey. He wouldn't be missed.

He arrived at the Anchor at the same time as Stan and Ethel, and noted that the rest of the guests were strung out up the road with Cordelia and Peggy bringing up the rear with Daisy in her pushchair. He waited for them and winced as he heard the wheels squeaking.

'I did ask you to oil them, Ron,' Peggy chided without rancour. 'They're making the most appalling racket.'

Ron promised he would see to them later and then helped Cordelia down the steps and got her settled in her chair where she had a good view of everything. He looked around for Rosie, but she was fussing over everyone and so he helped himself to a glass of beer and waited until he could get her alone.

He finally caught up with her as she went out the back to get more sherry glasses. He slid his arm around her waist and gave it a squeeze.

'Hello, my darling,' he murmured appreciatively. 'You're looking especially lovely this afternoon.'

She giggled and kissed his cheek. 'That's more than can be said about you last night. I didn't think you'd make it out of here, let alone escort Stan home and get back to Beach View.' She smiled into his eyes as she wiped her lipstick from his smooth cheek. 'But you do look handsome today, and I admire your close shave. Very kissable.'

He pulled her closer and kissed her to shouts of encouragement from the rest of the party. 'We'll continue this conversation after that lot have gone home,' he said with a wink.

'I doubt you'll be in a fit state for anything much by then,' she teased, 'but we'll see.' With that she hoisted up the carton of glasses and shot off.

Rosie had done them all proud, thought Ron as he finished his meal. Following the delicious pea and ham soup there had been roasted chicken and potatoes with spring greens and leeks, followed by bread pudding which had been drenched in fruit, demerara sugar and thick custard. Wine and beer had flowed, and there were even a few bottles of champagne set aside for the toasts and the cutting of the magnificent cake which took pride of place on a side table. How on earth Ethel had managed to filch that much icing, fruit and marzipan was a mystery.

Remembering suddenly that he was expected to give a speech, he urgently patted his pockets for the slip of paper he should have brought with him. There was no sign of it, and he gave a sigh of annoyance as he realised he'd left it on his bed. He'd just have to wing it – like he did most things these days.

The chatter and laughter grew louder as the alcohol began to take effect, and as cigarettes and pipes were lit and people surreptitiously eased their feet out of tight shoes and loosened belts, it was time for the speeches. Fred Gough who'd given the bride away was clearly delighted to share a bit of the day's limelight, and seemed to enjoy the sound of his own voice. Everyone was getting restless by the time he proposed a toast to the bridesmaid.

The applause was generous, perhaps out of relief that he'd finally shut up, and then it was Ron's turn.

He stood and smiled at everyone. 'I'll not be making a long speech,' he said. 'Because I left it back at home.' This was greeted with laughter. 'I just want to say that I've known Stan man and boy, and if I was to tell you about the things he got up to over the years, we'd be here all night.'

As everyone chuckled, he smiled beatifically at the radiant couple through an alcoholic haze. 'I'm delighted that he's found such happiness with Ethel, and I wish them a long life and happiness together.' He raised his glass. 'To the bride and groom.'

Stan swept Ethel into his arms for a smacking kiss and made her hat slide over her eyes. This was greeted with laughter and a few ribald remarks about their wedding night.

Stan rose from the table and waxed lyrical

about his love for Ethel, his pride in Ruby, and the joy with which he'd welcomed April back into the family fold. He blithely ignored Ethel's glower at this and thanked Rosie for a wonderful spread; his friends for their dubious influence the night before; and Ron for the excellent way he'd handled being his best man.

He raised his glass. 'Here's to Ethel, Ruby and April – and all the rest of you wonderful, wonderful friends. I salute you.'

The glass was almost at his lips when his hand faltered and his smile faded into a frown. The glass shattered on the flagstones and Stan clutched at his chest with a look of utter astonishment. He staggered and the astonishment turned into a grimace. And then, with a deep groan, he slowly toppled like a felled tree and landed with an almighty crash on the floor.

26

In the stunned silence that followed Stan's collapse everything seemed to go into slow motion. April stared dumbly at the sprawled figure on the floor, unable to make sense of what she was seeing, as people half rose from their chairs and Ron appeared to wade through an invisible sea to get to his old pal.

Ethel's piercing scream galvanised them all and everyone started shouting as she fell to her knees and threw herself across Stan.

April was at the far end of the table with Ruby and they both rushed to Stan's side just as Fran pushed her way through the crush of people now surrounding him. 'Get off him, Mum,' Ruby yelled, grabbing her arm and pulling her away. 'He can't breathe with you on top of 'im.'

'He's dead,' she screamed, clinging to him and trying to shake him awake. 'My Stan's dead.'

'He's not dead,' said Fran in a commanding voice. 'Stand back, all of you, and give me some room – and Ruby, get your mother away. Now.'

Ruby was having the devil's own job trying to pull Ethel away, so April grasped her other arm and tried to help.

Ethel wrenched her arm from April's grip, her face full of hatred. 'Get yer 'ands off me, you filthy slag,' Ethel yelled. 'It's your fault my Stan's dead, and I'll kill you for this.'

April dodged the clawed fingers, shocked at the venom spewing from Ethel.

Ruby grabbed her mother more firmly and gave her a sharp shake. 'Stop it, Mum. You ain't 'elping. Just sit down and shut up while Fran takes a look at 'im.'

'He's dead, he's dead,' moaned an overwrought Ethel, collapsing against Ruby with a pitiful wail.

'Someone run down to the hospital and get an ambulance,' shouted Fran above the hubbub, 'it'll be quicker than phoning – and give Ethel a brandy.' As Rita went flying out of the door, Fran and Ron rolled Stan onto his side, checked that his airway was clear and kept a finger on the pulse in his neck. 'He's not dead, Ethel,' she said evenly. 'Please try and stay calm.'

'That's no thanks to you,' snarled Ethel, glaring at April through her tears. 'If you 'adn't come down 'ere flouting yer condition to all and sundry 'e wouldn't've been so anxious these past weeks.'

'I'm sorry, Ethel,' replied a stricken April. 'But he seemed to be all right about it. Really he did.'

'Yeah, well I know better,' she yelled, jabbing a finger at her. 'He were worried sick about the trouble you'd cause – and now look what you done!'

April could only stare at her in bewilderment and disbelief, for Stan had shown no sign of worrying about scandal – and she was horrified at the thought that she could have in some way been the cause of today's collapse.

'I'm sorry, April,' murmured Ruby above her mother's wails. 'She knows it ain't your fault really. She's just in shock and doesn't know what she's saying.'

April had no reply, for Ethel had been bottling things up for weeks and now, in her fear and shock, the truth of her feelings had come pouring out.

'Come on, April,' said Peggy. 'We all need to calm down and give Fran some room while we wait for the ambulance.'

'Was I to blame?' she asked tearfully.

'Of course you weren't,' soothed Peggy, steering her and the others from Beach View to the far end of the room. 'Ethel's just being hysterical.'

April sat down next to Cordelia as the other guests slowly moved away from the stricken man and formed little groups, their voices muted, their expressions solemn as they listened to Stan's ragged breathing and waited for the ambulance. Rosie brought a pillow and blankets downstairs to cover Stan as Fran continued to monitor his pulse and Ron knelt at his side, his face quite grey with anxiety.

April sat in mute distress while Peggy got the men to shift the table and chairs away from Stan, and the women to rally around Ethel so that she stopped that awful wailing and calmed down. There was nothing anyone could do, and the wait for the ambulance seemed interminable.

And then the clanging bells heralded its approach and it screeched to a halt outside the Anchor.

There was absolute silence in the pub as the doctor examined Stan and spoke quietly to Fran. Then, like the parting of the Red Sea, the gathering shifted and Stan was placed on a stretcher and loaded into the ambulance. Ethel and Ruby clambered in, the doors were slammed shut and it roared off back down the road.

'Well done, Fran,' murmured Peggy. 'Stan's very lucky you were here, because I doubt anyone else would have known what to do.'

Fran lightly shrugged off her praise. 'I suspect Ron would have coped,' she replied, glancing across to where he was shakily downing a nip of brandy. She looked around at the stunned guests. 'Poor Stan,' she sighed. 'And poor Ethel. What a thing to happen on your wedding day.' She grabbed her handbag and gas-mask box. 'I'll go to the hospital and keep you posted. Better everyone stays here and not turn up in Casualty – the staff have enough to do.'

As Fran slipped out through the door Rosie tapped a spoon against a wine glass. 'I'll let you know as soon as there's any news,' she said, 'but for now I think we ought to raise a glass to Stan and Ethel and wish them the very best of luck.'

Glasses were filled, the toast given with heartfelt emotion and slowly the conversation stuttered into a muted flow. However, the mood of the day had been ruined and as time went on and still there was no news from the hospital, people began to drift home.

April sat with Peggy, Cordelia and the other girls, none of them sure what to do for the best, but reluctant to leave until Fran telephoned with news. April couldn't dismiss Ethel's accusation and, although she realised Ethel had been hysterical with fear and grief, her words ate away at her as time slowly passed. She wanted desperately to see Stan, and all this sitting about not knowing what was happening at the hospital was absolute torture.

'I'll go and help Rosie with the clearing up,' she said to Peggy. 'I can't bear doing nothing.'

'I feel the same,' she replied, and they went across the room to where Rosie was reluctantly clearing away the detritus of the abandoned wedding table. Ron and his pals were huddled in a solemn group nearby, so April got them to carry the magnificent cake upstairs with a warning to stow it away well out of reach of the dogs. Then, while Ron cleared all the bottles away, Fred, Alf and Chalky stacked the extra chairs and carried them back into the cellar as their wives helped the barmaids wash and dry the many glasses.

The bunting and paper streamers hanging from the rafters and the balloons bobbing in clusters from above the inglenook and bar seemed suddenly highly inappropriate, so it was agreed that they should all be taken down. Within minutes there was little sign of the celebrations but for a few tiny pieces of confetti that drifted across the flagstone floor as a sad reminder.

The blackouts were drawn against the twilight, most of the guests had gone home and another pot of tea had been made by the time Fran came through the door. Everyone fell silent, waiting breathlessly to hear her news.

'He's had a heart attack,' she told them. 'But the prognosis is good and the doctor doesn't see any reason why he shouldn't make a full recovery – as long as he takes better care of himself. Ethel and Ruby are with him now, but he's heavily sedated, so it's best to leave visiting until tomorrow.'

'But he will pull through, won't he?' asked an anxious April.

Fran nodded. 'He'll have to stay in for quite a while so he can rest and recoup, but there's no reason to think the worst. The doctor will put him on a really strict diet, though, and weigh him regularly. It was the added weight that caused this, April, no matter what Ethel said, so please don't take it to heart.'

'Do you think she'll let me visit him?'

'Stan's already asked to see you, so I don't think Ethel has much choice in the matter.' Fran patted April's hand in sympathy. 'None of this was your fault, April,' she soothed, 'and I'm sure that once Stan's back to his old self Ethel will come round.'

April very much doubted that, but now was not the time to voice her opinion on Ethel's outburst. Regardless of the fact she'd been less than friendly over these past two weeks, April felt terribly sorry for her. It was an awful thing to happen at the best of times, but for it to ruin their wedding was a terrible blow.

And yet it was Stan she truly worried about, and the memory of him lying helplessly on the floor like that made her want to weep. She'd come to love and admire him so much and he'd been happy, full of the joys of life and looking forward to a sunny future with his new wife. Now she could only pray that he would indeed recover.

'Will she be going back to the cottage tonight as they'd planned?' asked Peggy.

Fran shook her head. 'She'll stay with Ruby until he's safely on the mend.'

'That's probably for the best,' murmured Peggy. 'Oh dear, poor Ethel. We must all rally round and make sure she's coping.'

There was a general murmur of agreement before Alf, Chalky and Fred said their goodbyes and escorted their wives home. The residents of Beach View sat in silence round the table by the inglenook, each with their own thoughts of Stan, unwilling to leave this snug, familiar place where so many memories had been made.

'I should probably telephone my mother,' April murmured to no one in particular.

'There's not much she can do to help Stan from Tunbridge Wells,' said Peggy.

'I know. But I think she ought to be told. Just in case...'

The words hung between them and Peggy's eyes were dark with sorrow as the awful possibility overshadowed them. She finally blinked and made a concerted effort to remain clear-headed and practical. 'Go and do it now before everyone gets home,' she advised. 'It'll be quieter.'

April gathered up her things, said goodbye to the others and headed for Beach View. Mildred probably didn't give a hoot about her brother's health, and April didn't really relish the thought of having to talk to her at all – but she couldn't in all conscience keep such news from her.

Queenie came to greet her at the back door demanding to be fed, and once April had filled her saucer and replenished her water bowl, she shrugged off her coat and went into the hall.

Glancing at her watch, she realised Bertha would still be on the switchboard, and would no doubt be listening in. But she didn't want to leave the call until tomorrow – doctors didn't always get things right and she'd never forgive herself if anything happened to Stan before Mildred had been warned. Her hand trembled at the thought as she lifted the receiver, and her voice was unsteady when she gave Bertha her mother's number and waited for her to answer.

'Mildred Wilton.'

April gripped the receiver. 'Mother, it's me.'

'I'm just about to go out to dinner,' Mildred said impatiently. 'What is it?'

'It was Uncle Stan's wedding today,' April said through gritted teeth, 'and unfortunately he's been

389

taken ill.'

'Well that's a shame, I'm sure. But what do you expect me to do about it?'

'I don't expect you to do anything,' April replied shortly. 'I just thought you should know that Stan's had a heart attack and is in hospital.'

'Heart attack?' Mildred's tone sharpened. 'How bad is it?'

'The doctor's hopeful he'll recover. But he will be in hospital for a while yet.'

'He never did look after himself properly,' said Mildred crossly. 'I suppose he's still fat?'

April took a deep breath and tamped down on the rush of anger. 'I just thought you should know what's happened,' she said. 'I'm sure he'd appreciate a visit if you could find the time.'

'There's no need to take that tone with me,' snapped Mildred. 'You know how difficult it is to get anywhere these days – and as you're already down there, it would be very little hardship for you to keep me informed of his progress.'

'I'll ring when I have any more news,' said April and disconnected the call before she said something she might regret. How any two siblings could be such opposites confounded her.

Feeling restless and utterly useless, she fetched her coat and went up to her bedroom. Stripping off the borrowed clothes and placing them back in their bag, she pulled on a shirt, dungarees and a sweater. Lacing up her shoes, she then carried the hat back to Cordelia's bedroom, the bag to Sarah's, and the fake pearls to Ivy's. Carrying the dress and coat down to Peggy's room, she hung them up in the wardrobe.

Wandering into the kitchen, she put the kettle on, realised she didn't want another cup of tea, and took it off the hob again. There was something niggling at her, but she couldn't identify it, and that made her even more restless. The upset over Stan and the deep hurt inflicted by Ethel's attack was bad enough, and although the only thing she wanted to do was go to the hospital, she knew there'd be no point if he was heavily sedated.

'I feel so damn useless,' she said to the uncaring cat. 'Surely there must be something I could do?'

She glanced up at the clock, wondering when the others would return from the Anchor, then began to tidy up the chaos in the kitchen. As the time ticked away and there was still no sign of anyone, she decided to go for a walk. She simply couldn't hang about here any longer worrying about Stan, and perhaps a bit of fresh air and exercise might clear her head and help her to sleep.

The bombers were taking off from Cliffe, roaring across the Channel with their escorts of night fighters, the sound of them reverberating in the very ground beneath her as they virtually skimmed the water to evade the enemy's radar. The moon was full, hovering above the horizon to the east and casting a silver sheen over the glassy surface of the calm sea.

April stood on the promenade and watched until the last plane disappeared before shrugging up the collar of her old raincoat and striding out. She had no idea of where she was going, but the simple act of walking in this lovely still night was enough to soothe her anxieties and help her to think.

It was as she'd almost reached the kiosk and looked up the High Street that she realised what it was that had been niggling ever since she'd telephoned her mother, and she began to walk with fresh purpose up the hill towards the station.

The platform was deserted and all was dark and still as she walked up the cinder path to the cottage and rapped on the door.

An elderly man peered round the blackout curtains and hurriedly turned off the light before opening the door just a crack. 'What is it?'

'I'm the stationmaster's niece, and I need to have a word with you.'

He grimaced, shoved his glasses up the bridge of his nose and then grudgingly opened the door wider. 'You'd better come in then.'

April stepped inside, and as he shut the door and switched the light back on, she came straight to the point. 'I'm afraid I have a bit of bad news, Mr...'

'Eric Flint,' he said gruffly, his eyes magnified by his bottle-thick glasses. 'Stan's had a heart attack, hasn't he?'

'Yes, but how did you know?' she stammered.

'He didn't look right this morning,' he muttered. 'A man that size is asking for trouble, if you want my opinion.'

April didn't, but let it go. 'He's in hospital,' she said evenly, 'so of course he won't be able to work for a while. I was wondering if you could stay on for a few days?'

He sucked his false teeth. 'Well, it's not very convenient. The wife and I were planning to go away next week.'

'Would the railway send someone else, do you think?'

'It would be difficult. We're short on manpower these days, what with the war on.'

April felt he wasn't being at all helpful but she tried not to let her exasperation show. 'But Mr Flint – Eric,' she coaxed, 'if you could stay on for just a few more days, perhaps you could teach someone to take over until Stan's better.'

His lips turned down and his eyes glinted behind his glasses as he thought about this. 'Looking after a station isn't as easy as you might think,' he said finally. 'The railway company doesn't allow just anybody to run their stations willy-nilly. I can't do anything without permission from my superiors.'

April felt a flicker of hope. 'But you would consider staying on to train someone up if they did give permission?'

'That depends,' he said thoughtfully.

'On what?'

'On what the wife says and whether or not the railway will pay me extra to train someone. It's a big responsibility.'

'Then let's find out what the company says about it,' said April, her gaze flitting to the telephone on the wall.

'There won't be no one in the office at this time of night,' he said grumpily.

'Then will you stay here and telephone them in the morning?' She pasted on what she hoped was a winning smile. 'There will be no one with your skills to deal with the early morning trains, and I'm sure the company will be most relieved to discover that Cliffehaven station is in such

393

capable hands.'

She could see from his expression that he wasn't sure whether he was being flattered, or just buttered up, and she waited nervously for his reply.

'The wife won't like it,' he grumbled. 'I was supposed to go home after the last train.' He glanced round the cosy room and jingled the coins in his trouser pockets as he considered his options. 'Still, I could ring her, I suppose,' he said after a long silence. 'There is a war on, and the trains do have to be kept rolling, even in backwaters like this.'

'That would be marvellous if you could. And I'm sure your wife would understand that in these times a man's duty must come first.'

'I know my duty,' he said crossly. 'There's no need for that sort of talk.'

April reddened. 'Sorry, it's just that it's so important things are kept running smoothly while Stan's recuperating.'

He eyed her keenly. 'And who did you have in mind as a replacement?'

April realised she hadn't really thought this through, but as Eric seemed to be wavering she needed to press her advantage. 'There are several candidates,' she said quickly. 'I'm sure Stan's wife would do an admirable job, as would her daughter Ruby. There's Ron who can turn his hand to most things, and if all else fails, there's always me...' She tailed off.

He eyed her up and down and chuckled. 'Well, you're a game little thing, I'll say that for you – and you've got the cheek of Old Nick besides – but the company is very wary of employing women. Let alone ones in your condition.'

'But that's ridiculous,' she gasped. 'Women are doing all sorts of jobs now the men are away fighting. I'm as capable as anyone to do the job, and so are Ruby and Ethel.'

He shook his head. 'The company won't wear it,' he said stubbornly. 'If I'm to train anyone, it'll have to be your friend Ron.'

The voice from the doorway startled them both. 'And what exactly am I to be trained for?' asked Ron. He slammed the door and folded his arms as Harvey sniffed the cat and then collapsed with a grunt in front of the fire.

They both started talking at once and after a few seconds Ron held up his hand. 'I get the gist,' he rumbled, 'and to be sure the wee girl must have been reading me mind, for it's been bothering me about Stan's security here, which is why I came up.'

'I realise it's his home as well as his job,' blustered Eric, 'but if he's ill for too long, the company will have no other choice but to retire him.'

'Unless you teach me or one of the girls to do the job,' said Ron. 'I'll not be letting Stan lose everything after all the years he's served that company.'

The little man peered at both of them through his thick glasses and gave in. 'All right,' he sighed. 'I'll stay tonight and ring the office in the morning. If they agree I'll teach you, but I doubt they'll let a woman anywhere near the signal box.'

'Ethel will be too tied up with caring for Stan and holding her job at the factory – as will her daughter Ruby. But April's at a loose end for a few months, and as she used to service and repair

395

Royal Navy gun boats, I think she'd be eminently qualified to pull a few levers, blow whistles and wave flags, don't you?'

Mr Flint looked at April with new respect. 'It's a bit more complicated than that,' he muttered, 'but I'll speak to my superior in the morning and see what he has to say.'

'Aye, that would be grand, so it would.' Ron gave him a beaming smile and shook his hand. 'We'll both be here for the six o'clock train and our first lesson. Might as well start as we mean to go on.' With that he clicked his fingers to summon Harvey, turned off the light and opened the door.

April shot the little man a smile of gratitude and followed Ron out into the night. 'Thank goodness we both had the same idea,' she said as they began to make their way back home. 'I could never have persuaded him on my own.'

'You're a naughty wee girl to hire out me services without asking me first,' he said on a chuckle. 'It's a good thing I was already planning to offer anyway – and that's a first, let me tell you. I've spent my life avoiding volunteering for anything.'

'I'm sorry about that, but I got the idea and didn't really think it through,' she admitted. 'Stan loves his job and that cottage; it just would have been too cruel for him to lose them after what happened today.'

'Aye, well you've talked yourself into a new career, young April, so I hope you'll not have regrets about it.' He chuckled again and paused to light his pipe. 'I never thought I'd be playing with trains at my age, but life throws up many a

396

surprise along the way, doesn't it?'

'It certainly does. I just hope Ethel doesn't chuck a spanner in the works by refusing to let me set a foot over the threshold.'

'You leave Ethel to me, April. I know how to handle women like her.'

'I wish you the best of luck with that,' she replied drily.

Ron gave her an awkward hug before linking arms with her and continuing their journey home. 'She'll be putty in my hands,' he said. 'You just wait and see.'

Ron and April told the rest of the astonished household about their plan to run the station for Stan until he was well enough to go back to work, and although Peggy was worried that it would all be too much for April, she didn't have any other sensible ideas as an alternative, so had to accept her decision.

Ron went to bed that night feeling rather excited about this new venture. He'd longed for a train set as a boy but his family was too poor to get him one, and so when his grandsons came along he'd rushed out to buy a set and had spent many a happy hour playing with it. Now he was going to be in charge of real locomotives, carriages, goods trains and all manner of things, and the thought thrilled him.

He set his alarm clock and switched off the light, the animals curled on either side of him like furry bolsters. As he lay in the darkness his thoughts went over all that had happened today, and although he was really looking forward to tomorrow, the excitement was tinged with sadness, for he'd have given anything for his best friend to be hale and hearty and in his rightful place on that platform.

He turned over and struggled to get enough blanket from beneath the animals to cover his shoulders. April had surprised him by showing such initiative, and she'd certainly earned his respect today, not only for bearing the brunt of Ethel's venom, but for caring enough about Stan to do something practical that would really help him. It would be interesting to see how she got on tomorrow – and how Ethel would react.

27

April had felt much calmer once she'd actually achieved something important for Stan, and consequently had slept surprisingly well. She woke just before her alarm went off and quickly dressed in the dungarees, shirt and sweater before quietly using the bathroom. The rest of the household were asleep, and it was still dark outside, so she tiptoed down to the kitchen where she discovered Ron was already tucking into hot porridge, tea and toast.

'I'm glad to see you're an early riser,' he said.

'I got used to it in the WRNS.' She helped herself to the porridge and returned the pot to the warming oven. As she ate, she glanced across at the sturdy old man she'd once been so wary of and couldn't help but smile. He'd clearly got dressed in the dark, and had thrown on whatever he could find. His shirt was creased and stained, his baggy corduroy trousers were held up with garden twine, the sweater had more holes in it than a colander and he was wearing odd socks.

'Well, you'd have to be a very early bird to beat me in the mornings,' he boasted. 'I've already walked the dog and fed him and the cat.'

April finished the last bit of porridge and smiled at him. 'It might be an idea to get dressed with the light on though,' she teased. 'Your sweater's on back to front and you've buttoned your shirt up all wrong.'

'Ach, minor details,' he said airily. His bright blue eyes regarded her from beneath his bushy brows. 'I don't know what you've let us both in for, but I'm hoping it will not prove too much for you. There's bound to be some heavy lifting involved when the mail train comes in, and you'll need to be careful you don't strain yourself.'

'I'm sure I'll manage,' she assured him. She finished the cup of tea and carried their dirty dishes to the sink where she began to wash them. 'But I do think that once we know what we're doing and can be left in charge, we should sort out some sort of roster.'

His bushy brows shot up. 'This isn't the navy,' he protested.

'It certainly isn't,' she replied with the ghost of a smile. 'But that doesn't mean we shouldn't be organised.' She set the last cup on the drainer and dried her hands. 'Neither of us can spend all day and night at the station,' she explained, 'and you have the pub and your Home Guard duties to fulfil. I'll have doctor and midwife appointments, and Stan's allotment will also need to be tended. And then of course we'll both want to visit Stan and keep an eye on Ethel. It would only be sensible to work out a proper schedule, don't you think?'

'Aye, you're right, wee girl,' he replied with a twinkle in his eyes, 'but let's see if the railway company will employ us first, shall we?'

April smiled and reached for her coat and gas-mask box as Ron hauled on his long poaching coat and squashed his cap over his hair. 'I have to admit that I'm quite excited at the thought of running a station,' she confided. 'Trains have always fascinated me.'

'Aye, me too.'

They shared a delighted grin, firmly closed the door on the cat, and then set off through the deserted, silent streets for the station, Harvey padding along beside them.

Eric Flint was already in the signal box. He checked his watch and stood poised to pull down one of the two large levers as a bell pinged repeatedly from a board above his head. 'The bell warns me the train is approaching, and this lever has to be pulled down to guide it onto the right line,' he said importantly. 'If you don't do that, it will go off on the branch line half a mile back and end up at the wrong station – and that won't do at all.'

He pushed a smaller lever forward and there was a click as the signals changed and the metal flag dropped, then he made a great show of

400

hauling down the big lever and pressing a button several times. 'That bell is to confirm to the locomotive driver that the track is ready for the train,' he said.

'And if it isn't?' asked April.

'Then you don't press the button.'

'But what if a tree's fallen over the line or you need to contact the driver in an emergency?' she persisted.

'Then you put your thumb on that button and hold it there until he gives two pings back to let you know he understands. Of course you would have inspected the track first thing for any such occurrence, and if there was a tree on the line, you would ring through on the emergency line which is there.' Looking a bit disgruntled by all the questions, he jabbed his thumb towards the old-fashioned telephone fixed to the wall before he clambered down the short flight of steps to the platform.

Stan and April glanced at one another, rolled their eyes, and then meekly followed him.

'You're lucky this is just a single track to deal with here,' Eric continued rather pompously. 'As long as you ensure the train doesn't go off on the branch line, it's simply a case of it coming in, stopping and going back again.'

Unfurling his little red flag, he stood to attention and solemnly waved it as the steam train slowly chuffed to a standstill within inches of the buffers. 'All change. All change,' he bellowed. 'Cliffehaven, Cliffehaven, this is Cliffehaven. All change.'

April caught Ron's eye and had to look away. Eric looked very silly in that over-large uniform,

401

and his show of self-importance was so comical, it was difficult not to laugh.

'Collect the tickets,' Eric said as a few passengers alighted. 'And make sure they're valid. Some people try to use the same ticket twice.' His suspicious gaze followed a group of chattering factory girls as they headed for the exit.

While April checked the tickets and answered all the passengers' questions about Stan, Ron helped an elderly woman down from the train and carried her heavy case towards the exit. He then unloaded the tightly bound stacks of newspapers and the huge hessian sacks of mail from the guard's van. These were collected by the newsagents who were now gathered on the platform, while the mail was carried off in the back of the Post Office truck.

April had finished collecting tickets and she smiled in amusement as Ron appeared through the smoke and steam armed with two enormous wooden crates filled with squawking chickens. They were labelled clearly and destined for the dairy where the owner was branching out into eggs and poultry to subsidise his milk round.

Once everything was unloaded and the train doors had been shut, Eric put the whistle to his lips and raised his flag. As if conducting the London Symphony Orchestra, he held it aloft, paused – and then waved it with an unnecessary flourish. The engine driver shook his head, winked at Ron and April and gave a long blast from the funnel before setting the train back down the line.

The next hour was spent listening to Eric, who made it very clear that although there were only six trains a day and the job might appear to be simple, it was in fact highly skilled and very important. Ron and April tried to keep a straight face, but it was almost impossible, and by the time he'd left the signal box to go and ring his superiors, they were aching from the need to burst out laughing.

They went and sat in the sunshine to drink their tea. 'Good grief,' spluttered April. 'It's more difficult to run the telephone exchange than this. Is this *really* all Stan does every day?'

Ron nodded. 'But he keeps busy, what with the allotment and his garden.'

'I think we'll manage between us and still have lots of time to do other things, don't you?'

He shrugged. 'That all depends on what Eric's got to say. The job's not guaranteed, April.'

They watched the little man bustle towards them, his eagerness to share his news clearly exciting him. 'Head Office has agreed to me training you both,' he said as he plumped down on the bench and took the proffered mug of tea from Ron. 'And my wife is happy to do her bit for the war effort by letting me stay on for another day just to get you settled in.' He beamed with pleasure. 'So that's all sorted.'

'And Stan will keep his job?' asked Ron.

'Oh yes, at least for the duration. But it's keeping the line open for all the troop trains that's the important thing.'

'And the wages?'

'They will be split between you. The company can't afford to pay two people to man such a quiet station.'

'That's all right,' said April. 'We've already

agreed to give our wages to Stan, anyway.'

Eric regarded them both. 'It strikes me Stan's a lucky man to have such good friends. There's not many who'd do that.'

'Maybe not,' muttered Ron, 'but Stan's an institution in this town, and it's our way of showing how much we appreciate all the things he's done for us over the years.' He finished the last drop of tea in his mug. 'Well, April, it seems we're about to embark on our new adventure, so how about refreshing that teapot so we can celebrate?'

Peggy's thoughts had been with Stan since she'd woken that morning, and as she did her housework and then tried to keep Daisy amused with her toys in the garden, she fretted over the lack of any news.

'Fran did say she'd ring us if there was any change,' said Cordelia from the depths of the old deckchair. 'It's a terrible worry, I know, but there's absolutely nothing we can do to change things, and fretting over him won't help at all.'

'I do realise that.' Distractedly, Peggy filled Daisy's little bucket with sand and then tipped it out again. 'But I can't help thinking there must be something we can do.'

'Ron and April are doing the most practical thing,' said Cordelia. 'He'd be devastated if he lost his home and his job because of this.'

'And that's another thing,' sighed Peggy. 'April shouldn't be lifting heavy things and dealing with dirty trains in her condition. She'll do herself a damage.'

'Oh, I suspect she's tougher than she looks,'

murmured Cordelia. 'With a mother like that she's had to be.'

'I wonder if Mildred will come down to see Stan?'

'I doubt it,' said Cordelia with a sniff. 'From what little April has told us, she's far too taken up with her own concerns to worry about others.'

Peggy thought how sad that was, and she just hoped Mildred wouldn't expect to stay here if she did deign to put in an appearance, for she doubted she could keep a civil tongue in her head after the disgraceful way the woman had treated her daughter. She glanced at her watch. 'I'll do us both a sandwich for lunch and then go to the hospital,' she said. 'Visiting time's at two, and I can't stand the suspense any longer.'

Under normal circumstances, Stan avoided the hospital like the plague. Matron might be a fellow rose enthusiast, but she had all the tact and grace of a bull in a china shop when it came to ordering everybody about, and as for idling about in bed and being assaulted with needles, damp flannels and bedpans when there were more important things to do – it was against Stan's nature.

However, he was feeling as weak as a kitten, and so tired he could hardly keep his eyes open. He lay propped up on pillows, the starched sheet and rough blanket virtually tying him to the bed as a machine beeped regularly and a drip fed drugs into the back of his hand. He ached from stem to stern, had a bump the size of an egg on the back of his head, and was finding it difficult to focus on the beloved figure who clung to his

405

hand at his bedside and watched his every move.

He only had a vague memory of a terrible pain in his chest that had taken his breath away, and the sound of hushed voices and Ethel's wailing. He supposed he came here in an ambulance, but several hours must have passed before he'd been able to comprehend what was happening, for he'd noted – even through the haze of medication – that Ethel had changed out of her wedding finery.

Stan looked at her now and felt a great rush of love. Her sweet face was drawn, her eyes dark with weariness and worry as she gazed at him intently. Had she been here all night? 'Go home, Ethel, love,' he said, squeezing her fingers. 'You need to rest.'

'I ain't leaving you, Stan. Not until the doctor's been to check you over again.'

Stan recognised that mulish look and knew it was pointless to argue even if he did have the energy. He closed his eyes, too exhausted to be able to think straight, let alone talk. It felt as if he was floating in a thick haze that muffled sound and distorted his senses, making his thoughts sluggish and his limbs heavy. Something important was trying to emerge from that fog of confusion and unreality, but try as he might, he couldn't quite grasp what it was. The effort to identify it became too much and he let it slip away.

'Hello, Ethel. How is he?'

'He's not right, Peggy. Not right at all.' Ethel's voice wavered. 'I nearly lost him, you know.'

'Have you been here all night on your own? Where's Ruby?'

'She went home earlier to get me a change of

406

clothes, and then went off to work. There's a rush on at the factory and she didn't like to ask for time off, but she promised to be back later.'

Stan struggled to open his eyes. 'Make her go home, Peggy,' he managed.

'I really think you should,' said Peggy. 'You won't be doing him any good by making yourself sick. There're nurses and doctors to look after Stan, and I'll sit with him until Ruby gets here.'

'I dunno. I promised Ruby I'd be 'ere, and I don't like leaving 'im like this.'

Peggy's tone revealed her impatience. 'Ruby shouldn't have gone to work, not at a time like this. I'm sure the factory could have spared her for a day or two.'

'That's as maybe, but I made her go. What with Stan laid up and me working much shorter shifts so I can be with him, we're going to need the money.'

Stan realised suddenly what the important thing was that he hadn't been able to grasp earlier, and emerged momentarily from his stupor. 'The station,' he gasped. 'Who's looking after the station?'

Peggy patted his hand. 'It's all right, Stan. Ron and April are up there now learning how to run the place until you're better. And you won't be out of pocket,' she added hastily, 'because you'll still be getting the wages.'

'The railway are paying all three of us?' he asked in astonishment.

'Well, no,' Peggy admitted. 'April and Ron's combined wage is the same as you've been receiving, but they're passing it straight to you so you're not out of pocket.'

Stan was stunned at their generosity.

'I ain't takin' no charity from the likes of 'er,' snapped Ethel.

'Then you're a fool,' said Peggy flatly. 'If it wasn't for her quick thinking there would have been no one to run the place and Stan would more than likely have lost his job – as well as that lovely cottage. So think on, Ethel, and wind your neck in.'

'You ain't got no cause to speak to me like that. Not with my 'usband on 'is death bed.'

'I'm not dying, Ethel,' Stan rasped, 'but if I hear any more talk like that against my April, I'll tell the nurses not to let you visit again.'

Ethel's eyes narrowed and her lips thinned. 'So, you'd take 'er side, then?'

'There are no sides, Ethel,' he said wearily. 'You're both family and I love you. Please try and be a little charitable towards her – for my sake, if nothing else.'

Ethel clamped her lips together and folded her arms tightly 'Well, if that's what you want, I suppose I'll just have to put up with it,' she said stiffly. 'But I don't like it, Stan. Not one little bit.'

The short exchange had drained the last of his energy. 'Just go home, Ethel,' he sighed.

'That's good advice, Ethel,' said Peggy. 'You both need to rest, and you don't want him worrying about you, do you?'

'I suppose not,' she said with bad grace. 'But you'll stay with 'im for a bit, won't you? I need to know someone's keeping a close eye on 'im.'

'Of course,' said Peggy. 'And Ethel – go straight home. April's a good girl doing her very best in a bad situation. This isn't the time to stir up trouble.'

'If you say so.'

Stan felt Ethel's lips brush his cheek and her hand sweep back the lick of hair that drooped over his forehead, and as her footsteps faded and the ward door swung behind her, he opened his eyes. 'Thanks, Peg,' he muttered. 'I know she means well, but it's difficult to relax with her watching my every breath.'

'Well, you can relax now, Stan,' she soothed. 'I brought my knitting, so if you fancy a bit of a snooze, you carry on and don't mind me.'

'It's kind of April and Ron to take over the station,' he murmured. 'You will thank them for me, won't you?'

'You'll get the chance to do that yourself when they visit. Now close your eyes and stop worrying.'

Stan drifted off to sleep, content to have the quiet, understanding Peggy calmly knitting at his bedside. He was a lucky man to have such good friends, and all he could pray for now was that Ethel and April would find a way to rub along together.

As there were no trains due for a couple of hours, and the hospital restricted visiting to two people per patient on Stan's ward, Ron took Eric off to Stan's allotment to admire his friend's roses. It turned out that Eric was an avid gardener, and something of a self-proclaimed expert on roses, so Ron had steeled himself to withstand two hours of pontificating.

April had swept the platform, watered the vegetables in the large tubs and given the Nissen hut a good spring clean. Stan clearly spent a good deal of time in there, for there was a caddy of tea, a bottle of Camp Coffee, and a tin of biscuits stowed away alongside piles of books and magazines on gardening, and a collection of hand-tools which he was in the process of mending. Once it was neat and tidied to her satisfaction, she locked the hut and carried the illicit tin of biscuits to the cottage. She'd noticed earlier that Eric seemed to be averse to cleaning up after himself, and she didn't want Ethel turning up and complaining.

The vast ginger tom was waiting for her on the doorstep, and she lifted the latch and went in, leaving the door open to let in the fresh air. The fire had gone out, the cat's bowl was empty and the sink was full of dirty crockery. Flinging open the small windows, she appeased the cat's hunger and then set to and started cleaning the cottage.

She took the embroidered tablecloth outside to shake the crumbs from it, polished the table and plumped the cushions of the two easy chairs. Having relaid the fire with kindling and screws of paper, she swept the floor and put the rubbish in the dustbin, before hurrying upstairs to make the spare bed Eric had used the night before.

She was just tackling the washing-up when she heard footsteps on the cinder path, and she turned from the sink to be confronted by a sour-faced Ethel.

'I might have known it wouldn't take you long to get yer feet under the bleedin' table,' Ethel snapped.

April refused to rise to the bait. 'I came in to clean up and feed the cat,' she said, calmly drying her hands.

'Snooping, more like,' Ethel snarled. 'Well, you can sling yer 'ook.'

'I have a perfect right to be here,' April said evenly, 'and I'll leave when I'm good and ready.'

Ethel sneered. 'You can drop that snooty act. I ain't impressed. And you can shove yer charity right up yer arse, an' all. I know what you're really after.'

'And what's that, Ethel?' she asked quietly.

'This place. Suit you good and proper, wouldn't it, to move in and take over?'

'That's not why I'm here at all. This is your home, yours and Stan's, and I respect that and would never presume to have any call on it.'

'Humph. All yer fancy talk don't impress me. I ain't soft like Stan, and if it were up to me I'd send you packing with a flea in yer ear.'

'I feel sorry for you, Ethel,' April said. 'You're so blinkered you can't see that you're destroying everything Stan holds dear.'

'Oh, yeah? How's that then?'

'Family means everything to Stan, and he's welcomed me despite my situation and the scandal it might cause. He wants a simple life – a life in which he can enjoy the company of the people he loves and who love him. But he can't have that if you continue to be so spiteful.'

'He could if you left us all in peace,' Ethel retorted. Her eyes were suspiciously bright and her chin trembled as she looked at April defiantly. 'We was doing all right before you come along. It was you what spoilt it.'

'I'm truly sorry, Ethel,' she murmured. 'And if I could change things, then I would. But we both

411

know that's impossible.' She took a step towards her and put out a hesitant hand that didn't quite touch Ethel's tightly folded arms. 'Can't we at least agree to be civil to one another for Stan's sake?'

'It's what 'e wants,' Ethel admitted grudgingly.

'And so do I,' said April softly.

She watched the inner battle that was clearly going on in Ethel's heart and mind, noting the spark of tears in her eyes and the way she was holding back her emotions by keeping her back stiff and shoulders squared. 'Oh, Ethel,' she sighed as she put her arms around her. 'Don't try and carry this awful burden on your own.'

Ethel was rigid in her embrace, but April could feel the tremors running through her and the dampness of her tears on her blouse collar. 'I know you're frightened,' she soothed, 'and that it feels as if your world is crashing down around you. But Stan is strong. He'll come through this.'

The trembling increased and the silent tears became great wails of anguish as Ethel fell against April and clung to her. 'But he's so 'elpless,' she sobbed. 'I see 'im lying there hardly moving and so pale, and there ain't nothing I can do. I don't want to lose 'im – I can't lose 'im!'

April held her close as her own tears rolled down her face. She could almost feel Ethel's pain and fear, and being well acquainted with such emotions, she understood what the other woman was going through. There were no words that could really soothe, just the warmth of a pair of arms and the comforting knowledge that she wasn't alone in her grief.

They stood in the middle of the room welded together through their love for Stan, and when Ethel's tears had ebbed and she eased from the embrace, she couldn't quite look April in the eye. 'I don't know where that come from,' she said, fumbling for a handkerchief.

'From the heart,' said April, mopping at her own tears. 'And from fear and worry and a lack of sleep.' She smiled at her. 'Don't be ashamed of those tears, Ethel. They're not a sign of weakness, but of love.'

Ethel nodded and shot her a wary glance. 'I been tough on you,' she admitted, 'and now I feel a bit ashamed 'cos of the way you've been so kind. I'm surprised you didn't lump me one a long time ago.'

'That's not my way, Ethel.'

'No, I can see it ain't.' She gave a hesitant, fleeting smile. 'So where do we go from 'ere?'

'We put our differences behind us because we both love Stan and want him to get better. It might be a bit awkward at first, but I'm sure we'll find a way'

Ethel lit a fag and slumped down into one of the fireside chairs. 'I got you all wrong, didn't I?' she said on a sigh. 'You're like my Stan; loyal and kind and devoted to family – but I didn't want to see that because I resented you. I was jealous,' she admitted softly. 'Jealous of all the attention Stan was paying you, and of the joy he felt at having found you.'

Her rueful smile was watery as she looked back at April. 'Silly, weren't I?'

April patted her shoulder. 'You're worn out with

worry and lack of sleep,' she said softly. 'Why don't you go up to bed? I'll wake you when it's visiting time again and, if you agree, we could go and see Stan together. That way he'll stop worrying about us and can concentrate on getting well again.'

Ethel nodded. 'That's a good idea. But don't you have trains to meet?'

'Ron's doing the evening ones.'

Ethel slowly climbed the narrow wooden stairs and April waited until she heard her footsteps overhead and then the creaking of the bedsprings. She turned away from the stairs and was startled to see Ron standing on the doorstep. 'How long have you been there?'

'Long enough,' he said as he tramped into the room and gave her a hug. 'Well done, April. I couldn't have handled that better myself.'

April smiled as she hugged him back. Ethel had certainly not been as easy as putty to mould, but they'd reached an understanding which hopefully would blossom into friendship, and that was all that really mattered.

28

A month had passed since Stan's heart attack, and Peggy was delighted that he seemed, at last, to be on the mend. The restrictions on the number of visitors had been lifted now he'd been transferred to Men's Medical, so everyone at Beach View had managed to see for themselves how well he was doing.

Ethel was working part-time at the factory and helping Ruby keep the allotment in order when they weren't sitting with Stan, while Ron and April had worked out a schedule to keep the trains running. Ron was rarely at home now, what with his trains, his Home Guard and fire-watch duties and the jobs Rosie needed doing at the Anchor, but Peggy was relieved that he was being kept fully occupied, for it meant there would be no more nonsense concerning Gloria Stevens.

As for April, she was blooming now that she and Ethel had reached an agreement to rub along together and make the best of things for Stan's sake. The fresh air and sunshine, and the knowledge that she was doing her bit, had brought colour to her face and a sparkle to her eyes. Her pregnancy was now evident for all to see, but strangely enough there was very little condemnation of her situation by the local gossips, and Peggy put that down to her relationship with Stan and the willing way she'd mucked in during a crisis.

Peggy had written a long letter to Jim about all that had happened – though she hadn't mentioned his father's suspected dalliance with Gloria, and the fact that April's baby would be brown, for what he didn't know wouldn't hurt or worry him. Now she was waiting impatiently to hear back from him.

She continued packing the comfort boxes which were due to be sent out to the Allied troops in India, hoping that perhaps one that she'd packed might find its way to Jim. The odds were against that happening, but she packed each box with

415

loving care just in case, and added a picture post-card of Cliffehaven wishing the recipient well.

Her thoughts turned to April again as one of the babies in the crèche began to wail. She'd gone with her to the adoption place yesterday to sign the second lot of papers, and although she'd put a brave face on things, Peggy knew she'd become attached to the little one growing inside her and would find it agonisingly hard to give it up. The girl was making a brave decision, but Peggy did agree that it was the right one. Miss Franklyn had managed to find a couple who were desperate for a baby, and as the prospective parents were of mixed race, the child would grow up with a clearer sense of its identity, and not be picked out as different amid all the white faces.

Peggy finished taping the box and glanced up at the clock. Her three hours of volunteering were up and it was now time to collect Daisy from the crèche. She would pop into the uniform factory on her way home to make sure Shirley was coming to tea with her mother the following day, and have a quiet word with Alf about the possibility of a bit of extra beef suet to make the potato pastry tastier on the Woolton pie she planned to cook tonight. This was one of the more successful recipes dreamt up by the rationing people and involved cooking vegetables in a pastry case – but the potato pastry turned a nasty grey when cooked, and it would be lovely to have a bit of fat mixed in for a change.

Ron hurried along the hospital corridor keeping a wary eye out for Matron, who was inclined to appear unexpectedly and put the wind up him. She'd never quite forgiven him for discharging himself and leaving on the back of Rita's motorbike after he'd been injured at the start of the war, and so he did his best to avoid her.

He eased through the door into the ward and grinned at the little nurse sitting behind her desk. 'How's the patient today?'

'Getting restless,' she replied with a wry smile.

'Aye, I know the feeling.' He tipped his cap to her and strolled down the ward to Stan's bed. 'I hear you're causing trouble,' he said cheerfully as he plumped down in the chair. 'You want to watch it, Stan, or you'll have Matron after you, and to be sure that's no fun at all.'

Stan looked rather gloomy as he fidgeted in the bed. 'I only asked if I could go to the lav on my own,' he replied. 'You'd have thought I wanted to climb onto the roof.'

'Aye, well they take things seriously in here, and you've got to be patient.' He chuckled. 'Get it? As a patient you have to be patient.'

Stan rolled his eyes. 'Very funny. But I'm bored, Ron, and all this lazing about isn't doing me a bit of good. I should be back at the station, starting my new life with Ethel.'

'There's no need to worry about the station. April and me are keeping it running as sweet as a nut, and Ethel pops in to keep an eye on us when she can. She and Ruby are looking after your allotment and making a grand job of it, so they are. And you can be assured that both April and Ethel are getting on like a house on fire.'

This was a bit of an exaggeration, for though

417

things were better between them, there was still an element of frostiness on Ethel's part. He leaned back in the chair and began to fill his pipe. 'I must say, Stan, it's money for old rope working at that station. What on earth do you do to keep yourself busy?'

'There's plenty to keep me out of mischief, never you mind,' Stan said solemnly. 'And talking of mischief, are you going to tell me what you were up to with Gloria Stevens?'

'Well now, Stan, I would – but I'd have to shoot you.'

Stan's eyes widened and then his face creased into a broad smile. 'You had me going there for a minute. A fling with Gloria is hardly a shooting offence – unless it's Rosie holding the gun, of course.'

'Aye, you could be right there, old pal. There's nothing more fearsome than a woman scorned.' Ron had spoken lightly in the hope that Stan would drop the subject, and he continued to fill his pipe.

'So? Are you going to tell me? Or will I go to my grave never knowing?'

'You're not at death's door, Stan, so don't pull that one,' Ron said mildly. 'Curiosity killed the cat, remember?'

'Ah, yes, but satisfaction brought it back. I really don't understand why you're so reluctant to talk about it, Ron. In your position I'd have been bursting to share my good fortune at having two women after my body.'

It was clear that Stanley wasn't going to give up on this, so now Ron had to decide whether he

418

should tell his pal the truth, or spin him a line. He stuck the pipe in his mouth and spent a few more moments getting a good draw on it while he thought things through. The idea of lying to Stan didn't sit easily, but the truth was complicated and, once revealed, could have serious and far-reaching consequences.

'The thing between me and Gloria wasn't what you thought,' he said finally.

'So it's over then?'

'In a manner of speaking.'

Stan remained silent, his gaze steady on his friend's face. 'It either is or isn't,' he said flatly.

Ron puffed on his pipe and then examined the burnt tobacco in the bowl. He and Stan had signed the Official Secrets Act during the last shout, and because they'd shared some highly dangerous and top secret missions behind enemy lines which they'd kept to themselves ever since, he knew Stan could be trusted.

'Remember those papers we signed back in 1916? The oath we took then still holds.'

Stan regarded him evenly, his expression solemn. 'I know that.' He leaned forward, his voice barely above a whisper, 'But what on earth has that to do with Gloria?'

'Just promise to keep to that oath, Stan, or I'll say nothing more.'

Stan frowned in puzzlement and then nodded. 'I promise I won't breathe a word.'

Ron gathered his thoughts and then rested his elbows on the bed so he could keep his voice below the general chatter on the ward. 'I was contacted by someone in London a while ago. I can't tell you who, but they were important enough for me to go to the barber's and put on my best clothes for the meetings in Westminster.'

Stan's eyes were wide with astonishment as Ron glanced quickly over his shoulder to make sure no one else was listening before he continued. 'The person I met asked me to keep tabs on a certain group who'd formed a private gentlemen's club here in Cliffehaven and to keep special watch over their newest recruit.'

Stan was quick on the uptake. 'Are we talking about Fifth Columnists?' he muttered. At Ron's nod he gasped. 'What?' he squeaked. 'Here in Cliffehaven?'

'Keep your voice down,' Ron hissed, 'or I'll tell you no more.'

Stan looked warily round the ward and edged closer to Ron. 'But I don't understand where Gloria fits into all this.'

'The men met twice a week in the function room at the Crown – which is situated directly below Gloria's bedroom. The floorboards are loose enough to coax apart and the plaster's thin enough to overhear everything they said.'

'But surely, if she knew what they were she'd have refused to have them there?'

Ron grinned. 'It turns out there's rather more to our Gloria than we ever suspected. You see, she's been working for the government ever since the war began and is ideally placed to hear and see things that might threaten the nation's security. When she was approached by the leader of the group – someone who would never normally have darkened her door – her suspicions were aroused and she listened in to their first meeting. She immediately reported what she'd heard to her local contact, and was told to encourage them to continue meeting there so they could be monitored.'

'Well I never,' Stan breathed. 'Who would have thought it?'

'Things became difficult for her when her son was killed and her daughter-in-law and grandchildren moved in, so I was asked to take over recording the meetings until the little family could be found other accommodation.'

'But surely, if the government knows about these men, they'd be arrested and executed as Nazi spies?'

'Ah, well that's the clever part, see, Stan. Now they know who they are they can infiltrate the group, stay one step ahead, and supply them with misinformation.' He chuckled. 'The latest wheeze was for our mole to suggest they have a discreet club badge or tiepin to make their association look as valid as any other, and they fell for it hook, line and sinker – which means the police can easily identify them when it comes to their being arrested. Which they will be eventually.'

'Blimey, Ron,' breathed Stan. 'And here's me thinking you were dallying with Gloria.'

'It was a good cover, wasn't it?' He grinned and wiggled his eyebrows. 'Gloria's quite a woman.'

'But you didn't...?'

Ron shook his head. 'She was willing and I have to say I *was* tempted, but I love Rosie too much to cheat on her.'

Stan rested back against the pillows as he absorbed all that he'd learned. Then he leaned forward again. 'Who are the men involved?'

'I can't tell you,' Ron said firmly.

'What about the mole?'

'I can't tell you that either.'

'And do the men still meet at Gloria's?'

Ron could just imagine Stan letting his curiosity get the better of him to the point where he couldn't resist visiting the Crown in an attempt to nose out who the Fifth Columnists were. 'They now meet at a private house further along the coast,' he said truthfully. 'I think they realised their regular meetings at the Crown would be noticed if they went on for too long, so they found somewhere out of the way and far more discreet.'

'But how did these men find each other in the first place? That sort of warped thinking is hardly something to brag about.'

Ron shrugged. 'Through old school ties, clubs, bars, who knows. We're all drawn to like-minded people, and it only takes a word or a gesture to squirrel them out.'

Stan flopped back against the pillows and gave a low whistle. 'Well, Ron, you've certainly livened up my afternoon and given me something to think about. I shall be looking at every man differently now I know what's going on in our quiet little town. And as for Gloria... My goodness, I never would have guessed.'

'It's a dangerous game, Stan,' he said. 'And the oath we took all those years ago is as binding now as it was then, because lives are at stake as well as the security of our country. You have to forget everything I told you and carry on as normal.'

'You can count on me, Ron. But the man who's

infiltrated the group is taking a terrible risk. They'll kill him if they discover what he's up to.'

'Aye, but it's a risk he's more than willing to take.' Ron put his cold pipe in his pocket as the bell went to announce the end of visiting time. 'See you tomorrow, Stan.'

As Ron headed back to Beach View to collect Harvey for his late afternoon walk, his thoughts turned to Bertie Grantley-Adams. To the rest of the world, the dapper, mild-mannered and popular little man seemed content to spend his retirement playing golf and whist or driving Cordelia about. In reality he'd been one of England's best undercover agents during the first war, and his work had saved countless lives.

Like Ron, Bertie had also been approached by MI5 to come out of retirement and infiltrate the cadre of Fifth Columnists in Cliffehaven, which he'd done willingly, for he was staunchly patriotic and still as brave as a lion despite his advanced years. In fact he'd spent almost three weeks living rough on the streets of London as he kept close watch on one of the leading members of the group – Jasper Cliffe – and no one suspected that his so-called attack of malaria was a ruse to cover for his absence. Bertie knew Ron was part of this vital mission, but like the consummate undercover men they were, neither acknowledged it – but Ron's admiration for the man was unbounded.

April had taken to wearing dungarees beneath the railway uniform jacket, for they were more comfortable than anything else now she was so enormous. She ran her hand over her swollen stomach and eased her back, but the baby was restless today and she was suffering a bit from indigestion – which according to Shirley was a sure sign it would be born with lots of hair.

She smiled wistfully at this and then determinedly set about watering Stan's tubs of flowers and vegetables which were thriving in the July sun that streamed down onto the platform. There were less than seven weeks to go before the birth, and she was dreading the moment she'd have to hand her baby over to strangers. And yet she did find small comfort in the knowledge that there were two people out there who longed for the gift of a child, and that regardless of how painful it would be for her, she could be assured that her baby would be treasured.

She blinked back her tears, then set the watering can down by the standpipe and opened the tin of Spam sandwiches Ethel had brought to the station earlier. Perching on the hard wooden bench, she gazed down the empty track as she ate and watched the butterflies flitting above the embankment.

Her relationship with Ethel was still a bit awkward, for words spoken in the heat of the moment couldn't be taken back, and entrenched points of view couldn't be changed overnight. However, there was a definite thawing between them, and although neither broached the subject of April's pregnancy – that would have been a step too far for Ethel – there were the occasional small signs that Ethel's attitude was shifting.

She'd arrive with a pint of milk she said she had

no need for, or a couple of buns which she insisted would go stale if they weren't eaten – and once, she'd even turned up with a pair of sandshoes for April's swollen feet, saying she'd found them in the lost property at the factory and as no one had claimed them she thought April might as well have them. April had gratefully accepted these gruffly given tokens, realising it was Ethel's way of trying to make amends without actually admitting she was warming to her.

The sound of hurrying footsteps drew April from her thoughts and she smiled with pleasure as Shirley – came bustling towards her looking very pretty in a floral cotton dress and white sandals. 'Hello. I didn't expect to see you today. I thought you were working?'

Shirley smoothed back her hair and sat down. 'I should have been, but something's happened, and I needed to talk to you before you heard it elsewhere.'

April eyed her friend with some alarm. 'It's not James, is it?'

She shook her head. 'He's with Mum at the bed and breakfast. And you'll never guess who arrived last night,' she added, her eyes shining. Before April had a chance to speculate she blurted out, 'My dad!'

April grinned in delight. 'I can see by your face that his arrival wasn't a disaster – but how did this change of heart come about?'

Shirley dipped into her white handbag, found her cigarettes and lit one. 'Well,' she said, settling in to her story with relish. 'You know Mum came down two days ago to visit me because she thought he was up north on one of his factory inspections? What she didn't know was that his inspection had been cancelled and so he thought he'd surprise her by joining her.'

She blew smoke and grinned. 'But he had to hunt about her things to discover where she was staying, because she'd been deliberately vague about it – and that was when he found my letters and the photographs of James which I'd sent to her. She'd kept them in her needlework box along with her diary, and he only found them when he tripped over it and everything spilled out.'

'Gosh, that was lucky.'

'I don't think Dad thought so at first,' said Shirley. 'He admitted he'd been shocked to discover the extent of Mum's deceit, but as he'd sat there amid the spilled cottons and needles, his curiosity got the better of him and he began to look at the photographs and read my letters.'

She sighed happily. 'I'm so glad he did, because it made him realise what he was missing – for not only had he lost a daughter and turned his wife against him through his pride, he was also in danger of losing his only grandchild.'

'I bet you and your mother were shocked to see him,' said April.

'I'll say. I thought he'd come down to read me the riot act and Mum got all flustered and started babbling, but he just wrapped his arms around us both without a word and we all started crying.' She smiled at the memory. 'That started James off, of course, and Dad took him and soothed him wonderfully, and before we knew it, we were a family again and making plans for the future.'

April looked at her sharply, guessing the reason behind her unexpected appearance today. 'You're going back home, aren't you?'

Shirley nodded. 'We're leaving tomorrow morning, which is why I had to see you.' She stubbed out her cigarette and took April's hands. 'You've been a wonderful friend, April, and I shall miss you. I'm sorry I won't be here in September to help you through things, but I'll be by your side in spirit and will never forget you.'

They hugged fiercely, both close to tears. 'Promise you'll keep in touch,' pleaded Shirley as they finally drew apart and she slipped a piece of paper into April's hand. 'This is my address and telephone number, and if you're ever down my way, you must come and visit.'

April doubted she'd ever see her again, for Shirley's village was well off the beaten track, but she nodded anyway.

'And please say goodbye to Peggy and apologise about our not going to tea with her tomorrow,' Shirley continued. 'She's a marvellous, warm-hearted woman who wasn't afraid to stand up to bullies like that old cow down at the kiosk, and I know she'll take very good care of you.'

She squeezed April's hand and reached for her bag. 'Good luck, April. I hope Stan gets better soon and that Ethel comes to appreciate what a truly lovely person you are. Now I must go and pack.'

They hugged for the last time and then Shirley was walking swiftly over the bridge and down the High Street.

April stood and watched her until she was lost

amongst the factory girls and Allied servicemen who thronged the pavement. Her best friend's story had ended happily and she was truly delighted for her – and yet she felt a twinge of envy, for it was highly unlikely that she'd ever be welcomed back into her own mother's life.

She turned away and headed for the signal box. The five o'clock train was due, and after that Ron would take over until the last one at ten.

April dealt with the train and the questions about Stan from all the regular passengers, but her mind wasn't fully focused on the train driver's teasing or the usual chit-chat from the stoker, for her conversation with Shirley had stirred mixed emotions within her and she was finding it hard to contain them.

She watched the train leave the station and stood on the platform deep in thought. Mildred's coldness towards her had never been explained or even discussed apart from a few vague comments that Stan had let slip. The need to know and understand the woman who'd all but abandoned her was suddenly more important than ever, and she decided then and there that she would visit Stan tonight and coax the truth out of him.

Peggy had just put the Woolton pie in the oven when, to her surprise, April came into the kitchen. 'Hello, dear. I thought you'd be visiting Stan tonight?'

'I was going to, but Chalky, Alf and Fred were there, so I just checked he didn't need anything and left him to it.' She shed the uniform jacket and cap and hung them on the back of the door alongside her gas-mask box. 'And I've got some news about Shirley,' she said, reaching for the teapot.

Peggy was delighted to hear of Shirley's happy news. 'Well, that certainly clears up a mystery,' she said with a smile. 'I went to the factory on my way home and was told she'd given in her notice. I shall miss having her and the baby around, but she's much better off being with her own family again.'

She sat down and sipped her tea. 'But you'll miss her more, I suspect. Shirley was a good friend, wasn't she?'

'I certainly will, but as you say, she's back where she really belongs.'

Peggy caught the wistfulness in April's face and took her hand. 'There's still a chance your mother might relent,' she said softly.

'I doubt she will, and even if she does, I don't know how I'll feel about it. There have been too many years of coldness between us, and after this...' She ran her hand over her bump and then sighed. 'I thought I'd ask Uncle Stan to help me understand why she's been like she is. He's hinted that she'd had problems of some sort when I was small, but then clammed up.'

'Perhaps it's better not to pry,' said Peggy thoughtfully. 'It might just make things worse for you.'

'I don't see how,' April retorted. 'She's virtually ignored me for most of my life, hasn't bothered to write or telephone, and certainly hasn't put herself out to come and see Stan.' She gave a wry smile. 'That makes me sound bitter, doesn't it? And yet, despite everything, I just need her to love me.'

Peggy's heart lurched and she rushed to hug

429

the girl to her. 'Oh, my dear, I so wish things were different for you,' she murmured. 'If you were my little girl I'd move heaven and earth to ensure you knew you were loved.'

'I know,' April replied tremulously. 'And I love you for that, Peggy, really I do.'

They embraced in silence for a moment until they had their emotions and their tears under control, and then Peggy returned to her chair. She sipped her tea and lit a cigarette, but her hand was still unsteady, and she could see that April was trying her best to put a brave face on things.

'Did you know my mother?' April asked finally.

'Not really. We were at junior school together, but then she got a scholarship to a posh school in Eastbourne, and was rarely seen at home after that.' Peggy sighed. 'I know from Stan that she went on to university to take a degree in law because he was immensely proud of her and told everyone.'

April stared at her in shock. 'Mother studied law?'

Peggy frowned. 'You didn't know? But surely she must have said something? After all, that's where she met your father.' She realised the girl was stunned by this news, and was immediately contrite. 'I'm sorry, April. I wouldn't have said anything if I'd known how it would affect you.'

April shook her head. 'I'm glad you did. But what I can't understand is why she didn't continue to practise after I was born. For an ambitious woman to give up on something like that is incomprehensible.'

'Well, I don't know, dear,' said Peggy. She'd said

enough and had no wish to add anything more in the light of the girl's shock. 'That's something only your mother can tell you.'

'Uncle Stan might know. Perhaps that's what they fell out about all those years ago. Though I can't see why.' April fiddled with the teaspoon, then let it rattle into the saucer. 'I wish I'd asked more questions when Daddy was alive,' she said on a sigh.

'It's a regret we all have,' replied Peggy. 'I wish I'd talked more to my parents about their lives, and the family history. But I was too busy with my own life to take much notice of their reminiscences, and now they're gone, it's too late, and all I have are old faded photographs.'

She pushed back from the table and checked on the pie. The suet Alf had supplied had turned the potato pastry to a golden flaky topping, and just looking at it made her mouth water. She transferred it to the smaller oven where it would keep warm but not overcook and then turned back to April.

'I understand your need to know more about what makes your mother the way she is, but do try not to badger Stan about it, dear. He isn't as strong as before, and I'm sure none of us want him to suffer any undue stress.'

Of course not, Peggy. I'll just ask him a few questions and see how willing he is to talk about her. If there's the slightest sign that he's getting upset, then I'll leave it.'

Peggy gave an inward sigh of relief, for what she'd heard about Mildred from Stan over the years wasn't edifying, and she was almost certain

431

that he would find talking about her to April extremely difficult. Especially as April was so vulnerable still and only weeks away from giving birth.

29

Stan was such a popular man that there were always visitors at his bedside when April went in to see him, and so it was another ten days before she could catch him on his own. It was a lovely early August afternoon and April had made a point of arriving at the hospital early, in the knowledge that Stan would probably be in the small garden at the back and that she could sneak out there without Matron discovering her.

It was a walled garden, with a patch of grass at the centre and deep flower beds stuffed with hollyhocks, lavender, Canterbury bells, yellow-centred daisies and all manner of blooms that wouldn't have looked out of place surrounding a cottage. Roses and honeysuckle trailed along the mellow brick walls, and the wooden trellis above the paved seating area was positively dripping with purple clematis and clambering sweet-scented scarlet roses.

April saw Stan immediately, for he was alone on the sun-dappled terrace and dozing peacefully in a wicker chair in his pyjamas and dressing gown. He looked remarkably well, for his colour was good and he'd clearly lost quite a bit of weight. She tiptoed over and sat down, reluctant to disturb him, but worried that the opportunity to talk to him privately might be lost by the arrival of other visitors.

He gave a little grunt and blinked sleepily at her before breaking into a wide smile. 'I must be getting old,' he said ruefully. 'I never usually drop off during the day.'

'Oh, I think you've earned a nap after all you've been through,' she said fondly. 'I'm sorry if I disturbed you.'

'Well, don't be. It's lovely to see you and have you all to myself for once. How are you?'

She brought him up to date on everything and assured him she was feeling very well indeed. 'And what about you, Uncle Stan? You're looking very trim, I must say. Any news on when you might be coming home?'

He patted his stomach and beamed with pleasure. 'I've lost two whole stone and feel much better for it, even though I'm missing Ethel's cooking something rotten. And the really good news is that I should be out of here early next week.'

'That's marvellous to hear. I bet Ethel and Ruby are thrilled.'

'They don't know yet, so keep it under your hat. I want to surprise them when they visit this evening.' He fiddled with the braid that edged his tartan dressing gown. 'Of course I won't be allowed to rush about like I used to, or lift heavy things, or work in my allotment – not at first, anyway. But you wait, April, I'll be back to my old self before you know it once I can get out of here and back home where I belong.'

433

'You just make sure you don't overdo things, Stan,' she said firmly. 'We don't want you to have another attack.'

'Ethel will keep a close eye on me, never fear,' he replied comfortably. 'And I certainly never want to feel pain like that again.' He laced his fingers over his much reduced stomach and regarded her thoughtfully. 'I get the feeling you've been wanting to talk to me about something these past few days, April.'

'There is something I want to discuss with you,' she admitted, 'but I'm not sure if this is the right time, or even if you'd be willing.'

His gaze was steady as he regarded her. 'This is about your mother, isn't it?' At her nod he gave a deep sigh. 'I knew we'd have to have this conversation one day, and I can't say I've been looking forward to it.'

April felt a pang of guilt. 'Then we won't take it any further.'

He was silent as he gazed out to the garden, following a pair of red admiral butterflies which were darting back and forth above the flower beds. 'No,' he murmured. 'It's right you should know – especially as you're about to become a mother yourself.'

April waited for him to gather his thoughts.

'I loved my sister,' he said. 'She was such a bright little thing, with an enquiring mind and a winning smile that could charm the birds out of the trees. My parents were overjoyed when she was born, for the loss of little Daphne to scarlet fever had been the most terrible blow, and it seemed to them that Mildred had been a gift

434

from God in their later years.'

April kept still and silent, not wanting to break the spell.

'I suppose we all spoilt her because we loved her so – and that, unfortunately, was her undoing.' Stan took a deep breath and raised his face to the sunlight dappling through the tangled branches of the clematis and roses. 'We all realised she was very clever, and my poor parents were at their wits' end because they simply couldn't afford to send her to the sort of school that would challenge her. And then she won a scholarship to a fancy place in Sussex. There were still some fees to pay, and of course things like books and uniform to buy, but my parents scrimped and saved and Mother took on cleaning jobs and extra laundry so Mildred could take advantage of this life-changing opportunity.'

He dipped his chin, his expression betraying his sadness. 'Mixing with all those privileged girls changed Mildred, and opened doors to a whole different world that dazzled her. It was inevitable, I suppose, that as time went on she drifted away from us. She spent her holidays at grand country houses or London apartments and took on hoity-toity mannerisms and started talking as if she had a plum in her mouth.'

April could just imagine it, but she said nothing, realising that now Stan had opened up to her, he meant to tell her all he knew.

'When she did come home she treated Mum and Dad like servants, and refused to have very much to do with me or my pals because she thought we were common oiks. She became demanding and would sulk for days when our parents confessed they simply couldn't afford the luxuries she'd become used to.'

April could just imagine the heartache that must have caused. 'She sounds as if she was an absolute horror,' she murmured. 'Your poor parents.'

Stan shrugged. 'They just wanted her to have the education and privileges they'd never had, not realising it would lead to her resenting their lowly status, and perhaps even being embarrassed by them. She never invited her friends to stay, and as time went on she simply didn't bother to come home at all.'

April tensed as Stan fidgeted in his chair, for she suspected that what was coming wasn't easy for him. She reached over and clasped his hand. 'You don't have to go on if it upsets you,' she murmured.

'I've kept silent too long, and you've earned the right to be told the truth.' He clasped her hand and took a deep breath. 'What has your mother told you about her life before you were born, April?'

'Nothing very much at all. But I understand she went on to college and then university to study law. So she was obviously very bright.'

Stan nodded. 'She was a clever girl, and to begin with she worked hard and set her goals high.' His smile was wry. 'But Mildred wanted it all: a career, a wealthy husband and the sort of life her upper-crust friends enjoyed. She latched onto your father because he fitted the bill, but her studies suffered because of her social life, and at the end of her second year she failed her examinations quite dramatically and was sent down.'

April frowned. 'So she never actually qualified? Is that why she became a secretary?'

Stan chuckled. 'I don't know where you got that idea from. Mildred would never lower herself to be someone's secretary.' He looked at her in puzzlement. 'How come you don't know any of this, April? Surely one of your parents must have talked to you?'

'I didn't think to ask about their lives before I came along – especially after Mother made it so clear she had no wish to discuss it. I just sort of assumed they'd always lived in Tunbridge Wells where my father had his solicitor's office.'

'I see.' Stan fell silent and gazed once more at the garden. 'Well, there's a reason why they were both so reluctant to talk about those early years, April.' He turned to look at her, his expression concerned. 'But it won't make pleasant listening. Are you sure you want to know?'

April's pulse was racing and she was finding it hard to breathe, so she just nodded and steeled herself for what was to come.

'Your father was a few years older than your mother, and I think he was dazzled by her to the point where, for the first and only time in his life, he allowed his heart to rule his head. He came from a distinguished and wealthy family who numbered Queen's Counsels and judges amongst their ranks, and I don't think they approved of Mildred at all.' He gave a sigh. 'I think she was regarded as rather flighty, and of course her background was hardly top drawer.'

April remained silent as this entirely different

437

Mildred slowly came to light.

'Your father was a respected lawyer who was a rising star and expected to be awarded his silk earlier than most. Your mother was a striking girl who'd used her influential friends to get her onto the board of some prestigious arts council, and she too became quite a star in the world of the arts, and was the darling of the society press. She and your father became the golden couple and their society wedding was recorded in most of the newspapers.'

He heaved a regretful sigh. 'The first I knew about it was when the papers were delivered by the mail train. My parents were dead by then, thank God, so they couldn't be hurt, but I was cut to the quick.'

'But that's awful,' breathed April. 'How could she simply ignore her family?'

His expression was grim. 'The way she did everything – with no thought for others' feelings.'

'So what went wrong, Uncle Stan? How did this golden couple with such bright futures end up in Tunbridge Wells?'

Stan hesitated and then rushed on. 'Your mother had an affair with the head of your father's chambers.' April gasped and he gripped her hand in empathy. 'She was bewitched by this man's looks, his eminence and his vast wealth. He was a decade older than Mildred, but seemed to have the world at his feet and the key to open doors otherwise closed to her. I'm afraid she found your father dull and pedestrian by contrast.'

April had painful memories of how her mother had never missed an opportunity to snipe at her father and belittle him. 'Poor Daddy,' she managed through her tears. 'How could she *do* that to him?'

'Once Mildred set her sights on something she was like a terrier,' Stan replied bitterly. 'She was bored with your father even though they lived quite the high life amongst their smart London set. She wanted to experience the glamour and excitement that this man could offer. Unfortunately his wife stood in the way of her ambitions.'

April gasped again. 'He was married?' She thought swiftly. 'So it all had to come to an end,' she said, 'and she had to go back to Daddy. Did he know about the affair?'

'He knew, as did half of London, because Mildred was about as subtle as Wallis Simpson when it came to pursuing her man.' Stan's expression was dour as he continued. 'The affair went on, with this man stringing Mildred along with promises he had no intention of keeping – and then something happened to change everything.'

April found she was holding her breath and she released it with a trembling sigh. 'Mother got pregnant, didn't she?' At his reluctant nod she could only stare at him, unable to ask the question that clamoured in her head.

Stan took a handkerchief from his dressing-gown pocket and wiped his perspiring face. 'Mildred confessed to me that she didn't know at first whose baby you were, but she used her pregnancy to pressurise her lover into divorcing his childless wife and marrying her.'

'That sounds more like the Mildred I know,' muttered April.

439

'Mildred was manipulative and sly and concerned only with what she wanted. It didn't matter to her whose you were as long as she could use you as a bargaining tool.'

April felt a pang of hurt at this. 'So, what happened, Uncle Stan?'

His smile was wry. 'Her lover had an ace up his sleeve that even Mildred couldn't have predicted.' He chuckled. 'You see, despite all his wealth, he'd been born with some condition that made him infertile, and although he'd consulted the best doctors in the world, he had yet to find a cure.'

April burst into tears of relief. 'So I am Daddy's after all,' she sobbed. 'Oh, thank God, thank God.'

Stan put his arm round her shoulders and waited until the storm was over. 'I only met your father once, but he seemed to me to be a good man who loved you very much, April, and that is something to cherish.'

'And I do,' she replied hoarsely. 'Just as I treasure you for so willingly opening your heart to me, and reliving those dark memories.' She drew from his embrace and gathered her thoughts. 'But there's more to tell, isn't there?'

'Unfortunately, there is,' he murmured. 'The man in question wanted nothing more to do with her, but Mildred is vengeful, and she threatened to expose him as a liar and cheat with an unfortunate defect if he didn't settle a considerable amount of money on her.' He grimaced. 'She'd had high expectations, and was determined to get something out of the affair.'

April was horrified She'd always known her mother was grasping, but she'd never suspected

440

she could stoop that low. 'Did he pay?'

Stan's smile was wry. 'Not in the way she'd hoped. He called her bluff, you see, and was wealthy and powerful enough to quash any mischief by threatening to sue her for libel and attempted blackmail.'

'Good for him,' said April tartly. 'Though the pair of them sound as if they deserve one another.'

Stan chuckled. 'I think you're right, April.'

April giggled. 'I bet she was seething.'

Stan nodded. 'She'd certainly met her match, and there was absolutely nothing she could do about it.'

'Was that why she and Daddy moved to Tunbridge Wells?'

'London can be a very small place when rumours start circulating and careers are put in jeopardy. Your father's position in chambers suddenly became untenable, and Mildred was voted off the board due to the rumours that were now affecting the council's respectability. Your father decided they needed to leave when it became clear that his career had been stalled by Mildred's lover, and that their child would be born under a cloud of malicious gossip and speculation. They moved to Tunbridge Wells and he became a suburban solicitor.'

'And Mother hated every minute of it, didn't she? She resented me because I was the reason her affair came to an end and she lost not only her lover, but her career and reputation. She was stuck with a baby she hadn't wanted, and a husband she clearly didn't love in a town she loathed for its middle-class snobbery. No wonder she couldn't even bring herself to like me.'

'I'm sorry, April. I wish I could find the words to make things better for you, but Mildred always had to blame someone else for her misfortune, and nothing will change her now.'

April chewed her lip, thinking of how Mildred's bitterness had coloured her life and her father's. 'But I don't understand, why she didn't hire a nanny to look after me if that was how she felt. Then at least she could have immersed herself in the snobbish community in Tunbridge Wells.'

Stan shifted in his chair. 'I don't know all the ins and outs of it; Mildred didn't bare her soul entirely to me when she came down with you all those years ago. I think her confidence had been badly shaken, and she didn't have the heart to start again once she'd left London.'

'That's rather sad, isn't it?'

'I suppose so, considering how much promise she'd shown in her early years. But Mildred was the architect of her own downfall, and it wasn't fair of her to punish you and your father for it.'

'I'm surprised she confided in you at all,' April murmured. 'She's never been one to let her feelings show.'

'It was unusual. But that night she'd been drinking quite heavily, and as I was feeling emotional after losing Barbara, I made some remark about what a lovely little girl you were, and didn't she realise how lucky she was to have you when Barbara and I had been denied children. I then made the mistake of asking her why she was so cold with you – and that set her off.'

He gave a deep sigh and tears glistened in his eyes. 'It was quite shocking how the bitterness poured out of her, and I'm afraid I ended up telling her a few harsh home truths. She left the following day, and I haven't seen her since.'

April kissed his cheek and gripped his hand. 'But we've found each other again,' she said, 'and for that I'll always be thankful. You've helped me to understand her now, and funnily enough, I can even empathise with how trapped she must have felt. No wonder she was so furious with me for getting pregnant. Although the circumstances are different, it was history repeating itself – and that must have brought it all back for her.'

'Aye. I think you could be right. But her anger shows that despite everything she does harbour some feelings for you, April.'

April felt a spark of hope as she thought about that, but it was soon extinguished by cold reality. Mildred's anger hadn't come from love, but from fear that her daughter's disgrace would bring yet another scandal to blight her life.

Stan got to his feet and stretched. 'Let's go and find a cup of tea. I'm parched after all that talking.'

April left the hospital a while later to take over at the station from Ron, who had an important Home Guard meeting that evening. Her thoughts were still going over all she'd learned from Stan, and although she felt she knew and understood her mother more clearly now, it saddened her to realise that no matter what the future held, their relationship would never change.

However, there was a part of April that couldn't

help but feel sorry for Mildred, and tears blinded her as she plodded up the hill. Mildred had clearly led a lonely, frustrated life, and although she'd brought it all upon herself, she'd paid a high price. Perhaps a letter might ease things between them – or would it only make it worse? Mildred would know immediately that Stan had told her everything, and therefore he'd be dragged into it all again. And he didn't deserve that.

April was deep in thought when a great shout went up in the bar of the Crown. Startled, she didn't have time to get out of the way as the doors slammed back against the wall and a struggling, swearing, fighting group of black and white GIs crashed straight into her.

She was knocked off balance, and as she fought to stay on her feet she was shoved in the back by someone, caught a flying fist in her midriff from someone else, and an elbow in her jaw, which sent her headlong into the road, cracking her head sharply against the unforgiving tarmac.

The fighting men hadn't noticed. They punched and wrestled, their heavy boots trampling within inches of April's sprawled body as the skirmish spread into the street and Gloria bellowed at them to stop.

Winded by the punch to her midriff and stunned by the crack to her head, April found she couldn't move even though a Military Police truck was now hurtling towards her. The men on board clearly hadn't seen her, for they were fully focused on the brawl.

She tried to shift out of the way, to call out for help. But a terrible weight seemed to be pressing her to the ground, and the punch had stolen her voice. She froze in terror. There was a squeal of brakes and the truck rocked on its chassis, tyres screeching, the driver fighting to get it under control.

But it was going too fast, and looming ever closer. As horrified screams rent the air, April fainted.

Ron had left the station with Harvey in search of his tea before he went to tonight's Home Guard meeting. April was probably already on her way to relieve him, and he expected to see her coming up the High Street as he crossed the little bridge.

He and Harvey froze as the high-pitched scream rent the air and tyres screeched on tarmac. Ron took in the scene in an instant.

An army truck was skidding out of control and rocking dangerously on its chassis. A group of Yanks were having a set-to nearby, and Gloria Stevens was pushing her way through the melee with fists and elbows to get to the still figure lying right in the path of the truck.

With a whine of concern, Harvey shot down the hill as Gloria stood over the prone figure, arms waving and yelling blue murder. The fighting had come to an abrupt halt and the High Street had turned into a horrified, transfixed tableau.

Galvanised into action, Ron raced after his dog, his fearful gaze taking in the careering truck, the girl on the road and the brave woman resolutely guarding her as the heavy wheels and armoured fender bore down on them.

Harvey was now also standing guard, barking

445

furiously at the truck as the bystanders watched open-mouthed, seemingly incapable of moving.

Ron was running at full pelt down the hill, and he caught up with the truck as it slew to a juddering halt within inches of Gloria's outstretched hands and Harvey's nose.

There was a moment of absolute silence but for the ticking of the truck's hot engine, and then, with admirable aplomb, Gloria yelled, 'Someone get an ambulance. Now.'

Ron could see she was ashen beneath the heavy make-up. Sweat beaded her top lip and her hands were trembling as she dropped to her knees and quickly drew April's dress over her sprawled legs before gently brushing the girl's hair from her face.

He pushed a frantic Harvey out of the way, knelt down and searched for April's pulse in her unresponsive wrist. It was weak and irregular, and the colour had drained from her face, making her look ghastly. 'She's still with us,' he breathed, 'but only just.'

'Get that bloody ambulance,' Gloria yelled to no one in particular. 'Go on, move yer ruddy arses. As for you,' she said, looking up at the four American MPs who'd climbed shakily out of their truck. 'Arrest the lot of 'em,' she ordered, jerking her thumb at the stunned GIs who still stood dumbly by, 'and someone fetch blankets.'

Ron could see the dark swell of a bruise on April's jaw and suspected there were probably others beneath her clothes. 'What on earth happened, Gloria?'

'A fight broke out 'cos I were serving them

446

black GIs,' she snapped. 'Before I knew it they were outside and April got caught up in it.' She grabbed the blanket someone had brought and tenderly placed it over April's swollen belly. 'Gawd knows what damage's been done, Ron.'

Very gently, Ron held April's wrist, once more searching for a pulse, praying his fears would be unfounded. But her pulse was so faint he could barely locate it, and there was a blue tinge to the delicate skin above her lips that didn't bode at all well. It would be a miracle if she and the baby survived.

30

Peggy was in the middle of packing a supper of Scotch egg, fresh garden salad and two slices of thick bread with a scrape of real butter for April's tea. She would take it up once the others had eaten and keep her company until the last train had come in, then they could walk home together.

She was just thinking how pleasant it would be to stroll up to the station on this lovely warm August evening without the hindrance of Daisy and her pram, when the telephone rang. She turned to Sarah who was laying the table. 'Get that, dear, would you? And if it's Doris, tell her I've gone out. I can't be dealing with her today.'

She placed the tin of supper in her basket, musing on how nice it was to get the chance to escape motherly duties now and then and just be herself when Sarah came back from the hall. One look at her pale, shocked face told Peggy that something bad must have happened.

'That was Gloria from the Crown,' said Sarah. 'April's had an accident and Ron's gone with her to the hospital in the ambulance.'

Peggy stared at her, unable to absorb what she was hearing. 'Gloria? April? Accident?' Then she snapped out of it and reached for her handbag, gas-mask box and jacket. 'At the hospital with Ron, you say? Did Gloria give you any details?'

'She just said she's been badly hurt and that we should get to the hospital pronto.'

'Right, tell the others when they get in and look after Daisy. I'll phone the moment I get any more news.' Peggy kissed Daisy's curly head hastily and then ran out of the back door, bag, gas-mask box and jacket flying.

She ran all the way down Camden Road, ignoring everyone and swerving impatiently around knots of gossiping women and ambling walkers. Skidding round the imposing pillars at the gateway to the hospital, she pulled on her jacket as she took the steps two at a time and then headed through the vast reception area into the Casualty department.

Ron was grim-faced and pacing the floor at the far end of the waiting room, and Harvey lay still and mournful-eyed beneath a row of chairs. Peggy knew then that April's accident had been serious. 'How is she?' she panted.

In reply, Ron gently took her by the shoulders and pressed her down into a hard wooden chair. He took her hands in his. 'She's with the doctor

448

now, Peggy,' he said solemnly, 'being prepared for an operation.'

Peggy could only stare at him as awful images flashed through her mind.

'There's a hairline fracture in her skull, and another in her jaw. The surgeon assures me that under normal circumstances such operations are almost commonplace and the patient is expected to fully recover.' He gripped her hands. 'But there are complications with April.'

Dread weighed heavily round her heart. 'What complications?' she managed hoarsely. 'Is it the baby?'

'It certainly has a bearing,' he said gruffly. 'You see, April caught a fist in the midriff which broke a rib and caused some bruising to her intestines.'

Peggy reeled back in shock. 'A fist! Someone punched April?'

'It's not like you think, Peggy, and I'll explain it all later,' he soothed. 'For now you have to listen to me and try to stay calm.' His gaze was steady, his hands gripping her to keep her still. 'Do you think you can do that?'

Peggy didn't think she'd ever be calm again, but Ron looked so determined to have his say, and Rita was hurrying towards them, her face such a picture of anguish, that she swallowed her rage and did her best to get her emotions under control.

'What's happened, Auntie Peg?' Rita asked. 'I saw you run past the fire station so I knew something must be up.'

Ron repeated what he'd told Peggy. 'I was just explaining that there are complications,' he said.

'Having suffered a blow to the abdomen, the surgeon is afraid that April might go into early labour during the operation. And if she does, then he and the gynaecologist might have to face the almost impossible option of saving either the baby or the mother.'

Peggy closed her eyes. 'Dear God in heaven,' she breathed. 'How can any mortal man be expected to do such a thing?'

'To be sure 'twill be God's decision in the end,' Ron muttered. 'But when I was a boy I remember my mam telling me that in such circumstances Catholics believe that the child should be saved.'

'But April's not a Catholic,' said Rita. 'And I can't see how leaving a child motherless can do it any good at all.'

'Surely there must be a way to save them both?' breathed Peggy, who was trying very hard not to cry.

'He promised he and the consultant gynaecologist will do their very best,' said Ron. 'And you never know, she might not go into labour, in which case they'll both have a fighting chance of coming through this.'

Peggy struggled to keep calm as Ron told them what had happened outside the Crown. She was shocked that a group of men could have been so caught up in their fight that they were oblivious to the vulnerable pregnant woman in their midst and horrified to learn that she'd been punched by a flying fist – the owner of which should have been clapped in irons! Patiently, Ron answered her and Rita's questions, then the three of them fell silent and sat there deep in their thoughts as the busy life of the department went on around them. Harvey crept beneath the chairs until he was curled behind Ron's sturdy legs out of sight of the bustling nurses and doctors and the omnipresent eye of Matron.

Peggy struggled to keep her worst fears at bay as the clock on the wall ticked away the time and still there was no word from theatre. Rita went off to try and track down Fran, but she was in theatre and not expected out for at least another two hours, so she got everyone a cup of tea and returned to the waiting room. Ron telephoned Beach View and the Anchor to pass on the news, and shortly afterwards, Gloria Stevens came marching in with Rosie.

'I bumped into Rose outside,' said Gloria. 'How's she doing?'

Peggy was surprised to see them together, for she knew they didn't really like one another. But then news travelled fast in Cliffehaven – especially bad news – and in times of crisis people put aside their differences and came together. She noticed that Ron looked decidedly uncomfortable as he relayed the news again, and Peggy suspected his conscience was troubling him now he was faced with the two women.

Gloria pulled a small bottle of brandy from her vast handbag. 'I thought you could all do with a snifter,' she said. 'I know I could.' She filled the metal measuring cup and swigged it back before passing the bottle and cup to Ron.

When it came to Peggy's turn she drank gratefully and handed the almost empty bottle back. She was about to ask Gloria for all the details of

451

what had happened when she caught a heart-warming sight.

Sarah was in charge of Daisy and her pushchair, and Ivy had tight hold of Cordelia's arm as well as a large basket as they walked into the waiting area and made their slow way towards them. And behind them were Ethel and Ruby.

'I thought Ethel should know,' said Sarah, parking the pushchair. 'And none of us could bear staying at home not knowing what was happening, so once Bertie brought Cordelia back, we packed up the supper and brought it along with fresh flasks of hot, sweet tea. I didn't think you'd mind the added sugar, not at a time like this.'

'Not at all,' said Peggy. 'It was a lovely thought, but I doubt any of us have an appetite just now.'

Cordelia was clearly upset, and she dabbed her eyes with a handkerchief. 'Is there any news on how the operation's going?' she asked.

'We just have to wait,' said Peggy, taking her soft hand and giving it an encouraging squeeze.

Ethel plumped herself down and started rolling a cigarette. 'You'd better tell me what's going on,' she muttered. 'I don't want Stan 'earing about this and getting the wrong end of the stick and worrying 'imself silly.'

Gloria and Ron took it in turns to tell everyone the full story. When Ron repeated what the doctor had said, he was met with a stunned silence. Cordelia was pale and on the verge of tears, and Ruby and the other girls did their best to comfort her, although they too were reeling in shock.

'It's probably best he saves April and lets the baby go,' said Ethel into the heavy silence. 'After

452

all, she were going to give it away anyway.'

Everyone gasped and stared at her in disgust. Ruby shot her a furious glare and gave her a sharp jab in the ribs with her elbow. 'Mum, that sort of talk ain't called for,' she hissed.

'If you ain't got anything sensible or kind to say, Ethel,' snapped Gloria, 'then I suggest you shut your gob.'

'There ain't no need to speak to me like that,' huffed Ethel. 'I only said what everyone were thinkin'. April didn't want it in the first place – and in the second place, she's still young enough to find 'erself an 'usband and 'ave more kids. It'd be the best thing all round, if you ask me.'

'Nobody asked you nothing,' growled Gloria. 'And if you don't shut your filthy gob right this minute I'll flaming well shut it for you.' Gloria's meaty fist was now wavering inches from Ethel's nose.

'That's quite enough from both of you,' snapped Rosie. 'April could be dying on that operating table – the baby too – so either shut up or get out.'

Gloria had the decency to look ashamed at her outburst, and uncurled her fist. Ruby glowered at her mother, still appalled at her cruel tongue, and Harvey crept further behind Ron as if to keep well out of the firing line.

Peggy saw Ron give Rosie a sly wink, then he glared beneath his brows at Ethel, who was now puffing furiously on her cigarette, arms tightly folded, avoiding everyone's gaze. The fraught atmosphere had been further soured by that show of nastiness, and Peggy wished Ethel would leave. She clearly didn't want to be here, and for all her recent show of warming to April, she seemed not to really care what happened to her or her baby.

They drank the tea and smoked cigarettes as the time ticked away and no one came to tell them anything. Daisy began to get restless and was making a bit of a nuisance of herself, so Rita offered to take her back to Beach View and put her to bed.

'I don't know about you, Rose,' said Gloria, 'but I got a pub to run, and that new girl ain't too reliable.' She gathered up her things. 'But I tell yer what, mate, there ain't gunna be a Yank of any flamin' colour in my pub again – not for a long while. More trouble than they're flamin' worth, with their fightin' and the filthy way they talk to them coloured boys.'

'It'd certainly be something to consider,' sighed Rosie. 'I've had a couple of incidents lately, but luckily managed to nip it in the bud before it got out of hand. I really can't understand why the Americans can't get on with one another – after all, they're all fighting the same bloody war.'

Gloria nodded in agreement. She shot a venomous glance at Ethel and then turned to Ron. 'Let me know the minute you hear anything – no matter what the time. I probably won't sleep easy tonight anyway.'

After she and Rosie had left, Ethel looked at the clock and picked up her bag and gas-mask box. 'It's time to visit Stan. I won't say nothing to 'im. Don't want 'im having another heart attack, do I?'

Ruby glowered at her. 'He'll never forgive you if she dies and you said nothing. He has a right to know, Mum.'

Ethel looked at Ruby with narrowed eyes. 'I know what's best for Stan,' she said crossly, 'and don't forget you got yer late shift tonight. We still got rent to pay and food to buy, no matter what's going on.' With that, she stomped off.

With Ethel gone the atmosphere lightened somewhat, but the continued silence from the surgeon was beginning to make them all fearful. 'Do you think I ought to telephone her mother, Ron?' Peggy asked.

'Aye, it might be wise, but it'll take her time to get here.'

'If she bothers at all,' said Peggy acidly. She dug about in her handbag and gave an exasperated sigh. 'Have you got any money on you for the phone box? Only I don't seem to have brought my purse.'

Ron handed over all his loose change and Peggy hurried off. It would mean making a trunk call, which was expensive, but this was an emergency and Mildred had a right to know that her daughter's life hung by a thread.

The red telephone box was just outside the main entrance and Peggy stepped inside, letting the door swing closed behind her as she piled the money on top of the coin box and searched in her bag for her address book. Once she'd found Mildred's number, she lifted the receiver and was relieved when Vera Gardener answered. She quickly explained what had happened and was put through immediately.

The telephone rang and rang and Peggy didn't think Mildred could be at home, but just as she was about to hang up, the receiver was lifted at the other end, so she quickly fumbled a coin into the slot and pressed button A.

'Mildred? It's Peggy Reilly,' she said breathlessly.

'If she's gone into labour then I'm not a bit interested,' said Mildred.

Peggy tamped down on the stab of anger and quickly told her the reason she was telephoning.

There was a long silence at the other end.

'Mildred, are you still there? I know this must come as an awful shock to you, and I'm sorry to be the bearer of such terrible news, but I really do think you should come. April needs you.'

'I can't possibly just drop everything in the middle of the night and get on a train,' said Mildred indignantly. 'I'll do my best to get a travel permit tomorrow once I've organised someone to take over my business establishment, but I can't promise anything.'

Peggy was filled with such fury she could barely speak. 'Your daughter and her baby might be dead by then, Mildred,' she said icily. 'But if you can live with the knowledge that you turned your back on them in what could be your daughter's last hours, then God help you.'

She slammed down the receiver and had to take a moment to get her breath back. But she swore then and there that if Mildred didn't come, she'd damned well go to Tunbridge Wells and drag her here.

Stan had been permitted by Matron to get dressed

456

and sit in the visitors' lounge as he was due to be discharged within a few days. He kept glancing eagerly at the door, waiting for Ethel and Ruby to arrive, but as the other visitors came in and the time ticked away, he began to feel uneasy. They'd never been late before, and had both promised to come tonight, so where were they?

He fidgeted in the easy chair, flicked through an old magazine and then tossed it aside. Something must have happened. He could feel it in his bones, and it made him shiver. A glance at the clock told him there were only twenty minutes to go before the bell went for the end of visiting time. He couldn't just sit here, he thought fretfully, he'd go mad with worry.

Stan hauled himself out of the chair, checked on the number of coins he had in his pockets, and made his way along the corridor to the pay-phone at the end. He could feel his heart begin to thud, and his breathing was a bit ragged, but he had to telephone the station and speak to April. The worst thing about being incarcerated in this place was the suspicion that no one told him anything of any importance in case it upset him, and he was fed up and frustrated at being kept in the dark. But April was a good girl, and if she realised he was worried, then she'd tell him straight if something had happened.

He was on the point of lifting the receiver when he heard the unmistakable sound of Ethel's voice. 'What you doing out 'ere, Stan?'

He turned guiltily and shot her a smile of relief. 'I was about to telephone April and find out where you'd got to,' he said after he'd kissed her.

'I was worried something had happened to you and Ruby.'

'Silly old sod,' she said with affectionate impatience. 'I were late off shift, that's all, and Ruby 'ad to go in early.'

There was something in her manner that made Stan look at her more sharply. 'Are you sure that's all it was? Nothing's happened I should know about?'

Her gaze slid away from him and she began to dig in her handbag for her cigarettes. 'Course not,' she retorted. 'Whatever give you that idea?'

Stan was more certain than ever that something was going on. He stilled her hand and drew her towards him. 'Look at me, Ethel,' he said evenly. 'Look me in the eye and tell me the truth.'

She reluctantly lifted her chin, and although she tried to appear defiant, her expression told him she was hiding something. 'You'd do better to go and sit down,' she said. 'I can tell you ain't feeling the full ticket.'

'That's because I'm worried,' he replied. 'What's the real reason you were late?'

She took a deep breath and let it out on a sigh. 'I'll tell you, but you gotta sit down first. I don't like the sound of yer breathing.'

Stan didn't much care for it either and as his chest was feeling tight, he meekly allowed Ethel to steer him back to the visitors' room. He plumped down in the chair and fixed her with a steady gaze. 'Tell me.'

As Ethel hesitantly told him what had happened his heart rate increased and his chest seemed to tighten. He fumbled in his waistcoat pocket for the little pill the doctor had given him for such occasions and slipped it under his tongue.

'I knew I shouldn't have told yer,' said a frantic Ethel. 'But you went on and on and now look at yer. I'm getting the doctor.'

'Stay where you are,' Stan ordered weakly. 'I'll be fine as long as you don't make a fuss.'

He tried to relax and let the pill do its work as Ethel sniffled at his side, but he was frightened at how easily he'd become unwell – and terrified that his beloved April might die before he got the chance to see her again.

'Oh, Gawd, Stan, I wish you'd let me get a doctor to see to you.'

He waved his hand dismissively at this suggestion, wishing she'd be still and let him concentrate on getting his heart rate back to normal.

'I should never 'ave told yer,' she sobbed. 'I knew it weren't right, despite Ruby insisting I should.'

His breathing finally became easier, and the tightness in his chest slowly disappeared. 'I'm glad you did,' he said. 'April's very dear to me, and if anything happened to her, I'm afraid I would find it hard to forgive you for keeping silent.'

'I'm sorry, Stan,' she said, mopping up her tears. 'But I were that worried about 'ow you'd take it. I thought I were doing the best thing.'

'I know that, love,' he replied wearily. He took her hand and held it to his heart. 'There, feel that? Running as good as gold again, so you've no need to worry.'

She blinked back her tears and gave a tremulous smile. 'She'll be all right, Stan, I'm sure of it,' she murmured. 'April's young and strong, and they'll look after her 'ere.'

Stan thought about that and prayed Ethel was right, but the realisation that he could lose April before the night was out weighed heavy. 'I have to find out what's happening,' he said, struggling to his feet. But the floor seemed to tilt beneath him and the room spun alarmingly, sending him slumping back into the chair.

'Right, that's it,' snapped Ethel. 'I'm getting the doctor whether you like it or not.'

Stan was too drained and dizzy to argue. He closed his eyes as she bustled out of the room and the next thing he knew he was back in his bed, a little nurse hovering at his side. 'Where's Ethel?' he managed.

'It's after ten o'clock, Mr Dawkins,' the girl replied, checking his pulse. 'I sent her home over two hours ago.'

Stan grasped her hand urgently. 'I have to know how my niece is doing,' he rasped. 'Her name's April Wilton and she had emergency surgery tonight to save her and her baby.'

'I'll see if I can find out, but you've got to promise to try not to worry, Mr Dawkins. You don't want another attack, do you?' She noted down his temperature and pulse on the chart and hung the clipboard over the end of the bed. 'I'll get Doctor to give you something to help you relax.'

Stan was asleep by the time the nurse had managed to get any news on April.

Four hours had passed since April had gone into theatre, and with no news from anyone, Ron was restlessly pacing the floor. He'd been up to the station to see to the trains, had informed his superior at the Home Guard meeting that he wouldn't be attending, and had eaten the Scotch egg with a lettuce sandwich and drunk half a flask of tea. Now the food seemed to be churning in his stomach, and the only way to stop it was to keep on the move.

Ruby had left to go to her night shift at the factory, and Ivy had gone back to Beach View to take over babysitting duty from Rita and to snatch some sleep before she went on shift at five the following morning. Although visiting time was long over, there had been no further sign of Ethel – which was a huge relief, because Ron had come to dislike her intensely.

'I'm wondering if Ethel told Stan,' he muttered. 'To be sure the poor wee man has a right to know, but he'll take it hard.'

'Who knows what that woman will do,' said Peggy. 'I know her heart's in the right place despite her prickliness, but I do wish she'd think before she speaks. Poor old Stan will find the news hard enough to take, but if she comes out with the sort of things she said earlier...'

'Hopefully she'll have more sense,' Ron replied grimly.

As Peggy, Cordelia, Sarah and Rita sat in doleful silence, Ron could see by their faces that they were desperately worried and struggling with their consciences. However, he had no words of consolation for them, only a deep sense of regret for how he'd first reacted himself when he'd discovered that April was in the family way and expecting a brown

461

baby. What did it matter in the scheme of things? No one was perfect, and mistakes happened. Who was he to pass judgement when his own sins were so numerous?

He heaved a deep sigh and reached for his pipe and tobacco. That it should come to this didn't bear thinking about, and although he rarely prayed, he sent up a silent plea for the miracle that would save April and her baby.

'I really do think they could have sent little Fran to tell us what's happening,' said an anxious Cordelia. 'All this not knowing is making me feel quite ill.'

'She must still be in theatre,' said Peggy. 'I wonder if she's one of the team working on April?'

'We can only hope that no news is good news,' muttered Ron. 'But to be sure I'm feeling as impatient and worried as you with all this hanging about.'

Cordelia sniffed back her tears and dabbed her eyes. 'Poor little April. Such a sweet girl despite everything. I feel so guilty that I wasn't as kind to her as I might have been.'

'Now, Cordelia, you mustn't think like that,' Ron insisted. 'This was none of your fault, and although I know you didn't approve of what she'd done, you did very well to hide it, so I'm sure she never realised.'

'I hope so,' she murmured. 'It would be awful if she left us and never knew how much we cared for her.'

Sarah took Cordelia's hand. 'I feel guilty too,' she said quietly. 'I should have been more supportive, and not let old prejudices colour my judgement. If anything happens to her, I'll never forgive myself.'

'Then let's hope she pulls through,' said Peggy. 'It's bad enough that her mother doesn't seem to care, and even though I know you and Cordelia have found it awkward to accept her situation, now is the time to put all that aside. Of course you feel guilty, we all do – and as we've none of us lived blameless lives, it's right we should feel ashamed.'

'Ach, Peggy, you've no call to feel that way,' protested Ron. 'You've mothered that wee girl and looked after her with more love and care than Mildred ever did.'

Peggy was about to reply when Fran came hurrying towards them. 'She's out of theatre and in the recovery ward,' she said quickly. 'The baby was delivered by Caesarean section during the op as its little heart was struggling and Mr Hooper feared the worst.'

'But April's all right?' asked Peggy, leaping to her feet. 'She's expected to recover fully?'

'It's very early days, Peggy. She's gone through a traumatic time, and has yet to come round properly from the anaesthetic.'

'But surely the doctor has some idea of whether she'll recover?' Peggy's face had drained of colour and she had to sit down again.

Fran took Peggy's hand, her expression solemn. 'None of us have any way of knowing,' she said softly. 'She's been through a great deal, and it's going to depend on how strong she is to fight her way back to health.' She gave Peggy a warm, consoling smile. 'But she has the best team of

463

doctors and nurses looking after her, so she won't have to fight alone.'

Peggy patted her hand, the tears running unheeded down her face. 'Don't let her die, Fran. Please don't let her die.'

Fran made no reply, but put her arm round Peggy's shoulders as she met Ron's concerned gaze over her head. 'We'll do everything possible,' she murmured.

'And the baby?' asked Cordelia tearfully, gripping Sarah's hand.

Fran bit her lip, her green eyes dulled from weariness and care. 'She's five weeks early and so very tiny and had to go straight into an incubator. Mr Hooper is monitoring her closely, because she's premature and her underdeveloped lungs are struggling.' Her voice became ragged. 'I'm sorry, Cordelia, but he doesn't hold out much hope that she'll survive.'

'Poor little mite,' wept Cordelia, 'and to think...'

Peggy was battling her own tears as she looked at Fran. 'When can we see April? She'll need us more than ever now.'

'Not tonight,' said Fran. 'She has to come round properly and then sleep naturally for a while before she's told about the baby. It's probably best you all go home. I'll ring if anything happens in the night – if not I'll let you know how things have gone when I come off shift in the morning.'

'I don't like the thought of leaving her,' fretted Peggy.

'I'll keep an eye on her, Peg,' said Fran, 'and be with her should the worst happen. I promise.'

Peggy patted her cheek. 'Bless you, Fran. You've

a good heart, and I feel easier knowing she won't have to go through this alone.'

'It's why I'm a nurse, Peggy. But, to be sure, 'tis a hard calling at times.'

Fran bustled off back to work, and Peggy and the others wearily gathered up their discarded coats, bags and baskets, and made their slow way home through the dark streets. It was a beautiful night, the air soft, the sky a canopy of stars above the mirrored surface of the sea, but in their hearts lay the chill of winter.

31

Stan woke long before the early morning cups of tea were due to be handed out, and as he was feeling much stronger, he clambered out of bed, pulled on his dressing gown and shoved his large feet into his slippers. He had a suspicion that the doctor had given him a sleeping pill the night before, and so even if the nurse had been able to discover what was happening to April, he'd have been out cold, and that made him more determined than ever to see April for himself.

There was no sign of any nurses on the ward, so he pushed through the doors and went into the sluice room where they were chattering over cups of tea.

'Mr Dawkins,' gasped the little nurse he'd spoken to the night before. 'You shouldn't be in here.'

465

'I need to know about April,' he replied, 'and I'm not leaving until you tell me.'

The nurse took his arm and tried to steer him out of the sluice. 'She came through the operation, Mr Dawkins, so you've no need to worry. I expect you'll be able to visit her in a couple of days.'

Stan stood firm, blocking the doorway. 'And the baby?'

The girl looked up at him, her expression telling its own story. 'I'm sorry, Mr Dawkins. She's premature and very frail. The doctor doesn't expect–'

'But she's still alive?' he interrupted.

'She was last night, but...'

Stan didn't wait to hear any more. He went back to the ward, pulled the curtains round his bed and grabbed his clothes out of the bedside locker. He had to get to April and her baby before it was too late.

He was just doing up his fly buttons when the curtain was whipped back with such force he nearly jumped out of his skin.

'And what exactly do you think you're doing?' demanded a stern-faced Matron.

'I'm going to see my niece and her baby,' he muttered, dragging his braces over his shoulders.

'You'll do no such thing,' she countered. 'Get back into bed immediately.'

Stan reached for his jacket. 'I'm not a schoolboy to be bullied,' he said with uncharacteristic firmness. 'And you can't stop me.'

She stood in front of him, arms folded, her steely eyes boring into him. 'You're my patient,

466

and I'm in charge,' she barked. 'Get back into bed.'

Stan placed his great hands gently but firmly on her arms, lifted her off her feet and set her to one side. 'I hereby formally discharge myself,' he said before heading down the ward.

'You can't do that. Come back at once.' Her voice followed him as he cut a swathe through the startled nurses and slammed through the doors.

Stan walked as quickly as he could along what seemed to be endless corridors, and finally found a sign for the intensive care wards. He slowed to get his breath, and realised he was still wearing his slippers and probably looked very wild as he hadn't shaved or combed his hair. Shrugging off these minor details, he pushed through the first door he came to.

The light was dim and the atmosphere hushed but for the steady pulse of machinery, and the soft squeak of rubber-soled shoes as the nurses tended their patients. He tiptoed up to the desk where two nurses were dealing with a great stack of patients' notes. 'I'm looking for April Wilton and her baby,' he whispered.

The nurse took in the fact he was wearing slippers and looked rather dishevelled and wild-eyed, and although her eyes widened in surprise, she didn't make a fuss. 'Miss Wilton is not well enough for visitors,' she said quietly. 'You'll have to come back this afternoon.'

This was an awful blow, and Stan's level of concern soared to even greater heights. 'I promise not to wake her,' he whispered urgently. 'I just need to see her. She's my niece, and I'm all

467

the family she has.'

The nurses exchanged glances. 'All right,' the girl said. 'You can take a look at her, but you're not to touch her or say anything. Is that understood?'

Stan nodded dumbly, the dread for April making his heart thud. He followed the girl down the quiet ward, and when she stopped beside the bed and he looked at the still figure lying there, he gasped in distress.

He hardly recognised April, for her head and jaw were swathed in bandages, her skin was waxen, and she looked so tiny in that bed he could hardly believe she was more than a child. He wanted to touch her pale hand which curled on top of the sheet; wanted to kiss that deathly little face and tell her he was here and that he loved her. Tears blinded him as he watched the barely perceptible rise and fall of her chest. At least she was still alive – but for how long?

'Can I sit with her?' he breathed. 'I promise not to wake her.'

The nurse shook her head. 'You have to go now,' she whispered.

He looked down at April and realised he could do nothing to help her, so he nodded and reluctantly followed the nurse to the door. 'You won't let her die, will you?' he pleaded.

'We're doing our very best to make sure that doesn't happen,' she replied with a consoling pat on his arm.

'Where's the baby? Why isn't she with her mother?'

A shadow seemed to flit over the girl's eyes. 'If

she didn't pass away in the night, she'll be in the special care baby ward,' she replied softly. 'I'm sorry.'

Stan nodded and set off down yet more corridors in search of the special baby ward. A nurse was just coming through the door loaded with laundry, and on seeing him standing there, she took pity on him. 'Mr Dawkins?'

'Yes, but how...?'

She placed the laundry in a heap on a nearby chair. 'Matron telephoned and warned me you might come. But it's all right, she's given special permission for you to see baby Wilton.'

'Is that because...?' He couldn't voice his fear.

She nodded. 'Baby Wilton is struggling, Mr Dawkins. All we can do is hope she stays with us long enough for her mother to be able to hold her.'

Stan closed his eyes momentarily, forcing the tears back and steeling himself for what was to come, and then followed the girl into the room.

There were six incubators lined up on one side and half a dozen cots on the other. The incubators were like see-through boxes on square stands into which oxygen was being pumped. There was only one incubator in use, the tiny occupant being closely monitored by a plump, sweet-faced nurse.

'What's that in the tank below the baby?' he asked in a whisper.

'It's water being heated by a small pump to keep her warm,' the nurse replied as she led him across the room. 'This is Sister Black, who is looking after baby Wilton. You can stay as long as there isn't an emergency.'

Stan acknowledged the sister and then looked down at the miniature scrap of human life curled beneath a soft pink blanket in the cocoon of warmth and oxygen that was keeping her alive. Her light brown skin was wrinkled as if it was too loose for her bones; her hair was thick and dark, and her perfect miniature feet and hands could have fitted through a wedding ring.

His heart melted and tears welled as he sank into the nearby chair and just gazed at her in awe. She was perfect, and he was overwhelmed with a love he'd never known – a powerful, all-consuming love that he could only pray she could feel and take strength from.

None of them had slept well, and so it was a dispirited group that gathered in the kitchen at Beach View early that morning. As Fran hadn't telephoned there was a spark of hope that April and her baby had survived the night, but it wasn't enough to give any of them an appetite for dried egg and gritty wheatmeal toast smeared with foul-tasting margarine.

Sarah and Rita reluctantly had to leave for their workplaces, promising to telephone if they could for any news. Cordelia, who usually devoured the newspapers in the morning, sat staring into space, and Ron was grim-faced as he returned from meeting the mail train to feed the animals and clean out the ferrets and the chicken run.

Peggy gave up trying to help Daisy with her spoon: a bit of egg spilled was unimportant in the scheme of things, and her mind was too taken up with April to be able to concentrate on anything else. She glanced up at the clock, urging the hands to move more quickly – but they seemed not to move at all.

She cleared away the dirty plates and washed them up while Daisy nagged Ron to read her a story, but Peggy could tell that he too was preoccupied, for he kept drifting into silence, his gaze repeatedly going to the clock on the mantel.

At the sound of the latch clicking on the gate they all stiffened and looked towards the door as hurrying footsteps came up the path. Fran came in smiling and they let out a sigh in unison.

'April woke up half an hour ago, and although she's still groggy from the anaesthesia, and unable to talk because of her wired jaw, she's aware of what's going on around her, and can even scrawl what she wants to say on a notebook.' Fran took off her cape and cap and unpinned her hair, letting the copper curls tumble down her back.

'So she will get better?' asked a tense Peggy. 'And there are no repercussions after the damage to her head?'

'The doctor is hopeful that she'll make a complete recovery, with no side effects from that fractured skull. It will be a while before they can remove the wires from her jaw, and of course the Caesarean scar will take some time to heal. All in all,' she said on a sigh, 'she's been very lucky.'

'Has she been told about the baby?' asked Peggy fretfully.

Fran nodded. 'I was with her when the doctor explained everything. I thought she might want a familiar face at a time like that, and she seemed to appreciate me being there.'

471

She sat down, her expression solemn. 'I think she was shocked more than anything at first, and then when it sank in, she cried as if her heart was breaking. It was only moments later that she scribbled a note demanding to be taken to see her. The doctor was adamant she shouldn't, but I'm not sure he was right. April needs to see her baby before...'

Cordelia gave a tremulous sigh. 'Have *you* seen her, Fran?'

'I popped into the neonatal unit after seeing April, which is why I'm a bit later than usual coming home. She's very small, and terrifyingly fragile, but she's clinging to life still. The sister in charge said that the next forty-eight hours were crucial, and if she passed that milestone her chances of survival should improve every day.'

'Should?' asked Peggy sharply.

Fran placed her hand over Peggy's. 'There's no guarantee with such premature babies, I'm afraid,' she said softly. 'Their lungs aren't fully formed, there's a risk of infection and myriad other things that can crop up unexpectedly. All any of us can do is hope.'

'Poor wee mite,' muttered Ron. 'April should be with her. It's not right she should be in the care of strangers, however kind, at such a time.'

Fran smiled. 'She's not alone, Ron. Stan's discharged himself and is sitting beside her incubator in his outdoor clothes and slippers, willing her to pull through.' She blinked away her tears. 'He hasn't shaved or combed his hair, and is clearly not too well himself – but I've never seen such love in a man, Ron. It was emanating from

472

him like a glowing aura.'

Cordelia mopped her eyes. 'He always was ruled by his heart and not his head,' she said gruffly. 'It's all very well getting over-sentimental, but if that baby survives it will be adopted, and he'll never see it again. How's he going to feel then?'

Peggy swallowed the lump in her throat. 'Surely it's better that Stan and April should love her for the short while she'll be with them? I can't bear the thought she might die without hearing her mother's voice or feeling the touch of her hand. It would be too cruel.'

'If April comes to love the baby and it survives it would be far crueller,' said Cordelia. 'A mother's love is the most powerful thing in the world, and she'll find it impossible to give her away.' She shook her head as fresh tears threatened. 'Oh dear, poor little April. What a terrible, terrible dilemma.'

'Whatever happens, April's going to need our love and support more than ever now,' said Peggy firmly. She looked across at Fran. 'Will we be able to visit her later today?'

'Only if the doctor agrees, but as she's in the special ward, there'll be a restriction on the number of visitors – probably one, maybe two at the most – and only for a matter of minutes. She's still very weak, and the drugs they're giving her to ease the pain and fight infection are making her sleepy.'

'Then I'll go this afternoon, and sit outside the ward if necessary until someone lets me see her,' said Peggy. 'Ron, you'll have to take Daisy with you to the station – talking of which, shouldn't you be on your way there now for the next train?'

473

Ron glanced sharply at the clock, grabbed his coat and cap and whistled to Harvey. 'To be sure, it's not easy running that place single-handedly when I have so many other things to do,' he grumbled. 'But if you get to see April, tell her I wish her well.'

April opened her eyes and blearily surveyed her surroundings. The blinds had been pulled down over the windows, the overhead lights were dim and the nurses moved from bed to bed with only the rustle of their starched aprons and the soft pad of their rubber-soled shoes marking their passage. Voices were murmurs against the steady rhythm of the machines that were keeping some of the patients alive, and although the atmosphere was sombre, there was a sense of quiet efficiency and optimism which in any other circumstance might have comforted her.

The ready tears blinded her, and she didn't have the strength to brush them away as they ran down her face and soaked the bandages. Every part of her yearned for her baby who was just down the corridor fighting for her life – and it was such a powerful need that it overrode the pain that was beginning to emerge from the haze of medication. She had to see her, to be with her – and perhaps even hold her – for surely the touch and sound and smell of her mother would imbue her with the strength she needed to survive.

April shifted on the pillows and winced as that slight movement sent a stab of pain through her stomach. She lay still for a moment, her hand resting on the bandages that encased her from

474

midriff to thigh beneath the hospital gown, waiting until she felt strong enough to defy that pain and get out of bed.

When she felt ready, she concentrated on her breathing and kept an eye on the nurses in case one of them should spot what she was doing, and then surreptitiously drew back the sheet and thin blanket. The room spun as she lifted her head, and she gasped in agony as she tried to swing her legs to the side of the bed. Panting from the effort and desperately trying to stop the room from spinning, she inched her bottom towards the edge.

'What on earth are you doing, Miss Wilton?' Firm hands grasped her upper arms, stopping her from going any further.

'Baby,' she panted. 'I have to see my baby.' But even she could hear that her words were unintelligible through the wiring in her jaw. She lashed out with her hand, ignored the agony that tore through her and pushed forward. 'Baby,' she persisted. 'See baby.'

'I can guess what you're trying to say,' said the nurse, 'but you simply aren't well enough. You have to have complete bed rest for at least two weeks. The doctor said so.'

April swiped at her again, and pressed against the restraining hands. She had to make the woman see that she would not be denied.

'Please, Miss Wilton, don't fight me,' pleaded the nurse. 'I will get into the most fearful trouble if Doctor or Matron comes in.'

April was in agony, the sweat soaking her bandages as pain roared in her head and sent daggers of fire through her belly and into her ribs. 'No,' she keened. 'No.'

The nurse relaxed her grip on her arms and looked into her face, her expression concerned. 'Miss Wilton, April,' she said softly. 'You simply aren't well enough, and if you persist in doing this, you'll undo all the good the doctor has done for you.'

Tears mingled with the sweat as April looked back at her and realised just how weak and wracked with pain she was. 'But I have to see her,' she sobbed. 'I don't want her to die alone.'

The nurse guessed what April was trying to say. 'She's not alone, dear. Your uncle has been with her since first light and there's a whole team of specially trained nurses and doctors looking after her.'

April stared at her through the fog of distress, giddiness and pain, and tried to absorb what she was telling her. 'I should be there too,' she managed, gripping the older woman's hand. 'Please, please let me go to her.'

The nurse regarded her solemnly for a long moment and then gave a deep sigh. 'I suppose you'll only try again when my back's turned, won't you?'

April managed the slightest of nods.

'In that case, will you let me get you back into bed properly, and promise me you'll stay there while I go and have a word with Sister?'

'Yes,' she breathed, the hope rising and making her pulse race.

'I can't promise anything,' the woman warned, 'but I'll do my best.' She eased April back into the centre of the bed, pulled up the sheet and blanket and bustled off with a crackling of starched apron.

April was exhausted, but she watched the woman's every move as she spoke to the sister in charge of the ward. Was this simply a ruse to keep her imprisoned in this bed? Her fingers sought the hem of the blanket, ready to try again should this prove to be the case.

However, as she watched, the nurse nodded and turned towards her, striding down the hushed ward with what looked like a sense of purpose. April's fingers tightened on the blanket.

'Sister hasn't dismissed the idea entirely,' said the nurse, 'but the decision isn't really hers to make. That's up to Matron and your doctor.'

April's spirits plummeted as she gripped the blanket. It was highly unlikely she'd get permission, so the only option open to her was to try again and just hope she'd find the strength to make it out of here.

'I can see what you're plotting,' said the nurse with a wry smile, 'which is why I'm going to wait with you until Sister gets back.' With that she folded her apron neatly over her lap and sat down on the nearby chair.

April closed her eyes, the tears seeping from between her lashes. She had to see her baby, had to be with her for her final hours and get the hospital padre to christen her. If she didn't get permission, then she'd find another way to be with her. And then she remembered that her Uncle Stan was already with her, just down the corridor.

'Uncle Stan. I want to see him,' she said determinedly.

'What's that, dear?'

April tamped down on her impatience. 'Uncle Stan. See him,' she said as clearly as she could through her wired jaw.

'I promise I'll see if he's still here once Matron arrives,' the nurse said. 'I'm not risking you trying to escape again.'

That promise was enough to lift away some of her anxiety, and although she was exhausted and it was all too tempting to give in to the need to sleep, she concentrated hard on the doors to the ward, determined to have her say and get her own way.

The doors finally swung open and Matron appeared. Her gimlet glare swept the ward, the nurse beside April hastily stood to attention and all the others found something important to do so they didn't meet her gaze.

April watched as she strode down the ward like a galleon, her starched cap billowing like a sail, her apron as rigid as her features. She was a formidable figure, and if April hadn't been so determined to have her way, she might have been instantly cowed.

'What's all this nonsense about getting out of bed?' the woman snapped.

'Baby,' April retorted. 'I want to be with my baby.'

'I hardly think that's appropriate in the circumstances,' Matron replied. 'Your child might not live, but if it does, I understand it will be adopted. It would be very foolish to get involved with her, Miss Wilton, and remiss of me in my duty if I permitted it.'

'She's my baby and I want to see her. And if

you don't let me, I'll do it anyway.' The words might not have been intelligible, but the force of their meaning was perfectly clear.

Matron glared at her, clearly not accustomed to patients answering back. 'It seems wilfulness runs in your family, Miss Wilton. I have had similar dealings with your uncle only this morning.'

'Are you taking my name in vain, Matron?' boomed Stan as he loomed up behind her with a frantic little nurse in tow.

'You are not allowed in here,' she snapped. 'Nurse, remove him immediately.'

He easily warded off the little nurse's attempts to shift him by standing as steady and immovable as a rock. 'I heard April was awake and asking to see her little one, so I've come to collect her,' he said, wrestling the wheelchair from the flustered little nurse and pushing it up to the bed. 'Your carriage awaits,' he said, winking at April. 'I nicked it from down the hall.'

'If you move her you could be responsible for setting her recovery back days if not weeks,' said Matron. 'I forbid you to go anywhere near her, and insist you return that chair to where you found it.'

Stan looked down at her and his grim expression softened into a beaming smile as he continued to take charge of the wheelchair and ward off the nurse's feeble attempts to shift him. 'Matron, we've known each other for years through the Rose Growers' Association, and I know that under all that starch beats a kind, caring heart.'

He raised his hand to halt what she was about to say, and carried on. 'April will not recover as

479

long as she's fretting over her baby – and her baby needs her to help her fight for life. By bringing them together, they will both be strengthened by the bond that binds mother and child.'

'And if, as expected, the baby dies?'

'Then at least April would have had a chance to be with her. And although her passing will break her heart, the pain will not be as great as it would if she'd been forced to abandon her.'

April gazed at Stan with gratitude and love. She couldn't have put it any better.

Matron cleared her throat and folded her hands at her waist. 'You put forward a strong argument, Stanley Dawkins,' she said. 'And although it is against my better judgement, you may take April to see her baby.'

She held up her hand as Stan eagerly pushed the wheelchair forward. 'But,' she said forcefully. 'You will stay for fifteen minutes only and then bring her back.'

April could have kissed the old trout, but knew it wouldn't be at all the thing to do, so she gingerly reached out her arms to Stan and hugged him as best she could.

Matron turned to the little nurse who was all but hidden behind Stan's bulk. 'Nurse Logan, stop dithering there and help Sister Black and Nurse Dunn prepare Miss Wilton.' She turned a beady eye on Stan. 'You wait outside the ward until we're ready.'

Stan nodded and lumbered off in his carpet slippers.

Afraid that Matron might change her mind, April didn't dare make a sound or show any sign that she was in a great deal of pain as the nurses helped her, into a hospital dressing gown, and then eased her towards the side of the bed. With Matron orchestrating their every move, the two nurses lifted her between them and carefully lowered her into the chair, before Sister tucked a blanket over her knees, slid her feet into slippers, and checked that the drip needle hadn't come loose from the back of her hand.

Her heart was thudding; thunder seemed to fill her head and lightning strikes shot through her torso, but she managed to stifle her cries through sheer determination and the knowledge that she would soon see her baby.

Matron handed her a glass of water and two pills. 'Take these,' she ordered. 'I know you're in pain.'

April hesitated, not wanting to take anything that would knock her out.

'They're only aspirin,' said Matron. 'You can have the rest of your medication when you return to the ward.'

Once April had meekly taken the pills, Matron swept back the curtain, grasped the wheelchair's handles and pushed it down the length of the ward and through the swing doors to where Stan was anxiously waiting. 'You have precisely fifteen minutes,' she reminded him. 'I shall be timing you.'

Stan pushed the chair down the long corridor. 'It's no wonder Ron did a runner,' he said. 'That woman's a menace. But at least we got our way in the end.'

They came to the special baby ward and he drew to a halt and leaned over April. 'Your baby's beau-

481

tiful, April. I'm so glad you're getting a chance to see her.'

April took his hand. 'Thank you, Uncle Stan. I couldn't have done it without you.'

'Don't try and talk, my dear, I can see how painful it is.' He quickly cleared his throat and carefully pushed the wheelchair through the swing doors into another hushed room where the light was diffused by thick shades to protect the babies' eyes.

April saw the surprise on the nurses' faces, but her whole being was centred on the small mound beneath the pink blanket in the incubator. As Stan pushed the chair close to it, she leaned forward and touched the glass in wonder.

Her baby *was* beautiful, with tiny fingers and toes, a button nose, rosebud mouth and surprisingly thick dark hair. Her skin was wrinkled as if she'd been in a bath for too long, and it hung loosely from her delicate bones – but it was the colour of golden honey, as if she'd been out in the sunshine.

A flood of love swept through her, so powerful she wondered that her baby couldn't feel it through the glass. Gazing in awe, she smiled as that darling little face screwed up and she squirmed and waved her tiny arms and legs about. She was so fragile, so small she would have almost fitted in the palm of her hand, and April felt a fierce and overwhelming desire to gather her to her heart and protect her for ever.

'She's lovely, isn't she?' murmured Stan. 'Quite stolen my heart, she has.'

April couldn't tear her gaze from her baby, but

she reached out and caught hold of his hand. 'And mine,' she managed. 'She has to live,' she breathed, 'just has to.'

'Your love will help her grow strong, April,' he said gruffly. 'Talk to her if you can, and let her know you're here.'

'Hello, precious little girl,' she murmured, as clearly as she could through the wiring in her jaw. 'Mummy's here now, and she loves you very much.'

A nurse approached the incubator and took note of the temperature and level of oxygen before she opened the glass panel on the side and measured the baby's pulse.

'Can I touch her?' asked April.

The nurse nodded and Stan pushed the chair to the other side of the bed so April could reach into the incubator.

April's hand almost dwarfed the baby, but as she softly stroked the little fist it opened and the tiny hand curled around April's finger as if to let her know she was aware of her and put her trust in her.

Tears rolled down April's face and as she sat there joined once again to her daughter, the agonising flare of pain through her body was lost in the tumult of a much stronger sensation – the indestructible force that is a mother's love.

32

'I don't know what you was thinkin' of, Stanley Dawkins,' stormed Ethel as she plonked herself down beside his bed that afternoon. 'Discharging yerself and causing trouble with Matron – and then making things worse by traipsing all over this place with April.'

Stan had already explained why he'd done it, but it seemed Ethel was in such umbrage she wasn't actually listening to him. He realised it was only because she cared, but he was too tired to talk any more, so he just let her rabbit on while he dozed against the pillows.

He'd been rather fortunate that Matron had taken one look at him when he'd returned April to her ward, and ordered him to get into the wheelchair. He hadn't argued then either, for he was an emotional and physical wreck, and wouldn't have managed to get any further than the corridor on his own. He'd been whisked back to his old ward, swiftly undressed and tucked into bed, where he'd fallen into a deep sleep for almost four hours. It had only been the sound of the visiting, bell that had stirred him, and Ethel's furious voice that had fully wakened him.

'Well I'm glad to 'ear April's on the mend,' said Ethel, the ash on her cigarette trembling as she spoke. 'But I don't reckon you did right by 'er, taking 'er to see the kid. It'll only get 'er all fired up and confused about things.' She paused. 'Are you listening to me, Stan?' she said sharply.

'Yes, my little flower, I'm listening,' he said wearily. 'I'm just resting my eyes for a bit.'

'What's it look like then? Her kid. How dark is it?'

Stan's eyes flew open and he stared at her in shock. His thoughts whirled. He could deny the baby's heritage, or try to bluff his way out of why he hadn't confided in her – but then he'd always been a lousy liar and Ethel could see right through him. He felt her steady gaze boring into him and the heat suffusing his neck and face, and knew there was no escape.

'You don't need to say anything,' muttered Ethel crossly. 'Yer guilty face tells me all I need to know.' She puffed on her cigarette and folded her arms tightly.

'But I suspected as much,' she continued. 'She were too tight-lipped, and I wondered right from the start what that girl was trying to hide.' She wagged a finger at him. 'I told you she'd be trouble, Stan, but you wouldn't listen, would you?'

He glanced at her from beneath his brows, shamed by his deceit, and unwilling to tell her straight why it had been kept from her.

'Well, it's a great pity you didn't think to tell me. After all, we're married, and I 'ave a right to know these things.' Her eyes narrowed. 'How long you known, Stan?'

'Since she told me she was expecting,' he admitted shamefacedly.

'Did Peggy and the others at Beach View know?'

He nodded. 'They were shocked at first, but

485

they'd come to like April, so they set aside their doubts and decided to support her.' He reached for her hand which was tightly gripping the strap of her handbag. 'I didn't tell you because you'd made your feelings clear on the subject, and as the baby was to be adopted, I didn't see the point in upsetting you any further.'

Her lip curled and she eased her hand away from his. 'Just how dark is it?'

Stan was the most patient of men, but Ethel had a way of making his blood boil at times and he was finding it hard to remain calm. 'She's not an "it", Ethel. She's a baby – and a very sick one at that. April calls her Paula after her best friend who died in the air raid on Portsmouth,' he said evenly.

Ethel glared at him. 'Answer my question, Stan,' she said tartly.

'Paula's hair is black, and her skin is light brown as if she's been kissed by the sun. She could easily pass as Mediterranean.'

'But we all know better, don't we?' she retorted. 'I hope the silly girl doesn't get carried away and decide to keep it – 'cos as sure as eggs is eggs, the truth will come out eventually.'

'That decision can only be April's,' he said sadly. 'But I tell you what, Ethel, if Paula survives and April decides to keep her, then I shall support them both in any way I can.'

There was wariness in Ethel's eyes. 'Even if I don't like it?'

'Even if you don't like it,' he replied, firmly holding her gaze.

Ethel looked away. 'Well, I'll have to think on

that, Stan.' She fiddled with the handbag strap, clearly agitated. 'Has my Ruby been keeping this from me an' all?'

'I didn't tell her, but she's got closer to April these past few weeks, so they might have discussed it.'

Ethel took the butt of her cigarette out of her mouth and dropped it into the beaten metal ashtray on top of the locker. 'Well, if they did, she kept it to 'erself,' she said tightly. She abruptly gathered up her things and got to her feet. 'I'd better go.'

'Ethel, darling, please try and understand why I didn't tell you,' he pleaded, reaching for her hand.

She ignored his plea and avoided his reaching fingers. 'I'll see yer tomorrow.'

Her kiss on his cheek was fleeting before she walked away, and Stan wondered fretfully whether he'd lost her and the golden future he'd planned for them – or if Ethel would find it in her heart to forgive him and embrace a softer, more charitable outlook on the sins of others while examining her own conscience.

Peggy had received no word from Mildred, and her repeated attempts to get through to her on the telephone throughout the morning had been un-answered, so she'd come to the conclusion that she was either on her way, or, more likely, had decided to just ignore what was happening. Which made Peggy so hopping mad, she could barely speak.

She was in a furious bate by the time she de-livered Daisy to Ron at the station 'Honest to goodness, Ron, I could swing for that woman, really I could.'

He put his arm round her shoulder and gave her a swift hug. 'April has you, and that's enough,' he replied. 'Leave Mildred to stew; none of us needs her here anyway.'

Peggy was still nettled, but by the time she'd walked back to Camden Road and the hospital, she'd calmed down enough to realise that Ron had been right. Ethel would be difficult enough to deal with, and they certainly didn't need Mildred poking her snooty nose in and causing poor little April even more trouble. Her absence would undoubtedly hurt the girl, but Peggy suspected she'd actually be relieved not to have to face her.

She looked at her watch and realised it was a bit early for visiting time, so she popped into the Lilac Tearooms for a cup of tea and a fag to restore her spirits before she headed for April's ward.

The nurse was most apologetic, but the doctor was with April, so Peggy would have to wait outside until he'd gone. When she asked the nurse how April was doing, she learned of her and Stan's visit to see the baby that morning, and her heart gladdened at the thought that Stan was championing the girl. Though how Ethel would take it, was another thing entirely.

Her spirits had revived, and as she stood outside the ward, she decided to use the time to go and see if she'd be allowed to visit the baby. She had to admit she was curious, for she'd never seen a premature baby before, let alone a brown one.

Asking a nurse the way to the special baby ward, she found it was almost at the very end of the long corridor. But as she headed towards it, she came to an abrupt halt and dodged behind a nearby pillar. Ethel had emerged through the doors ahead of her, and was clearly most upset.

Under any other circumstances, Peggy would have rushed to console someone in tears, but as it was Ethel, and she'd come to dislike the woman intensely, Peggy stayed where she was. She watched as the other woman dug in her cardigan pocket for a handkerchief, wiped her eyes and then took a deep breath before hurrying off.

'Well I'll be blowed,' muttered Peggy. 'I never thought I'd see Ethel here – and certainly not in tears.' She stood in the lee of the pillar for a long moment, her thoughts racing. Ethel would know now that they'd all been keeping the truth from her, and must surely have realised the reason why. Were her tears a sign that she was at last softening her attitude? Peggy very much hoped so, but with Ethel it was hard to tell which way the wind blew.

She waited until Ethel had turned the corner and was out of sight before she approached the door and tapped on the window to attract a nurse's attention. 'I'd like to see April Wilton's baby,' she said to the girl at the door, before explaining who she was.

The girl smiled. 'My goodness. Baby Wilton is popular today. You're her fourth visitor.'

'Yes, I saw Ethel leaving. She looked very upset,' said Peggy, hoping the nurse would enlighten her on this uncharacteristic behaviour.

The sweet-faced girl nodded and frowned. 'Some people find it very distressing to see such small babies struggling for life, Mrs Reilly. Mrs Dawkins stood for ages just looking at the baby, and then she asked all sorts of questions about how she was doing and if she was expected to survive.'

The girl's expression was infinitely sad as she continued. 'The doctor isn't too hopeful, I'm afraid, and when I told Mrs Dawkins that, she burst into tears and left. I'd've run after her to make sure she was all right, but I can't leave the ward until the end of my shift.'

Peggy felt a jolt of alarm, all concern for Ethel wiped away in the nurse's words. 'The doctor isn't hopeful? You mean...'

'There is always hope, Mrs Reilly,' the girl replied softly. 'But baby Wilton is still very frail, and she's struggling.' She opened the door wider. 'You may come in just for a moment. The doctor will be back to check on her soon.'

Peggy followed her to the incubator and, like Ethel before her, just stood and gazed at the impossibly tiny baby. There were needles in her thin arms, wires leading to miniature pads on her chest and thick gauze taped over her eyes – probably to protect them from the light and a machine attached to the wires was beeping at the side of the incubator.

Tears blinded her as she remembered how sturdy and strong her own babies had been compared to this little one. She looked so vulnerable, tightly curled up like a rosebud waiting to blossom, and Peggy ached to take her in her arms, to run her fingers over the silky black hair and instil some of her own strength into that delicate little being that was clinging so desperately to life.

'It must break your heart working here,' she whispered to the nurse.

'It can do,' she admitted, 'but there are always the ones who make it against all the odds – and they bring the greatest joy.'

Peggy looked back at April's baby. 'Thank you for letting me see her. May I come again?'

The girl smiled. 'Any time you like. She might not see you, but I'm sure she knows when someone comes, and gains strength from that. Her heart rate steadied considerably when her mother was here this morning, and it was quite lovely to see her tiny hand curled round April's finger. I'm very hopeful that once we can express some of her mother's milk, she'll start to thrive.'

Peggy could no longer stem her tears, and with a muttered apology fled the room before she made a complete show of herself. She understood now why Ethel had been so deeply moved.

April's determination to be with her baby as much as possible led to Matron granting her permission to visit as long as her own health was improving. Paula was putting up a terrific fight now she had her mother's milk to sustain her, and had survived through those critical forty-eight hours, but April knew the battle was not yet over and could only pray that her baby would defy the odds set against her.

April's daily routine was ordered by medicine rounds, doctors' rounds, visiting hours and mealtimes, but in between, she would be wheeled into the hushed, dim nursery and sit beside Paula just watching her breathe as her tiny hand clasped her finger. She was so very precious, and with each passing day April felt closer and ever more protective of her.

Stan, Ruby, Gloria and Rosie, and everyone at Beach View, had all been marvellous. They'd popped in to see her and Paula at every chance they could snatch, even though they led such hectic lives. Peggy had knitted the sweetest little pink hat for Paula to replace the hospital one, and Cordelia had brought in one of her delicate bed jackets for April to wear over the lovely sprigged nightdress the girls had clubbed together to buy for her. Gloria had brought in a sheaf of brand new magazines, and Rosie had arrived armed with new slippers and a bottle of cologne.

Stan was back at the cottage now, on strict instructions not to overdo things and to stick to his diet, but he still insisted upon visiting her and Paula every day. Ruby was filling in at the station when she wasn't working, to give Ron some time off, and the two men had brought in the most glorious flowers from the allotment.

As yet, there had been no sign of Ethel or April's mother, and although she could understand Ethel's reluctance to visit after being kept in the dark by everyone, she was deeply hurt by her mother's continued silence.

April sat in the hushed room, her eyelids slowly drooping from exhaustion. She'd hardly slept these past few days, for she'd refused to take the nightly sleeping pill, and had spent those long, dark hours fretting over Paula, wanting to be with her But some hospital rules could not be broken, and the nursery was off limits from eight at night until ten in the morning.

'Come on, April,' said the nurse. 'You need to get some proper sleep.'

She jerked up her head and blinked. 'I'm fine,' she insisted.

'I'll be the judge of that,' the nurse replied firmly. She grasped the wheelchair handles and steered her out of the ward before she could protest further.

April had to admit that her bed was a welcome sight, and once the nurse had helped her into it and tucked the blanket over her, she sank into the pillows, closed her eyes and was asleep before the nurse had left her side.

'April. April, dear, you need to wake up.'

She shrugged off the hand that was shaking her shoulder and turned over, anaesthetised by exhaustion and still heavy with sleep.

'April, you must wake up,' said the voice with some urgency. 'It's Paula.'

She was awake in an instant, bolting upright, careless of the deep pains that shot through her. 'What's happened?'

'She's showing signs of distress,' the nurse whispered. 'The doctor thinks you should come.'

April swung her legs out of the bed, reached for her dressing gown and eased herself into the wheelchair. She clung to the arms of the chair as the nurse swiftly pushed her down the ward, through the door and towards the baby ward. The fear was rising with every passing second and she couldn't speak.

As they entered the nursery she saw that Paula's incubator was surrounded by nurses and doctors frantically working on Paula. 'What's happened? What are they doing?' she managed.

'Paula has a chest infection and it's affecting her heart and lungs,' the nurse explained. 'The doctor is giving her medication to clear the infection, but she needs help to breathe, so they're going to transfer her to a special baby-sized Both-Nuffield respirator. It might look frightening to you, April, but it is Paula's only hope.'

'You mean she's going to die?' she asked brokenly.

'Not if that machine can take over while she fights the infection,' the nurse replied. 'And I've witnessed many a miracle, so don't give up hope.'

April's heart thudded painfully as she watched through her tears. They were putting her precious little girl into an ugly plywood box which was plugged into a small generator she'd never noticed before. Now the machine seemed to be breathing, the flow of air hissing in and out. She'd heard about 'iron lungs', but she had no idea how they worked – but at this very moment she didn't care as long as it did its job and kept her baby alive.

'Hundreds of those machines have been donated by Lord Nuffield to hospitals all over Britain,' said the nurse. 'The pressure inside can be regulated as the oxygen flows, and that helps to keep the chest cavity open – so in essence, the machine is breathing for Paula.'

April was frantic with worry and desperate to reassure herself that her baby wasn't being smothered. 'Can I go to her?'

'When they have the machine regulated and it's clear that Paula is no longer distressed.' The nurse squatted at April's side. 'Is there anyone you'd like me to call?' she asked softly.

'Peggy,' she said hoarsely, her gaze fixed on the top of Paula's head which was all she could see of her. 'I need Peggy.'

'I'll make the call now.' The nurse hurried away.

The shrill ringing of the telephone pierced the silence of Beach View and brought Peggy stumbling from her bedroom to answer it.

She listened with deepening dread and by the time she'd replaced the receiver she noticed that the girls had come down to the hall, Cordelia was at the top of the stairs and Ron was standing in the kitchen doorway. She could tell by their ashen faces that they'd guessed what the call was about.

Tears were streaming down her face and her heart felt as if it was encased in ice. 'It's Paula,' she choked. 'She's not expected to make it through the night and April needs me.'

Without waiting for them to respond, she closed her bedroom door behind her and swiftly, got dressed. Daisy hadn't woken, and she paused for a moment to kiss her soft, warm face, silently thanking God that her baby was healthy, and then grabbed her handbag and left the room.

Ron was dressed and waiting for her in the kitchen, Harvey at his feet. 'I've rung Stan,' he said. 'He should be there too in case...'

Peggy nodded, and together they left the house to the pitiful sound of Harvey whining behind the firmly closed back door.

495

'I can't imagine what April must be going through,' said Peggy as they hurried down Camden Road in the blackout. 'I just hope we're in time to be there when... If...'

Ron dug his chin into the collar of his coat and didn't reply, and she suspected he was as anguished as she was, for he'd seen Paula and she knew how fiercely protective he'd become of her.

They reached the hospital, took the steps two at a time and raced towards the ward. Out of breath and shaking with dread, Peggy peered through the window in the door and was admitted immediately.

'I'm sorry, Mr Reilly,' said the nurse, 'you'll have to wait outside.'

Peggy went straight to April and folded her into her arms. The girl was as white as a sheet and trembling as her tears streaked down her face and she clung to Peggy. 'Thank you,' she wept. 'Thank you so much for coming. I don't think I could bear this on my own.'

'You don't have to, April,' she soothed, stroking back her hair. 'I'm here, and I won't leave you.' She waited for the girl to get her emotions a bit more under control, and watched fearfully as the doctors turned knobs and switches on that terrifying-looking machine. She'd seen iron lungs before during the polio epidemic before the war, and although they looked more like iron coffins than life-savers, they'd proved to be miraculous inventions, so she could only pray this one would preserve Paula.

As the medics clustered round the respirator, Peggy held April close and encouraged her to tell her what had brought about this sudden change in Paula's condition. None of it boded well, and Peggy's heart twisted at the thought of that innocent little soul trembling on the very brink between life and death.

April finally loosened her grip on Peggy and mopped her face with an already sodden handkerchief. Her gaze never left the huddle around the machine that inhaled and exhaled in the corner, but her tears slowly continued to roll down her face. 'I'd like to have her christened,' she murmured. 'Do you think the hospital padre would agree to do it?'

Some clergy were still reluctant to christen illegitimate babies, and as Peggy hadn't met the hospital padre, she had no idea what his feelings were on the subject. However, she wasn't going to discuss that with April at such a traumatic time. 'We'll only know that if we ask him,' she replied. 'But I doubt he'll be in the hospital at this hour.'

One of the younger nurses overheard and came over. 'Padre John is always here,' she said. 'He was wounded at El Alamein, and is now living in the small annexe at the back of the hospital. Would you like me to ask Mr Reilly to go and find him?'

Peggy looked across the room at the machine and the medics surrounding it and nodded. 'I think it would be best,' she murmured.

Ron's heart was heavy as he tramped along the endless corridors, for to call upon the services of the clergy could mean only one thing, and the thought that brave little Paula was losing the battle made him want to weep.

He finally found his way to the annexe, and his knock was answered almost immediately, for the padre had yet to retire despite the late hour. 'I'm Ron Reilly and I've been asked to fetch you,' he said gruffly, surprised at the other man's youth. 'There's a wee soul in the special baby ward that needs you.'

'Last rites?' he asked, reaching for his dog collar and small black bag.

'I'm thinking her little mother wants her christened,' Ron replied. 'But aye, it could be that too.'

The younger man closed the door and limped along beside Ron as they navigated the stairs and winding corridors back to the baby ward. 'Mortar fire at El Alamein,' he said when he realised Ron had noticed his halting gait. He paused, breathing heavily. 'Sorry,' he panted. 'The lungs aren't what they were. Why don't you tell me something about the mother and her baby so I don't go in there and say the wrong thing?'

Ron eyed him thoughtfully. 'I don't know how you feel about such things,' he said hesitantly, 'but the mother's not married.'

The younger man smiled as they set off again at a slower pace. 'I'm not worthy to judge others; that's up to God. But if you remember your Bible, Mr Reilly, Jesus blessed the little children and called them to Him, for the Kingdom of Heaven was theirs.'

Ron nodded and dug his nails into the palms of his hands as he struggled to keep the image of that wee, innocent soul leaving this earth for the benign and loving arms of a bearded Jesus. It was at times like this that he almost wished he was religious, and could still believe in some omnipotent being who could solve everything and forgive all sins. But Ron had lived for too long and seen too many horrors to be swayed by tales spouted by priests and nuns, and he preferred to live by his own creed – do unto others as you'd have them do to you.

As they turned the corner, the two men came to a halt and stared in amazement at the sad-faced group of people conducting a silent vigil outside the doors to the ward. 'Who are they?' whispered the padre.

Ron was almost blinded by his tears and his heart swelled as he looked at them all. Gloria and Rosie sat next to Cordelia, and were holding hands; Rita was in charge of a sleeping Daisy; and Ruby and the other girls from Beach View were ashen-faced as they also held hands – and at the end of the row of chairs, clinging to Stan's arm, was a tear-streaked Ethel.

'They're April's family,' he replied. 'And they're here to show how much they love her and little Paula.'

Whether it was the outpouring of love, the care of the doctors and nurses and their infernal machine, or simply the will of God and the padre's blessing, Paula survived the night. Normal life was all but put on hold by everyone at Beach View and Railway Cottage, and as day followed worrying day those who'd come to love April and her brave little baby would arrive from their places of work to sit and wait their turn to go in and see them.

No one castigated Ethel, for they could tell she was truly sorry for having been so unkind, and desperate to make amends. It was also clear that she'd come to care for Paula, for she would sit at her side, talking quietly to her and humming snatches of lullabies as she knitted endless tiny bootees, jackets and bonnets.

Peggy came out of the ward five evenings later with a beaming smile. 'She's clear of infection and breathing on her own again,' she said excitedly. 'They're going to move her back into the incubator for a bit, but the doctor's hopeful that within a couple of days she'll be strong enough to go in a proper cot.'

Stan drew a sobbing Ethel into a bear hug, Ruby, Fran and Rita grinned at each other in delight, while Sarah and Ivy clasped hands, and Cordelia burst into tears. Ron dug his hands into his pockets, found a grubby handkerchief and blew his nose so loudly the sound reverberated right down the corridor, which earned him a sharp dig in the ribs from Gloria and Rosie.

'I think we should let April have some time alone with Paula,' said Peggy as she comforted a weeping Cordelia. 'This is a special moment for her after all the worry she's gone through, and I've told her we'll see her tomorrow, so she won't think she's been abandoned.'

'I got something to say before we leave,' said Ethel in her usual straightforward manner. When they all stilled and turned to look at her warily, she shook her head. 'I ain't gunna say nothing unkind no more,' she said. 'But I reckon we got an important decision to make now Paula's pulling through.'

'And what would that be?' rumbled Ron suspiciously.

Ethel folded her arms and glared defiantly back at him. 'April ain't gunna want to let Paula out of her sight after all this,' she said. 'And I don't blame 'er. But she ain't the sort of girl to ask favours off no one and is probably scared of asking us to 'elp when Paula's discharged.'

'Then I'll make certain she knows she and the baby can come and live with us,' said Peggy.

'You're a good woman, Peggy, and I know you'd look after 'em as if they was yer own. But a boarding 'ouse ain't no place to bring up such a delicate baby, if you don't mind my saying so, and as we're proper family, so ter speak, I reckon she should move in with me and Stan. Until she finds 'er feet like.'

Peggy might have taken umbrage at this, but she realised Ethel was, as usual, talking without thinking, so she smiled and gave her a hug. 'That would be perfect,' she murmured. 'I'm so pleased you've come round, Ethel.'

'Yeah, well, someone's got to look after them proper, ain't they?' she said gruffly.

Stan grabbed Ethel and kissed her until they were both breathless. When they came up for air, he took her hands. 'Let's go in and tell April now, and put her mind at rest.'

Ethel poked him in his much-reduced stomach. 'Soft old sod,' she murmured affectionately.

Epilogue

April stood beneath the branches of the gnarled apple tree in the cottage garden and watched the sun dappling through the blossom onto the pram. She'd been living with Stan and Ethel ever since she'd been discharged from hospital back in September, and had brought Paula home here just before Christmas.

That first Christmas had been the best she'd ever experienced, for although there were no expensive presents and rationing meant they'd had to go without a turkey, the warmth of family and the delicious weight of her child in her arms made her heart sing.

Now spring was in the air, there were bright heads of daffodils bobbing in the light breeze, and drifts of pink and white blossom floated like confetti across the vegetable patch she and Ruby tended under Stan's watchful eye. Distracted from her musing by Paula's chuckle, she smiled fondly as the little girl laughed up at her, kicking off her blankets to wave her chubby little legs and arms about.

The doctors had warned her that Paula would always be small for her age, but she'd put on weight, and looked marvellously healthy. Her hair was still dark and the curls were silky around her sweet face, and there were faint reminders of her father in the delicately formed nose and cheekbones, and in her olive skin, but her eyes were the darkest, deepest brown without any hint of that treacherous tawny gold.

April gazed at her. She was the most beautiful baby in the world as far as she was concerned, and in very great danger of being spoilt rotten by everyone, especially Ethel and Stan. She became aware she was being watched and turned to see Ethel standing in the doorway with an indulgent smile, tapping her watch rather pointedly.

'Yes, I know, I'll be late for work if I don't get a move on.'

She smiled back, then kissed her baby's irresistible little feet and fingers, nuzzled her sweet neck and reluctantly headed for the telephone exchange. Vera Gardener had surprised her by offering to take her on again when the unpleasant Bertha had suddenly decided she'd make more money working in one of the factories. The smelly Winston had passed away and Vera had turned her affections to Paula, proving to be an attentive and caring babysitter when Ethel had to be at the factory.

April kissed Stan on her way through the station – he was looking very much healthier now he'd lost so much weight – and then crossed the bridge. As the sunshine warmed her face and the sea sparkled at the end of the High Street, she felt she'd at last found her rightful place in the world. The continued silence from her mother was almost a blessing, for she'd realised a while ago that she didn't need her approval, or even her love. She had all the love she needed right here in Cliffehaven.

503

A Map of Cliffehaven

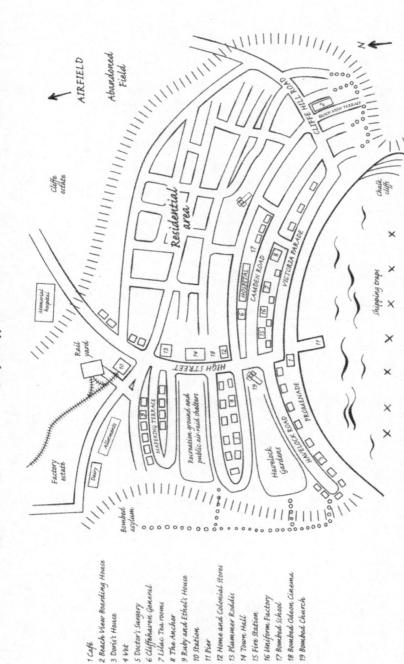

AIRFIELD

Abandoned Field

Cliffe estate

Memorial hospital

Factory estate

Rail yard

Dairy

Allotments

Bombed asylum

Residential area

CLIFFE HILL ROAD

BEACH VIEW TERRACE

HIGH STREET

MAFEKING TERRACE

Recreation ground and public air-raid shelters

Havelock Gardens

HAVELOCK ROAD

PROMENADE

VICTORIA PARADE

CAMDEN ROAD

HOSPITAL

chalk cliffs

Shipping traps

1 Café
2 Beach View Boarding House
3 Doris's House
4 Vet
5 Doctor's Surgery
6 Cliffehaven General
7 Lilac Tea rooms
8 The Anchor
9 Ruby and Ethel's House
10 Station
11 Pier
12 Home and Colonial Stores
13 Plummer Roddis
14 Town Hall
15 Fire Station
16 Uniform Factory
17 Bombed School
18 Bombed Odeon Cinema
19 Bombed Church

Dear Reader

April's story was one I'd wanted to write for some time, but rather lacked the courage to do so until now. It's an emotive subject, played out during a time when strict moral codes were adhered to – or at least were seen to be followed – and the language and attitudes would not be acceptable in these more enlightened days. I have no wish to offend, but to keep the story authentic it was vital to use words and phrases I would never normally dream of using. There is little doubt that the girls were naïve sexually, for it wasn't a subject to be talked about except in extremely vague terms by embarrassed mothers. The influx of dashing young men in the uniform of the foreign services, their perceived sophistication and the very uncertainty of the times proved irresistible to some, which led to clandestine affairs, and quite often, heartache.

The arrival of the black GIs certainly caused a stir, just as they had during the First World War, and not all of them abandoned their children. And yet the prejudice of inter-racial relationships was rife on both sides of the Atlantic, and it was a very brave girl who defied the conventions of the time and married her black American, or kept his baby. Pressure from family combined with the lack of any of the financial benefits available today, and the unwillingness of employers to hire an unmarried girl with a child of any colour, meant that many girls were cast out of their homes, with the inevitable result that many of these babies were placed in orphanages.

I thought long and hard about April's baby, and what her outcome would be, and came to the conclusion that she had to survive and stay with her mother. April had the love and support of Stan, Ethel and Peggy, but realistically, there was still a tough battle ahead in a world not yet ready to accept she'd made a mistake, and was doing her very best to atone for it. Baby Paula had come to represent all the 'khaki babies' born during those times, and I wanted her to have the love and warmth of a proper home denied to so many others.

Between the two wars and after 1945 the orphanages were overcrowded, the mainly church-funded institutions unable to support so many unwanted children. It is during these times that the churches began to send the children abroad, mainly to Australia where, despite the promises of a better life, they were often abused and used as slave labour in some of the harshest environments on earth. I have explored and researched this era of the 'Empty Cradles,' for my book, *Savannah Winds*, which I wrote under the pseudonym of Tamara McKinley.

I hope you enjoy *Shelter From the Storm*. Please let me know what you think. You can contact me through www.ellie-dean.co.uk, or on Facebook.

Ellie x

The characters

PEGGY REILLY is in her early forties, and married to Jim. She is small and slender, with dark, curly hair and lively brown eyes, and finds it very hard to sit still. As if running a busy household wasn't enough, she also does voluntary work for the WVS, makes tea and sandwiches for anyone in need and is always there to listen and to sympathise.

   She and Jim took over the running of Beach View Boarding House when Peggy's parents retired to a bungalow further along the coast. Peggy has three daughters and two sons, and when war was declared and the boarding house business no longer became viable, she decided to take in evacuees. Peggy can be feisty and certainly doesn't suffer fools, and yet she is also trying very hard to come to terms with the fact that her family has been torn apart by the war. She is a romantic at heart and can't help trying to match-make, but she's also a terrible worrier, always fretting over someone – and as the young evacuees make their home with her, she comes to regard them as her chicks and will do everything she can to protect them.

JIM REILLY is in his mid-forties and was a

projectionist at the local cinema until it was bombed. He was a young engineer in the First World War, in which he served alongside his brother, Frank. Jim is handsome, with flashing blue eyes and dark hair, and of course the gift of the Irish blarney, which usually gets him out of trouble. He likes to flirt with women and although he would never be unfaithful to Peggy, she still keeps a close eye on him. Jim also likes to make a dishonest quid here and there, and is not averse to dabbling in the black market. He's shocked and horrified that he has once again been called up to fight in another war, and this is heightened by the fact he's been sent to India.

RONAN REILLY (Ron) is a sturdy man in his mid-sixties. Widowed several years ago, he's fallen in love with the luscious Rosie Braithwaite who owns the Anchor pub, and although she isn't averse to his attentions, she's keeping him at arm's length. Ron is a countryman, a poacher and retired fisherman who tramps over the fields with his dog and ferrets and frequently comes home with game in the deep pockets of his coat. He doesn't care much about his appearance, much to Peggy's dismay, but beneath that ramshackle old hat and moth-eaten clothing beats the heart of a strong, loving man who will fiercely protect those he loves.

ROSIE BRAITHWAITE is in her fifties and in love with Ron, but as her husband is in a mental asylum, she is unable to get divorced. She took over the Anchor twenty years ago and has turned it into a little gold-mine. Rosie has platinum hair, big blue eyes and an hour-glass figure – she also has a good sense of humour and can hold her own with the customers. She runs the pub with a firm hand, and keeps Ron at bay, although she's not averse to a bit of slap and tickle.

CORDELIA FINCH has been living at Beach View for many years. She is in her late seventies and is rather frail from her arthritis. But Cordelia has a twinkle in her eye and loves being an intrinsic part of the lively household. She enjoys singing along to the wireless and having too many sherries in the Anchor. As deaf as a post, she regularly forgets to turn on her hearing aid which can lead to many a convoluted conversation, and although she tries very hard with her knitting, it usually turns out to be a disaster. She adores Peggy and looks on her as a daughter, for her own sons emigrated to Canada many years before and she rarely hears from them. The girls who live at Beach View regard her as their grandmother.

HARVEY is a brindled lurcher, with a mind of his own and a mischievous nature – much like his owner, Ron. Clever and intuitive, he hunts for game with Ron, and once war has been declared, proves to be a heroic rescuer of people trapped in the ruins of their homes. He sleeps on Ron's bed, steals food from the table and has recently blotted his copybook by seducing a pedigree whippet and producing a son, Monty. Harvey adores everyone but Doris.

DORIS WILLIAMS is Peggy's older sister and married to the long-suffering Ted who is manager of the Home and Colonial store. She lives in the posh part of town, Havelock Road, looks down on Peggy and the boarding house and is a terrible social climber. She's a leading light – or would like to be – in Cliffehaven society, is on the board of several charities – because it brings her into contact with Lady Chumley – and insists upon calling Peggy Margaret because she knows it winds her up like a clock.

ANTHONY WILLIAMS is the son of Doris and Ted, and before the war was a teacher at a private school. He's now working for the MOD, and has recently got married to Suzy who was a lodger at Beach View Boarding House.

RITA SMITH came to Beach View after her home in Cliffehaven was flattened by an air raid. Her father is away in the army, her Italian neighbours who took her in have been interned and so she goes to Peggy, whom she's known since childhood. Rita is small and an energetic tomboy who is a fully qualified mechanic, having been taught from an early age by her father. She has a motorbike which she roars about on, and can usually be seen in heavy trousers and boots, and a First World War leather jacket and flying helmet. She works for the Fire Service, and in her spare time has been organising motorbike races to raise money for a Cliffehaven Spitfire.

FRAN is from Ireland and works as a theatre

nurse at Cliffehaven General alongside Suzy. She has been living with Peggy since before the war, and has become an intrinsic part of the family. Fran is a little inclined to wear her heart on her sleeve, and has already had an unfortunate run-in with an over-persuasive and very married American serviceman. She's a dab hand at hair-dressing, much to Ron's disgust – but has proved to be a very talented violinist. She plays the violin at the Anchor for the sing-songs, and has fallen in love with Robert who was Anthony and Suzy's best man.

PEGGY'S CHILDREN

ANNE is married to Commander Martin Black, an RAF pilot, and they have two small girls. Anne has moved down to Somerset for the duration, and although she is teaching at the local village school and getting on with her life, she misses Martin and of course her mother, Peggy.

CICELY (Cissy) is a driver for the WAAF and is stationed at Cliffe Aerodrome. She once had ambitions to go on stage, but finds great satisfaction in doing her bit, and has now fallen in love with a young Spitfire pilot.

BOB and **CHARLIE** are Peggy's two young sons of fourteen and twelve, who are also living in Somerset for the duration.

DAISY is the youngest child, born the day

Singapore fell. She can sleep through air raids, can throw awful tantrums and simply adores pulling Ron's wayward eyebrows. She and Harvey are best friends.

The publishers hope that this book has given you enjoyable reading. Large Print Books are especially designed to be as easy to see and hold as possible. If you wish a complete list of our books please ask at your local library or write directly to:

Magna Large Print Books
Magna House, Long Preston,
Skipton, North Yorkshire.
BD23 4ND

This Large Print Book for the partially sighted, who cannot read normal print, is published under the auspices of

THE ULVERSCROFT FOUNDATION